PISTOL GRIP

"You're either a very courageous man," Lunsford said, "or a very stupid one."

Morgan approached the judge's small desk. "While you're trying to figure out which, Judge, I suggest you hear what I have to say."

"I'm under no obligation to give an audience to a suspected fugitive."

Morgan once again drew and cocked the Colts. He leveled it at Lunsford's head and leaned a little forward when he spoke. "Yes, you are, Judge, in this case."

Morgan learned something at once about Judge Arlo Lunsford. He was not a man easily intimidated. He leaned back in his chair. "I can have you arrested or, if necessary, killed, Mr. Morgan, and when either one is done, no one will question me about it. If you live, you'll end up in Yuma prison. Killing me won't stop the process, except that if you lived, you'd hang."

PEACEMAKER PASS

The girl Morgan found was better than most, even in Denver. They were settled nicely in Morgan's bed and the gunman was just beginning to apply his skills to the girl's breasts. He knew he'd locked the door but it came open anyway, without breaking. The telltale sound was the little squeal in one of the hinges when the door was about half open.

Morgan rolled to the side of the bed opposite the door, landed hard, his pistol in his hand. The girl's scream was cut off.

The light of the lamp flared up and Morgan peeked cautiously over the edge of the bed.

"I'm sorry, Mister Morgan, for having to spoil your fun, but business is business ...."

Other *Double Buckskins* from Leisure Books:

PISTOL GRIP
PEACEMAKER PASS

BUCKSKIN

KIT DALTON

LEISURE BOOKS   NEW YORK CITY

A LEISURE BOOK®

January 1992

Published by

Dorchester Publishing Co., Inc.
276 Fifth Avenue
New York, NY 10001

Printed in the United States of America.

PISTOL GRIP

Dedicated with love to:
My Sis and her family
Marilyn, Bill and Billy Sturdivant
of
Miles City, Montana

1

Lee Morgan rode into Cheyenne, Wyoming in the midst of a blizzard. He was cold, ass tired, hungry, irritated and damned near broke. The circumstances made for a very short temper and a potentially volatile situation.

He found a stall for his horse but Morgan's appearance prompted the liveryman to ask for payment in advance. Morgan couldn't blame him but it didn't do much for his attitude. It also made him wonder what he'd run into at the Cattlemen's Hotel.

"A single, three nights," Morgan said. He got the onceover from the desk clerk and Morgan heaved a sigh. "I'll give you one night in advance and the balance by checkout time." The clerk smiled and reversed the registration book.

The clerk scrutinized Morgan's signature for a moment and then looked up and smiled.

"That will be three dollars, sir." Morgan frowned. The clerk eyed him and then added, "I assume you wanted the bath included. Without the . . . ."

"Never mind," Morgan said, "the bath is fine." The clerk nodded. "The dining room will be open until six o'clock, Mr. Morgan."

"Yeah," Morgan said, picking up his gear, "thanks."

The room was plain. Morgan chuckled to himself. Just a few short weeks earlier, he'd been ensconced at the Brown Palace in Denver. Still, this was not the worst room he'd ever rented. He tossed his gear in the corner, pulled back the bed covers and the sheets. Nothing was crawling. He raised the window shade. It was a back room, not much of a view.

A single picture hung over the bed. It was crooked. Morgan hated crooked pictures. He straightened it and then looked at it. He chuckled again. It depicted a lone wolf atop a snow covered hill. It was howling at the moon. "I don't blame you, pal," Morgan said.

It was nearly four o'clock in the afternoon before Morgan woke up. He threw some cold water on his face and got dressed. He looked out of the window. It had stopped snowing. His circumstance was no better, but he sure as hell felt better. A shave, a bath and a few hours sleep gave him some of the energy he'd need to accomplish his next task. Figuring out what the hell he was going to do.

Morgan's luck at investments had always been on the down side. The Spade Bit ranch had floundered under his ownership, albeit an absentee ownership. He'd tried other things. A horse ranch which was raided, and the Spade Bit again, which was burned out. His most recent business venture had been in a stage line. At the outset it looked promising. Five months later the main office was nailed shut and one Jedediah Welsh had disappeared with what was left of Morgan's money. It was another chuckle. Welsh, thought Morgan, was a most appropriate name for his ex-business partner.

Morgan counted his money before he went to the dining room. If he paid two more days rent, ate light and got damned lucky in a poker game, he might get through the week. He'd come to Cheyenne with a plan in mind, however. The local cattlemen were growing more and more restless over the invasion of sheep. Several ranches had advertised for hired guns. Morgan wanted to check the validity of their claims, and if true, he'd hire his and he wouldn't hire cheap.

The beefsteak was good and Morgan topped off the meal by treating himself to a shot of good whiskey, the last in his own supply. He knew it might be a long dry spell. The idea of hiring his gun didn't bother him, he'd done that, in one form or another, most of his adult life. What did bother him was just how quickly he could do it. Many of the advertisements requested that letters be written to the ranchers. After all, it was winter and how much trouble were they having right now? Morgan was gambling on his skill and perhaps his reputation. He would try to hire on as a kind of gun hand's ramrod.

The casino proved to be another obstacle for Morgan. The smallest table stakes he could find were fifty dollars. Hell, he didn't have anywhere near fifty dollars. A house man told him he would have to come back on Monday night when there were several tables open to what the house man called, "penny ante" players.

Morgan considered bucking the cold weather and wandering around trying to find a game he could afford but the warmth of the bar changed his mind. That, and the fact the barkeep seemed to assume Morgan wanted his drinks charged to his room bill. He was told it was a new policy being instituted by many of the finer hotels in the country. Morgan decided he'd drink tonight and worry about the cost tomorrow.

"Just leave the bottle," Morgan said. The barkeep nodded.

Morgan returned to his room about nine o'clock. He was not drunk but the effects of the whiskey were evident. He read the evening paper and then simply sprawled out on his bed. A little more than an hour later, he was aroused by a gentle knock at the door. The whiskey hadn't dulled his senses or his reflexes that much and he was on his feet, gun drawn and far enough away from the door to avoid being shot.

"Yeah?" There was no reply but the knocking was repeated. "Who is it?"

"Please, sir, just let me in." The plea was whispered, the voice feminine. Morgan moved again, pressing his back against the wall next to the door.

"It's open." The girl came in and Morgan got a good look at her and made certain she was alone before he spoke. The girl's eyes were still adjusting to the semi-darkness, and when Morgan finally did say something the sound startled her.

"Who are you?" She blinked, looked down at the gun and stepped back. Morgan had forgotten about it. He holstered it. "Habit," he said. Then he repeated his question.

"Tamara Winfrey," came the reply. "I'm called Tammy."

"I won't bother introducing myself," Morgan said. "You either already know or you've got the wrong room. Which is it?"

"I know who you are and I've come to ask for your help."

"How do you know who I am and how did you know I was in Cheyenne?"

She smiled and relaxed a little. Morgan began to think she was somewhat older than she appeared. "May I sit down?"

"No need if you're not going to be here that long," Morgan said. He walked to her. "And you're not if I don't get some answers."

"Very well. I had a man, a man who worked for me, go to Fort Laramie to find you. You'd already left. He found out you were coming here and sent me a telegraph cable. Then he was going to follow you and make the contact with you himself." She opened a small bag and produced the cable. Morgan read it and looked up.

"You said he was going to contact me. Where is he?"

"Dead." She winced a little and swallowed and licked her lips and said, "May I have a drink?"

"Of what?"

"Whiskey would be nice, if you have any left." Morgan eyed her, his head tilted to one side. "I saw you in the saloon. I saw the bottle."

Morgan didn't say anything but instead walked to the chiffonnier and poured the last two drinks from the bottle. He carried hers back to her and then silently held his glass out in a mock toast. They both drank. "Thank you," she said. Morgan nodded. "May I sit down now?"

"Who killed your man, and why?"

The girl sighed. "I know why," came the reply and then an added touch of disgust in the tone, "but if I knew who, I wouldn't be trying to hire you."

"And what makes you think I can be hired?"

"You're broke and you won't get on with anybody around here 'til next spring. What I want you to do is immediate and it could pay very well."

"Could?"

"Look, Mr. Morgan, I've had a very tiring and somewhat frightening day. I don't mind answering your questions, but I would appreciate doing it from the comfort of a chair. I've just come in from a very cold and exhausting one hour walk." Morgan considered her again and then nodded. He took a chair across the room.

"All right, Tammy, let's hear it all."

"My brother and I have inherited some land. We were told it was pretty much worthless and someone made an offer to buy it from us. We were going to accept the offer when we received this message." She'd been fishing through some papers while she talked and now she produced one and handed it to Morgan. He read.

Don't sell. Get help but don't sell.

Morgan looked up. "It doesn't impress the hell out of me, Tammy," he said. "Unsigned and rather poorly written."

"I felt the same way until I turned it over." Morgan frowned and then turned the message over. There was one more line.

Find Lee Morgan. Hire him and then come here.

Morgan looked at Tammy and she was holding out the envelope in which the message had arrived. "Look at the postmark." He did.

"Tombstone, Arizona? Just where in the hell is this land of yours?"

"In California."

"Jeezus! You barge in here, wake me up,

want to hire me to find a killer in Wyoming, tell me it might pay fairly well, and all I have to do is follow you to Arizona on the strength of an unsigned letter to find out about some land you own out in California." Morgan got to his feet. "Tammy, you're crazy."

Tammy stood up also. She had a half smile on her face. "I'm very sure it must look that way but it isn't. My brother will be here in a few minutes and I'll have more answers."

"Like what?"

"Like who wrote this message and, well, maybe why."

"Yeah," Morgan said, "That would be a good start. For all I know there never was a hired man who got himself killed and there is no land and you wrote this."

"Please, Morgan, just bear with me. I swear to you that what I've told you is the truth. You have to believe me." Morgan shook his head. "No, Tammy, that's where you're wrong. I don't have to believe a damned word of it."

"Will you just wait for my brother, please."

Morgan considered her. Actually, he was looking at her for the first time as a woman rather than an intruder. If he had plenty of other doubts, he had none about her womanhood. He snorted and grinned and thought of the messes he seemed to get himself into.

"I'll wait," he said. "The one thing I feel pretty sure about is that you're not going to all this trouble just to rob me." There was just a moment when Tamara Winfrey thought Morgan

14

was serious. Suddenly the tension broke and they both got a big laugh out of it.

Almost on the schedule Tammy had predicted, her brother showed up. He became the second thing about which Morgan was sure. Tad Winfrey was his sister's twin. There was, according to Tammy, just two hours difference between them. Both were twenty-seven. After the appropriate introductions, Tad said, "I've contacted a lawyer friend of mine in Phoenix. We'll know our mystery man soon."

Tad Winfrey was a well groomed, well dressed man who carried no weapons. By Morgan's reckoning, he probably had very little use for them. He was big, husky and, according to him, a skilled pugilist. Morgan knew that boxing wouldn't stop a bullet but it could stop the man with the gun. Tad also proved as long on brains as brawn.

"You know, Mr. Morgan, you've asked a lot of questions of my sister and me. I understand that but I think it's time you answered one, if you can."

"Yeah? What's that?"

"Who do you know in Tombstone, Arizona who would recommend to us that we find you and hire you?"

Morgan couldn't argue the validity of the question. As a matter of fact, he had been somewhat surprised that Tammy hadn't asked it. He was glad she hadn't and was somewhat embarrassed by Tad's having asked. All that aside, it deserved the best answer Morgan could give.

"I don't know a living soul in Tombstone, Arizona," he said. A knock at the door turned all three heads toward it and then glances back at one another. Tad answered. It was the boy from the telegraph office. Tad ripped open the cable and read. He looked up. "My friend used his position as a lawyer to get our answer for us. The sender of the mystery message was Wyatt Earp!"

2

Morgan sold his horse. The move was one of simple practicality. It was cheaper to sell him than to transport him. The Winfreys footed the bill for the trip to Tombstone. All but the last leg of it was by rail. They called it an investment but Morgan was quick to point out that he had agreed to nothing more than making the trip.

Morgan reckoned that if Wyatt Earp had actually sent the message, it deserved his attention. If the sender proved to be an imposter, the sender deserved his attention. Either way, in Morgan's view, the long trip was justified.

Enroute, Morgan gave Tad and Tammy the only plausible explanation of which he was aware for the message from Wyatt Earp. Earp, Morgan told them, had been a close friend of

Morgan's father, Buckskin Frank Leslie.

Morgan felt a bit of excitement within himself as the trio walked from the train depot down along the main street toward the Oriental Saloon. At one point along the way, Morgan stopped and stared and pointed to a sign. It read,

O K Corral

"October of eighteen and eighty-one," Morgan said.

Tad Winfrey shook his head and then said, "Sure, I remember reading about the gunfight at the O K Corral." He turned to Morgan. "Was your father in it?"

Morgan shook his head. "I heard that he would have been except for a rainstorm that held up a stagecoach for two days. No, as I remember him telling me, it was the three Earp brothers, Doc Holliday and a gang called the Clanton-McLaury gang."

"Did many die?" Tammy asked.

"Three. Two of the Earp brothers were wounded. Even Doc Holliday got hit, I think, but Wyatt never got a scratch. The other side took the heavy losses."

The three checked into the hotel next to the Oriental and at Morgan's urging got adjacent rooms with a connecting door. Only a few minutes after they were settled in, Morgan knocked.

"You two stay put." He handed Tad a rifle.

Tad frowned. "You know how to use it?"

"I do but. . . ."

"No buts," Morgan said, "not until I find out what's going on. You open the door for me, no one else. If there's more trouble than you can handle," he added, "go through my room and out onto the roof. You can drop from the roof at the far end."

"Are you always this cautious?"

Morgan eyed Tammy and nodded. "Try to remember your hired man."

The Oriental Saloon was jam-packed. Morgan got the eye from one or two of the still unoccupied ladies. One caught his return attention. She was a beautiful octoroon with raven hair pulled into a comb and draped, seductively, over her left shoulder. Morgan made a mental note to inquire about her later.

"What'll you have, mister?" the barkeep asked. Morgan wasn't paying attention and the barkeep repeated the question with a tone of irritation.

"Beer," Morgan said. He was eyeing the back bar and the fancy paintings. There were many tintypes about. The great and near great who had frequented the Oriental over the years. The famed Birdcage Theatre brought them to Tombstone and the Oriental entertained them as they entertained the citizens of Tombstone.

Lily Langtry, Sarah Bernhardt, Georgia Drew and, of course, the famed Little Egypt were among the women. Male entertainers had been equally welcomed however and included the likes of Jack Langrische, Edwin Booth, Maurice Barrymore and the ever popular Eddie Foy.

As Morgan drank his beer, he also considered the infamous who had frequented Tombstone's palaces of pleasure. The Earps, Doc Holliday, John Ringo, Morgan's own father and a score of men Morgan had only read about.

"Another beer, mister?" Morgan blinked, looked up and nodded.

"You look like your father. At least the way he looked when I first knew him." Morgan's head jerked around and he found himself staring into a set of deep blue eyes and a rugged face. The man sported a thick and drooping handlebar moustache, flecked with gray. The skin tone was brown and the texture a bit leathery.

The barkeep returned with Morgan's beer. He took the money and then cast a casual glance at the man who'd moved in next to Morgan. "Evenin', Mr. Earp."

"Charlie."

"I'll be damned," Morgan said. He stood up straight and held out his hand. "You're Wyatt Earp." The man nodded.

"I have a private table in the far corner. Shall we?"

"Sure," Morgan said. Morgan took note of those whose eyes were upon them as they crossed the room. Earp was no doubt one of Tombstone's most colorful characters and he had been one of its first citizens and lawmen. Now the glances carried in them the curiosity of

Morgan's own identity. He was glad when they reached the table.

Morgan had a score of questions. He decided to wet down his throat before he began and took a long swallow of beer. He never got to the questions.

"I sent a message up to Tammy Winfrey. I have to assume she got it and found you. Did all three come with you?"

"Three? Tammy is here and her brother Tad."

Wyatt winced. "Jake Miller?"

"Sorry, never heard of him," Morgan said. Suddenly it dawned on Morgan about the man Tammy said she'd hired. "Tammy told me she had a man working for her. He came looking for me at Fort Laramie. Missed me by a day or two. Got himself killed on the way back to Cheyenne."

Wyatt Earp looked suddenly tired. The sparkle was gone from his eyes and his mouth curled down at the corners. He shook his head back and forth in an almost imperceptible motion. He looked up. "Jake Miller was an old and dear friend. One of the oldtimers in this country. We rode more than one trail together. If Tammy didn't mention him, then he never got to her. It wasn't Jake on that trail but with him dead too, they know about me."

"They? Who the hell is they?" Morgan asked.

Wyatt Earp shook his head again. "The impatience of the young."

"You were never impatient?"

"I was but it's a bad habit for any man who makes his way with a gun."

"I'm not making my way with a gun right now," Morgan said. "I'm trying to get some sensible answers out of somebody, anybody who can give them and when I keep asking and don't get them, I get damned impatient."

"Your father was that way. Impatient as hell, except when he was waiting for a man to make his play. Are you as good as he was?"

"Not from what I've heard. Not from the one time I saw him draw."

"Kid Curry, wasn't it?" Morgan nodded. "I don't think it would have happened that way if Frank Leslie had been your age when he faced Curry." Wyatt scooted his chair back from the table. "I'll be up to see you all tonight, midnight likely, twelve-thirty at the latest." Wyatt Earp got to his feet and it was the first time Morgan noted that the old lawman wasn't carrying a gun.

"You feel safe not toting a piece?"

"Naked is more the word for it," Wyatt said, "but I made a promise to my family. Probably the dumbest promise I ever made and I'll tell you the damned truth, I've never felt comfortable since the day I took it off for good."

"You're not that old," Morgan said, standing up. "And it's obvious you're involved in something here."

"Indirectly is all. I'll tell you about it tonight, Morgan, but I'll tell you this much now.

Tamara and Thaddius are kin to me and I'll not see them hurt. I want the best I can get to help them. In my opinion," Wyatt concluded, smiling, "you're the best around."

"That's a hell of a smooth way to enlist a man's help."

Morgan was surprised to find Wyatt Earp already at the Winfreys' room when he arrived. Wyatt poured Morgan a drink, handed it to him and said, "Morgan, I'd like you to meet these youngsters a second time. This is Tamara and Thaddius Winfrey, the twin children of my sister." Wyatt downed his own shot of whiskey and shook his head a little. "Actually, she was my half sister." He added, quickly, "But I wouldn't have felt any more kinship if she'd have been full blooded Earp."

"Alright," Morgan said, "I'm convinced your request is legitimate. Now how about some of those answers?"

Wyatt nodded, sighed and took a chair. "It could get to sounding like just another frontier tale if I'm not careful, so I'll do my best to keep it simple."

"I'd appreciate that, Wyatt," Morgan said.

"My sister's name was Lileth. She married Holt Winfrey, who could best be described as a dreamer. A prospector with a few more brains than most, but still a dreamer. After about twenty-five years of poking around the rocks trying to find that dream, he did. Big!"

"How big?" Morgan asked.

"Eight to ten million dollars." Morgan's

eyebrows raised and he let go a long, low whistle. Wyatt nodded. "Yes, sir. That's one helluva dream."

"Where'd he hit this Mother Lode?"

"The Palo Verdes range, along the Arroyo Seco at the southeastern tip of California."

Morgan pondered the information for a moment and then looked up and said, "I'm no mining engineer." He grinned, "I wouldn't even qualify as a good prospector but I've never heard of any big strikes in that part of California. What the hell kind of ore was it?"

Wyatt glanced at Tad and Tammy and then back to Morgan. Morgan had caught the glance and now he frowned. Wyatt didn't wait for Morgan to push the issue. "It wasn't ore. It was gold. Pure gold, already mined, already smelted."

"What?"

"Tad," Wyatt said, "maybe you should take it from here."

"My father found the Peralta treasure. I'm sure you've heard of that."

Morgan got up, poured himself another drink, downed it and refilled his glass one more time. Then he turned around and his expression was a mixture of serious doubt and possible anger. "Yeah, I guess damned near everybody who ever rode west of St. Louis, Missouri has heard of the Peralta treasure." Morgan looked down for a moment, obviously in thought. A moment later he looked up, eyed Wyatt and then Tad and Tammy. "I also heard it was bullshit."

Morgan looked at Tammy somewhat sheepishly. "I'm sorry," he said. She smiled and nodded her understanding.

"Tammy's heard a lot worse," Tad said, "from me. I didn't believe it either and I know there must be a thousand legends about buried Spanish gold."

"If you know that, Tad," Morgan said, pouring himself another drink, "then you also know that not so much as one twenty dollar gold piece has been found."

"Yes, I know that, too, but this is different."

"Sounds that way, if he actually found gold. Have you seen it?"

"He didn't find the gold, I mean, not the gold itself." Morgan laughed. Tad's face flushed with the first hint of anger. Morgan downed his drink and looked at Wyatt. Morgan was rather hoping for some support from the old lawman. Wyatt's expression didn't indicate that he was about to give in.

"What the hell did he find, Tad? A damned map?"

Wyatt Earp said, "Do me the favor of hearing the story, Morgan. I'm no damned fool for Spanish gold. I listened and I changed my mind."

"I'm here," Morgan replied, coldly, "and my expenses are paid. Listening to another treasure story seems little enough to do to earn my keep." Morgan sat down, crossed his legs, folded his arms across his chest and said, "Go ahead, Tad, I'm listening."

"I promise I won't bore you with another Spanish gold legend."

Morgan admired Tad's spunk but he really didn't want to hear another tale of buried treasure. "I'll hold you to that," Morgan said.

"Simply put," Tad began, "Francisco Peralta rode into California seeking land, not gold. He stumbled into an Indian village in which the tribe used gold for virtually everything. Their tools, dishes, replicas of their Gods. Peralta got the fever. He wiped out the village and then spent six months rounding up wild horses and breaking them for pack animals."

"And what went wrong?"

"The usual. Internal at first. Men who weren't content with a bonus in their pay. They wanted a share. The longer it went, the more they became unhappy. Only a raid on the Spanish camp by Mexican bandits unified them again."

"And the gold?"

"Still with them but Peralta knew he'd never get it back to Spain. Besides, by that time he was already considering some pretty horrible alternatives."

"Like keeping it all for himself?" Morgan smiled. He'd heard it all before. Different names and places but the same story.

Tad knew that Morgan didn't buy any of the story. It angered him somewhat, but he tried to remember that, at first, neither had Wyatt Earp. He ignored Morgan's question and just continued. "Peralta ordered eighty percent of the gold loaded onto the newly broken horses. Twenty percent he loaded onto the expedition's pack mules, then he split the two groups. The smaller of the two carried the most wealth."

"And the other one was a decoy, a sacrificial lamb he sent to the slaughter."

"Exactly."

Morgan smiled again. It was like reading an old newspaper. "Did it work?"

"It did. The smaller force was attacked and wiped out. It gave Peralta enough time to reach the mountains."

"The Palo Verdes."

"No. A range to the south which, at that time, didn't have a name. Today it's called the Cargo Muchacho range. The mountains of the remorseful boy." Morgan cocked his head. Tad went on. "There were about two hundred boys riding with Peralta. They were the newest conscripts into the army and he'd asked permission to take them on the five year trip so that they might return home as men. Among them was his own grandson."

"That's all he had with him in the main body? Boys?"

"No. There was still a contingent of troops under an officer who completely trusted Peralta. The Spaniard had chosen a plan and now set it in motion. He sent the captain and the rest of the soldiers south, ordering them to find a passable route through the mountains and into Mexico.

"But they didn't find it and Peralta, stuck with a pack of rug rats, had to bury the gold."

Tad was becoming increasingly irritated by Morgan's chiding. He looked to Wyatt for support but the old lawman just smiled. Tad turned back, his jaw set, his eyes piercing.

"No, Morgan, they didn't find it. What they found were Indians and Mexican bandits and death. It was exactly what Peralta had hoped they'd find."

Morgan frowned. "You saying he planned it that way?"

"That's what I'm saying, yes. You see, almost the instant the soldiers rode out, Peralta ordered the boys into groups of about fifty each. Four of them. They divided up the gold and over the next four days, rode in four directions and buried it. Peralta's grandson accompanied each of the four groups and made a drawing of the burial spot. By the time the last group had returned, Peralta had the only map depicting all four areas. No one else, not even his grandson, knew all four locations."

"I'll be damned," Morgan said, "now that's a new one."

"Yes, Morgan, it is, so to speak, a new one and not the only new one where the Peralta gold is concerned."

"I'm listening."

Tad smiled. For the first time, he believed Morgan really was listening. "The soldiers had not returned. If the captain had been easily persuaded by Peralta's manner, you can imagine how he handled the boys."

"He ordered them into the field?"

"Not only that, he split them up again. Groups of fifty in four directions. This time, they were told not to stop until they found a way out."

"Jeezus! How many made it?"

"There are no records that any of them made it. If they did, they were too damned scared to ride back or try to tell their story to anyone."

"Peralta?"

Tad held up his hands. "I'll get to that." He walked across the room, warming now to a subject he'd obviously researched very thoroughly. "Peralta had kept two other people behind when he ordered the last contingent of troops away. One was the priest. The other, a metalsmith."

"The priest for the boys, the metalsmith to melt the stuff down into," Morgan paused, "into what? Coins? Bricks?"

"You're right about the priest, Morgan. Not to have kept him back with the boys would have aroused too much suspicion. The metalsmith is another story."

"I'm still listening."

"Peralta's wife had presented him with a brand new brace of pistols before he left. Pistols with wooden butts. Now, Peralta ordered the metalsmith to fashion new grips for them. Grips of gold, each of which would depict a portion of the four burial sites of the treasure. Only someone with both pistols would have the complete map. As each grip was completed,

29

Peralta destroyed the accompanying map made by his grandson."

"And he'd have to destroy the metalsmith and the priest too."

"Exactly," Tad said.

"And Peralta? Did he make it?"

"Only one person rode out of that mountain range, Morgan."

"The grandson! What the hell happened?"

"That we don't know for sure. Maybe no one ever will."

"The kid didn't get the gold either," Morgan said, "and that's the remorse."

"If the grandson followed in his grandfather's footsteps, yes. But there was plenty to be remorseful about without the gold. The boy's grandfather was dead, the soldiers were dead, his friends were dead. He was twelve, maybe fifteen. He was all alone."

"Well," Morgan said, walking over to the whiskey bottle again, "it's one of the best gold stories I've heard." He poured a little shorter shot and downed it and then turned to face the trio. He smiled. "I'll give it that." None of them smiled back.

Tad Winfrey crossed the room to a chair in the far corner. Draped over its back was a set of saddlebags. Tad stepped into Morgan's line of sight, removed something from one of the bags and turned around. Morgan stared. His smile faded. He was looking at the rusty frame of an old flintlock pistol. A pistol with a gold grip.

3

Morgan slept on what he'd heard and seen and there were plenty of questions to which he wanted answers but he'd decided to throw in with Wyatt Earp. He'd agreed to meet Wyatt the next morning and he assumed Wyatt would want an answer. He was wrong.

At ten o'clock, Morgan strolled into the Arizona Bank & Trust Company and soon found himself in company with Wyatt and the bank's president, John Hemmings. After the introductions, Morgan got his biggest surprise yet.

"Read this," Wyatt said, handing Morgan what appeared to be an official document. Morgan read. His expression hardened as he read and when he finished he tossed the paper on the desk.

"You mind if we talk privately for a moment, Mr. Hemmings? Morgan was looking at Wyatt Earp the whole time he was speaking. It was Wyatt who responded.

"I'm sure he wouldn't mind Morgan, but there's no need. He's involved in this thing a helluva lot deeper than I am right now." Wyatt leaned forward, "Mr. Hemmings here is puttin' up the money and I won't let 'im do that unless the man that I recommend for the job is wearin' a badge."

"I don't much like wearing badges, Wyatt."

"And I don't much like hired gun hands, Morgan, which is exactly what you'd be without the badge. Take it or leave it."

Morgan had an odd sense of obligation, somehow, and he resented it. Wyatt Earp had been almost as much a legend to him as the Peralta treasure, until now. He eyed both men.

"I don't like the idea of justifying hiring out my gun by pinning on a tin star."

Wyatt leaned back and smiled. "Then don't justify it, I don't give a damn and I'm sure Mr. Hemmings doesn't either. But without the badge, you can catch the afternoon stage back north. You got expenses for both directions."

"Why did you wait 'til this morning to spring this on me?"

"Because if you didn't believe the rest of it, there was no need for this morning."

"Who says I do believe it?"

"You showed up."

Morgan leaned forward. "I showed up because you're Wyatt Earp, not necessarily because I believe that gold legend or a rusty old pistol with a shiny grip."

"Then sign that paper for the same reason, Morgan, and do us both a favor." Wyatt reached into his vest pocket and pulled out a small cloth sack. He said, "You know, if you come out o' this in one piece, you could be a wealthy man." He put the sack on the desk in front of Morgan. Morgan eyed it.

"When I sit in a poker game," Morgan said, "I like to know ever'body who's going to play."

"When you're ready to play," Wyatt Earp countered, "I'll be glad to tell you as much as I know." He pointed at the cloth sack. Morgan picked it up, undid the draw strings and let the contents spill into his hand. It was a badge. A shiny brass badge.

United States Marshal

"Real pretty," Morgan said.

"It was given to me by John Fremont when he appointed me marshal right here in Tombstone back in the summer of eighty. I only wore it once," Wyatt said, "had a silver one for ever-'day."

"Go to meeting badge, was it?" Morgan asked.

"I'd reckon that's what Fremont had in mind, but I didn't wear it for that. I wore it on the twenty-sixth day of October, eighteen and eighty-one."

Morgan's eyes widened. "The shootout at the O K corral?"

Wyatt nodded. "Put it on that mornin' and left it on 'til they'd buried Tom and Frank McLaury and Billy Clanton. Never pinned it on again. I'd like you to wear it." Wyatt had a carpetbag next to him and he opened it and handed Morgan a Buntline Special.

"I've heard about this gun, but this is the first one I ever saw."

"More'n likely be the last, too," Wyatt said. "The folks up to Colt don't figure on makin' any more of 'em. Now, Morgan, I want that badge back." Morgan looked up. Wyatt was smiling. "No hole in it, neither." He nodded toward the long barreled pistol. "That gun is yours to keep, whether you ride in this thing or not." Morgan looked puzzled. "I owed your daddy." Wyatt paused in obvious remembrance. "Helluva man, your daddy. Sometime I'll tell you about the marker he held on me. In the meanwhile, I'd like you to accept the gun for him."

Morgan looked up. He knew Wyatt Earp was not a man to offer a bribe to get what he wanted and he was thinking to himself exactly what Buckskin Frank Leslie would be saying to him. He'd have told Morgan to ride for Wyatt just because Earp asked him to, no other reason necessary, no questions asked.

Lee Morgan had become his own man, no question about that, but he was now being exposed to a part of his heritage which was becoming almost as scarce as buffalo herds. The code, his father called it. The unwritten, un-spoken tie which linked certain men together. There were times and places for questions and for caution and for saying no. Morgan remem-bered what his father had said. "You don't say no to a friend. That's the code."

"You've got yourself a gun," Morgan said.

Wyatt Earp smiled. "I could have got a gun in a half a dozen places, Morgan. It's the man behind it I was picky about." He extended his hand and Morgan gripped it firmly. He'd ridden many trails for many reasons, but he'd never ridden one for the code. It was time he did.

Lee Morgan learned another quick lesson about the code. It was one lonely sonuvabitch! The Winfreys had their own set of duties to perform and would be making the trip to California nearly two weeks after Morgan was already there. As to Wyatt Earp, he had a family and a promise to them and home. He went back to it.

Morgan received five hundred dollars in expenses from the banker, Wyatt standing good for it, and a letter of credit for any additional funds he might need. His destination was the little desert town which Holt Winfrey put together after he'd made his discovery.

Morgan rode through a pass in the Cargo Muchacho range and down into the God for-saken desert below it. It was land on which, Morgan reckoned, a man couldn't raise hell with a fifth of whiskey. Holtville, California, offered little in the way of respite from it.

Morgan bought himself a new wardrobe in Tombstone and it included a fine cowhide vest. Beneath it, pinned on his left shirt pocket, he wore the marshal's badge. He decided he'd likely end up a target for somebody before this trail ended but he didn't intend to make it easy for them.

The Holtville Hotel had some things in common with some of the finest establishments in the country. A front door, at least one window in each room, and a chamber pot. If there were other similarities, Morgan was damned if he could find them.

"How long will you be with us, sir?"

"Not sure," Morgan said, "looking to buy some land hereabouts and there seems to be plenty of it to see. Could be quite a spell." The desk clerk was giving Morgan the once-over all the time Morgan was talking. He took particular note of Morgan's rig and the extra special rig which Morgan now wore in a cross drawn fashion on his left hip. It was Wyatt's Buntline Special.

"You, uh, well, you don't look the cut of a land buyer." The clerk looked at the registration book and frowned. The name meant nothing to him. Morgan picked up his gear. He looked the clerk right in the eye.

"Funny," he said, "you don't look like a desk clerk."

Morgan settled in and then took a turn around the town. It wasn't much. He reckoned that it had been at one time and he was certain that Holt Winfrey had good intentions. The town just didn't match the dream. A third of the buildings along the main street were boarded up. There were half a dozen run-down saloons, a drug store, a mercantile, a tonsorial parlor, one eatery which boasted home cooked meals, a law office, the Holtville Bank and the sheriff's office.

Morgan's tour was kept to the main street, although he got a glimpse of a railroad depot and one or two rather large and pretentious looking homes on a tree-lined side street. He promised himself a more thorough tour later.

The door to his room was ajar and Morgan tensed up. He approached cautiously and he could hear voices.

"You check that carpetbag?"

"Not yet. Nothin' important in these saddle bags, though."

"Looks like our visitin' land buyer just bought himself some new clothes. Don't appear these duds been wore yet."

There was a loose and squeaky floor board just outside Morgan's room. By whatever chance applies, he'd missed stepping on it when he checked in. Now, he found it.

"Shit," he mumbled, looking down. The door flew open and Morgan didn't see the meaty fist coming. It connected.

Morgan reeled backwards, slammed into the wall across the narrow hall and found the wind half knocked out of him. He shook his head and brought his arms up to defend himself. It was already too late. The man who'd hit him was built like a battering ram. Short and stocky and solid and with a head like a boulder. He doubled up and put the boulder right into Morgan's middle. The gunman folded up over the man's muscular shoulders. He lifted Morgan, spun around and literally tossed Morgan through the door to his own room. He felt his arms being pinned behind him by the second man and he could see the battering ram coming at him again. It was the last thing he saw for some little time.

What Morgan saw an hour later seemed to be floating. He blinked and some things looked more solid. He drew a breath and moaned. A moment later, a bearded face came into view as Morgan pushed himself up on his elbows. He blinked again and the last of the blur disappeared, replaced by a clear vision of iron bars.

"Glad to see you're still with us, Marshal. I've seen more'n one gent stove up for a month or more after tanglin' with Shorty." Morgan got to his feet. Instinctively he felt for his gun. "Got your hardware out here, Marshal." The man pulled the cell door open. Obviously, it hadn't been locked.

Morgan noted that there were only two cells, with no one using either but him. The bearded man had already gone into the small office at the building's front. Morgan now followed. The bearded man was gathering up Morgan's guns. He turned around just as Morgan's eyes fell on Shorty. The bearded man grinned.

"I'm Sheriff Prather," he said, stepping

quickly in between Morgan and Shorty. He handed Morgan his six-gun and the empty holster in which Morgan had been carrying the long barreled Buntline. Morgan frowned. "Got that fancy pistol in muh desk drawer there. Didn't want to chance anybody stealin' it." The sheriff wiped his hand on the seat of his pants and then extended it. "Tyson Prather. Most call me Ty," he said, and then added, "when they git to know me."

Morgan declined the handshake and strapped on his rig instead. The sheriff stepped aside, gestured toward Shorty with his left hand and said, "I think you two already met but I'll introduce ya jist the same. This here is one o' muh deputies, Shorty. T'other one's eatin' his supper. Name's Luther." He motioned for Shorty to stand up. The deputy did, grinning the whole time. "Shorty, this gent here is a honest to God Yewnited States Marshal name o' Lee Morgan." Ty Prather turned back to face Morgan. "Shorty, he never met no real marshal before."

"You've got a lousy welcoming committee in your town," Morgan said, stepping by the sheriff and moving to the desk. He opened the top drawer, glanced down, slammed it shut, and opened a side drawer. In it was the Buntline. He took it out and slipped it into the holster. He looked up. Ty Prather was frowning at Morgan's audacity but Shorty was scowling.

"We don't git too many strangers in Holtville, Mr. Morgan, and I can't recollect the last time we had a visit from a Yewnited States Marshal. As the duly elected lawman in town, it's muh duty to find out a stranger's name an' intent."

"Did you ever hear of asking questions?"

Sheriff Prather shuffled his feet, looked down and then ran his fingers through dirty looking, stringy hair and said, "Well, sir, now I just got to apologize fer that there. Ya see, I was out o' town on important business an' Shorty here, he kind o' takes the job too serious sometimes." Prather looked up. "I'd likely do more to both of 'em, Marshal, but them bein' named Prather too," he grinned, "well sir, you can see muh problem. Them bein' kin an' all."

"Yeah, Sheriff," Morgan said, "I understand." He came from behind the desk and walked straight over to the two men. "Now you understand something. I'm going to be with you for a spell and I'm here officially. I hope nobody gets in my way."

Morgan saw Ty Prather's hand move backwards and still a threatened move by Shorty. Morgan had been ready but there was no need to stir more trouble than he'd already encountered.

"As one lawman to another, Mr. Morgan, I sure would feel better if we could work together, yessir. An' I'll see to it nobody gits in your way. You can count on me, Marshal, sure enough you can."

Morgan said nothing else and didn't bother acknowledging Ty Prather's commitment. He wasn't certain just exactly how the brothers

Prather had managed the only badges in town, but he was certain it wasn't by the Democratic process. He vowed to find out and to be a helluva lot more careful in the days to come.

Behind him, in the office of Sheriff Ty Prather, the grimy looking lawman picked up his hat and used it to flog his brother about the head and shoulders.

"Goddam it, Shorty, I tol' you a hunnert times, if'n I tol' you once, you don't do nuthin' less'n you ask me first." He flogged some more and only the arrival of Luther, or Lutey as he was known generally, stopped the flogging. Ty proceeded to administer a like punishment to Lutey and then said, "Shorty, now you ride on out to the ranch an' you tell Judge Lunsford what we found an' what we got. You hear?"

"How's come I got to go? Lutey eat his supper, I ain't."

Ty Prather let go another barrage with his hat. "You go 'cause I said you go. If I wanted Lutey to go, I'd send Lutey."

Morgan found himself some supper and more sore stomach muscles than he'd first believed and a lot of curious citizens. He ate and departed as quickly as his digestion would allow. He did want to make one more stop before he returned to his room. He found the off duty desk clerk playing poker. The clerk sensed Morgan's presence next to him and looked up. He looked puzzled.

"If you pass out anymore keys to my room, you and I will meet again and it won't be to talk.

41

You understand me?" The man sitting next to the clerk stiffened. He was a burly man with a thick neck and a face scarred from a bout with the pox.

"You make threats against my friends, mister, you make threats against me." The man pushed back from the table and the clerk smiled. The man got up. Morgan was in no mood to get caught off guard and let somebody else get in the first lick. As a matter of fact, at that moment, he was not even in the mood for a good old, one on one, fair fight barroom brawl.

"Mister," Morgan said, calmly, "I'm not talking to you." He drew the Buntline and laid the barrel across the man's head.

Morgan washed down with the coolest water he could find and stretched out, shirtless, on his bed. He was dozing in a few minutes, but his right hand was firm around the butt of the Bisley Colts. The squeaky hallway floor board worked again. This time to Morgan's advantage.

His eyes opened, fast and wide. He moved quietly but quickly off the bed. The door was locked and he fixed his gaze to the knob. It turned once, then again. Morgan waited. The floorboard squeaked and Morgan made his move.

He was at the door, had it unlocked and wide open in almost one fluid move. The door opened in and to the right of someone on the inside. He flung it open and stepped left. He heard footsteps pick up speed. He peered cautiously to his right and then wheeled into the hallway in a crouch, Bisley at the ready.

"That's far enough, unless you want a walking stick for a spell." The intruder stopped. "Turn around." The intruder complied. "Jeezus!" The intruder proved to be a kid, twelve to fifteen years old, Morgan reckoned. He stood up and motioned for the kid to come to him. Still, he kept the Bisley aimed at him.

"Buenas noches, señor Morgan."

"Good evening hell! *No habla Ingles."*

The boy shrugged. *"No habla Ingles."*

Morgan stuffed the Bisley into his waistband. He thought a moment. *"Como te llamas?"*

"Me llamo Felipe."

It had been sometime since Morgan had to test his Spanish. He paused again and then said, *"En que' puedo servirle?"*

"He came for me, *señor."* Morgan looked up toward the end of the hall. The girl he saw standing there was one of the most beautiful he'd ever seen. Clearly she was Spanish but she had breeding. The inky black hair was swept up and held in place with combs. Most of it, Morgan reckoned, was hidden beneath the flat, black hat. She wore leather britches, a white silk blouse and a short leather vest atop it. The britches were molded to shapely hips and thighs and Morgan could see the considerable stress on the silk blouse.

"Why?" Morgan asked.

"I knew you would not kill a boy."

Morgan smirked. "That right." She nodded. "But you didn't figure I'd have any trouble

43

gunning down a woman."

"I didn't mean that," she said. Just then, the boy bolted away and hurried to her. Morgan eyed them both. "He is my brother."

"Damned dangerous thing to do, lady, sending in a kid."

"I was," she hesitated, and then sighed, "I was wrong."

"Uh huh, you were but now that you're here, you may as well come in."

"I will send Felipe home first."

"I wouldn't. I've had other visitors since I hit town and they weren't quite as friendly with their approach."

In Morgan's room the woman and the boy stood in the corner huddled together. They both looked scared but Morgan could see a look of determination in the woman's eyes. He'd seen the look before. The look of a woman who'd been wronged or scorned. He remembered something about the wrath of a woman scorned. He also knew it applied to a woman wronged.

"You said someone visited you earlier. May I ask who?"

"Your friendly local deputies."

"They are evil men. They enforce only one law."

"Their own?"

"That of Don Miguel Carbona."

Morgan's ears picked up. It was a name he recognized and he didn't know why.

"Carbona? It's familiar to me." He considered the woman. "Any idea why it should be?"

"Perhaps you read of him, *señor*. He was charged with financing a raid on the Mexican border town of Tecolote."

"Yeah," Morgan said, nodding, "I remember now but they acquitted him, didn't they?"

The woman smirked. "Of course they did. Would it be otherwise when his best friend is Josiah Lunsford?" It was another name which struck a familiar chord. Morgan came up with that reason on his own.

"I saw that name on one or two of the stores in town."

"More than that, *señor*, but his main business is what saved Don Miguel."

"And what would that be?"

"He is the Federal Judge."

Morgan pondered the names and the obvious power which they had behind them and began to wonder just what the hell he was into.

"Seems to me it's time to talk about you, lady. Who you are and why you're here."

"I was told to contact you when you arrived. I had to make certain you were the right man. There is much at stake, *señor* Morgan."

"Who told you to contact me?"

"I cannot say that now but I know you are Lee Morgan, and I know you are a U.S. Marshal."

"And who the hell are you?"

The woman took a deep breath and said, "Estralita Peralta."

45

4

Morgan found sleep elusive following the woman's revelation. Neither the Winfreys or Wyatt Earp had bothered to tell him there were Peraltas still around. He wondered if, in fact, they themselves knew it. He was up and down a half a dozen times and it was well after two o'clock in the morning before he finally dozed off.

The shotgun blast tore a hole in the room's door big enough for a man's head to pass through. The second blast ripped into the center of the bed and showered Morgan in a blizzard of ticking. The gunman had already vacated the bed even before the first blast, however, and now it was Morgan and not his assailant who had the edge.

Morgan had rolled from the bed with the

first sounds in the hallway. He picked the side nearest the door and then pressed his back to the wall nearest the door. After a second blast, Morgan jerked open the door, spinning into position at the same time. He fired two shots and two men died.

He'd fully expected to see the two seedy deputies, but neither of the men in the hallway were men he'd seen before. Moments later however, the deputies did arrive. One at each end of the hallway. Shorty approached Morgan while the one called Lutey stood by with a shotgun. Morgan eyed them both.

"Lawman or no lawman, mister," Shorty said, grinning, "we don't tolerate no gunplay in Holtville."

"There was no play to it," Morgan said, "these two tried to leave their brand on me with shotguns."

"That so? Well now, mister fancy ass Marshal, we'll jist let the judge decide that. We got a good 'un here, ya know."

Morgan remembered Estralita Peralta's description of the good judge. A Federal Judge, no less. Lunsford, Morgan recalled. He also remembered that the Federal Territorial Prison was too damned close for comfort. The worst Federal Prison in the country was at Yuman, Airzona.

Morgan shrugged and dropped his pistol. At the same time he glanced down the hall toward Lutey. "Oh shit," he screamed, pointing at the same time. Lutey was predictable. He whirled around. By then, Shorty was about five feet from Morgan. The gunman would have liked nothing better than to take Shorty out back and beat the piss out of him but there simply wasn't time.

Morgan telegraphed his right leg with deadly accuracy. He wished he had his boots on but the ball of his foot found the target, Shorty's balls. Morgan expected Shorty to bend forward. He did and Morgan's knee greeted him on the chin.

Shorty went down like a poled ox and Morgan vanished into his room. By then Lutey knew he'd been sharked and when he saw Shorty, he bellowed at the top of his lungs and came charging down the hall. Morgan couldn't afford to kill a deputy sheriff and the man was brandishing a sawed-off.

Morgan grabbed his bedroll and freed up the black snake whip. He had it uncoiled just as Lutey reached the door. By then Lutey's brain was working and he stopped short of coming into view.

"Shorty. Shit! Goddam! You kilt 'im, ya sonuvabitch. You'll hang fer this, sure."

"You've got me," Morgan said. He tossed his pistol into the hallway. Lutey displayed a sudden show of smarts which Morgan wouldn't have imagined he possessed.

"You ain't foolin' me none, Marshal," he said, "you still got the long barreled pistol." Morgan smiled and shook his head. He slipped the Buntline from its holster and tossed it into the hallway as well.

"You're too smart for me, deputy." The compliment now also took effect and turned Lutey's brain back to mush. He stepped into view and Morgan unleashed the black snake. The shotgun flew into the air as the whip's end wrapped itself around Lutey's right wrist. Morgan worked the whip again.

Lutey was howling at the top of his lungs and holding his wrist. He didn't even see the second attack. Morgan aimed low and put two coils around Lutey's legs just below the knees. Morgan pulled and Lutey Prather ended up on his ass. Morgan walked himself along the whip, freed Lutey's legs and then pressed Lutey's own shotgun against the deputy's belly.

"I've got some questions, Deputy, and as long as I keep getting answers, this shotgun won't go off." Lutey stopped howling and he was scared, but brother Ty had trained him well.

"You won't shoot no lawman. You're one yourself." He forced a half smile. Morgan half straightened up, gave Lutey a weak smile in return, shrugged, turned the shotgun end for end and swung the butt in a short arc. The end of it caught Lutey on the chin and the obese little deputy joined Shorty in a heap.

Morgan didn't wait for morning. He gathered his gear and slipped out a side entrance. The man at the livery emerged from his quarters in long johns, bleary eyed and toting an old single shell shotgun. Morgan simply flashed the brass badge and the man returned to his quarters without a word. Morgan rode out, headed east. He was supposed to meet Estralita Peralta and he'd decided he wanted to be at their meeting place ahead of her.

The sand hills were strung out for two hundred miles in a diagonal pattern which ran from northwest to southeast. It was country in which a man could easily lose his way, either by accident or design. The wind was perpetual and made short work of tracks. Morgan had agreed to a meeting place with which he was already familiar. There were four roads through the sand hills. They converged at one point and Morgan had been there when he rode into the country.

As he sat and waited for the Peralta woman, he grew more and more uneasy. His mind was reeling with unanswered questions and each passing day brought new threats, new faces, more questions and no goddamn answers. The Winfreys and even Wyatt Earp had been of no help in that sense. They gave him information and directions and legends but no answers.

Morgan's horse snorted and pawed the ground. Morgan looked up and the animal had turned and was looking toward a nearby rise to the southeast. Morgan levered a shell into the Winchester and got to his feet. The horse snorted again and turned its head to the right. So did Morgan, then back to the left and then straight ahead.

"Jeezus!" The entire crest of the ridge of sand which overlooked the road junction was covered with riders. Morgan could only guess how many, and he did, in his mind. A hundred, he guessed.

Lee Morgan had been potato-sacked over a saddle only one other time in his life. He'd been scouting for the Army and found himself the unwilling guest of a Sioux war party. Now, he was the equally unwilling guest of a small army of Mexican bandits. Making matters worse was a blindfold and a gag and some damned sore ribs from his first meeting with Shorty.

Morgan estimated an hour on the animal from the road junction to the camp where they eventually ended up. He was untied. Then his captors trussed him up with his wrists bound to his ankles, his arms pulled behind him. He was dumped finally and only then did he lose the blindfold and the gag. He saw no one. He found himself in what he reckoned was a two-man Army field tent.

The day wore on, the sun grew hot, the thirst great and still Morgan saw no one. He kept conjuring up a vision of that beautiful face in the hallway. Estralita Peralta had considered the possibility that Morgan might gun her. Right at that moment, he thought, it would not only be easy but it might be pleasurable.

Morgan did his best to roll and find a new position and a little more comfort. Too, he knew he mustn't let the blood circulation get too low in his legs. His eyes got big.

The scorpion was on his leg, just above the knees and working its way up. Another was crawling along the sand about four feet away, headed straight for Morgan's face. He didn't move and he was wondering if scorpions had ears. If he shouted, would they hear him too? The tent flap opened and Morgan was momentarily blinded by the brightness.

"Don't move, for Chrissakes," he said, "I've got two scorpions on me."

"I know," came the reply, "I turned them into the tent to see if you'd scream. Most men do." A moment later the insects were dead in the sand and Morgan's wrists were free of his ankles. The girl was on her knees next to him, smiling. "Would you have screamed?"

"Why the hell didn't you wait it out and see?"

She smiled. "I would have, Mr. Morgan, but you would have been stung and died and there are others here who seem to think you have very valuable information."

"But you don't agree?"

"That's right. Now, can you sit up by yourself or do you want some help?"

"Why the hell don't you cut me loose? If that little army I saw is outside, I'm sure as hell not going anywhere." The girl ignored him. "Do you want help or not?" He nodded.

The girl looked vaguely familiar but she was not the girl in the hallway. She was not Estralita Peralta. She got Morgan to a sitting position. In spite of everything, Morgan could not ignore the girl's body or her soft touch or a faint feminine odor which stirred something deep within him. He had a need which had not been fulfilled for too long.

"I can tell you, lady," Morgan said, "you're right and your friends are wrong. I don't know a damned thing that will be of any use to them."

She smiled. "And even if you do, Marshal, you're the kind of man who would die before you'd reveal it."

"Your percentage just went down, lady," Morgan said, "on that one, you're wrong."

"I don't believe you, Mr. Morgan, but I can assure you of one thing," she said, turning around, "we will both have ample opportunity to put it to the test." She crawled out of the tent.

"How about some water?" Morgan hollered. There was no reply. He began at once to test the strength of his bonds. He cursed under his breath. These were not amateurs. The bonds were leather and short of his Bowie knife, or someone else's, they would not be removed. "Spanish fucking gold," he muttered. "Nice move, Morgan, real nice move."

Morgan's next visitor, perhaps an hour later, was no shapely, attractive, sweetly scented female. Morgan was yanked from the tent by his hair and found a boot resting on the side of his neck while a second man cut his bonds. Slowly, Morgan got to his feet. He'd barely done so when the big Mexican rammed a rifle butt into his soler plexus. Morgan's knees, already tingling from the bonds so lately removed, buckled.

"You stay on your feet Yankee dog, in the presence of our leader." Morgan was pulled back to his feet, his arms were pinned behind him and the second man struck three solid blows. Morgan went down again when he was turned loose. He shook his head and gulped in air. He tensed his muscles and struggled to his hands and knees. He could see a leg being drawn back.

"That's enough, Paco. He's no good to us dead." The voice was feminine and Morgan recognized it as that of the girl he knew as Estralita Peralta. A few minutes later, he found himself in a large tent attached to a make shift lean-to. He was pushed into a chair. He sat facing a big, muscular man whose dress was most definitely that of a Mexican bandit. What happened next surprised Morgan even in his condition.

"I'm certain you expected to be dragged before some kind of animal with a name like El Lobo or El Diablo."

Morgan eyed the man. He was dressed in typical Mexican attire and the trappings matched. A silver band around the base of the crown of his hat, silver encrusted, crossed bandoliers, twin, ivory gripped pistols, twin, bone handled Bowie knives and a bolo knife in a shoulder sheath. Its grip protruded above the man's left shoulder.

"You sure as hell look like one or the other," Morgan said. The man smiled. He turned to the girl and said, "Get Mr. Morgan some water." She nodded. He turned back to face Morgan. "Later some tequila or even wine perhaps." Morgan said nothing until he had consumed two large cups of water. He asked for a third and dumped it over his head.

"If you worked for me, I'd have you shot for what you just did."

Morgan mopped the water out of his eyes and face and then looked up and said, "If I worked for you, I'd have done it a long time back."

The man smiled. "You are a man who makes hasty judgments. You don't know me and you don't know what I do or why I do it, yet you have already acquired a dislike for me."

"That's a powerful bit of understatement," Morgan shot back.

"Then let me give you some information."

"Why not just give me back my belongings and my horse instead?"

"I'm afraid that's quite impossible. I'm surprised you'd even bother to ask."

"My daddy used to say you never know unless you ask."

"Frank Leslie, wasn't he?" Morgan was surprised. He showed it. He nodded.

"I know a great deal about you, Mr. Morgan, and now I propose to tell you a little about myself. My name is not El Lobo or El Diablo. I am not the Mexican bandito or the comanchero you would read about in the American press or the dime novels. My name is Joaquin Francisco Marin." Estralita brought Marin a flask. He opened it and took a short pull. He released it, handed it back to her and said, "Medicinal only."

"Get to the point, Marin."

The man cocked his head. "Very well. Let me

spell it out for you. My family was Spanish, not Mexican, not at the beginning in any event. The gold which was, shall I say, confiscated by *señor* Peralta belonged to my family. It was Marin money which financed the expedition, not Peralta's."

"Uh huh. So you've come up from Spain to claim your rightful heritage. Just a nice, neighborly fellow riding at the head of a gang of gun slinging, knife toting cutthroats."

"There is somewhat more to it than that, but you don't seem interested in hearing the truth or the details."

"The truth? I've met damned few people in the last few weeks who know the meaning of the word and none of them live within a day's ride of here. Just what the hell do you want from me, Marin?"

"The pistol with the gold grip. Don't bother denying your knowledge of it. Now you either have it or you know who does and therefore have access to it. I want it and I have a deadline. Produce it and you save your life."

"And you're going to take my word for what I tell you, let me ride out of here and get it and bring it back, that right?"

Marin smiled and shook his head. "You Americans and your sense of humor. It has seen you through many ordeals, hasn't it?" Morgan didn't reply. "Of course, you will simply tell me what I need to know. Your own life is the best security for both of us. If my men return with the pistol, you go free. If they do not, I'll have you killed." Marin got to his feet, held up his hand at a point when it appeared Morgan was about to speak. "I want you to think about it. Think about it very carefully," he paused, "until tomorrow."

"I do have one question Marin, before tomorrow." Marin stopped and turned back. "Why the hell is a girl named Peralta in your camp?"

Marin cocked his head and shrugged. "A lie, sir. I wasn't certain what you knew or did not know. I was sure of only one thing. You would meet a Peralta, not a Marin."

Morgan didn't have to wait long before he found himself once again in company with the two Mexicans. This time, however, he was also joined by Estralita Peralta, or whoever the hell she was.

"There is no need to bind him, Paco." Morgan had steeled himself to resist being tied up again. He hadn't the vaguest idea what he intended to do after he won the fight with Paco, if indeed he won the fight with Paco, but the consideration became academic. "You will ride with us to the house," she said. Morgan didn't say anything but he was wondering where the hell this house was located. He soon found out.

It was Spanish architecture at its finest. A tree-lined, green oasis in the middle of nowhere and with more security, Morgan reckoned, than Yuma prison could boast.

Morgan was given an upstairs room with an adjacent water closet and sunken bath. He was in need of both and ignored the barred windows and half a hundred armed guards.

Morgan's eyes were closed and he let the warm water soak into his bruised, aching muscles. Escape, deals, gold, the Winfreys, even Wyatt Earp could not rouse him now. He was dead ass tired and if he died tomorrow he intended to enjoy today.

He heard the movement behind him so he wasn't being careless. He just didn't give a damn.

"Wine?" He nodded. He heard the liquid being poured, a soft hand touched his arm. He put the glass to his lips and savored the taste. It was good wine and cool on his parched lips and throat. He still hadn't opened his eyes. Now, the same soft hands became more firm in their touch. Fingers dug in and worked on taut shoulder and back muscles.

"That's good," Morgan said.

"What? The wine or the massage?"

"Both and I'll take more of both." Morgan thought that Wyatt Earp would tell him he was fraternizing with the enemy. "Go to hell, Earp."

"What?" Morgan took a second glass of wine, smiled and opened his eyes. "Who did you say?"

"Nothing," Morgan replied, "forget it." He looked up. It was the girl who called herself Estralita. "What's your real name?"

"Teresa Marin. The other, the one who came to you before in the camp tent, she is my sister, Felisa."

"And Estralita Peralta?"

"She lives. She is the last of the Peraltas. My father wishes her dead." The girl frowned.

"You don't sound like you approve?"

"It is of no importance what a Marin woman thinks."

"It's important to me," Morgan said. He scooted up in the bathtub and did a half turn. His eyes met the girls and both knew what the other was thinking and what they wanted. Morgan had a flash of thought about her age but it passed quickly. He didn't give a damn about that either, as long as she was old enough to know her own mind.

Teresa Marin left the room. Morgan got out of the tub, dried himself and wrapped a towel around his waist. It proved to be a more modest act than any by Teresa. She was nude and on the bed and waiting. Morgan glanced at the door and back at her.

"It's allright," she said. "Everyone has been given orders to leave you alone. My father wants you to realize that he is a civilized man who has been wronged."

"Yeah," Morgan said, "I'm sure he does." He dropped the towel and moved to the bed. Hands reached up to welcome him.

Morgan's mouth began with Teresa's lips. He moved, slowly and sensuously down. Down along her throat, he kissed the indentations on each of her shoulders and let his tongue explore the cleavage between the modest but firm breasts.

Teresa wiggled and shivered with each of Morgan's movements and soon he had his hands working in conjunction with his mouth. He caressed her thighs, buttocks and paused at her hip bones when he got an extra reaction. He immediately moved down and let his tongue take over where his fingers had been.

Teresa Marin had been with a man before. Morgan felt less guilty but chuckled internally at himself. Certainly, he reasoned, there had never been that much guilt. He moved his hands up to her breasts and began to massage her nipples. They hardened at once under his touch and Teresa moaned with the joy of it.

Morgan moved down still further and let his tongue track along her inner thighs and finally come to rest on the black bush of her womanhood. This was no little girl. This was a woman and the scent alone brought Morgan very near to a climax. He had been celibate far too long.

He was so engrossed in giving pleasure and in turn feeling it by the very act he performed, he heard nothing.

The first realization of anyone else in the room came with a touch. A soft touch on his back, just between his shoulder blades. He thought nothing of it at first but then he realized it could not possibly be Teresa's hands. He stopped. He raised up and looked at Teresa. She was smiling and then her eyes shifted just a little to the left. Morgan turned his head. Felisa Marin was smiling at him, her hands still on his back. Her body naked.

"Holy shit," he mumbled. The two women now gently prodded and pushed Morgan until he was in the position they wanted him. He was on his back and the girls knelt on either side of him. Teresa began kissing his chest, his nipples, his upper abdomen. Felisa worked her wonders below that. She stopped short of taking him in her mouth but instead used her tongue with an expertise which Morgan didn't know existed outside of a whore house.

The number had been doubled, the sensation became astronomical. Two sets of hands, two sets of lips, two tongues, but with only one purpose, to give Lee Morgan total pleasure. The sisters seemed not only to sense Morgan's capacity but the limits of their own pursuits. Each time Morgan thought he was going to explode with pleasure, the sisters called a halt and changed positions.

They re-positioned Morgan lower on the bed. His legs were hanging over the end of it, his feet just touching the floor. Teresa Marin got on her knees between Morgan's legs, leaned forward and began licking him. Felisa had already climbed on the bed and positioned herself above him. He serviced her both orally and with his hands on her breasts. Unlike Teresa's tiny breasts, Felisa's were large, pendulous and highly sensitive.

Both women were moaning and Felisa's lips were grinding with the pleasure of every movement of Morgan's tongue. Still, they showed a self restraint which almost equalled Morgan's.

At the very height of their pleasure, they stopped and switched positions. Morgan was fast reaching a point of no return. Indeed, such a point was finally attained and Morgan couldn't help but wonder how they would split him up now.

Teresa straddled Morgan's face and Felisa assumed a similar position over his crotch. Between them, they kept his tongue, shaft and hands totally obligated to them. Teresa broke first, emitting a little howl of pleasure and writhing like a trapped animal. Her eyes were closed and her hands were busy on her own breasts as the pent up passion released itself.

Only a moment later, Felisa found release and Morgan couldn't hold out any longer either. Their bodies became one.

"Morgan," Teresa said, kissing his cheek, "next time you will make love to me." Morgan blinked. He was totally exhausted and the girl was talking about a next time. No, Morgan thought, not a girl, but two girls. He nodded, weakly. Felisa Marin slithered onto the bed beside him and kissed and nibbled at his ear.

"And next time," she said, softly, "I will feel your mouth on me."

They dressed and departed and Morgan downed two glasses of wine and smoked and thought about what had just happened and said aloud, "To hell with tomorrow." Lee Morgan climbed onto the bed and dropped into the deepest sleep he'd had in weeks.

5

Joaquin Marin ordered Morgan rousted out of bed well before sun up. As Morgan dressed, he pondered the realities which could face him when he faced Marin. He was none too sure about the discretion of either of Marin's daughters and he'd already considered his odds of escape. They were slim to none.

"I trust you slept soundly and comfortably, Mr. Morgan?"

"Very well," Morgan replied.

"Coffee?" Morgan nodded. "How do you take it?"

"Black, thanks." Marin handed Morgan the cup and at that moment Morgan decided to go over to the offensive. "The pistol is well hidden. It is in my possession. That is to say I have rather immediate access to it. I'll deal with you."

"You've made a very wise decision," Marin said. "I hope for your sake that you carry your end of it clear through."

"Believe me," Morgan said, "I fully intend to do just that." Morgan got up and served himself a second cup of coffee. He also helped himself to a cigar. Marin considered him. Morgan let the Mexican ponder him while he lit the cigar. Then he said, "A hundred thousand dollars, Marin. Fifty thousand to be hand delivered to me, right here, today."

Joaquin Marin frowned at first and then he smiled. "More of your Yankee humor?"

Morgan walked over, glanced out of the window and saw the man called Paco and his nameless shadow. Morgan refilled his coffee cup and turned around.

"Humor? Not hardly." Morgan gestured toward the window with a nod of his head. "Go ahead and call your monkeys, Marin. You've got plenty of them out there. Hell, kill me. You'll never see that damned pistol." He eyed the man and judged that he was making some headway. All he had to do now was to keep himself from rushing it.

"You think I won't order your death, Morgan?" Marin got to his feet. "I tried to be reasonable to you yesterday. I am not a man who gives his word lightly. I meant what I said. Give me the pistol and you will save your life."

Morgan strolled around the room with an air of total nonchalance. He looked at Marin's paintings, read a few of the book titles on the shelves and showed particular interest in an antiquated Spanish blunderbuss. Suddenly, Morgan turned around.

"I heard you yesterday, Marin, and I have no doubt that you'd order me killed in a heartbeat," he paused, "if you were a stupid man." Morgan smiled. "But you're not."

Marin moved toward the door. Morgan had anticipated him. He set his coffee down, walked to the window, pushed it open and hollered. "Hey, Paco. Your boss wants you in here. Right now!" Morgan, uncertain as to the amount of English the men understood, added a touch of sign language. Both looked stunned when Morgan pulled the window shut. Even before Marin could react to Morgan's action, the two men were at the door. They didn't bother with knocking.

Both eyed Marin and then Morgan. Morgan smiled, sipped his coffee and took a long, deep drag on the cigar. The scenario made no sense to the two strong arms.

"You had something to say to these uh, gentlemen, Mr. Marin?"

Marin, for the first time, was flustered. It turned to anger. He vented it on the men. "Get out! Get out and don't come unless I call you personally." They looked, for the first time, as stupid as Morgan imagined them. Both backed through the door. The advantage had moved to Morgan's side of the table. Marin glowered at Morgan and said, "Make no mistake, Yankee, you've won nothing. Nothing! Do you understand me?"

Morgan smiled and replied, calmly, "I'm not out to win anything, Marin, just negotiate the best damned deal I can get. He picked up the coffee pot. "Coffee?"

Marin walked back to the table. He took the coffee Morgan offered and then a seat. He looked up. "Perhaps I have underestimated you. Perhaps, we can discuss uh," he waggled a hand in the air, "some sort of arrangement."

Morgan pulled out a chair and turned it around. He sat on it opposite Marin, finished his coffee, ground out the cigar and said, "The discussion is over. Fifty thousand now, today," he jabbed at the floor, "here. The balance when you get the pistol."

"Don't push me too far, Morgan."

"And don't try treating me like one of your trained gorillas," Morgan shot back. "I'm no goddam U.S. Marshal. I'm a hired gun and a helluva lot better one than anybody you've got but the pickin's are getting slimmer every year. I'm planning to retire and that Peralta pistol with the fancy gold butt is going to make it possible. Now you take it or leave it."

"You don't know what you've got and neither do I until I see it."

"That may damned well be, but I know that what you've got now isn't worth a damn to you." Morgan was gambling now, pure and simple. He had nothing to lose. "You need the fourth grip, or you don't have shit!"

"Your pistol has both grips?" The tone of Marin's question was one of excitement. It was also exactly what Lee Morgan had planned. If Marin had any of the grips at all, or the other pistol, this was Morgan's chance to find out. Marin had barely blurted out the question when he realized he'd been tricked. He leaned back, his face paled.

"The matching pistol? Is that what you've got, Marin? The Mexican no longer looked the powerful leader of a gang and the wealthy owner of a vast corner of California border land. Instead, he'd been slickered by an unknown gunsharp who'd ridden in from nowhere and was in possession of a sizeable share of one of the largest Spanish treasures ever recorded.

"I have only one grip." He looked up. "I was told that one pistol is missing a grip and the other has both." Bull's eye, Morgan thought. Marin had the grip he needed. The finishing hole looked promising and Morgan sure as hell had the right bait. Why stop now?

"The other pistol, Marin? Where is it?"

Marin looked up. He considered Morgan again but he decided not to tangle with him. At least not now and not with Morgan holding the high hand. "I'm not certain but I'm told it is in the hands of Estralita Peralta."

"And how do you know this Peralta woman is even alive?" Joaquin Marin looked up. His expression had changed somewhat. He didn't answer Morgan. Instead, he got up and walked to the door again. He put his hand on the doorknob but he turned back before he opened it.

"You may or may not be a lawman but you are certainly more than a trail dirty gun hand. You were both clever and resourceful this morning but don't press me. My family has waited for centuries to claim its heritage. Your arrival is a bonus I wasn't expecting so if I lose it, I'll be no worse off."

Morgan didn't need pictures drawn. He'd been too long at the poker tables to overplay his hand. He'd bluffed and it had raised the pot but now he'd been called.

"I don't give a damn about heritage," he said, "yours or the Peraltas or old family feuds. I told you what I want. Give it to me and I'll keep my end of the bargain."

"We'll see, Morgan," Marin said. "We'll see." After Marin left the room, Morgan cursed himself. Perhaps he'd already gone too far. He poured himself another cup of coffee and looked around until he found a bottle of brandy. He laced the coffee with a healthy dose and sat down to await the outcome of his charade. Morgan wondered how Marin knew about him and he was even more curious as to why the Winfrey name hadn't come up.

When Joaquin Marin returned nearly half an hour later, Teresa was with him. Morgan had to struggle to keep his eyes off of her. The once or twice he did glance at her, he was amazed at her restraint. Teresa bade Morgan a good morning when she came into the room but nothing else was said. Marin carried a leather pouch with him. He walked to the far corner of the room, removed several books from a shelf and exposed a wall safe. Morgan grinned to himself.

After the Mexican had locked the safe and replaced the books, he walked to Morgan and handed him the pouch. "Fifty thousand dollars, Morgan. Fifty, one thousand dollar bills, Yankee dollars." He smiled. "A great deal of cash, even for me." He jabbed at the pouch. "It's all there but you'll have plenty of time to count it. Now, Morgan, where is the pistol?"

Morgan tossed the pouch back to Marin and the Mexican caught it. The reflex action was good. Morgan noted it, assuming the man had equal skill with his guns. "I tell you where the pistol is, your men bring it back here and then you've got the pistol, the money and me. Shit! What the hell do you take me for, Marin?"

"The question, Morgan, is the exact opposite of that. What do you take me for? An easy mark? A good metalsmith could have made you a simple forgery."

"No offense intended," Morgan said, getting to his feet, "but it appears to me that we have a Mexican standoff." Teresa had been busying herself cleaning up the coffee cups and the pot. She stopped her work and eyed both men.

"Why not a compromise, Daddy?"

He scowled at her. *Señoritas* did not stick their noses into the business of their men. Morgan was at the window again. He turned around.

"Yeah, Marin, why not? You pick some men and you come along. Bring the rest of the money and I'll take you to the gun." Morgan pointed at Teresa. "She's your daughter, you must trust her. Let her take it to town and have it verified. You and I wait it out together."

"And what stops me from having you killed when Teresa returns?" Marin smiled.

Morgan smiled. "I will," he said, "because I don't ride one goddam foot 'til I get back my belongings. Horse, possibles and loaded weapons." Morgan walked straight to Marin. "You've got enough men to do me in," he continued, "and I'd likely only get off one shot. Guess who my target would be?"

"And what stops me from having you trailed and killed after we conclude our business?"

"I'll take my chances," Morgan said.

"Teresa!" The girl looked at her father and he nodded toward the door. She quickly gathered up the dishes and took her leave. "Morgan, I heard about you from a longtime friend. A man who himself was once connected to the Yankee gunfighter Wyatt Earp. Do you ride for Earp, or someone else?"

The question caught Morgan a little off guard. He thought he'd pretty well satisfied Marin's curiousity about him. Obviously that was not the case.

"I ride for Lee Morgan."

"It is a clever response from a clever man, but not a truthful one. I know there is more to you than meets the eye. Perhaps there is not the time to find out but I want to warn you. If you remain in this country, if I see you after our arrangement is complete, I will order you killed, or I will kill you myself. Is that clear?"

"Can't be much plainer," Morgan said.

"And one more thing, Marshal. I am not the only threat you face. My daughter did not lie to you when she spoke of the local sheriff in Holtsville or of Judge Lundsford and Don Miguel Carbona."

"That right?" Morgan feigned a lack of interest he sure as hell didn't feel but he knew if he was going to accomplish anything, he had to stay alive. That meant shaking off Marin.

6

Morgan knew full well the gamble he was taking when he made his deal with Marin. Morgan didn't have the pistol and, in fact, had no idea of when the Winfreys were liable to show up. He'd bought himself some time, nothing else. Now, as he rode in company with half a dozen of Marin's men, Teresa and Marin himself, Morgan was trying to figure out just how to best use that time.

He was not all that familiar with the country and was therefore limited on choosing a phony hiding place. He could sense Marin's impatience by the time they reached the road junction where he'd been captured.

"Hold up here," Morgan said. "You, your daughter and I will go on from here. She takes

the gun and goes to town. You and I wait,"
Morgan said, "alone."

"I won't have Teresa going to Holtville
alone."

"Why?" Morgan asked, sarcastically. "You
didn't mind when you sent her in to con me?"

Marin scowled but held his temper. "There
was no one else involved then. There is now. I
won't have it."

"Then send a man or two with her. I don't
give a damn. But when she comes back to us, she
comes alone." Morgan could tell Marin didn't
like it but he wanted the pistol even more.

"Very well. Teresa, after Morgan gives you
the pistol, you will ride back here. Take Paco and
Juan with you."

"Yes, Father."

Marin turned back to Morgan. "How far
and in which direction?" Morgan smiled. "You
never give up, do you? You just stay behind me.
We'll head in the proper direction when we're out
of sight of your men." Morgan didn't wait for
approval this time, he spurred his horse and
trotted off to the northwest.

His selection was not a random one. He
recalled a dry stream bed he'd crossed when he'd
first ridden in from Arizona. That arroyo seemed
the most promising opportunity for him to make
his break whenever he got the chance. Once he
felt they were a safe enough distance from
Marin's men, Morgan turned to the northeast.

They'd been riding for about a quarter of an
hour and Morgan had still not seen a sign of the

stream bed. Where in the hell was it? Maybe he had the wrong area completely. The country sure as hell all looked alike. He knew Marin would soon lose his patience. It came sooner than later. Morgan heard the lever of a rifle click behind him. He reined up, and did a half twist in his saddle.

"You've been giving the orders," Marin said, "for more than long enough, Morgan. I want the pistol. I want it now."

"It's under a rock in a dry stream bed just east and a little north. Not much farther." Joaquin Marin raised the barrel of the rifle until it was pointed at Morgan's head.

"You're a liar, Morgan. I think you've been lying to me all along but I know you're lying now." Marin put the rifle to his shoulder.

"Daddy."

"Shut up, Teresa! This man is lying." Morgan knew Marin had caught him, but how? Where had he gone wrong? Suddenly, it hit the gunman. He clenched his teeth, "Shit," he whispered to himself. He'd pulled a greenhorn stunt. "He is not stupid," Marin went on to Teresa, "and he would not hide so valuable a possession in a dry stream bed. A simple thunderstorm in this country could turn that bed into a raging torrent in minutes. Mr. Morgan is very much aware of that."

Morgan was like a little kid who just got caught with his hand in the cookie jar. Anything he said would only make matters worse. He had to gamble again. He shrugged. "I don't have the pistol, Marin, I've never had it. I hoped to get you isolated enough that you'd listen to a deal. I know where it is but I need help getting it. I figured I had a better chance out here than at your ranch."

Marin raised the barrel of the rifle just a hair and fired.

Morgan's hat flew from his head but the gunman was unperturbed. Now, his years of experience took over. He'd made a tactical error in his dealings with Marin, Marin had made a strategic error. Morgan's speed rendered the rifle, for all practical purposes, empty.

Morgan catapaulted himself out of the saddle, drew the Bisley and fired low all in the same motion. Marin took the hit high up on his left leg. The velocity was considerable at that range and the pain was intensified when the bullet cracked the bone.

Marin lost the rifle, grabbed for his leg and his horse reared in reaction to the proximity of the shot. Marin went down. Teresa Marin was wearing a gun. Morgan discovered she could use it but her own horse was even more spooked than her father's bronc. After rearing, it bolted and Teresa had to drop the pistol to stay on the horse.

Morgan literally leaped onto his own mount's back and took off in pursuit of Teresa. He knew there would be Paco and Juan and the others on his ass in minutes. He caught up with Teresa and she was spouting language the likes of which he hadn't heard since the last time he was short of funds in a house of ill repute.

He leaped from his own horse and took Teresa down.

"Yanqui bastardo," Teresa screamed. She swung but Morgan was too fast for her and he didn't have time for the social graces. He cold cocked her with a right to the jaw.

Morgan reckoned that Marin's men would have easily heard the shots and riding hard would cover the distance in a third less time than it had taken him. His own mount had kept Teresa's horse from straying too far and he was counting on Marin's wound to pull off one or two of the men. He'd just have to deal with other events as they developed.

He held Teresa Marin in front of him and led her horse until they'd covered another couple of miles. He worked north but he wasn't certain that town was the place to go. At least not right away. Teresa was beginning to stir when Morgan stopped again and he decided to tie her onto her horse. By the time he'd finished, she was fully conscious. He took another moment to give her a drink of water and a warning.

"I've got no time for trouble, Teresa, so don't give me any or I'll put you back to sleep." She considered him but there wasn't much to think about. He'd done it once and she harbored no doubts that he'd do it again. She nodded passively.

Two shots rang out and Morgan saw the sand near his horse's hooves fly up. He looked back and saw two riders.

Morgan slapped Teresa's mount on the rump and the mare bolted off over a nearby hill. He freed his Winchester from the boot, chased off his own mount and turned to face the two riders. They were coming hard now, heads down. He smiled to himself. They figured him to run.

The first shot he fired was low, deliberately. The rider on the left reacted first, putting his horse into a half gallop and returning fire with his hand gun. The range was too great. Morgan's second shot took the man out of the saddle. Morgan didn't worry whether he'd killed him or not.

The second rider was good, very good. At full gallop, he unsheathed his rifle, worked the lever and with both hands free of the reins, raised the weapon to his shoulder. Morgan had no options to weigh. He killed the man with his third shot.

He didn't have to go far to find his own horse or Teresa Marin. He mounted up. "There will be more trouble in town and Paco and Juan will be coming after us. "I know a place, I've known of it for sometime." She swallowed. "You would have to go there sometime anyway. I will take you. Trust me, Morgan, I don't want my father in this. It is evil. The Peralta curse is upon that gold and my father refuses to admit all the truth of the story. Trust me."

"Where is this place?" Morgan asked, adding "and what is it, exactly?"

"It is just over the border in Mexico. A house. We can hide there and you can figure out what to do next." She looked back, nervously. Morgan knew she was right about one thing. Her father would send men swarming all over the hills looking for him and her.

"Whose place is it, Teresa? I don't need to trade one set of troubles for another?" Morgan frowned. "You said I'd have to go there eventually anyhow. Why?"

"To see Estralita Peralta."

The horizon blurred and the terrain between the riders and the horizon appeared to be undulating. The heat waves were distorting everything and the heat itself was taking its toll on both riders and mounts. Morgan had rationed the water by swallows when he'd learned that Teresa's canteen had been lost. It was nearing three o'clock in the afternoon, the very hottest part of the day, when the last of the water was used up.

"How the hell much farther is this place."

Teresa shook her head. Morgan thought she looked about ready to cry. "It's been so long. I," she paused and looked both right and left then dead ahead. "I'm just not sure. I'm sorry."

"Look, we must be close, if you're telling me the truth."

"I am, I swear it. I've been trying to get. . . ."

Morgan didn't let her finish. "Never mind that right now. You stay put. There's no use in killing both horses if we're lost. I'll ride ahead. You get under your mount, stay as much in the shade as possible and I'll be back inside half an hour."

Morgan veered gradually east as he rode. He was acting on the best possible description of the terrain that Teresa could furnish. He was nearly ready to turn back when the wind carried to him the sounds of a barking dog. It was faint but it was real.

Two sizeable sand dunes separated Morgan from the sound but atop the second one, he saw the house. It was not unlike the Marin house in terms of the terrain. Several trees surrounded it and Morgan could see a well behind it. There was a creek flowing nearby, fed from the more frequent moisture which fell on the nearby Cargo Muchacho range.

Morgan eyed the spread carefully. There were two out buildings and the house. One of them served as a small barn and he could see there was some stock. The other was the biffy. There were no visible signs of human life but anyone with brains would be inside anyway. Morgan turned back to get Teresa.

All the way back, Morgan wondered to himself if he'd made another mistake. He'd gotten by with one earlier but he was not in a position to make another. If Teresa Marin was gone, he'd simply ride, hell bent, back to the little house and check it out. He was certain of Teresa's sincerity in only one thing. She'd gotten them lost.

Teresa was asleep and Morgan was relieved. He gently awakened her. "Any trouble?" She shook her head, rubbed her eyes and then used her blouse to mop the perspiration from her face and forehead. "I found it. Log, small, a small barn and a johnny?" She nodded and smiled. "Let's go," he said.

There was no one at the house but there was food, firewood and several items which attested to the presence of a woman. Morgan went straight to the well. He grinned when, after the third pump, water spewed from the spout. He filled two buckets and returned to the house. Minutes later, he was back at the well toting more. He made six trips altogether, thinking to himself that his present circumstance was as good a reason as any for not having gotten married.

Teresa Marin wanted a bath. She got one and then she wanted Morgan. She would have probably gotten him, too, but the owner returned. Estralita Peralta, Morgan decided, was all woman.

Estralita hugged Teresa as though they were long lost kin. Both had tears in their eyes. Estralita displayed little interest in Morgan at the outset. Finally, Teresa introduced them.

"So you are the famous Lee Morgan?" Morgan found it difficult to keep his eyes from roaming over her body. She had massive breasts, although not out of proportion to the rest of her. She was, Morgan reckoned, about five feet, eleven inches tall. Her legs were long, accounting for much of her height. The waist was narrow and the hips flared but again not out of proportion.

Estralita's face was almost angelic and the features were soft, presenting a molded appearance. Her lips were her most sensuous facial feature and she pursed them just right when she spoke. Morgan imagined them in other uses and felt the fire in his groin again. Here was a woman he wanted to bed, soon too, he thought.

They had looked each other over with almost microscopic detail. A fact that did not go unnoticed by Teresa Marin but Morgan thought she didn't seem to mind. His own thoughts went back to the Marin house and his experience with Teresa and her sister. He wondered if such a scenario could be repeated out here in the middle of nowhere with Teresa and Estralita.

"I don't know how famous I am," Morgan finally said, "but I am Lee Morgan. I sure as hell didn't know you existed, however."

Estralita smiled. "I asked them not to say anything. You might call me the final proof for the claims of Tad and Tammy Winfrey and Marshal Earp." She looked quizzical. "I heard you were a hired gun. I wanted the law on my side. I deserve it." Morgan showed her the badge.

"You know, I don't think it's too damned smart of you to live out here alone."

"I'm flattered by your concern," Estralita said, "but it's misplaced. I am not here alone." Morgan now sported the look of surprise. He'd made a rather thorough reconnaisance of the place and had not seen another living soul or any sign that anyone else had been near the place.

The door opened and a shadow filled the room, almost literally. The shadow moved and blurred and the room went into semi darkness. A great hulk, bending low to avoid a banged head, stepped inside.

"Morgan, meet Cho Ping." Morgan looked up and he kept looking up. There before him was the one biggest bastard Lee Morgan had ever seen. "Cho Ping was a Shaolin in China. He is seven feet tall and weighs nearly three hundred pounds."

"I retract my observation," Morgan said, "you're sure as hell not alone." Morgan smiled up at Cho Ping. He got no smile in return. Instead, the giant Chinese stretched out his right arm, touched Morgan's shoulder and then quickly slammed the arm, diagonally, across his own chest.

"He likes you," Estralita said, "and he approves of you being here and bringing the little Spanish flower. That's what he calls Teresa."

"I'm overjoyed that he approves," Morgan said. The girls both laughed. Morgan watched the big Chinese back out. He shook his head.

"Did you see Cho Ping's belly?" Teresa asked. Morgan shook his head. He'd been too busy looking up. "He was shot there once. Three times wasn't it, Lita."

"Yes, from some sixty feet away by a gunman. Cho Ping still ran the distance, zigzagging to avoid being shot again. He broke the man's neck in a single blow."

"Yeah," Morgan said, "the only stopping him would have to be a shot between the eyes."

"Easier said than done. He moves much quicker than you might imagine."

"I don't care to put it to the test either way," Morgan said. "Did I hear Teresa call you, uh, Lita?"

"Yes. All my friends call me that. It's my own choice and much easier than Estralita Madalena Desiree Lomacinda Lucia del Peralta."

Morgan shrugged, deadpanned her and said, "A little." It was the first laugh for any of them in sometime.

Feeling total security with Cho Ping standing by, Morgan rode off for nearly two hours just before dark. He was pleased to report on his return that he had seen no sign of anyone trailing them. After a hearty meal, Morgan made his contribution to the little party. He had a full bottle of bourbon and they all enjoyed an after dinner round of drinks.

"Tell me about the Peralta treasure," Morgan said. "Does it exist?"

"Yes. Up there," Lita said, pointing northeast, "in the Cargo Muchacho." She turned to Teresa. "Would you mind moving, please? Your chair, too." Teresa thought the request odd but she complied. "Do you have a knife, Morgan?" He nodded and handed her his Bowie. Lita poked a bit in the dirt floor until there was a sharp noise of metal striking metal. She probed and prodded some more and finally scraped away a three-inch layer of dirt. She handed Morgan his knife. "You will find a metal ring down there, Morgan. Pull on it."

Morgan put his back to it and finally a heavy door broke free and he slowly pulled it up. Lita stood nearby with a coal oil lamp. "There are snakes down there. Mostly harmless I think, but a rattler or two and plenty of scorpions." She handed him a long pole with a metal hook on its end. "Feel around with the hook until you detect a handle. Hook it and bring it up. It isn't nearly as heavy as the door."

The chest was wood and metal, somewhat resembling a stave barrel with one flat side. Morgan was reminded of the pirate's treasure chests he'd seen pictures of as a boy. This one was considerably smaller, however. Morgan cleaned it of dirt and cob webs and the placed it on the table.

"Its latch is no doubt rusted shut. Break it if you have to." He did and a minute later, he opened the lid. There was a small tray just beneath the lid. It contained a few odd looking chunks of gold and others which were obviously spear and arrow heads. They were also gold. Morgan removed the tray and found himself staring down at a piece of yellow oilcloth.

"You've seen the pistol the Winfrey's possess, of course." Morgan nodded. "It is rusty, aging and has one grip missing so I'm told."

"You are told right." Morgan eyed Teresa and then undid the leather thong tie around the oilcloth and opened it.

Morgan stared down, incredulous. Resting inside the oilcloth was a flintlock pistol with gold grips. Its condition was nearly perfect. "Damn!" He looked up. "Is that it? The real thing?" Lita nodded. Morgan reached for it and then stopped and looked up again. Again, Lita nodded. Morgan picked it up and scrutinized it carefully. He didn't really know what he was looking for, he was simply looking and thinking of the story the Winfreys had related to him.

"The barrel itself and the rest of the gun's frame are iron I guess but the plating, save for the grips, is silver, not nickel." Morgan looked at Lita. "As far as I know, the weapon is functional but, of course, its worth isn't in its value as a pistol."

Morgan put the pistol back into the oilcloth. "How long have you had it? How long has it been here? Where . . ." He caught himself and smiled. "You want to tell the story?" Lita smiled and nodded. Morgan glanced at Teresa.

"She has known for sometime about the pistol and its location. She could have told her father, she could have betrayed me. She has not."

"Why?" Morgan addressed his question to Teresa. "You did mention something about your father and all of the truth of the Peralta story. Is that the reason?" Teresa nodded.

"Enrique Peralta, the fourteen-year old

grandson of Francisco Peralta, walked out of the Cargo Muchacho mountains. I'm sure the Winfreys told you that much.''

"Yeah, and they said no one knew for sure what happened to old Francisco or to the pistols.''

Lita continued, "That is partially true. But we do know that Francisco kept one of the weapons. He gave his grandson the other.''

"The kid buried this one,'' Morgan asked, pointing to the pistol.

"Yes. More than once. There was nothing here then, of course, but Enrique survived and determined that he would stay in this country, never returning to Spain.''

"And that's how we end up with Peralta here.'' Morgan leaned back, poured himself some more whiskey and held up the bottle. The women declined. "I'm still listening.''

"There are as many stories of what happened to Enrique Peralta as there are people to tell them. I do not think any purpose is served by repeating all of them and trying to figure out which one is the real one. The facts are somewhat more clear cut and simple.''

Morgan drained his glass. "Yeah. We have two pistols, three gold grips which are supposed to be a map and a lot of greedy folks.''

"Again, simply put,'' Lita said, "yes.''

Morgan leaned forward and eyed the pistol and then asked, "How did we end up with so damned many players in the game? I mean outside of the obvious greed involved, the men

I've heard about or seen all claim ownership of the Peralta gold."

"As the writer would put it, Morgan, the plot thickens. First, *señor* Carbona."

"Uh uh," Morgan interrupted, waggling a finger in the air, "first we have the Winfreys."

Lita sighed. "Yes, of course, you are quite right."

Morgan smiled and added, "No climbing old family trees here, just simply put."

"Enrique Peralta's granddaughter married a Lutheran missionary named Josiah Winfrey. Enrique survived the rest of his family. The stories say he lived to be a hundred and nine years old." Lita pointed in several directions. "He is supposed to be buried out here somewhere, a few hundred yards away at most. This place was once the mission of Josiah Winfrey."

"Did old Enrique reveal the truth before he died?"

"We must assume he revealed some of it, certainly. It seems old Josiah considered the story a miracle from God. He went looking for the treasure. He found a rusty pistol."

"Okay, we have a Winfrey with a rusty pistol."

"Almost. Josiah died in the Cargo Muchacho. Indians perhaps, we don't know for sure. What we have is a Peralta who, by marriage, is also a Winfrey. And we have a rusty gun." Morgan pondered the story and said, "Let me hazard a guess. Our missionary friend didn't practice celibacy."

Lita smiled and shook her head. "He did not."

"So we have little Winfreys with Peralta blood. Now what?"

"A recognition of reality on the part of Mrs. Winfrey. The Winfrey name meant nothing. Most missionaries were not accepted at all. Those who were allowed to live were certainly not considered good business risks."

"She dropped her married name and we're back to the Peralta name."

"Quite correct. That name carried both legend and reality with it. Enter a business partner with money, Louis Encino Carbona."

"It's getting crowded," Morgan said.

"Very," Lita agreed, "and that doesn't even take into consideration the outsiders who heard the legend and came seeking the Peralta gold."

"We have Peraltas, Winfreys and Carbonas."

"And finally," Teresa said, "we have Marin."

Morgan shook his head. "Yeah. Hard as hell to keep it simple, isn't it?"

"Centuries produce people, Morgan. It is the way of the world."

Morgan grinned and said, "I know that but why the hell do all of them have to be looking for the Peralta treasure?" The women laughed. Morgan turned to Teresa. "Your daddy lays claim to it because the Marin family supposedly paid the fare for the Peraltas in the first place, simply put. True?"

"As far as my father cares to venture into the truth, yes. What he does not say," she looked down, Morgan sensed she was feeling shame, "what he does not say," she repeated, "is the fact that the Marin family in Spain took the Peralta fortune by force. Franciso Peralta wrote one letter back to his family after he'd found the gold. One of my ancestors was present when it arrived. Up to that time, they had been friends."

"But then, the Marin family took the Peraltas by force and sat back to await Francisco's return, gold and all."

"Yes."

"They must have had one helluva wait." Morgan shook his head at the turns and twists in the story but he understood now how a mix of legend and fact could prove a deadly lure.

"It sounds as though Carbona has more of a claim on a share than your daddy does," Morgan said to Teresa.

"I agree it sounds that way, Morgan," Lita interjected, "but this Carbona's father was as cruel and greedy a man as was Teresa's Spanish ancestors. He took the land to which our present day Carbona holds title, by force. He killed, brutally and ruthlessly to get it."

"Peralta land?"

Lita nodded and said, "Some of it. Two of the factions in the tale did make their peace and family branches no longer quarrel. They are willing to share the spoils of their victory."

Morgan looked puzzled now. "What factions and what spoils?"

"The Peraltas and the Winfreys. Recently, for the first time, the United States Supreme Court took up the issue of Spanish land grants. The Spanish were meticulous in that effort. Hundreds of maps and deeds exist. Some of them deal with bits of land barely more than five acres in size. Others cover vast regions which, if valid, would make some people the owners of entire states."

"Yeah," Morgan said, pondering Lita's revelation, "I remember reading about some of those decisions." He looked at the two women.

"Carbona lost his claim. So did Teresa's father."

"So they're going to do what runs in their families. Ignore the law and take it by force."

"Yes, Morgan," Lita said. "Once, I didn't believe the legend of the gold either. I didn't even care. Then, my father died and I found papers. Deeds and grants and his formal request to the courts."

Morgan saw the expression on Lita's face undergo a change and he could see the pain. "Your father, how did he die?"

"A fire. They say a horse kicked over a lamp in the barn."

"You don't believe it?"

"I don't know," she paused, "now."

Morgan pondered what she'd just said. "You spoke of a barn and horse. Your place?" She nodded. "Where is it?"

"Gone. It all burned. It was a windy night, very windy. There was no saving anything. The hands ran away. Most were peons. Two of my father's top men also died in the blaze," she took a deep breath, "supposedly."

Teresa Marin spoke up now. "I cannot bring myself to believe that my father would do such a thing or order it done. But I cannot deny the possibility."

"Either he or Carbona." The girls nodded.

"When all of this happened, I decided to ask for help. I received an offer on my land from Carbona and I was aware that he had made a similar offer to the Winfreys. The common denominator between us was Wyatt Earp."

"You made the contact and he got to the Winfreys."

"Yes. My father and their mother were kin too, by marriage."

"Their pistol and their father, Holt Winfrey. What's the tie there?"

"Much as you heard it from them, Morgan. Now of course, Holt Winfrey's death is also suspect and there is one other uh, well, story or legend or whatever you want to call it."

"And what's that?"

"This pistol has both grips, the Winfrey pistol only one. One story has it that Holt Winfrey subsequently came into possession of the fourth one. The story says he built the town of Holtville for two reasons. One as a base camp from which he could search for the Peralta gold. The other to hide the fourth pistol grip until he could locate the second pistol."

"You put any stock in the story," Morgan

asked, "either of you?"

Teresa Marin answered. "We don't know. Apparently my father does and so does Miguel Carbona. Our belief doesn't seem to matter."

"It matters a helluva lot to me," Morgan said. "And a few other things make more sense."

Lita frowned. "Like what?" she asked.

"Like a sheriff and two deputies in somebody's hip pocket. Whose?"

Teresa answered. "Indirectly, as I told you that first day, Miguel Carbona. But they take daily orders from Judge Lunsford."

"Uh huh, and just what the hell is his interest in the whole thing?"

"Why, he's filing the appeal to the Supreme Court to get them to overturn their decision. He's preparing evidence based on a precedent set on Indian lands. It has something to do with the law of Manifest Destiny."

"But in the meanwhile, he doesn't mind overlooking a few indiscretions or illegal acts committed by his client." It was a statement and not a question and Morgan looked worried. He finally looked up at both of the girls. "He is the most dangerous of the men we face. A helluva lot worse than any gang or fast gun or would-be dictator. Few men in this country wield more power than a Federal Judge." Morgan thought back to Wyatt Earp's insistence that he wear a badge. Now he knew why. "I also figure there's another reason for Lunsford and the sheriff."

"What's that?" Lita asked.

"What better way to keep tabs on a missing treasure and keep others with the same interest out or jailed or dead, legally!" The women looked at one another. Neither had considered that possibility. Teresa was more inclined to suspect her father of misdeeds than to suspect a man who wore the robes of a Federal Judge.

"My God! How do we fight that kind of power? What chance do we have?

"You fight fire with fire," Morgan said "and power with power."

Teresa considered him. "You have a plan then?"

"One damned good short term plan, yeah," Morgan replied. Teresa leaned forward in anticipation. Morgan smiled. "Let's get some sleep."

In the darkness, Morgan let his mind relax and soak up more slowly the vast amount of information he'd taken in. His thoughts were interrupted several times however, with visions of Estralita Peralta. He found himself wishing that he and she were alone in the shack.

Morgan closed his eyes and tried to sleep. He thought about Wyatt Earp and Tad and Tammy Winfrey. He chuckled. How had he ended up in no man's land looking for a damned pistol grip?

7

Morgan didn't mind riding away from the little shack. He knew the two women would be as well protected by Cho Ping as by Morgan himself. The trio had breakfasted together, in spite of the fact that it was still well before sunup. They had agreed that Teresa Marin would stay with them. If nothing else, it would keep her father engaged, believing her kidnapped by Morgan. If Morgan had any remaining doubts about Teresa, she virtually eliminated them with her private pledge to Lita Peralta.

Morgan pondered many possibilities after he rode away. He did not have a long range plan, he knew he must be ever alert to actions by those in the opposing camps and finally, he felt he could do little in the way of direct action until the

Winfreys arrived.

He did have one course of action, however, and he was determined to follow his own advice. Fight power with power. He had two methods in mind at the outset. Holtville boasted a tri-weekly newspaper. He would start there. His second stop would bring him into a direct meeting with Judge Arlo Lunsford.

When Morgan rode into Holtville, it was still early and as best he could, he stayed to the back of the buildings. He didn't want to attract any more attention than was necessary.

Morgan reached the office of the *Holtville Courier* and found it manned by a single individual. The man behind the desk didn't even look up when Morgan walked in. Instead, he motioned with his hand toward a chair and said, "Have a seat and I'll be with you in a few minutes." Morgan didn't argue but neither did he take the seat. Instead, he positioned himself where he could see the street.

He was still looking out of the window when the man finally looked up. "Jehosophat! You're Marshal Morgan, aren't you?" The title sounded funny to Morgan but he turned and nodded. "D'ja know there's a warrant out for your arrest? Sheriff Prather claims you beat up his deputies and may have gunned down two men in cold blood."

Morgan grinned. "That bad, eh?"

The man nodded and then wiped the palms of his hands on his ink covered apron. He stuck one of them out. "I'm mighty glad to metcha,

Mr. Morgan, yessir, mighty glad."

"I appreciate that," Morgan replied, "particularly in view of my first introductions to your community and the most recent news about myself." Morgan fished into the breast pocket on his shirt and withdrew a folded paper. "I know you can make more of this than I've written but that will tell you enough that you may get yourself a story out of it. Give it a try."

The little editor took the sheet and read it. His eyes grew bigger with each line and Morgan could feel a rejection coming. The editor looked up. "I'm Cyrus Black, Mr. Morgan, and if what I read there is the truth, you can be sure I'll print it. Can you substantiate it?"

"When do you go to press, Mr. Black?"

"Two o'clock is muh deadline, sir."

"I'll be back and you'll have your substantiation." Cyrus Black watched Morgan ride out of sight and then picked up the sheet of paper and read it again. He smiled. It would either assure him a lasting place in western journalism and put the *Courier* out front as a hard-hitting news source or it would get him run out of town. Or worse, he thought.

Morgan made no bones about his presence in town now. He rode down the main street and straight to the building which was used as a town meeting hall and, when the occasion arose, a courthouse. He knew he was being watched and at least two men went scurrying off in the direction of Sheriff Prather's office.

Inside, he found two small offices. One was

used by the court clerk and the other by Judge Arlo Lunsford. The court clerk leaped to his feet and started for Lunsford's office. The barrel of Morgan's gun slowed and then stopped him.

"You find yourself a hole," Morgan said, "and crawl into it until I complete my business with the judge." Morgan punctuated his demand by cocking the Colts. The man nodded and disappeared back into his office. Morgan pulled the door closed.

Judge Lunsford had heard some of the commotion and looked up but he was back to reading a transcript when Morgan walked in.

"You're either a very courageous man," Lunsford said, "or a very stupid one."

Morgan approached the judge's small desk. "While you're trying to figure out which, Judge, I suggest you hear what I have to say."

"I'm under no obligation to give an audience to a suspected fugitive."

Morgan once again drew and cocked the Colts. He leveled it at Lunsford's head and leaned a little forward when he spoke. "Yes, you are, Judge, in this case."

Morgan learned something at once about Judge Arlo Lunsford. He was not a man easily intimidated. He leaned back in his chair. "I can have you arrested or, if necessary, killed, Mr. Morgan, and when either one is done, no one will question me about it. If you live, you'll end up in Yuma prison. Killing me won't stop the process, except that if you lived, you'd hang."

"Alright, Judge," Morgan said, holstering

his pistol, "let's play it your way." Along with
the badge Wyatt Earp had given him, Morgan
had also received a formal letter of his appointment as a U.S. Marshal. He produced it now and
tossed it on Lunsford's desk. The judge considered Morgan, glanced at the letter and finally
picked it up. He read. As he reached the bottom
of the page, he glanced up. The signature was far
more of a threat to Lunsford than was Morgan's
Bisley. It was signed by Lunsford's boss, the
President of the United States.

Lunsford tossed the letter aside, feigning a
nonchalance which Morgan knew he didn't feel.
"Just who the hell are you, Morgan, and what do
you want in Holtville?"

The gunman had gained a little edge and
now readied himself to expand on it. He moved
several things on the desk top aside so that he
might sit on the desk's edge. That done, he said,
"You know who I am, Lunsford, and you know
why I'm here and it isn't to have you insult my
intelligence by playing dumb."

Lee Morgan had only a pittance of book
learning but the times and the land in which he'd
been raised and now lived and worked, de-
manded a much more practical knowledge. At
that, Lee Morgan was possessed of a Master's
Degree. One of the skills he had honed to a fine
edge was his judgment of men's reactions. He
looked Arlo Lunsford square in the eye and let
him squirm.

Lunsford's body, tense with the potential of
a bloody confrontation, now relaxed, almost into

a slump. It was more of a telltale sign of Lunsford's feelings than were his harsh words.

"You think you can walk in here with a letter you claim is a Presidential authorization and threaten me?" Lunsford chuckled. "I've seen your kind for twenty-five years in my courtroom, Morgan. You're barely more than a common drover with a skill for killing and a mentality to match." Lunsford reached for a silver box on his desk. Morgan tensed. Lunsford had, for a moment, made a judgment of his own. He lifted the lid. "Cigar, Morgan?"

Dammit, Morgan thought to himself, I had him and I lost him again. Morgan accepted the cigar and both men sized each other up, both plotting their next thrust or parry while they lit the cigars. Morgan made a sudden decision. It was an all or nothing at all plan but, he thought, I've still got the Bisley.

"I'm here to gather every bit of information I can on a man named Carbona. While my jurisdiction is unlimited, Lunsford, by virtue of this letter," Morgan picked it up and returned it to his pocket as he continued, "I am doing my work for the State Department. Our relations with Mexico have somewhat deteriorated of late and State seems to feel Carbona is responsible.

Judge Arlo Lunsford's eyebrows raised and his mouth opened and closed. He shifted his position in his chair. Morgan made certain his own demeanor remained stern but unchanged. Lunsford was calling on every ounce of his judicial experience. He was trying to view Lee

Morgan the way he always had to view a man in his court. Was he telling the truth or not?

"I don't believe you," Lunsford finally said. "I think you've got the gold fever, same as every other man of your cut." Morgan had him. He knew he couldn't lose a second in his follow up punch.

"I don't give a damn if you believe me or not, Lunsford. As to the gold fever business, that's simple enough. The whole Peralta legend gets me to the people I need to talk to. Beyond that, it's just bullshit." Morgan heard the front door to the building open and so did Lunsford. That, Morgan knew, would be the sheriff or his deputies or both. He stepped to one side, out of sight. "I heard you were an independent and totally uncooperative man but I like to make my own judgments, so I ignored what I heard. Apparently, I was told right. Well now," Morgan said, his tone again threatening, "I'm going to tell you something. You cooperate with me on my investigation, Lunsford, or I'll see to it you end up facing your own peers, in Washington. You'd better believe that!"

Sheriff Ty Prather and the deputy named Shorty burst into the office. Morgan grinned. Both men had their guns out and the instant they saw Morgan, they threw down on him.

"Damned good protection you've got, Judge. If I'd have been here for any reason other than what I've told you, there'd be three dead men in this room right now." Morgan pointed his finger at the judge and added, "And you'd have been the first." The statement was both accurate and Morgan's *coup de gras.* Judge Arlo Lunsford had been baited, hooked and landed.

"Prather, you stupid twit! Did I send for you?" The sheriff's neck turned suddenly rubbery as he looked first at Morgan and then at the judge. Finally, he ended up scowling at his deputy. "Put those damned guns away and get the hell out of this office. You could have gotten me killed coming in here like that. Now get out!"

"He's a wanted man," Shorty said. Prather gasped at the audacity and stupidity of his deputy. Prather looked at Lunsford. Lunsford glanced at Morgan. He was very much aware of how foolish he was being made to look by the likes of Ty Prather. Morgan was very much in control. Lunsford forced a half smile at his sheriff.

"There has been a, uh, a little misunderstanding, Sheriff. If you will please, let me handle it." Prather stared and nodded.

After the sheriff's departure, Arlo Lunsford got to his feet. "What do you want from me, Morgan?"

"A commitment, first and foremost. I've taken the liberty of placing a story with the local newspaper." Morgan handed the judge a copy of it. "I told the editor I would be back in his office by noon today with your approval to run it. I hope you don't make a liar out of me, Judge."

Lunsford read it and Morgan watched his face. Morgan knew that if Lunsford could get away with it, he'd kill Morgan right on the spot.

He couldn't. He also couldn't refuse to acknowledge the newspaper story. It merely cited a State Department investigation into Mexican-American relations and offered up the district Federal Judge's full cooperation in the matter. Lunsford swallowed and Morgan knew he'd achieved what he'd come to do. He had Lunsford by the balls. Now all he had to do was squeeze.

Lunsford nodded weakly and handed Morgan the story. Morgan shook his head and said, "Keep it, Judge, for your file on the investigation." Morgan strolled to the door and then turned back. "I'll be in touch," he said. He walked out. Arlo Lunsford caught up with him some fifteen feet later. Morgan turned.

"If you've lied to me, Marshal, you're a dead man!"

Morgan returned at once to the newspaper office and found editor Cy Black elated with the judge's approval and commitment. He looked at Morgan however and said, "You know, this story could blow things wide open in Southern California, and it could also be your death warrant."

Morgan smiled and nodded. "So I've been told, Mr. Black. About a half a dozen times just this morning."

Cy Black considered him and then waggled the story in his face. "It could get us both killed but they won't look for any trouble out of me about it. They can shoot me, blow up my office or my printing press about anytime. You? Another matter. Watch yourself, Morgan. The good judge has got more than just drovers working for him."

"Thanks, Black. I'll remember."

In fact, Morgan didn't have to wait long for reminder. He'd decided to stay in town for awhile. For one thing, he didn't want to risk being followed and for another, he wanted to size up the competition. He was certain of one thing. One way or another, Judge Arlo Lunsford would try to do him in.

Morgan repaired to one of the smaller saloons along the main street to let the dust settle and await developments. He found himself the object of considerable attention, some of it, he thought, sincere but guarded.

" 'Scuse me, Marshal, like to buy you a drink." Morgan looked up. The man, he reckoned, was about fifty. He had the look of a ranch owner. A man who'd known his share of trial, tribulation and hard work but had prevailed. "Name's Lupton, Charles Lupton."

"Sit down, Mr. Lupton," Morgan said. Lupton sat. "What can I do for you?"

"No sir, Marshal, it ain't what you can do for me. If anythin', it's t'other way 'round. Course that kinda depends on the stories I been hearin.' "

"Such as?"

"Such as you bein' here to put Carbona an' Marin out o' binness. That true?"

"I'm not here to put anybody out of business," Morgan said. Lupton wrinkled his brow. "You might say I'm here to keep them from putting people out of business." The wrinkled brow disappeared and was replaced with a broad smile.

"Yessir, by God, that's what needs to happen awright. Yessir. Now then, Marshal, how many deputies you got ridin' fer ya?"

"Not a one, Lupton. I'm here all by myself." The wrinkled brow reappeared. "You tellin' me factual?" Morgan nodded. "Then, Marshal, yo're a by God bonafidey fool!"

"How many deputies do you figure I'll need?" Morgan asked.

"Carbona's got hisself close to a hunnert men ridin' fer 'im. Marin prob'ly half that many ag'in. You can kinda figger it out your own self."

Morgan considered the man and the facts. He'd known, of course, that both Marin and Carbona had plenty of men behind them but given his real reason for being there, he hadn't bothered to find out numbers. Now, he thought to himself, might be a good time to take complete stock of the enemy camp.

"You must have had something in mind when you asked to sit down here, Lupton. Assuming I had some deputies, what was it?"

"I could git some men to stand with you, Marshal. They be men who know 'bout fightin' an' ain't scared of it. Most are fair to middlin' shots an' can sit a horse an' take orders."

"And you'd be willing to get these men together if the need arose?"

Lupton got to his feet and shook his head. "I would o' been if'n I knowed they was somebody to lead 'em. Somebody who knowed what he was doin'."

"What makes you think I don't know what I'm doing?"

" 'Cause you come out here by yourself, Marshal, that's why."

Morgan stood up. "Before you make too hasty a judgment, Lupton, let me ask you a question." Lupton nodded. "How well do Carbona and Marin get on?"

" 'Bout as good as an ol' Blue Tick an' a bobcat. Why?"

"Just kind of curious," Morgan replied, nonchalantly. "Since they seemed to have about the same number of men riding for them, maybe I wouldn't need any deputies. Just a few men like yours standing by. If Carbona and Marin got mad at each other, looks to me like it'd keep 'em both busy. Maybe all we'd have to do is move in when it's over and pick up the pieces."

Morgan hadn't exactly come up with the idea stone cold. Several times he'd pondered the thought of open warfare between Carbona and Marin but he dismissed it for lack of a way that he could take advantage of it.

"Well, I'll be consarned," Lupton said, removing his hat and scratching the back of his head. "You be a mite smarter'n I took ya fer, Marshal. Yessir, a mite smarter. Besides, if'n you'd have brought deputies, they'd a tipped your hand sure. Bein' as how you're by yourself, I reckon Marin or Carbona either one is too worried 'bout ya."

"I don't know that I'd go quite that far,"

Morgan said, "but I would appreciate it if you would just keep quiet and wait 'til you hear from me, if you'd like to change your mind and help."

"You bet I will, Marshal, yessir. Now then," Lupton said, "I'm a friend o' Cy Black. He tol' me 'bout ya. Come time to git ahold o' me, he'll know how an' where."

"Good, Lupton, I'll look forward to it." Morgan shook Lupton's hand and watched him walk out of the saloon. It was, Morgan thought, one of the more positive things that had happened to him since he arrived in Holtville.

Morgan finished his drink, paid for it and headed for the door. The shot he heard was fired from some distance, but it had the easily distinguished crack of a high powered rifle. Morgan thought of a Remington Creedmoor.

Morgan hurried outside and saw a little knot of people about half a block away. Several of them were kneeling down. Morgan felt a twinge in his gut. He looked in both directions and saw no riders. He hurried down the street, arriving almost at the same time as Ty Prather did. Cy Black from the newspaper also came up. They all three pushed their way through the crowd.

"God, dear God. Poor Mary," Cy Black said. He looked at Morgan. "His wife." Morgan was still looking down. Down, into the face of Charles Lupton.

8

Morgan was fully aware that he was being trailed. He'd known it since he rode out of Holtville that morning. He'd stayed in town one day more than he'd planned, mostly to get a look-see at those who attended the funeral of Charles Lupton. There were many and most of the men in attendance looked like whipped dogs. Morgan reckoned they were not only mourning the loss of a friend but witnessing the burial of the only man who had shown any backbone and leadership.

He knew that Teresa and Lita would be beside themselves with worry but there hadn't been a damned thing he could do about it. There was no way to get a message to them and he considered it more important to snoop around as much as possible in Holtville. By the time of

Lupton's funeral, the word had spread of Morgan's presence and the alleged reason for it. The questions he was asking around town were all related to the line of bull he'd fed Judge Lunsford. Therefore, he was no closer to finding the fourth gold pistol grip.

Morgan rode nearly five miles out of his way to lead his trackers away from the Peralta shack. He also figured to double back on them and try to determine who they were and who was paying them. He didn't want a fight if he could avoid it. He couldn't.

Morgan ran his mount into a dry wash and then moved about a quarter of a mile away to an outcropping of rocks. By the time he got a good look at his pursuers, he realized that one horse carried only stuffed feed sacks.

"You can come down out o' the rocks, mister, or Slow Dog will kill you up there. It's no never mind to me." The man who was speaking now dismounted, slapped his horse on the rump and ran both animals about two hundred yards away. Morgan had been suckered but he didn't feel too bad about it. He'd been suckered by the best in the business.

As the man was shouting at him, Morgan heard the first noise he'd heard in the rocks. He turned slowly and found he was looking into the barrel of a rifle. Its owner was a full blood Apache. Morgan held his rifle up with one arm, stood up and began walking down the hill.

As he approached the second man, Morgan noted that he was not Mexican but American. He was big and mean looking. He was outfitted in buckskins and carried a single revolver stuffed in his waist band. The man spoke in Apache. Morgan's Apache was a little on the short side but he picked up enough to figure that he wouldn't ride out of here alive if the man had his way.

"You an' me are gonna palaver, mister. Now me, I'm gonna do the askin' an' you're gonna do the answerin'." Morgan shrugged.

"You be Lee Morgan, that right?" Morgan nodded. "Then I hear tell you're faster'n a rattler with that there hip pistol." The man spoke to the Apache called Slow Dog again and Morgan heard the lever action work. "Now, Morgan, you take hold o' that rifle o' your'n by both ends and you put it up behind your neck." The man grinned. "That'll keep them hands where I can see 'em an' where you can't move 'em none too sudden."

Morgan complied and then said, "You mind if I sit?" The man in the buckskins shook his head and Morgan crossed his ankles and sat down, Indian fashion, on the hot sand.

"The fella what pays muh wages thinks he'd like to do some palaverin' with you hisself. I tol' him you was a lyin', no-good but he's a little softer'n me. Anyways, we kinda reached middle ground. I said I'd run you down and git the lyin' streak outa you so's when he met ya, he wouldn't be wastin' his time."

"Damned big of you," Morgan said. The man moved toward Morgan and stopped when he was about ten feet away. "Now it's a mite hot out here an' I'm thirsty an' a shade irritable. I'd sooner not have to work up a sweat to convince ya, so when I ask, save us both a heap o' trouble an' tell me the truth the first time. Ever' time ya don't, Slow Dog there is gonna git a sign from me an' you won't like what it means.''

"Ask away," Morgan said, "I feel real truthful today."

"Where's the Peralta girl?"

"In a shack about eight, mebbe ten miles south of here." The man in the buckskins frowned. "That's mighty easy," he said.

"Truth tellin' is real easy when you've got an Apache at your back with a rifle and a man with your reputation asking the questions."

Another frown. "You think you be knowin' me, Morgan?"

"I'd make a guess. I'd guess you're Jessie Willow." The man grinned. "And I'd guess you're working for Don Miguel."

"Well now, I'm right flattered, Mr. Morgan, yessir, right flattered. Man with your reputation hearin' 'bout a no account like me."

"Don't feel too flattered," Morgan said, "there's a likeness of you in damned near every town south of the Canadian border and west of the Missouri River."

Jessie Willow's reputation could best be summed up in three words, cold blooded killer. Morgan was certain that Willow was the man who'd killed Charles Lupton. He was also convinced that Willow was his fastest route to Miguel Carbona.

"What you doin' wearin' law tin, Morgan?"

"I've got a connection or two who want a piece of the Peralta treasure. It's a helluva lot easier to move around when you're wearing a badge."

"Who are the Winfreys?"

Morgan had to struggle to keep his own expression from changing. He covered his surprise at the question with a cough. He looked up and he could see that Willow was expecting to hear his first lie. Morgan now reckoned that Willow wasn't asking any questions to which he did not already have the answers, or at least a damn good start to getting them.

"They're some kind of shirttail kin to the Peralta girl."

"How come they hired the likes o' you?"

Morgan detected a small opening. A chink in Willow's armor of knowledge. Morgan was betting that Willow didn't know about Wyatt Earp's connection. "The people I work for knew about them. That's the reason they gave me the badge. They figured the Winfreys would buy that quicker than anything else." Morgan smiled and shook his head in a gesture designed to add credibility to his answer. "They were sure as hell right."

"Where's the pistol with the gold grip, Morgan? An' where's Teresa Marin?" Morgan coughed again.

"The Winfreys have the pistol. Always have. The Marin girl is with the Peralta girl."

"An' the big Chinese fella," Willow said, grinning, "you jist walk right on by him, did ya?"

"Right now, the Peralta girl trusts me."

Jessie Willow considered Lee Morgan at length. Willow had made a promise of his own to Miguel Carbona. He would bring back Lee Morgan alive. Willow didn't want to incur the

wrath of his employer, but alive left a great deal
to Willow's imagination. He'd entertained visions of Lee Morgan being brought back, draped
over a saddle with just enough life left in him to
shake his head either yes or no.

"I'll tell you somethin', gunfighter," Jessie
finally said, "that girl gives you a heap more'n I
do by trustin' ya, but I'm gonna give a chanc'st
to prove me wrong. Git to yore feet." Morgan
strained a little to keep the rifle in position and
still get back to his feet but he did it.

"What have you got in mind, Willow?"

"We're ridin' to that there shack and we're
pickin' up them wimmin folk. Now when we git
close, you'n me, we're gonna sit tight while Slow
Dog moves on down an' slits that big China-
man's throat."

Morgan turned suddenly and started walking. "Let's do it," he said.

"Hold up, Morgan." Morgan stopped and
turned around. "I won't kill ya. I mean if I find
you been lyin' to me, I won't kill ya but I'll
promise ya, you'll wish I had of." Morgan eyed
the big man but said nothing.

"You un'erstan' me, gunfighter?" Morgan
nodded. "Say it."

Morgan was getting fed up with Willow but
he clenched his teeth.

"I understand you, Willow."

"Now one more thing. You toss that rifle to
me, real easy an' careful like an' after you done
that, you unbuckle that there gunbelt." Willow
pointed and added, "With yore left hand."

Morgan was about midway between Willow
and the Apache. He was in a half turn where he

could see them both with his peripheral vision. He'd first considered the possibility of making his move after they got to the shack. It was too risky and he wondered why he'd even considered it. The Apache might just do to Cho Ping what no one else had been able to do, kill him. In any event, if there was one slip up on Morgan's part, it would be too late to correct it.

"Here you are, Willow." Morgan let the Winchester slip into his left hand and he gave it a sudden toss, but a weak one. Jessie Willow's reflexes, Morgan reckoned, would do the rest. Rather than letting the rifle go, Willow would make an effort to catch it. At the instant Morgan moved his left arm to toss the rifle, his right one, which was on the Apache's blind side, moved in a blur of speed. Morgan drew, did a half twist and a drop to the ground as he fired. The Apache still managed a shot but it was harmless. He took Morgan's bullet between the eyes.

Jessie Willow realized the error he'd made even as he was making it. He also realized that a man didn't make an error when he was facing Lee Morgan without paying the price. The price Jessie Willow paid was the highest any man can pay, ever. Morgan's shot pierced Jessie's heart. The huge man's eyes bulged out and he glanced down at his chest as though he could will himself another chance. He staggered, he blinked and his knees buckled beneath him. Still, he reached for and drew his pistol and as he fell forward, he fired into the ground.

It took all Morgan's strength and the help of a rope and his horse to load Jessie Willow onto

the back of his own mount. Morgan didn't
bother with the Apache. He covered him with a
few rocks but took his headband. It would be
proof enough when the time came. Morgan also
felt a new and deep anger. He found a rifle boot
on the Apache's horse. In it reposed a Remington Creedmoor. The Apache had done the
dirty work but it was Miguel Carbona at whom
Morgan's anger was directed.

He arrived at the shack, relieved to find it
and its occupants intact. He quickly explained
what had happened in Holtville, who was involved and then what had happened on the trail.
The women both had the same question. What
next?

"We're pulling out of here, right now. Jessie
Willow knew more than I had a chance to find
out but if he knew some, you can bet Carbona
knows even more."

"But where can we go?"

"I had an invite to stop by the Lupton place
tomorrow evening. There's going to be a meeting
of some of the landowners. We're going to be
there."

"Morgan," Teresa said, "how can you be
sure about all of those people? What if my father
or Carbona has spies among them?"

"Yeah, Teresa, I thought about it and you're
right. We don't know who we can or can't trust.
Thing is, we're never going to be sure until we
get out of here. We can hide from now on or we
can make a move. Which way do you want it?"

Teresa looked at Lita Peralta. Their eyes
both told Morgan what they were thinking. The
time for safe choices had come and gone. Besides

that, he had to be back in Holtville quickly. The next stage was due to arrive in two days and it was more than likely that it would be carrying Tad and Tammy Winfrey.

Lita glanced out of the window and eyed the motionless form of Jessie Willow. She turned back. "What about him?"

Morgan smiled. "I'm sending him home. We'll be within five miles of Carbona's compound. The horse will do the rest."

Charlie Lupton's spread was one of the prettiest in the area. Morgan found it hard to believe the lush green surroundings were, in fact, in the middle of such desolate and otherwise barren terrain. The physical layout of the ranch put him in mind of his own home in Idaho, the Spade Bit. He grimaced each time he remembered that he no longer had a home. The Spade Bit had been burned out once and for all. Lee Morgan was a loner. No father, no mother, no living kin of which he was aware.

Lita Peralta's query jarred Morgan's daydream. "What if they don't want us and won't let us in down there?"

"Then we'll have a little better picture of where we stand in this thing." He looked at both women. "You go on ahead a ways. Any lookouts they've got posted will let you get closer than they would a man. Cho Ping and I won't be far behind."

The girls rode off, tentative about it, and both glancing back several times to reassure themselves that Morgan and Cho Ping were not too far behind. Morgan finally called a halt for him and the big Chinese. Cho Ping's head jerked around and he stared a hole through Morgan.

"I just wanted to tell you my idea. You stand guard at the corral. Anybody tries to ride out early, you stop 'em."

Cho Ping's expression rarely changed. Morgan had inquired of Lita about her reference to him as a Shaolin. Morgan learned that the Shaolin was a religious order which stressed physical as well as spiritual training. Somewhere in his training, something went wrong and Cho Ping had violated the Order's strict rules and was banned.

Now, the big Chinese grinned broadly. He held up his left arm and gripped it, high up, with his right hand. "No one will leave until you say." Morgan wasn't sure about Cho Ping's change toward him but he was damned grateful for it. They rode into the Lupton spread.

Morgan found the ranchers had posted two lookouts. Any greenhorn could have taken them out however. Too, with almost no questioning, they accepted the quartet inside. Morgan knew there would have to be many changes if this small band of human beings was going to stand up to the likes of Carbona and perhaps Marin as well.

Morgan sought out Mary Lupton and explained how he came to be at the meeting, how he had met her husband and that her husband's murderer was now himself, dead. It was, Morgan thought, damned little consolation but Mary Lupton struck him as a woman who had as much courage as that possessed by her late husband. Indeed, after she listened to Morgan's brief story, she proved it.

"We're holding the meeting in the barn, Marshal. I want you to come out there and let me introduce you and I want you to tell these people what you just told me." She smiled. "As to these girls, they're both welcome in my home and they can stay as long as it's necessary."

"Ma'am," Morgan said, "I appreciate it and so will they but I don't want you underestimating the dangers I mentioned. They are many and imminent."

"Dangers?" She smiled, wistfully. "I just lost my husband, Mr. Morgan, and without a fight, I'll lose my home. The danger I feel is in not doing anything about it."

While a few of the men in the gathering were hired hands, most were land owners and ranch operators. The Peralta gold, if it did exist, was of little importance to them. Their land and homes and families came first and they were ready to fight if they felt they had a chance. The problem seemed to be that most of them felt they did not.

The unofficial spokesman for the group was the owner of a small cattle operation. His name was Howard Leeds and he was in company with a couple of seedy looking gunslingers. Men he'd hired as personal bodyguards. One of them, Morgan noted, had been whispering to Leeds throughout much of the meeting.

"That there is real purty talk, Mr. Morgan," Leeds finally said, "but it don't say much. We're facin' two big powers here, Carbona and Marin, and by what I can figure, they got the only law that matters." Morgan was sizing the man up but Leeds wasn't through. "Besides that, I hear tell you ain't really no marshal." That one caught the attention of the gathering and a hush fell over them.

"Who told you that?"

Leeds ignored Morgan's question and continued. "What I hear is that you'd hire your gun to the man with the most money to offer. I hear your daddy was a killer name o' Frank Leslie." Leeds looked around, feeling the mood of support for his allegations. Leeds looked back at Morgan and added, "An' I hear tell the only reason you came here was to look for the Peralta gold. Now whatta you got to say 'bout those things?"

"Only one. There's a war brewing in this country and everybody in this room is going to be in it, unless they hightail it out of here tonight. Like any war, as soon as it starts, nobody gives a damn anymore about what started it. When this one starts, you'd better be gone or you'd better be ready to fight."

"You didn't answer his questions," someone shouted.

"The answers are none of his damned business."

"I'm makin' it my business," Leeds said, "I won't ride for no gunslingin' killer."

"Then I'd suggest you ride out, Leeds, right now." Mary Lupton pushed her way through the crowd and moved up beside Morgan. She scowled at Leeds.

"How dare you speak like that to this man?" She pointed to the two men who were in Leeds' company. "Your wife didn't even want you to hire those men you've got on your payroll and four of your best, hardest working hands rode away because of them.''

The two men now separated and so did the crowd. Mary Lupton sucked in her breath. Morgan had already sized them up. As a matter of fact, he knew one of them. A gunny named Jake Branch. Morgan had killed his cousin in a gunfight in Idaho some five years earlier.

"Move behind me, Mizz Lupton," Morgan said, calmly.

"But, Mister . . ."

"Now, Mizz Lupton!" She moved. "That's far enough, Branch."

Leeds eyed the two men and frowned. "No trouble, boys, I don't want no trouble. I just think we got some answers comin'." It was the man named Branch who responded. "Shut up, Leeds! Morgan there is the reason I hired on. The reason I come."

"What? Now just a minute here, Branch, I give the orders and you take 'em."

"Not no more, Leeds," Branch said, "an' I won't tell you again, shut up!" Branch grinned and addressed himself to Morgan. "Want you to meet Billy Baines. Best little gunhand you'll be likely to see fer the rest o' your life, Morgan, which ain't gonna be too much longer. Boys!" Branch was yelling to three more men who were supposed to have slipped in and positioned themselves in the loft. They had ridden there for the specific purpose of breaking up the meeting. It was as Morgan had figured, they were plants. It made no difference whether they worked for Marin or Carbona.

Branch got no answer to his cry. He tried

again. "Boys!" This time, he got an answer. Three bodies tumbled from the loft. They were clad only in their longjohns and they were hogtied and gagged.

"No boys," Cho Ping said.

Jake Branch's eyes got big and round and his jaw dropped open. He turned, looked up at Lee Morgan and said, "No, Billy boy!"

Billy Baines was barely twenty years old but the cut of his rig told Morgan he was the fastest of the two men by far and away. Morgan's eyes had never really been off of Billy.

Billy Baines blinked and drew and fired. He put a bullet through a lantern about two feet above Morgan's head. Morgan drew and fired and didn't blink. That was the only difference, almost. The other difference was Morgan's bullet. It went through Billy Baines' heart.

Morgan could have easily killed Jake Branch as well. He had plenty of time but Branch had an odd expression on his face, his right hand at the back of his neck and he was falling forward. Closer examination proved that his spinal column had been severed just at the base of his skull.

As Morgan and some of the other men were examining him, Cho Ping walked up. He knelt down and his powerful fingers withdrew a star shaped piece of metal from Jake's neck. Cho Ping held it up, smiled and said, "Shurikan."

9

The presence at the meeting of five men intent on killing Lee Morgan gave Mary Lupton the boost she needed to gain support for her "stand and fight" movement. Morgan found himself elected to the leadership by unanimous vote. It was a role he didn't want, but it offered a thin veil behind which he might carry out his real purpose.

The day had been long and harrowing and Morgan was glad when he was finally able to retire to the privacy of his own room. He'd agreed to stay on at the Lupton place until the stage's arrival.

He lay back on the bed and pondered the difficulties of his new role. He knew it would make his search for the treasure that much more difficult and any agreements with Marin or Cabona totally impossible. Under his breath, he was cursing Wyatt Earp as well as his own need of money.

The soft rapping at his door didn't bring the usual reaction. Somehow, he felt perfectly safe for the moment.

"Yeah?"

"May I come in, please?" The voice was barely audible but Morgan recognized it as Lita Peralta's. He sat up, rubbed his eyes and noted that he had a small headache. He squeezed the bridge of his nose between his thumb and forefinger.

"Yeah," he replied. He got off the bed and walked across the room to turn up the lamp. He didn't get to it.

"Please," Lita said, "leave it dim." Morgan turned to face her. She had on a very revealing, silk nightdress. "I wanted you to know how grateful I am, Morgan. I didn't want to wait because I don't know what the future will bring, but I am ever so grateful to you." A single tie string held the nightdress together. Lita untied it and the frock slipped from her creamy shoulders.

Lee Morgan lived his life by only a few hard rules. One of them dictated that there was a time and a place for everything and he knew that neither one was right for this. He also lived by the edict that states, for every rule there is an exception. He sucked in his breath at the beauty which stood before him and realized the latter rule prevailed in this case.

Estralita Peralta's body radiated heat and a musky, feminine odor which, of itself, could arouse a man. Morgan quickly forgot his aching muscles and mental concerns. Lita straddled him, leaned forward and began brushing his cheeks and lips with the mountains of flesh that were her breasts. Lita's nipples were soft and pliable but quickly hardened.

"Lick them," she said to him, softly. He did and she moved to alternate between them. She held remarkably still for him and manipulated the mounds to extract the maximum sensation from Morgan's efforts. Soon, Lita was breathing faster and heavier and she pulled away from him.

She repositioned herself and began kissing and licking Morgan's bare flesh, his chest and down along the center of his stomach. She worked lower until she could make contact with his manhood. She did and it was Morgan who was squirming. Lita pressed tighter against him, mostly in an effort to get him to lay quietly and enjoy what she was doing.

After a somewhat longer period of time than Morgan had spent on Lita's breasts, she got up again. She leaned forward and kissed him on the mouth and let her body slide down against him. They seemed to fit together perfectly and Morgan found a new sensation as the mass of Lita's public hair scratched and rubbed against his erection.

Lita finally rolled to her back and held her arms out until he filled them. They kissed and then Morgan resumed his oral ministrations on Lita's body. These exchanges of pleasure continued for nearly an hour. By then, both parties were at the very peak of their endurance. Lita Peralta pushed Morgan away, sat up, turned around and got on her hands and knees.

Morgan knew what to do and he did it and Lita moaned, writhed and seemed to find a whole new physical sensation to the act. It ended in a sweat soaked merger of two naked human forms whose sole purpose was to give and receive physical pleasure.

Morgan and Lita parted with a kiss usually reserved for the likes of a courtship but both had felt something very special between them. Neither spoke of it but both thought it went beyond the usual sexual experience. Morgan butted his cigarette and got into bed. He smiled as he wondered how much more grateful Lita might be later on, and if he'd be able to accept her expression of it. He dropped off into a deep sleep.

While Lee Morgan was accepting a somewhat unorthodox display of appreciation for a job he'd not yet done, Holtville Sheriff Ty Prather was arriving at his office. He was bleary eyed and not a little irate at having been summoned from his bed at such an unholy hour.

"Who the goddam hell is so important that they figger to pull me out o' bed at this time o' night?" The sheriff was speaking to the boy who'd brought the message to him. The lad now stood, hand out, waiting his pay. Prather looked at him and scowled. "Let him what sent ya pay ya boy. He owes ya."

The door to Prather's office opened and the sheriff looked up. A man said, "Pay the kid, Prather, and get in here." The sheriff swallowed, nodded and took out a quarter. "Give 'im a dollar, that's what he was promised." Prather swallowed and reached for a dollar. A moment later he stepped inside.

"Long time no see," Prather said, tentatively.

"Not long enough to suit me, Prather," the man replied, "but I didn't come to see you, just to give you a little advice."

Prather smiled weakly and said, "Little friendly advice never hurt no man."

"I didn't say it was friendly, Prather. Healthy advice is more accurate. The stage is due in later today, that right?" Prather nodded. " 'Bout eleven o'clock is usual."

"Leave town at ten-thirty, Prather, and take those mealy mouthed no-goods you call deputies with you. Stay gone until sundown."

Prather frowned. "Where am I s'posed to go?"

"I don't give a damn where you go, just make sure you're not inside the city limits of Holtville."

"I, uh, I'm not sure I can do that without . . ."

"You can do it or I'll kill you. It's up to you.

You can either make yourself scarce or make yourself dead.''

The man giving the orders to the Holtville sheriff was a gunfighter named Brock Haskell. He was one of the most feared men in California and possessed of the skills to keep it that way. Haskell was known to have murdered at least fifteen men in his life and had stood trial in the deaths of at least six of them. He'd received a verdict of acquittal in all six cases on a plea of self defense.

Haskell wore a customized Smith & Wesson, .44/.40 in a vest holster. He drew left handed and was credited with having faced down famed U.S. Marshal Billy Tilghman in an El Paso brothel.

"Damn, Mr. Haskell, I git muh orders right here in town an' I'd be in a dung pile if I did what you say without checkin' first.''

"You've been warned, Prather, and that's what I came here to do but I'll remind you of something.''

"What's that?''

"A dung pile beats the hell out of a pine box.''

Ty Prather left his office and headed straight for the Lazy L ranch, the Lunsford spread. The judge was none too happy about being yanked from his bed either but he listened to the nervous little sheriff's story.

"I figgered you oughta know. Whatta ya want me to do?'' Judge Lunsford gave Prather a pitiful look. "Just exactly as you were told, get the hell out of town. Haskell is, uh, on the payroll temporarily. He's going to handle a little job for us. Didn't he tell you that?''

Prather shook his head. "Never said nuthin." Every now and again, Ty Prather found a threadbare swatch of courage deep within himself. Most of it came from being in the employ and therefore confidence of a Federal Judge. He experienced just such a bravado at this moment. "Ya know, I'm on the payroll too, so to speak." He smiled, weakly again. "If they is a job to do, I'd reckon I ought to git first crack at it."

Judge Lunsford was in no mood to be amused but he couldn't resist a little smile at Ty Prather's veiled demand.

"Fine," the Judge said, "ride back and tell Haskell to forget it, that you'll handle it personally."

Prather bit. He smiled. "Sure Judge, sure. Uh, jist what is the job?"

"Kill Lee Morgan."

Sunrise was accompanied by a desert shower. They were infrequent and even the rain drops were hot but they settled some of the dust and gave the air a clean, fresh scent.

"Mornin', Mr. Morgan." Mary Lupton was pouring a cup of coffee with one hand and gesturing toward the table with the other. Morgan was surprised she was up and his look showed it. She smiled. "I've been gettin' out o' bed about four of a mornin' for nearly thirty years now, an' fixin' breakfast for a passle o' ranch hands or muh own man or both. Don't go spoilin' it for me by tellin' me you don't eat in the mornin'."

"I won't, Mizz Lupton."

"Mary is muh name, I'm not comfortable with anythin' more'n that." Morgan nodded. He heard footsteps and reached for his gun. "It's that big Chinese fella, Cho Ping. He was up when I come down." She smiled as she served up Morgan's eggs and said. "Now there's a man any woman ought to really enjoy cookin' for. He ate a dozen eggs, fifteen flapjacks an' two pounds o' hogback easy."

Morgan looked up, grinned and said, "Then, you've cooked breakfast for one man this morning and one kid." He held up two fingers, "I'll have two eggs, three flapjacks and about two medium thick slices of hog back." She laughed. Morgan liked her. She put him in mind of Idaho and his mother when she used to flit around the kitchen. He ate and as he did so he was aware of Mary Lupton's enjoyment in watching him.

"Morgan," she said suddenly, "I'm not usual a woman who sticks her nose where it might not fit but there's somethin' I think you should know."

Morgan was finishing off the last of his flapjacks and he washed them down with a swallow of coffee and then said, "What's that, Mary?"

"I don't think you know how much of an impression you've made on the Peralta girl. Oh, I know she's got some troubles right now but there's a look on her face I've seen before." Mary smiled. "Had it on my own once." She frowned. "Just don't be too hasty to chase her away if she comes 'round wantin' to say thanks."

If Morgan had been given to blushing, it was a perfect opportunity. As it was, a hasty departure suited him better. He looked at Mary Lupton, smiled and said, "I promise, I won't be hasty."

Morgan gave a few last minute instructions to the Lupton ranch hands and said his farewell to Cho Ping. Mary Lupton came out on the porch as Morgan was mounting up.

"Don't you go an' get yourself shot up, Morgan. We need you. Just meet that stagecoach and get those young people back out here as fast as you can."

"I will, Mary, and tell the girls to stay put and stay close to Cho Ping." He pointed to Mary. "And you do the same."

The same sunrise brought Judge Lunsford, for the second time, to his front door. He was prepared to give Sheriff Prather a sound reprimand. Instead, he found himself staring into the ugly, bearded faces of three vaqueros. The ugliest of the unsightly trio proved to be the spokesman.

"*Buenos dias, señor* Lunsford." He stepped aside and pointed toward the yard. "We have your *caballo* ready and Don Miguel awaits you."

Lunsford frowned, "I'm not riding out to see Don Miguel at this hour or, for that matter, anytime today." The big Mexican turned back,

smiled and telegraphed a meaty fist into Lunsford's middle. The judge crumpled into a heap at
the Mexican's feet.

"Juan, some clothes for the *señor*." Lunsford moaned. The Mexican named Juan went
inside and stood admiring the home's interior. A
moment later, Lunsford's wife appeared at the
head of the stairs.

"Who are you?" she shouted. "And what do
you want?" Juan didn't answer but started up
the stairs. Mrs. Lunsford started backing up.
Judge Lunsford got to his hands and knees and
looked inside.

"No," he said, weakly, "leave her alone, I'll
ride with you." Lunsford's wife backed into their
bedroom. Juan followed her. "Jeanette," Lunsford screamed, "give him my clothes."

The judge's wife darted across the room to
the closet and pulled down a pair of pants, a shirt
and some shoes. She threw them on the bed and
then hurried to the chiffonnier and found some
socks and a pair of galluses. When she turned
back, Juan was right in front of her. She stifled a
scream and held out the items. Juan pushed her
arm aside.

Downstairs, Judge Lunsford got back to his
feet with the help of the doorknob. He was
wobbly but he stepped inside and shouted again.
"Jeanette! Jeanette, are you all right?" He
turned and looked at the man who'd hit him.
Lunsford's look was missing the usual arro-
gance. His eyes were pleading.

Juan reached up, gripped the neckline of

Jeanette Lunsford's nightdress and pulled. It fell away like rotting lace and Juan stood licking his lips and taking in her total nudity with his eyes while she screamed. Downstairs, the judge turned and made two quick steps toward the stairs. The big Mexican unleashed another blow. This one to Lunsford's right kidney. The judge groaned, staggered and went down again.

"Juan, come, we must go." The scream stopped. Judge Lunsford felt hands pulling him to his feet. His clothes struck him in the face and fell to the floor. The Mexican picked them up and Lunsford saw Juan coming down the stairs, smiling. "The *señora's* teats, they are *magnifico señor.*"

Judge Arlo Lunsford had, at one point in his career, been one of the most promising members of the American Bar Association. He had been a strict disciplinarian and was possessed of one of the keenest legal minds in the country. There were even rumors of his consideration to the Supreme Court, easily its youngest member.

Things began to go sour for Judge Lunsford after a half a dozen unsuccessful business investments and a very costly mining venture. Soon, it was money and not justice which dominated Lunsford's decisions. The judge's connection with Miguel Carbona seemed to ease Lunsford's immediate needs. Thereafter, the temptation was for bigger and better, at any cost.

Now the Carbona relationship was coming home to roost. Carbona had placed great stock in

Judge Lunsford's promises to find the missing pistol grip. Carbona knew something else about its hiding place which no one else knew. There were, hidden with it, the names of those who had the two pistols.

Carbona had been patient and Lunsford had been stalling. He knew nothing more now than he had months before but there were new problems. New faces were appearing and now a fast gun with badge to back it up. Carbona wanted action and he had run out of patience. He sent his men to fetch Lunsford to him.

"You are looking peaked, *señor* Lunsford," Miguel said. He gestured to his men to leave them alone. "Have you not been feeling well?"

"You cannot send your dogs to my home and abuse my wife and assault me. You forget who I am, Miguel."

"Tsk, tsk," Miguel shook his head, "is that what happened this morning, *señor*? I shall speak to the men. Those who are guilty will be properly punished, I assure you." Lunsford knew it was a lie but discretion was definitely in order. "I know you must have missed your breakfast. Will you join me?"

"I'm not hungry," Lunsford said, "and I have a busy schedule. I would appreciate conducting our business and being on my way."

Carbona could not be hurried. He carefully tucked his napkin into his shirt collar, sampled his eggs and sent them back to the kitchen because the whites were not cooked to his liking. He sipped fresh orange juice and silently offered

Lunsford some coffee.

"You have been a disappointment to me, but I have displayed to you my generous understanding of your problem." Miguel looked up, smiled, reached inside his tunic, producing a throwing knife and placed it on the table.

Judge Lunsford was a man who understood threats and physical violence and was not easily intimidated by the mere threat of them. The earlier incident of course had been more than a mere threat. Lunsford did understand Carbona, however, and fully realized that Carbona would not hesitate to use physical violence, even to its ultimate end.

"I have failed to deliver as promised, Don Miguel, but I need only a little more time. I expect developments to take a sudden turn and when they do, we will have all of the information we need."

"You mean from the marshal with the fast gun? You can handle this one?"

"Of course I can," Lunsford lied, "I deal with his kind in my court room every day."

Carbona took a huge bite of egg and toast. Yoke dribbled down his beard. He took a swallow of coffee, swished it around to loosen the bits of food stuck to his teeth, swallowed it and then wiped his beard.

"Why then," Miguel asked, smiling, "did this man come to your office and threaten you and you let him get away with it?"

Lunsford assumed that Prather had ridden directly to Don Miguel and told him everything.

His assumption was partially correct.

Don Miguel called in his servant, spoke to her in a whisper and she departed. Moments later she returned with Judge Lunsford's court clerk in tow. Lunsford was clearly shocked. "I believe you gentlemen know each other," Don Miguel said, smiling. The smile faded and Don Miguel leaned forward toward Judge Lunsford. "You have taken my money and you have done far more than simply fail me." He pointed to the court clerk. "He has been on my personal payroll since my own trial and your every move, your every thought has come back to me."

"I . . ." Lunsford was suddenly frightened. He had a vision of his wife at the mercy of Juan and the others and of himself dying as he witnessed the atrocity, helpless to stop it.

Don Miguel motioned the servant and the court clerk out of the room. When the door closed, Miguel spoke again. "I am a man of infinite mercy, *señor.*" He extended his hands in front of him, palms upward, "I understand the things that plague others and I wish only to help them with their troubles." The act nearly made Lunsford vomit but he dared not defy it. "Therefore, *amigo,* I am giving you this last chance. A clean slate with old troubles and bad feelings put behind us. A chance to show me that my judgment of you was justified."

Arlo Lunsford was visibly shaking and pale. He looked up. "What do you want me to do?"

"I have employed a gunman, the very best gunman money can buy. Today, he will dispatch this marshal, this man Morgan. Then, Judge, your slate will be clean again. When it is, you will make up tax papers on the properties on this list." Miguel handed Lunsford a paper. He started to look at it but Miguel stopped him. "You may read that when you return to your office. Your clerk will replace the real tax papers with the ones you draft and the sheriff will serve them to the owners."

"But taxes have been paid already. They will have receipts on their property showing them paid."

"Then you will hold a hearing, an appeal hearing and you will declare the receipts are forgeries." Miguel smiled. "We will acquire all of the land on which the Peralta treasure can be hidden, *mi amigo*." Lunsford swallowed. He had done many things already which were illegal but they were all easy to hide, easy to justify through blaming others. He had done nothing which could be traced to him directly. If he did this, he knew there would be no escape if the scheme failed.

"Now, *mi amigo,* let me explain one more thing to you. If you fail in this thing, you will lose all you have. Your fine home will go to me." Miguel smiled. "Your fine wife to Juan."

"I, uh, it will take some time," Lunsford said. "It isn't something I can do in a few days."

Don Miguel smiled and shook his head and said, "Of course not. Of course not. You think me a fool?" Lunsford shook his head. Miguel's smile disappeared. "You have one week, *señor,* one week.''

The ride back to his home was the longest Judge Arlo Lunsford had ever endured. His head was swimming with what he'd been asked to do but even more, with the consequences of failure. There was something else in the back of Judge Lunsford's mind, however. Something which he believed even Don Miguel had not considered. What if Lee Morgan killed Carbona's hired gun? What then? Judge Lunsford began to calm himself down and by the time he reached home, he'd decided the last issue.

10

Morgan was less than five miles from Holtville when he caught the movement along the ridge to his right. He knew there was a rider up there and he'd suspected it for several miles. He decided if whoever was on his ass intended to act, they'd do it now. He opted not to wait.

At one point, the road was within fifty feet of the spiny ridge. Morgan would make his move at that juncture. He tensed himself for a sudden move as he approached the area but his thinking and effort proved needless. His pursuer had the same plan and made the move ahead of him, suddenly appearing in the road.

"Jeezus," Morgan mumbled. The rider was Felisa Marin. He rode straight up to her, carefully eyeing the terrain around him. He saw nothing but he still didn't like it. A man with a rifle up in those rocks had a clean shot at him now.

"I'm alone," she said, "and here to warn you." He considered her, remembering first, the warmth of her body. "Warn me about what?"

"Carbona has hired a man, a *pistolero*. He is already in town. He is supposed to kill you and then your young friends if necessary."

"That right," Morgan replied, still dubious. "Who is he?"

"Haskell," Felisa replied. "Does the name have meaning to you?"

Morgan looked down and then up again. "Yeah," he said, "it sure as hell does. It means the worst kind of trouble."

"Is he very fast, this Haskell?"

"Some say there's nobody around who's any faster." Felisa considered Morgan, herself remembering the warmth of his flesh and the gentleness of his touch. "And what do you say, Morgan?"

"I say you get back to your daddy and stay put."

"I can't," she said. "It is the other thing I have to warn you about." Morgan frowned. "My father has found something. Something new about the treasure. I'm not sure what it is but it has to do with Holtville."

"Shit!" Morgan thought a minute and then said, "Why can't you go back?"

"I stole it from his safe." She dipped into her ample cleavage and withdrew a carefully folded bit of old parchment paper. She gave it to Morgan. He quickly opened it and found it was a roughly drawn map of the center of Holtville. There were stains on the map which blotted out some of the old marks on it but two letters were clear, right in what was the center of town. The letters were M and C. Morgan looked up.

"No ideas as to what it means?" She shrugged. "Does he know you stole it?"

"Perhaps by now he does. If not, he soon will. When he discovers it missing, he will know it was me. No one else has the combination to the safe. He placed it in the safe in my bedroom. It was put there for my jewels, mine and Teresa's." She frowned. Morgan didn't need to hear the question.

"Teresa is fine. She is with Estralita Peralta and they are at the Lupton place. You go there too, now, fast." Felisa smiled and then moved her horse next to Morgan's. She leaned out of her own saddle and kissed him. "Come back," she said, "and Teresa and I will welcome you." Morgan felt a tug in his groin at the thought.

He watched her ride out of sight and then he rolled up the parchment into as small a roll as he could. Carefully, he stuffed it down into the barrel of his Winchester. He pulled the Colts and loaded the sixth chamber and then holstered it. He made two fast draws, flexing his grip around the butt and getting the feel of the weapon for a new day. Indeed, each day in the life of a gunman was one in which he must reassure himself of his skill. Yesterday's skills no longer counted and tomorrow's would only be put to the test if he survived today.

"Okay, Haskell, let's see if you're another John Ringo."

It was just after ten o'clock when Morgan rode into Holtville. There were not more than a dozen people on the main street and all but two of them scurried away when they saw him riding in. Three horses were tethered to the hitching rail in front of the Holtville Saloon. Morgan reined up there and dismounted. One of the men who hadn't fled was Cyrus Black of the *Holtville Courier.*

"Ty Prather and his lap dogs lit out before sunup. You got a reception committee waitin' for you, Morgan."

"Brock Haskell?"

Cy Black shook his head and said, "You ought to be a journalist, Morgan. I'm damned if you don't get information faster'n me. You know, a lot o' folks gave you up for dead 'til that meeting at the Lupton place. Now, the same ones are scared you'll stay alive and there'll be an all out war."

"That's a real familiar spot for me," Morgan said. "I'm damned if I do and damned if I don't," he grinned, "and I'm damned if I can figure out how I get into these spots."

"What's your plan?" Black looked at his watch. "If the stage is running on time, you've got about thirty-five minutes."

"My plan is real simple," Morgan said, "stay alive. Now I need a favor." Black looked at

Morgan quizzically.

"Name it, Morgan."

"The first chance you get, come get my rifle. Take it to your office and fish the paper out of the barrel."

"What?"

"Just do it," Morgan said. "After you've looked at the paper, do some research and find out all you can about it."

"And then what?"

"If my plan works, I'll be over to your office to hear what you found out. If it doesn't, see to it the information gets to Tad Winfrey. He and his sister will be in town today. If it works that way, there's one more thing you can do for me too."

"And what's that?"

"Send a telegraph to Los Angeles and explain what took place."

"Who do I send it to?"

"Wyatt Earp."

Morgan entered the saloon and took up a spot at the far end of the bar facing the batwing doors. There was no rear door. Two saloon girls were already plying their trade to the half a dozen men in the place. One card game was in progress and the barkeep was busy washing glasses.

"You drinkin'," the barkeep asked and then added, "Marshal?" Morgan glanced up. The barkeep was smiling.

"A beer." Morgan put out the money for it but the barkeep pushed it away. "Why so generous?''

"In about fifteen minutes, Marshal, there'll be more customers in here than I can handle." He pointed a finger, "An' most of 'em will be here to see you."

"You mean to see me get shot, don't you?"

The barkeep drew himself a beer. "I s'pose there's a few still bettin' that way but not most, not no more." Morgan considered the barkeep and the man reached down and produced a copy of the *Courier*. "Not since Cy Black put this story in his paper." Morgan glanced at the headline.

"Son of Famed Old Time Shootist in Holtville"

"Ain't you gonna read it?"

"I already know who I am," Morgan said. He sipped his beer and glanced toward the front door. One of the girls wiggled her way over to him.

"My name's Mandy," she said, "and if there's ever a time I can be of service to you, Marshal, just let me or Jack here know."

"I'll remember," Morgan said and then he turned and addressed himself again to the barkeep. "You mentioned bets. Just who the hell instigated that?"

Jack jabbed his own chest with his finger. "Not me, if that's what you're thinkin'." He pointed to the girl, "Not her neither or any o' the girls." Morgan finished his beer and the barkeep gestured toward the empty mug. Morgan shook his head. "It was Haskell himself."

"When?"

"Yesterday," Jack thought for a moment,
" 'bout noon as I recollect." There was a big
clock over the back bar. Jack turned and looked
up at it. "Yeah, 'bout noon." The barkeep turned
back. "He tol' folks to be back down here this
morning at quarter to eleven and that they'd
have drinks on the house and their money either
won or lost by eleven-thirty." Morgan looked up
at the clock. It was twenty minutes before
eleven.

"Did Haskell say anything about when he'd
be here?"

"Eleven o'clock sharp," Jack said, "right
here." Jack was pointing to a table in the corner
of the room near the front window. "Ya know,
this'll be the only gunfight Holtville has ever
had. Mostly them days are gone. Prob'ly never
be another chance to see one." Jack, the barkeep,
finished his own beer and then held up the paper.
"You really Buckskin Frank Leslie's son?"

Morgan eyed the barkeep, then Mandy and
then looked around the room. All eyes were upon
him. He supposed it was a legitimate question,
given the circumstances, and it probably deserved a legitimate answer. Nonetheless, Morgan didn't like it. These people were here to see a
native gunfighter stand up against the offspring
of a legend. It was of a hell of a lot more interest
and excitement to them than the Peralta gold or
the fact that their little town was about to be
torn asunder by a war of greed. Morgan said,

147

"That's what the paper says."

Jack had been right. People began pouring into the saloon. The batwing doors never had a chance to come together. As they entered, they'd pause, look around and then stare at Morgan a moment. Outside, their womenfolk were lining both sides of the street. Jack began serving drinks. Once, he got near Morgan and said, "I haven't seen this much activity in Holtville since the Fourth of July 'bout four years back. John L. Sillivan came through an' put on a exhibition bout."

Morgan had never seen Brock Haskell in person but the pictures he'd seen left no doubt about him when he walked into the saloon. Morgan's thoughts leaped back in time to the Spade Bit and the little shootist known as Kid Curry. Haskell was a little bigger but dressed in a store bought suit and a derby.

"Morgan," Haskell said, nodding his head. Morgan eyed the man but didn't respond. "Like to buy you a drink before I kill you." Morgan thought, "The sonuvabitch even acts like Kid Curry." Morgan remembered again when he'd first met little Harvey Logan and worse, when he'd bedded Harvey Logan's woman. Morgan was never sure how Logan ended up with the Kid Curry handle but it was Kid Curry who came after Morgan, all the way back to Idaho. It was Kid Curry who taunted and challenged him. It was, finally, Harvey Logan who stood against Morgan's father and they killed each other in the cookhouse at the Spade Bit Ranch. To this day, Morgan never knew who'd drawn first. He wondered if there would be witnesses to today's event who would think back and ask themselves the same question.

Morgan moved toward Haskell's table and the murmuring in the room stopped. Only the sound of Morgan's bootheels on the plank board floor could be heard. He scooted a chair out and sat down. Jack, the barkeep, brought a bottle of whiskey and two glasses. Brock Haskell looked up at the clock and then at Morgan. He smiled and poured them both a drink.

"I admired your daddy a lot," Haskell finally said. "I think the writers don't do him justice."

"Maybe he doesn't deserve it."

Haskell frowned. He was clearly puzzled by Morgan's first words.

Haskell considered Lee Morgan for several moments and then said, "Why do you say that? He was one of the best that ever lived."

"He's dead. Tying a man you pull on is the same as him beating you. You're just as dead." Haskell downed his drink. Morgan pushed his away. A faint moan rippled through the room. The onlookers were starting to weigh their betting decisions.

"You refusing to drink with me, Morgan?"

Morgan got to his feet, glanced up at the clock and then back at Haskell. He raised the volume of his voice just a bit as he said, "I haven't always been given a choice about who I have to kill and who I don't but I still have the choice of who I drink with, Haskell, and on a list of two, you'd come in third." Morgan wheeled and walked toward the door.

"You're a dead man, Morgan," Haskell said. Morgan pushed through the batwings and walked into the street. Inside, Brock Haskell's face was flushed. The men he'd challenged before had always drank with him, except those few he'd hunted down outside of a town. Haskell always tried to have his gunfights in a town. A town with a newspaper and a populace which was perpetually bored by lack of excitement. Then and only then could Haskell perpetuate his own legend. It was a flaw in Brock Haskell and Morgan knew it. What he didn't know was whether or not it was enough of a flaw.

Morgan walked to the center of the street, turned to his right and walked another thirty feet. He turned around and let his eyes scan the crowd on both sides. Among the mostly women spectators there was a scattering of men. A few were just the old men of the town but most, perhaps eight or ten, Morgan reckoned, were riders for both Marin and Carbona. Cy Black was in the front row of one group. Morgan couldn't see Judge Arlo Lunsford. No one could. Lunsford was peering from a window a half a block distant and muttering a prayer to himself.

The batwings came open and Brock Haskell stepped out. He, too, paused and looked in both directions. He smiled. He was obviously pleased at the turnout. He glanced at the sky and made a mental note of the conditions. It would enhance the story when he told it and told it and retold it. The day he'd gunned down the famous Lee Morgan, then serving as a U.S. Marshal. Haskell walked to the middle of the street and turned to face Morgan. Someone shouted from behind him, "Stage is comin'."

Cy Black thought it odd that even the pigeons on the town's clock tower seemed frozen to their perches. He eyed the crowd and jotted down short descriptions of facial expressions and what people were doing with their hands. He also noted the men in the crowd with their clenched jaws, squinty eyes and dry lips.

Something, perhaps the increasingly louder sound of the stagecoach coming, frightened the pigeons. Their wings beat an uneven rhythm as they sought more suitable environs. A single feather was fluttering down, almost midway between Haskell and Morgan. Both men saw it and both had the same thought. When the feather struck the ground, it would be time for someone to die.

The feather floated slowly downward with a typical rocking motion. Back and forth, to and fro, four feet, three, two! Brock Haskell's arm made a sweep so sudden it was not possible to follow it.

Inexplicably, a breeze violated the otherwise deathly calm air. The feather rose a few inches and blew three feet closer to Brock Haskell. His eyes caught the movement. As a result, they missed Morgan's draw. By the time Haskell's eyes had raised again, he was staring into a puff of blue-gray smoke. His own pistol roared and he could see the steely expression on Lee Morgan's face change almost imperceptibly. Morgan winced. A fraction of a second later, Brock Haskell's expression changed. Haskell died.

"You're hit," Cy Black said to Morgan.

Morgan nodded and felt his right side just at his waist. His fingers traced the bloody crease left by Haskell's bullet.

The wiry little newspaperman kept the crowds away. He and Morgan watched four or five men mount up and ride, hell bent, out of town in both directions. Morgan got his mount and walked with Cy back to the office of the *Courier.* They had just stepped inside when the stage coach rattled by.

"I'd sure like to be in two places at once right now," Cy said, grinning. "Out at Marin's place and down at Carbona's." He turned back to Morgan. The two men smiled at one another and Cy nodded his head toward the back of the building. Morgan pushed aside the curtain and stepped into the back room of the *Courier.*

"G'mornin'," he said. Tad and Tammy Winfrey both hurried to him, Tad shaking his outstretched hand and Tammy stretching up to kiss his cheek.

"They got here just after midnight," Cy Black said, "just like you figured it."

11

Tammy Winfrey doctored Morgan's wound and wondered at how close a thing the gunfight had been. Already, however, the talk around town was how fast and sure Marshal Lee Morgan had been and that his bullet had passed, dead center, through Brock Haskell's heart.

After Tammy treated his wound, Morgan dressed in the buckskins he often wore if he planned to be on the trail. That done, he brought the Winfreys up to date on the events in and around Holtville since his arrival.

"And you've actually seen the pistol," Tammy asked after hearing Morgan's story about Lita Peralta. Morgan nodded. She looked at her brother. "Tad, my God, maybe it's almost over at last." He smiled, squeezed her hand and nodded.

"I don't want to throw cold water on your excitement," Morgan said, "but we still don't have the fourth grip and even if that map locates it for us, we can't just walk out of here with it. Marin and Carbona both will make a try for it and I have to remind you that we're just a little bit outgunned."

"Believe me, Morgan, I've thought of little else," Tad Winfrey said, "but I do have a surprise of my own for you." Morgan frowned. "We'll have to make a short ride but," he continued, pointing to Cy, "thanks to him, it's well hidden."

"No disrespect intended," Morgan said, "but I've had about all the surprises lately that I can stand."

Cy Black walked over to Morgan and slapped him on the arm. "Go with the lad, no questions asked, Morgan. This is one surprise you won't mind and I need a little time to check some things about this map." Morgan looked at each of the three and finally shrugged.

"Lead the way, Tad."

The way proved to be rather rough. North of Holtville, the terrain was increasingly difficult unless one stuck to the trail. Tad and Morgan did not. After four miles, Tad dismounted. Morgan followed suit and was eyeing the huge rocks and the narrow openings into them which seemed to disappear into nowhere.

"We go the last mile or so on foot. The horses won't make it. Indeed," Tad said, looking at

Morgan now and smiling, "the mules barely made it."

"Mules?" Tad smiled again and started walking. He motioned with his arm for Morgan to follow. Both men were perspiring when they finally reached the top of a ridge. Below was a cut between the rocks, accessible only by the route they'd taken or by a narrow and treacherous trail. Indeed, Morgan saw a team of six mules grazing at leisure. Tad started down. At the bottom, Morgan got his first look at the huge cave hewn from the stone by nature.

At the cave's mouth was a heavy wagon. Beneath the canvas cover, Morgan saw case upon case of dynamite. The back half of the wagon also contained a number of unmarked boxes.

"Where in the hell did you get this?" Morgan asked. "And what's in those?" He was pointing to one of the smaller boxes. Tad smiled and motioned to him. They went just inside the cave and Morgan saw another canvas tarp. Ted eyed him and Morgan walked over, undid one tie down and threw back the covering. "Jeezus!" He was staring down at a brand new Gatling gun.

"It won't win the war all by itself but it sure will even things up a little."

"A little?" Morgan grinned. "It's worth a whole damned battalion and it doesn't bleed or run." Morgan replaced the tarp and walked back to the wagon. "Ammunition?" Tad nodded. "Where?" Morgan said and then cut himself short, "on second thought, Tad, don't tell me, I don't want to know."

Tad frowned. "You don't?"

"You got it here, that's all I need to know."

"Thing is," Tad said, "it's a full day's work to get it out of here. I'll need some advance notice before it's moved."

"Yeah," Morgan agreed, "but the dynamite will buy that."

Joaquin Marin listened carefully to the report of his men. While Marin had nothing but contempt for Don Miguel, he had hoped Miguel's hired gun would eliminate this new and increasingly irritating thorn in his side. He had, on one or two occasions, entertained the idea of trying to convince Carbona to consider a pact between them but Joaquin Marin's whole being rebelled at the idea. He waved his men out of his presence and sat back to ponder his next move.

He had assumed he'd be hearing from Morgan. Marin still believed that Teresa had been taken by force and was being held until Morgan could get his money. Marin called his valet. "Wake Miss Marin," he said. The man looked odd. "Well?"

"She is gone, *señor*. She was gone early this morning." Marin couldn't believe his ears but when he realized the implications of the information, he leaped out of his chair and hurried to the bedroom. The safe was shut and locked and he felt a moment of relief. Once he had it open, the earlier anxiety turned into full fledged anger.

He'd been robbed by his own daughter. Now, Marin thought, he had no course of action left to him but one. If he was to find the pistol grip in Holtville, he would have to occupy Holtville, all of it.

"Order the men to assemble at once."

A mere half a day's ride away, Don Miguel Carbona was making his own plans. Certain that Lee Morgan was now just one more dead gunfighter, Carbona called in his top man. "I want you to put three dozen men into the countryside, a dozen in three groups. Ride to the surrounding farms and burn one or more of the outbuildings. I don't want you engaging in gun play. Shoot only in defense of yourselves. Make your attacks at night, hit and run."

"But I thought you were taking over the ranches with tax delinquencies?"

"I do not pay you to think," Carbona growled. "Your thinking right now only strengthens my resolve that I was right about you. I will take them over with tax delinquencies but I want their owners frightened and ready to give up."

"*Sí sí*, Don Miguel." The man turned to leave but quickly turned back. "What of Marin?"

Don Miguel looked up. "When I have taken over everything else, Marin will be surrounded. So will his water and supply line."

Carbona smiled. "It is the perfect military operation, the equivalent of the great campaigns of Santa Ana."

The man frowned. The only campaign of Santa Ana's that he could recall was originally launched against the Alamo, hardly a great military victory. He decided against mentioning it.

Tad Winfrey and Morgan arrived back at the office of the *Courier* to find an elated Cy Black. He was about to share his findings with Tammy when the two men arrived. They waited as he put the old parchment map on a table and next to it, some of the original land deeds and lot markers.

"Here," he said, pointing, "and here and here." He looked up. "All of that property was once marked off for private ownership but it was later deeded over to the citizens' council appointed by the Winfreys' father, Holt."

"Part of the original plat for the town," Morgan asked.

"Right. Now then, we have these letters, M and C." Morgan's eyebrows raised. "Damn," he said, "That's easy enough."

"It is when you're not thinking too much about other things and you've got the plat marked off. Marin and Carbona."

Tad Winfrey studied the map for a few moments and then looked up. All right, we have some land that was once owned by them and they gave it to our father, I'm still confused about their significance here."

"So was I," Cy said, "until I did a little more digging. There is one spot in this town, one and only one, where the land once owned by those two men have a common boundary. Two blocks from here at the corner where the general store is now located."

"You mean the letters show where the grip is buried?"

"Well, we might have to do a little assuming and use a little imagination but this map isn't of much value if that isn't the case."

"Who owns the general store?"

Cy Black jabbed a finger into the air, "As Shakespeare wrote, 'Aye, there's the rub.' Lester King bought it but he had to borrow against it. Later, the bank sold the note."

"To whom?"

Cy shrugged. "That, Morgan, I don't know."

The front door opened, Morgan's Bisley came up and Cy held up a hand and moved to the curtain. He peered out, turned around and said, "My God, it's Judge Lunsford." Cy stepped out front. "Judge, what can I do for you?" Cy thought the Judge looked pale and even frightened. He frowned. "Judge?"

"Lee Morgan," Lunsford said, "is he here?"

"Why?"

"Please, Black, I must see him, believe me, I must. It's a matter of life and death."

Cy Black didn't trust Lunsford and he glanced outside to see if there were any of Carbona's men visible. He saw nothing out of the ordinary but he was very cautious. "Whose life and death Judge?"

"Mine, Black, and that of my wife."

Cy led Judge Lunsford to the back room. In a few minutes, the judge explained what had happened to him that morning and the order he'd been given by Don Miguel Carbona.

"I can't," he slumped into a chair, "I won't do any more for him." The judge looked up. "I promised myself that I would fight against Carbona and Marin and everyone else if you killed that gunfighter. I need help but I also come with some to offer."

"Just why in the hell should we believe you, Judge," Morgan asked.

The judge nodded. "Yes, why? I asked myself that same question before I left my office." Judge Lunsford got to his feet and looked Morgan straight in the eye. "I knew that Prather and his cronies were out of town and couldn't follow me here but then there was my court clerk. He came back with me. What could I do?

"What did you do, Judge?" Morgan asked the question and moved over near the curtain where he could keep an eye on the front door.

"I made certain I wasn't followed and I got your proof for you at the same time. You see, I'm not a violent man."

"What certainty and what proof?" Cy asked.

Judge Lunsford swallowed. "My court clerk. You see, I killed him."

Morgan moved quickly to the judge's office and confirmed the judge's story. He was still somewhat skeptical, given that anyone could have killed the clerk. Nothing would make it easier for Carbona than to get a man on the side of his adversaries.

When Morgan got back to the office of the *Courier,* he found Judge Lunsford going over the plat maps and parchment. Morgan was none too happy about it.

"I found the clerk but it only proves he couldn't follow. I don't know if the judge killed him or not and I'm still not certain about his motives."

Cy Black listened and then said, "Morgan, he saw the plat and all the rest. He asked about it and I told him. After all, he's settled a number of boundary disputes. Most important, however, is the fact that he told us who ended up with the deed on the mercantile store."

"Who?"

"Me," Lunsford said, "I own it now or I will when Les King can't meet his bank payment."

"How many others like that one, Judge?"

"A drawer full, Morgan, but they'll all go back and be set straight if you'll help me. My wife must be protected. I'll take my own chances but I can help you, too."

"How's that?"

"Carbona gave me another chance. Let me capitalize on it for you. You give my wife protection and I'll keep him busy. I told you what he wants from me. Well, he wouldn't know a phony tax bill from the real thing. I'll just take him the real ones."

"Uh uh," Morgan said. "In the first place, you told him you'd need some time. Go back too soon and he's liable to get suspicious. Besides, there's still Prather and his deputies to deal with." Morgan moved across the room, looking down and pondering this latest turn of events. "There may be a way." He studied Judge Lunsford's face. "You'd be taking one helluva life threatening risk, Judge, if you're sincere."

"I told you what I want of you. Protection for my wife. Nothing more."

Cy Black stepped forward. "Morgan, if you're thinking what I think you're thinking."

"I am. The Peralta place. It would keep Carbona fairly well occupied for a few days. In that time we might just find what we're looking for."

Morgan explained to Judge Lunsford about the Peralta place and drew a crude map of how to get there. "Now you have your wife here by sundown tonight, We'll see to it she's safe."

Judge Arlo Lunsford went on his way and Morgan turned his attention back to the mercantile store. "We're going to pay a visit to Les King this evening," he said. "We can't afford to waste time observing the proprieties."

"Agreed, Morgan, but where do we start?"

"Let's get a look at what we've got to work with from the inside first, then we make that decision, Tad. In any event, you won't be along."

"What? Why not?"

"You're work is cut out for you. When Mrs. Lunsford arrives this evening, she'll be able to lead you to the Lupton place. You take her and Tammy here out there."

"That's tonight. What about tomorrow?"

"And I'm not staying out there when everything we're doing is here in town," Tammy said.

Morgan held up both hands. "You hired me

to do a job and Wyatt Earp told me to watch after both of you. You can fire me and then all I'll do is what Wyatt asked me to do but if you think I'm going to risk his being mad at me, you've got another think coming." Tammy smiled and shrugged. "As to tomorrow, Tad, you'll take what hands you need from the Lupton place and get our other treasures down out of those hills."

"The Gatling? But where do I bring it? The Lupton place?"

Morgan jabbed a finger at the floor. "Here," he said, "to Holtville. Whatever else we find, we'll find right here in town." He set his jaw and added, "And whatever fighting we end up having to do will be easiest done here. We've got a water supply, food, ammunition, a doctor, everything our enemies don't have, except men."

"It'll take most of the day," Tad said.

"Mebbe not. Take two wagons from the Lupton place. A tow horse team to go with them. Split the load on the one wagon between those two and use the mules to pull the Gatling on the big wagon."

"It'll work, sure it will," Tad said, excitedly. "We may have trouble getting those horses into that canyon though."

"You can bet on it but do it, Tad, and get on back here as fast as you can."

Cy Black returned to the back room. He looked grim. "Ty Prather and his deputies just rode in. You can be sure they'll ride right straight down to see the judge."

"Then it seems to me," Morgan said, "that they need a little distracting."

"Like what?"

"Put the word on the street that I'm looking for them, all three of 'em, and add that I'm none too damned happy with 'em."

Less than thirty minutes after Cy spread the word of Morgan's search for Ty Prather, Prather was gone. One of his deputies rode with him but the one they called Shorty did not. He was convinced that Morgan was no man at all without his guns and he decided he'd prove it. On top of that, if he could deliver Morgan to Carbona where the fast gun had failed, he'd be Carbona's new ramrod.

Shorty found circumstances working for him when he saw Morgan and Cy Black leave Cy's office. They got even better when he barged in on Tad and Tammy. Tad might have made a little more account of himself had he not been taken by surprise. As it was, Tad was soon unconscious and suffering a cracked jawbone.

Shorty eyed young Tammy Winfrey but his mind was much more on greed and power than on lust. He'd have her anyway, he thought to himself.

"You take care o' the kid there, girlie, and keep your mouth shut an' mebbe you won't git hurt." Tammy was scared but she did a commendable job of hiding it. She knelt down beside her brother and kept quiet.

Morgan and Cy Black fared little better in what they were supposed to be doing. Morgan decided that they couldn't wait until evening to talk to Les King at the mercantile store. They'd talk to him then and hopefully be able to make a search.

As Cy and Morgan approached the mercantile store, a rider came into town at full gallop. He reined up when he saw Lee Morgan and Morgan recognized him as one of the Lupton hands.

"Mizz Lupton sent me," he shouted, never bothering to dismount, "one of our boys on the south range saw 'em, Marin's men. They're comin', ridin' hard this way, comin' to Holtville."

"Damn!" Morgan had wanted to get the man off his horse, calmed down and speak to him privately. Now it was too late. Several bystanders heard the warning.

"Get down to the newspaper office," Morgan shouted. Three men approached. One of them looked angry.

"You brought this grief down on us, Marshal. We wasn't havin' no trouble with nobody 'til you come in." One of the others doubled up his fists and moved toward Cy Black. Morgan watched, open mouthed, as Cy threw up both his arms, danced backwards, sideways and then threw three quick punches at the man which broke his nose, split his lip and knocked him down, in that order.

"You get the hell in the saloon," Morgan told the second man, "and you round up every man that wants to fight. If you want to save your town, that's what you'll have to do. It's up to you." The man eyed his friend on the ground and then shook his head and ran off. Cy Black was already trotting off toward his office.

The Lupton hand dismounted and stood by the doorway waiting for Cy and Morgan. Morgan caught up with the little editor.

"That was a helluva demonstration back there, Cy." Cy looked over and smiled. "Lightweight champion pugilist in my college class," he said. They both looked up and the door to Cy's office opened behind the man who was waiting for them. Both expected to see Tad or Tammy.

"Look out," Cy shouted. Morgan stopped, drew and fired. Shorty's gun flew from his hand and he clutched at his chest, staggered and fell face down on the board sidewalk. Cy stopped.

"My God! That must be eighty feet or more." Morgan holstered the Bisley and the two men hurried on. Shorty was dead. Tammy told them what had happened after they left. Tad was up and around but in a lot of pain.

"We'll have to make some plan changes," Morgan told them, "and we'll have to do it damned fast. Marin's men are on their way. My guess is that they plan to take over Holtville."

Tad could speak only with considerable difficulty but he managed to ask, "How do we stop them? There's not time to get the Gatling."

"But there is time to fetch some of that dynamite," Morgan said. He quickly wrote out a note and handed it to Cy.

"You're going to have to miss a newspaper today, Cy. You're the only one that can ride back to the Lupton place. I need this man here and every other one I can round up in town plus any that can be spared from the ranch. Take Tad and Tammy with you."

"I've never missed a deadline, dammit! All I have to do is set the type."

"Cy, there's just not time."

"I can set type. I worked as an apprentice for two years." They both looked at Tammy. "I won't go to the Lupton place, Morgan, I'll just ride off the first chance I get and come right back here."

"Damn!" Morgan glanced at Cy. "Get going," he said, "we'll get the paper out one way or another." Cy and Tad rode off toward the Lupton place and Morgan turned to the ranch hand. "I saw you at the meeting that night but I don't know your name."

"Jake Ledbetter, Mr. Morgan, and I'm damned proud to be ridin' for ya."

"Mebbe right now, I'll ask again later. All right Jake, you get down to the saloon and organize every man there. I'll be joining you in a few minutes. I've got to go to the livery and fetch a wagon and team." Jake nodded and hurried off.

Inside, Tammy was already busying herself with the type tray. "You really do know what you're doing, don't you?" She stopped and looked up and smiled. "Did you think I'd lie just so I could stay in town?"

"The thought crossed my mind. You know there won't be anybody around to keep an eye on you for awhile. I will be leaving some men at the saloon but I don't want them to split up just yet. Too easy for Marin's men to slip in one at a time."

"Don't you worry about me, I'll be fine. As soon as the paper is run, I'll deliver it to the saloon. Folks can pick one up there. I'll stay there too." Tammy moved over to where Morgan stood. "Take care of yourself."

"Not much to worry about this trip. It's what happens afterwards that matters." Morgan looked at the clock. "We could be back by dark if we don't run into any real trouble." She pulled his face close to hers and kissed him. It was a soft, gentle kiss but it belonged to a woman, not a little girl. "I'll be waiting," she said.

Morgan freed some very frightened but very grateful people. He told them to go on home and stay there. The fight, he told them, was only about to begin. That done, he returned to the saloon. All eyes were on him when he walked through the batwing doors but only one person spoke up. Morgan knew him as Obie Grant, a local cattle rancher who harbored almost no use at all for guns or gunmen. His own son had fallen victim to a wet-nosed gunny a few years back.

"You're a damned loose man with other folk's lives, mister. Some here might think you're quite a hero but what you did was damn dumb. What if it hadn't worked?"

Morgan poured a drink, downed it, turned to Grant and said, "Then you wouldn't be asking me the question."

12

Morgan went straight to Arlo Lunsford's office. The judge had just finished packing the things he would need to resume his position on the bench at some future date. He'd also written a letter which highlighted those things in which he had become embroiled.

"Morgan? What is it?"

"I want a court order authorizing me to enter the sheriff's office and confiscate the weapons he keeps. Joaquin Marin's men are riding toward Holtville now to take it over or sack it."

"My God! Morgan, I . . . I can't issue an order like that." He handed Morgan the letter he'd written. Morgan read it, looked up and then tore the letter into pieces.

"Let's play out the hand we talked about today, Judge. You can always write that letter when things are over, if you still feel the need and you're still able. That court order is a helluva lot more important right now."

The judge looked down at the torn bits of paper and then shook his head. "Yes," he said, "you're right, Marshal, it is." He quickly penned the order and as he handed it to Morgan, he said, "What about my wife now?"

"Do you know the Lupton place?"

"Yes but I . . ."

"Cy Black will be there by the time you arrive. He'll get you in. Take your missus out there and you stay put too until you get word from me or someone." Lunsford nodded and Morgan turned to leave.

"Marshal." Morgan turned back. "I owe you, sir. I've been a fool. I hope I'm not too late in recognizing it."

"It's easy to tell when it's too late, Judge." Lunsford looked quizzical. Morgan smiled and said, "You're not breathing anymore."

Jake Ledbetter had rounded up eighteen men by the time Morgan arrived. Some were skeptical about what they'd heard but most of them knew Jake and trusted him. Morgan climbed up on a table. "You're all deputized as of this moment." He pointed to three men in front. "You three go on over to the sheriff's office, break in and bring every weapon and all the ammunition you can find. I have a court order approving it and I'm acting in an official capacity. Bring back any tin stars you find, too. You boys lay claim to the first three you find."

The official sanctions made all the difference to all the men. Certainly none of them had reason to question Morgan's cool head or courage or speed or accuracy. They had a leader.

While the three men went after the weapons, Morgan sent Jake to roust Les King, the mercantile owner. Morgan was also going to confiscate whatever King had in stock which could help defend the town. While those men were so engaged, he addressed the others.

"Jake will be in charge. I want six men with me." He looked around. "I want the best shots left here and the best arm wrestlers with me. I need strong backs. I want three men to ride south toward the Marin's spread. I want to know where Marin is and how fast he's moving. As soon as you spot him, send one rider back with the news and a second back half way. The first will keep an eye on their movement and report to the second who will ride back to town again. Keep the relay working until we don't need it anymore."

"Where you an' your men gonna be, Marshal?" Morgan considered the man who'd asked the question. The tone of his voice indicated he didn't think much of a leader who was riding away from his men right off. Morgan saw the man was big, broad shouldered and with meaty, muscular arms.

"Tell you what," Morgan said, "I accept

your question as a commitment that you've volunteered to ride with me. I can use your brawn and you can use your brain to get the answer to your question first hand." The others broke into laughter.

Cy Black and Tad Winfrey had stayed to the dry washes which scored the landscape south of Holtville and out toward the Lupton ranch. By dusk however, they moved closer to the trail and by full dark, they were moving through the low, undulating hills which rolled into Lupton valley.

"Cy, look there, off to the southwest." Both men reined up. There was a red-orange glow in the sky. It appeared almost as a second sunset. "What is it?"

Cy Black knew what it was at once. He'd seen it before, many times and much worse. "Fire," he said. "Could be prairie or could be buildings but it's a fire sure. I saw more than I wanted to up north. Forest fires. A few big prairie fires, too, back when the Indians were still active."

"Don't strike me as being a lot of things on this particular prairie that would burn that big," Tad said.

"You're right, Tad, there isn't. Let's move faster."

Cy and Tad were not the only witnesses to the blaze. Joaquin Marin had opted to lead his own men to Holtville once he'd learned of his daughter's treachery. Now his point rider re-

turned to the main body and Marin halted his
gang. He had more than sixty men riding in,
more than enough as far as he was concerned to
either take Holtville or destroy it.

"It's a fire, sizeable," Marin said, "but
where?"

"I place it around *señor* Thomas's ranch,"
the point man said. Marin considered the opinion a moment and then concurred. "Yes, that
would be about right. Thomas has a huge barn
but nothing else would make such a large blaze
unless. . . ." he stopped himself. He watched the
blaze for a few moments more and then snapped
out a new order. "I want one more drag rider, two
more men on the flanks." He looked at the point
rider. "Keep a sharp watch, slow the pace just
slightly and watch for more such signs of a fire."
The man looked puzzled but he nodded.

Marin had originally planned to take Holtville that very night. Now, he opted to wait it out
until morning. He wanted a looksee at the town
before he made his move and if everything
looked normal, he would simply ride in at dawn
and have it before anyone could muster resistance. He looked at his pocket watch. At the new
pace he'd chosen, his men would have about
three hours to rest after they reached Holtville's
outskirts. Once again he turned and looked
toward the glow in the sky. He had a sinking
feeling in the pit of his stomach. He clearly felt
that something was wrong, something which
spelled trouble for him but he couldn't stop his
plan on that alone.

Less than an hour later, the point rider rejoined the main body again. There was a second and third fire now visible.

"Carbona *Bastardo!*" In Spanish, Marin ordered a patrol of six men to ride to the nearest of the blazes and confirm his suspicions. He also ordered a closing of his own ranks. He did want to maintain the pace he'd set however.

"We cannot," he told his point man, "afford to ride into Holtville after dawn."

Joaquin Marin was not the only man with decisions to be made and little time in which to make them. Only thirty minutes before his first arson patrol had struck, Miguel Carbona's men rode in from Holtville.

He knew they looked grim when they entered his study. He wrinkled his nose at the roady odor and dirty appearance. "Well?" None of the men wanted to act as the spokesman. Spanish history abounded with tales of the messenger who had paid with his life for the message he carried. Carbona looked at each face and he got his answer. "Was it a fair fight? A stand up fight between Morgan and Haskell?"

"*Sí.*" It was all any of them could manage.

Don Miguel waved the men out of his presence and poured himself a healthy quantity of tequila. He downed it and then sat down to ponder his problem and its most likely solution. He would not be stopped by a lone *Yanqui pistolero.*

The most accurate information about the

origin of the fires in the early evening sky was even then coming into the Lupton ranch. Half a dozen families had already arrived and were telling of the marauders who had ridden down on them, screaming, shooting and burning. Carbona's men had liquored themselves up before they ever took to the countryside and the fire they'd been ordered to set became only the climax of their raids.

One family reported the deaths of their three hired men, the theft of their stock and their own near brush with death. Those with young girls in their families were the most fearful and the night of terror was only beginning.

Mary Lupton gathered her foreman and the three women together as more fires were spotted and more families arrived.

"I'm ashamed to have to ask you this but we must know." She was looking at the Marin sisters and it was the recently arrived Felisa who responded.

"Is my father responsible for these fires and this horror?" She looked down, she glanced at her sister and then at Lita. Finally she looked back at Mary Lupton. "Do not be ashamed to ask such a thing. My shame is in the fact that I cannot give you an answer, I don't know. I do know that he is capable of it and I fear that he and Carbona may join forces."

"That has been my fear as well," Mary said, "but it seems both men are driven by a personal greed that has, so far, worked to our advantage."

Lita Peralta stepped forward. Mary Lupton saw the tears in her eyes. Mary started to speak but Lita held up her hand and then the oilcloth wrapping.

"This," she said, "is the cause of the trouble. When this began, I believed in the system of justice. I believed what was rightfully mine would be restored to me and that my family name would again have real meaning in California." She threw the pistol on the floor. "Instead, it has brought out the worst in men and now claims the lives and homes of innocent people. The very peons I'd one day hoped to help with the treasure. We must give up the fight. Let them have the gun and the gold."

Cho Ping entered the room. "Two riders come. Men. They come from the north."

Teresa turned. "Morgan," she said, softly.

The two riders proved to be Cy Black and Tad Winfred. They were ushered at once into the house. Mary Lupton began the introductions. They were halted when Tad and Lita met.

"I feel I have a family again," Lita said. She hugged Tad, gently touching his swollen jaw and kissing his cheek.

"I hate to put a damper on a family reunion," Cy said, "but we have some very real and immediate dangers to deal with." Mary Lupton quickly brought the two men up to date on the events of the past couple of hours. In turn, Cy Black told the gathering what had occurred in Holtville and what Morgan was planning to do about it.

"Lita wants to end it," Mary said. "She believes the Peralta gold is at fault."

"The Peralta curse," Lita said, "has become the reality. The Peralta gold remains only a legend." She turned to Tad. "Will you and your sister give up your claims so that we might end the bloodshed?''

"Whoa there, little lady," Cy Black said, "just hold on. The sincerity of your offer is above reproach. Of that, I'm certain. It's practical application is foolhardy." Tad Winfrey seemed to take umbrage with Cy's assessment and was about to say so. The newspaperman smiled, understandingly, at Tad. "These men won't stop." He looked at the Marin sisters. "Your father? You know him better than any of us? Would he stop driving people from their homes, taking their land and their pride if he had the treasure?''

Tad Winfrey was shocked. "Damn you, Black, that's the most crude and painful thing I've ever seen done in my life."

"You may well be right," Cy said, still looking at the Marin girls, "but the issue here is the truth of the words, not the grace with which they were spoken."

Felisa Marin responded but she addressed herself not to Cy Black or Tad Winfrey but to Estralita Peralta.

"*Señor* Black is quite correct," she began. "Our father and Don Miguel Carbona will not be stopped by giving them the gold, they will only become worse. They lust after power, not gold. They seek gold only because they know it will buy more power. You may give them the pistols and they may find the treasure but after that, they will only want more. Always," she said, her voice cracking with emotion, "always they will seek more power over lesser men. I know of only one thing which will stop our father."

"What then," Tad asked.

"His death!" Tad was sorry he'd asked.

Cy Black gave the moment only the time he felt they could afford. It wasn't much. "We've got to get these families organized and ready to move out of here. Holtville is our only chance and we can't wait beyond midnight to leave."

"I know most of these people," Mary Lupton said. "I'll inform them and my men can help ready them for the trip. I can use your help, girls." They nodded and the women took their leave.

"Cy," Tad said, "I'm sorry I shot off at you that way."

Cy smiled and slapped Tad on the arm. "Youth and pretty girls and their defense against old men with sharp tongues goes back several thousand years. No need to apologize for that." Tad's face flushed and he grinned. "By the by, how's the jaw?"

"Painful but if I keep busy, I don't think about it, so I'd like to keep busy. Someone needs to ride out of here, right now, back to Holtville. Morgan ought to know we're on our way and there may be some men available to come out a ways and escort these people, just in case."

"Are you volunteering?"

"No, Cy, I'm telling you that's what I'm going to do."

"Yeah, that's kind of what I thought. Watch yourself, son." Tad nodded.

13

If things had not gone well up to that time for Morgan, he couldn't quarrel with his latest efforts and plans. By midnight, only the Gatling gun was not yet in Holtville but it was on its way. The movement of the ammunition for the wonder gun and the transport of the dynamite had gone without a hitch.

Les King was also a Godsend. He had just received a huge dynamite shipment himself, to be used to clear land. Too, he had an inventory of twenty-five rifles and thirty-two handguns and plenty of ammunition.

Morgan found Jake Ledbetter to be an efficient man to leave in charge and by the time Morgan had returned from the hidden canyon, Jake had rounded up nearly forty men. He was using two dozen of them in a hastily conceived defense perimeter at the south edge of town.

"From the looks of the fires to the south, I'm betting that we won't get hit 'til sunup. By then," Morgan told Jake, "we'll have a few more surprises in store for our visitors."

"What have you got in mind?"

"Something to eat and a little sleep," Morgan said, "and I'd suggest the same for every man we can spare. Change the perimeter so that those men can get a break, too, and catch some shuteye yourself." Jake nodded. "I'll be back at three."

Morgan couldn't remember the last time he was so damn tired. He ached in every muscle and joint and his stomach must have believed that his throat had been cut. He wolfed down a steak, some boiled potatoes, two pieces of apple pie and a quart of milk. It was one-thirty when he got back to the newspaper office. He found a fresh pot of coffee and he took a few more minutes of relaxation with a cup of it and a cigar.

Cy Black kept a small cot in the back and Morgan didn't bother with a light. He slipped into the office, stripped off his boots, shirt and pants and started to climb in.

"I'm glad you're back," Tammy said.

"Goddam, I didn't know you were in here. You're supposed to be in a room at the hotel.."

"But I'm not." Tammy raised up on her arms and the thin sheet slipped lower. Morgan could see the pink top edges of her nipples and the little protrusions indicating their hardness.

"Dammit, Tammy!" Morgan pushed away from her and stood up. "I'll go to the hotel."

She swung her legs to the floor, stood up and let the sheet drop away. The body was young, firm, shapely and the fleecy, golden patch between her thighs revealed her most private asset.

"Don't you want me, Morgan?"

"It wouldn't make a goddam bit of difference if I did."

"Do you think I'm too young? Is that it?"

"I know how old you are," Morgan said, fumbling for the sheet so that he might cover her.

"Then it's my uncle, Wyatt Earp?" She giggled. "Surely you're not afraid of Tad." Morgan took the edges of the sheet, reached behind Tammy and started to drape the sheet over her shoulders. She grabbed his wrists, jerked and then put his open palms against her breasts. At the same time, she stepped forward and pressed against him.

Morgan backed up but Tammy moved with him, all the way to the wall. She stood on her tip toes and locked her fingers around the back of his neck. She pressed tightly against him and, in spite of himself, Morgan reacted.

"I am my own woman," she said, softly. "I don't answer to my brother or to my uncle."

"And I'm a damned fool," Morgan said. He pushed Tammy back to the bed and mounted her. He found himself wanting to be inside of her. Morgan liked to take it slow and easy with a woman, working up to a mutual moment of gratification. Now, here with Tammy, he felt an almost animal lust. He wriggled out of his under drawers and was not surprised to find her moist enough to accommodate him at once.

"Yes," she whispered, "Oh Morgan, yes. Take me."

The initial thrust by Morgan was met with Tammy's undulating hips but they soon dropped into a pleasure filled rhythm. Tammy's youth resulted in additional pleasure for Morgan and he didn't want it to end too quickly. He gradually slowed and then stopped his strokes. He pulled out of her and began bathing her body with his lips and tongue.

Tammy writhed and moaned and whispered her adoration of his efforts. Her only two previous experiences had been with boys. Lee Morgan was a man and he was treating her like a woman. While her mind may not yet have reached that stage, her physical attributes and needs both belied the fact.

Tammy felt new feelings and experienced new sensations as Morgan fondled, stroked, teased and mouthed her. Twice she experienced total fulfillment and learned that she was capable of even more. Morgan wanted no more from her than what she had already offered, herself, completely. Having more than satisfied her desires, Morgan now entered her again and fulfilled his own needs. Both were spent and they fell asleep entwined in total satisfaction.

Morgan's internal alarm didn't have a chance to function on this morning. Jake Ledbetter awakened him, virtually ignoring Tammy Winfrey's presence. Morgan sat up. Jake was holding a lamp.

"Get that damned thing out of my eyes," Morgan said. He got up and started pulling on his britches. "Sorry Jake." Jake stepped back. "What's wrong?"

Jake looked down now at Tammy. She appeared to be asleep. "Her brother just rode in. He's over at the saloon."

Morgan considered Jake and said, "Why'd he come back?"

Jake told Morgan as much as he knew and then added, "But I just found out we've got worse problems."

Morgan tucked in his shirt and then sat down and began pulling on his boots. "Like what?"

"The sheriff."

Morgan frowned. "Prather? What the hell problem is Prather? Hell, he rode out of here hours ago and I'd be damned surprised if he ever came back."

"Be surprised, Morgan." Tammy woke up, rubbed her eyes, turned over and sat up. She was bare breasted and grabbed for a blanket when she finally saw Jake. He smiled, sheepishly.

"Jake, dammit!"

Jake Ledbetter set the lamp on the table. He stood for a moment and then took a deep breath and said, "I didn't tell the men I posted about

Prather. Most still take 'im for a lawman. He came back, Morgan, with fifteen men. He's holed up in the stock stable down by the courthouse."

Morgan turned to Tammy. "Get dressed and go over to the saloon. Tad's there." She glanced at Jake and then nodded. "All right, so Prather thinks he can buffalo us with fifteen men. Hell, we'll blow him out of the damned place, if we have to."

Jake swallowed. "He's got Howard Tuck an' his wife an' little girl in there, Morgan. Tuck's the town banker. He tricked 'em into going with 'im. Now he's got 'em up in the loft with ropes around their necks. Threatens to push 'em off unless we give 'im what he wants."

"Which is?"

"You, Morgan, dead!"

Jake had trouble keeping up with Morgan as they hurried off to the saloon. When they got there, Morgan stopped just outside. "Do they know?" he asked, pointing inside.

"They know and most won't listen to too much. They all owe Tuck an' he's their friend. You're still a stranger to 'em. They'll fight with ya but when it comes to a choice between you an' one o' their own, it's no contest, badge or no badge."

Morgan smiled. "Why do you think I hate badges so much."

Morgan pushed his way inside. He spotted Tad and walked over to him. "What time did Cy figure to pull out of the Lupton place?"

"Midnight. They'll be pushed hard to beat

daylight."

"Jake," Morgan said, "you ride out, north."

"The Gatling?" Morgan nodded. "I'll git back as soon as I can." Jake set his jaw and then added, "Stay alive, Morgan. This town needs ya whether these folks know it or not." Jake pulled out and Tad Winfrey poured he and Morgan a drink and gestured with his eyes toward the men in the saloon.

"They're getting mighty edgy. What now?" He downed his own drink and watched Morgan slosh his around in the glass for a minute. Finally, Morgan downed it.

"I'll be back in a few minutes." Morgan passed Tammy at the batwings. They looked at each other and exchanged the faintest of smiles. Tammy hurried over to join Tad but Morgan was already near the end of the block. He drew the Bisley and fired into the air, twice.

Everyone in the saloon came out onto the street. They could see Morgan's silhouette but nothing in the barn. The only evidence of anyone was the exchange of dialogue and the men all recognized the high pitched squeak belonging to Ty Prather.

"Well if it ain't the big shot marshal with the real sudden gun. Now then, Mr. Big Shot Marshal, if you're ready to strike a bargain, ol' Sheriff Prather'll tell you what to do."

"I'm not interested in what you've got to say, Prather. I don't know why you think I'm in Holtville but let me set it straight right now. I came here for gold and I don't give a damn about anything or anybody else. I just came up here to warn you. If you get in my way, I'll kill you."

Ty Prather was peering between two rotten boards and he could see Morgan holster his gun, turn around and start walking away. He shouted, "Morgan! You walk away from me an' I'll hang these folks." He waited but Morgan kept walking. "Morgan, goddam you, I'll do it, I'll hang 'em, I swear it."

Morgan was looking straight ahead. The shock hadn't worn off yet and the men were frozen in awe. Morgan knew that once they realized he wasn't bluffing, they'd probably do something very stupid. He hoped he had enough time to prevent the situation from ever getting that far.

"Morgan! Here I am. I'll do it. I'll hang this goddam banker." Morgan had been able to see the Tucks fairly well. Indeed they were tied into chairs and he'd noted they were also gagged. He was grateful for that. Had there been screaming he didn't know if he would have been able to hold back the townsmen.

Morgan stopped and turned around. Now he could see Prather framed in the barn's loft door. He gauged the distance.

I'm tired of listening to you, Prather," Morgan shouted. "You're not going to hang these folks, one of your men will have to do that and after they do, I'll blow that barn all to hell. It was the first building we set with dynamite. The very first one. You're a real smart man."

"Your goddamn bluffin' won't wash with

me, Morgan. You're a mighty good man with a handgun but you can't out fox ol' Ty Prather." Prather stepped next to the chair of banker Tuck. "He'll be first an' just why the hell do you figger one o' my men'll hang 'em, 'stead of me?"

"I already told you that, Prather," Morgan said. He'd gauged the distance at about forty yards. "I told you, I'm tired of listening to you."

"So what?"

"Because I consider a man I'm tired of as a man who's in my way." Morgan drew and let his arm make a stiff arc until the gun barrel was at a forty-five degree angle and then he squeezed the trigger. No one who witnessed the shot could believe it, particularly Holtville Sheriff Ty Prather. In an instant, he became Holtville's late Sheriff, Ty Prather.

Morgan fired two more shots into the side of the barn. He placed them where he'd seen shadows of men. He hit no one.

He knew it didn't matter. He'd hit Ty Prather. The sheriff had just hit the ground. If Morgan's bullet didn't kill him, the fall did. He broke his neck. Morgan detected no movement inside the barn. He made his next move.

"Anybody else in there who thinks I'm bluffing, go on and move up to the loft and hang those folks. After you do, I'll keep my promise to you just like I kept it to the little weasel you were riding with. I'll blow that building all to hell."

Morgan was very curious about the quality of the men in that barn. Where the hell had

Prather come up with them? They weren't Carbona's men, that was sure. Had that been the case, one of them would have taken a shot at him, perhaps more than one. He was certain they were armed with rifles, or some of them anyway. He concluded they were mostly out of work drovers that Prather had enticed into the deal with the promise of some big payoff. Now, they were leaderless.

"If you're not going to hang those folks, then I'd suggest you get the hell out of that barn, right now!" A few moments later, Morgan did hear movement. Horses! There were only two or three at first, then many more. All of them were at the back of the building and moving fast, away from town. Morgan waited. After five minutes, he strolled into the barn.

14

Jake Ledbetter came through the batwing doors of the saloon and looked around. His eyebrows raised. He was impressed. He sought out Lee Morgan in the back office.

"You've done a helluva job out there," he said. "The place looks like an army headquarters."

Morgan was looking over a supply inventory which one of the women had just completed. He finished, looked up and smiled.

"If we're going to stay alive and save this town, that's the way it will have to function."

"The Gatling gun is in place and rigged just the way you ordered it. I'll, by God, say one thing. Those Amish folk might not fight but, I swan, they can build anything.''

"The sharpshooters in position?''

Jake nodded. "I've got two on each side of town. There are a dozen more men who rank close to the first eight. I got four o' them on the roof of the courthouse, two with the Gatlin gun and the rest for replacements.''

"Yeah, good, Jake, good." Morgan got up, pulled his shoulders back and worked his arms up and down to limber up the stiff and tired muscles. "The women will divide the duty here. Hot coffee, food, medical treatment as the doctor dictates it. Now, how about the dynamite?''

"Two lines of it buried about a quarter of a mile out and another line about a hundred and fifty yards from the outside defense ring. That'll cover us on the southwest and the southeast quadrant.''

Morgan reached out and slapped Jake on the arm. "You've done a helluva fine job yourself, Jake. It's a pleasure knowing you and I hope we can get drunk together tonight.''

"I'm countin' on it.''

"Well, there's no damned reason we can't start the day off right, is there?''

Jake grinned. "Not a damned one I can think of, Morgan.''

Down the block, Cy Black finished setting the type for the day's paper. There were two headlines and two sets of type for the main story.

The first read,

> Holtville, California Sacked
> and Burned By Marauders

Cy smiled and picked up the second lead plate. He gently kissed the top of it. "You're the one. You've just got to be."

> Bloodthirsty Marauders Meet Their Doom
> Holtville, California Their Waterloo

Cy placed both plates in his safe and shut and locked it.

Some ninety men were now in the confines of the town's buildings. Of that number, a dozen were too old to fight and eighteen more were of the Amish persuasion. Fifty-three were fully armed and considered the town's front line of defense. Five others, all with army experience, were in the field to watch for and report on the movement of either the raiders of Joaquin Marin or the small Mexican terrorist army of Don Miguel Carbona.

In fact, many of Carbona's men were sleeping off a night of too much tequila and too many *señoritas*. Carbona himself was waiting reports from the men he'd sent out the night before to burn buildings and put fear into the hearts of the ranchers. What they had succeeded in doing was to strengthen an already steely resolve.

While Carbona waited, Joaquin Marin

paced. His main body of men was still a hard two hour ride away from Holtville, and he didn't want to move until the patrols he'd sent out returned. He was irritated, too, by the fact that he'd sent out similar patrols the night before to bring him news of the many fires which had been seen. He'd heard nothing from any of them.

Unknown to either side, except by the participants, all but two of Carbona's raiders were dead. Half drunk and all crazy, they had run headlong into Marin's sober and prepared men.

The fight was short and one-sided but Marin's men did not escape unscathed. Forced from their mounts to fight in a skirmish line, their animals bolted and left them afoot. Indeed, the gods had made light of the mortals on this night and they were about to deliver their final, ironic touch.

Don Miguel Carbona was more than a little surprised to find he had an early morning visitor. When Judge Arlo Lunsford was ushered into his presence, Miguel gave him a long, studied look. He did not offer his usual greeting or gesture to a chair. Lunsford remained standing, holding a thick, official looking folder.

"I did not expect to see you very soon, my dear Judge."

"Nor I you, Don Miguel, but if we are to reconcile our misunderstandings and gain an ultimate victory, then we must move quickly. I saw fires on the horizon last night. I wondered if you did."

"I ordered them." Miguel said, calmly. "The

combination of fear and fact is often too much of an obstacle for the peon, whether American or Mexican. I have now provided the fear."

"And the facts, as you choose to call them, are here." Lunsford hugged the folder to him and touched it lightly.

"The taxes?" Miguel asked, leaning forward.

"Yes," Lunsford said and then invited himself to sit down. Miguel's smile faded. He leaned back and glanced at the big floor clock.

"You must have worked very diligently and very, very late to have had such sudden success." Miguel got up and walked around his desk, sitting then on its edge. "And you must have ridden out of Holtville very, very early to have arrived here at this hour."

"The important thing, Don Miguel, is not that I am here, but why." Judge Lunsford now launched into one the finer moments of his later years. He tossed the tax folder on Miguel's desk with an air of total disinterest. Now, he leaned forward. "I know where Estralita Peralta is, and I know the locations of all four pistol grips." Arlo Lunsford smiled. It was a smug look he gave Carbona and it did not go begging.

"You speak as though you have brought me more than what we had originally bargained for, my dear Judge." Carbona turned icy. "You have not. Even if what you say is true, it is no more than what you promised and some of it is long overdue."

"Indeed it is, Don Miguel, but the last part,

the last pistol grip, that isn't overdue and it is worth considerably more than merely clearing my obligation to you."

"I will not be blackmailed," Miguel shouted. Two *vaqueros* entered the room and looked at Carbona, awaiting their orders. Judge Lunsford smiled, leaned back in the chair and folded his arms.

"Are you going to order me shot then, Miguel?"

The big Mexican bandit had never been in quite this spot. He finally waved his two men away.

"What is it you want?"

"One third of the Peralta treasure." Miguel's jaw dropped. He was stunned by the request. Judge Lunsford let Carbona's stew reach a simmer and then he continued. "I will take you to the Peralta woman's hiding place. There, we will find one of the pistols." Lunsford stopped talking and Miguel Carbona couldn't stand it.

"Then what?"

"One step at a time, Carbona." Lunsford never addressed Don Miguel in such a fashion. It rendered him an equal by Carbona's tradition and he didn't accept it. He was miffed, angry and frustrated all at the same time.

"When do we go?"

"We don't," Lunsford said. "If we go there first, we may miss our chance at the other two grips." Judge Lunsford calmly got to his feet and walked to Carbona's liquor cabinet.

"A drink, Don Miguel?" The wily judge smiled when he asked the question but he also realized that he had pushed Carbona about as far as any man could. When he received no reply, Judge Lunsford shrugged, poured himself a shot of Carbona's treasured bourbon, downed it and then turned around. "Joaquin Marin will attack Holtville this morning. He intends to take it over or destroy it. If he does either one, we could lose our chance at the Peralta gold for good."

"You come with much talk, Judge Lunsford," Don Miguel said, picking up the folder, "and legal papers which you told me would take a week to produce." He threw the folder down. "Now you wish to share a third of the wealth which has been due to me for centuries." Carbona suddenly drew a pistol and cocked it. He held it at arm's length and pointed it at Judge Lunsford's head. "I could have killed you before for your lies but I was gracious to you. Now you come into my home, insult my intelligence with more lies and try to rob me with your words."

Arlo Lunsford had not played such a game with a man since his days as a young attorney in the court room of Ohio. He knew Carbona to be so volatile a man at times, that he would kill even if it meant losing the treasure. Lunsford was on very thin ice. He thought, *It's prima facie time.*

"We waste time, Don Miguel. I ride with you. If I'm lying, kill me then." Miguel straightened, steadied the pistol and took two steps toward the Judge. Lunsford suspected what was next.

"Where is Luis?" There it was, the key question! Luis, the court clerk, faithful to Don Miguel. His eyes and ears in Lunsford's life. Luis, the Judge's prima facie evidence.

"He is dead, Don Miguel. I killed him myself. I have suspected him for as long as you have suspected me. I told him what I had learned and his actions were predictable. He checked my story and my information and then he rode straight to Marin. I had him followed. When he returned, I killed him and came here."

Lunsford was counting on a number of things to work in his favor where Carbona was concerned but the shock effect of his story about Luis and the lack of time were his most potent allies. Now, he'd used them both. The first sign of Carbona's reaction was the pistol barrel. It wavered and then slowly came down. The second was Carbona's one, almost whispered response. "Luis, Luis."

Judge Arlo Lunsford had not killed the court clerk merely to remove an obstacle. The judge had also learned a truth. Luis was, in fact, Luis Manuel Carbona, Don Miguel's brother.

Judge Arlo Lunsford had found his own treasure. He'd lost it years before but now he had it back and he was bent on never losing it again. What he found was himself. While taking his wife to the Lupton place, they had met the people fleeing toward town and Lunsford then learned of Marin's plan. By the time Lunsford reached Carbona, he'd altered the plan he and

Morgan had worked out. Lunsford would not simply lead Carbona on a wild goose chase. He would attempt to pit Carbona and Marin against each other in a pitch battle. Let them destroy or at least weaken their forces and give the citizens in Holtville a fighting chance.

Don Miguel Carbona, resplendent in his black and silver garb and mounted upon a white stallion, personally led the first charge against Joaquin Marin's encampment. Carbona was beside himself with anger at his own lieutenants for their treachery and disobedience of the previous night but it was easy to stifle such feelings at this moment.

Marin was caught totally by surprise and suffered heavy losses before his own men could find suitable ground on which to make a stand. In Marin's favor was the fact that Carbona's men were scattered and by the time he could gather his entire force, Marin was prepared. Holtville, for the moment, got a reprieve.

In Holtville, Lee Morgan sequestered himself with Cy Black, the Winfreys, the Marin girls and Lita Peralta. They waited. They had talked, chattered as much as anything, during the last hour before sunup but their talk ran out and they busied themselves with their own thoughts now. Sunup came but the imminent attack from Joaquin Marin did not. Two hours past sunup, the attack had still not come. What did come was one of the patrol riders Jake Ledbetter had sent south to track Marin.

Jack burst into the office at the saloon and Morgan was on his feet in an instant. The others followed suit. Jake had been waiting for his man and was the first to get the news. He was grinning from ear to ear.

"How the hell it happened I don't know. Why, I don't know but Carbona and Marin are at war, all out, winner take all war!" He gave the little gathering the report he'd gotten from his man and a cheer went up. They danced around, hugged one another and would not have stopped save for Morgan.

"We've got a cheer or two coming," he finally said, "but we're a helluva ways from an all out *fiesta, amigos.*" Stern looks replaced the smiles when the reality of Morgan's observation soaked in.

Cy Black said, "You're right, of course. Can we exploit this?"

Morgan walked across the room, pondering the news and considering every possibility and each alternative to them. He stopped and turned to Jake. "A decoy! We need a damned decoy."

"I don't follow," Jake said.

"Look, neither Carbona or Marin want to die. They want the Peralta treasure. One or both of them is going to come to his senses before they've killed each other off. We're going to be facing whatever is left. A hundred men, fifty? Hell, I don't know and the worst possible scenario is, in fact, a peace and an agreement between them. We have to split up whatever is left."

Cy Black smiled. "Divide the enemy force and destroy the halves piecemeal."

"Yeah," Morgan said.

"A good plan, Morgan," Jake said, "but just how do we get them split up, if what you say happens."

"It'll happen, you can count on it and getting them split up is going to be your job, Jake." Jake frowned and looked at the others. They too were puzzled. "Take four men." Morgan thought. "Sharpshooters, take four sharpshooters. Make sure you've got plenty of ammunition for them. Take four wagons and load as much dynamite as you can. I want you to ride like hell for the Cargo Muchacho." He smiled. "You're going on a treasure hunt."

Throughout the night and in the hour before sunup, the quietest one of the group had been Estralita Peralta, Now, she came forward. She moved to the table and placed on it the pistol she owned and the parchment map and plat map of the town. She turned to Tammy Winfrey. "Do you have your pistol here?" Tammy frowned, looked at her brother and then nodded. "Get it, please." Tammy complied.

"Lita," Morgan said, "we're losing time."

"Why not make Jake's treasure hunt the real thing?"

"What? What the hell are you talking about? We don't have the time to look for the fourth pistol grip right now."

"We don't have to look for it, Morgan," she said, "I know where it is, exactly."

The others moved closer and Morgan moved to the desk. He gave Estralita a studied look and glanced down at the map. "Okay, explain."

"The letters, the M and the C. They had us all going. It was so simple. M and C could be nothing else but Marin and Carbona but we were wrong. Simple it is but so simple, we tried to make it difficult." She pointed to the city may. "There, that spot." She looked up. "What stands there?" Everyone thought but it was Felisa Marin who answered.

"It is the church, Our Lady of the Mountain."

"And in front of the church," she asked. Felisa thought, looked down and then said, "My God! It's the statue!"

Morgan thought. "Mary and the baby Jesus?"

"Madonna and child," Lita said, "M and C."

15

The fourth pistol grip reposed in the hollowed base of the Madonna and Child statue. Together, the four grips revealed a surprise of their own. Peralta had indeed sent the groups of boys out to bury the gold in small amounts and at all four points of the compass but he did not leave it so.

Peralta reclaimed eighty percent of the gold later, leaving only smidgens of it at the original four sites. The major portion was buried in the narrow confines of a canyon called El Cavidad, the cave or hole. It's location was well known to the longtime residents of the area and to the many Peralta treasure seekers over the years. It was considered inaccessible. It was not. A single trail led to its depths and finally to the Peralta treasure.

Even as the little band in Holtville stemmed their urge to celebrate prematurely and, instead, prepared Jake for his trip and themselves for the possible fight ahead, Morgan's prediction was coming to fruition.

It was, amazingly enough, Don Miguel Carbona who first displayed the white flag. It was little wonder Marin took so long to honor it. Carbona had been winning and Marin had been considering a withdrawal until he could reorganize.

"*Señor* Marin." Joaquin Marin got to his feet and gave Don Miguel Carbona the onceover. Finally, he extended an arm and gestured for Carbona to sit down. "We must stop our fighting. We face a mutual enemy in the *Yanqui* Morgan. It is he upon whom we should vent our wrath."

"You propose peace between us now, Don Miguel, so that we might defeat Morgan. But what of tomorrow?"

"Tomorrow we will share the spoils of victory. The Peralta treasure can be ours." Don Miguel swung his arm in a wide arc and said, "This valley and all that lives within it can be ours. Is there not enough for two?"

"There never has been before, why now?"

Carbona smiled. "Perhaps, *señor*, you and I do not share the same beliefs but hear me out and then decide. Each and every man who has sought the Peralta treasure for himself alone, has found instead, the Peralta curse. I, Don

Miguel Carbona, would rather rule half a land with half a treasure than be sole owner of a curse."

"I do not believe in curses, Carbona."

"Very well then, do you believe in Morgan?"

At Don Miguel's base camp, Judge Arlo Lunsford eyed the big white stallion just outside Carbona's field tent. Carbona had honored tradition by riding a wagon to meet Joaquin Marin.

Most of Carbona's men were on the line, at the ready against the advent of their leader's failure. Lunsford knew if he was to live, he would have to escape now. Carbona had left him in custody of Juan, the lecherous little man who had terrorized Lunsford's wife.

Juan stood just outside the tent. Lunsford knew he could not manhandle the Mexican and the judge had no weapon. Suddenly, Judge Lunsford saw the blue smoke of a cigar. He got to his feet and moved to the tent's opening. Juan turned quickly, frowning.

"I'm afraid I came off without my own cigars," he said. The judge didn't smoke. He was holding a twenty dollar gold piece between his thumb and forefinger. "May I buy one of yours?"

Juan smiled. It was a grimy toothed, drooling smile. "I have no *pesos, señor*. I would have to keep all of that."

"Of course," Lunsford said. Juan reached for a cigar and held it out. The judge took it, stretched out his hand which held the coin and then dropped it. "Sorry," he said. He looked

down and at once dropped to his knees. There
was sand and rocks and brush in abundance and
the coin had disappeared. By the time Lunsford
got to his knees, he'd already spotted it but he
put one hand over it and looked up.

Juan dropped to his own knees and Judge
Lunsford eyed the huge Bowie knife in a sheath
on Juan's right hip. They were facing each other
only a foot apart. Juan dug around in the sand.

"Be careful," Lunsford said, "you may
cover it up and we'll never find it." As he spoke,
he moved his hand slightly and tossed the coin
just to Juan's left and behind him. A moment
later, the judge said, "There, there it is." Juan
looked up and saw the judge pointing. Juan
turned to his left. The sun sparkled off the gold
coin's surface. Juan grinned, turned still more
and started to crawl toward it.

Arlo Lunsford thought the hardest thing he
had ever done in his life was to shoot a man.
When he shot Luis Carbona, he fought off his
nausea and he did not think he could ever kill
again. Now, all he could see in his mind's eye and
hear in his memory was Juan pawing Mrs.
Lunsford and her screams.

The judge reached out, grabbed the handle
of the knife and pulled, hard. Juan came up to his
knees and whirled around to face the judge. At
that moment, eye to eye, Arlo Lunsford brought
the big Bowie down from above his head in a
long sweep. Its point struck flesh just to the left
of Juan's breast bone and buried itself almost to
the hilt. Juan grunted, grabbed at the wound,

coughed a bloody cough and fell face down, dead.

Don Miguel Carbona returned to his own camp. He had made his point and, in his own mind, won the day. Joaquin Marin ordered his lieutenants to ready themselves for the attack on Holtville. Carbona would do the same. Now, once more, the gods awoke and resumed the games they play on mortal men.

Both Carbona and Marin had sent out patrols that morning to reconnoiter Holtville. Carbona's men left first and returned first, arriving almost as he returned to his camp. Juan's dead body and the Mexican's missing stallion were his first discoveries. The judge had tricked him. At first, his anger was almost out of hand but Lunsford's trick had backfired. Carbona and Marin were no longer enemies.

"The town," Carbona said, "what of the town?"

"Defended by perhaps thirty or forty men but we must attack before help comes back."

Carbona was puzzled at his man's report and statement. Help?

"What help? From who? From where?"

The man shrugged and said, "I do not know, Don Miguel, but four wagons and five men go east, there," he pointed, "toward the Cargo Muchacho. The wagons, they are almost empty. A few boxes, probably ammunition. I think they go to get more men." Don Miguel knew otherwise. Gold, not men, moved those wagons.

Carbona wasted no time. He ordered his men to ride north again but this time to watch for Marin's patrol. When they were found, Carbona told them, they were to be killed! Carbona himself rode back to Marin's camp.

"*Señor* Marin, I return with mixed news." Marin had already broken down his field tent and was about to begin his northward march.

"What news, *senor* Carbona?"

"Your own patrol was killed. A band from the town ambushed them. I ordered my men to ride to the north of the town. They have reported that the north is weakly defended. I will need two hours to position my men. I suggest you attack the south side in ninety minutes. That will draw their fire and their attention and I will sweep down upon them from behind."

"I wish to confirm what you tell me for myself!"

Carbona smiled. "Of course, *señor* Marin. If you do not find it as I have described, cancel your attack. I will hold until I hear gunfire. I have no reason to lie to you."

Marin's suspicion of Don Miguel Carbona was deeply rooted and not easily dispelled but he nodded and said, "If I find my patrol and see for myself the town's defenses, I will attack as you have suggested." Carbona smiled, waved and rode off.

Carbona issued orders to all but five of his best lieutenants. The main body of his force did, in fact, ride west and north, getting into position for the attack about which he had told Marin. Carbona himself had far different plans. His five most trusted men and ten of his best troops, led by Carbona himself, rode south and east, toward the Cargo Muchacho!

After a thirty minute march, Joaquin Marin found the truth of Carbona's last visit to him. Marin's men were lying slaughtered along the road. He doubled the men's pace and figured he would be in attack position right on schedule.

Arlo Lunsford was welcomed back with no small amount of attention. Joined, finally, by his wife, the judge reported what he had done and its result.

"I'm afraid," he concluded, "that it didn't work as I had hoped."

"The hell it didn't, Judge," Morgan said. "The only chance we ever had was cutting down some of the odds. Your plan did that for us. Now, we'll have to capitalize on it."

"I just wish," Lunsford said, "that I knew what Marin and Carbona agreed upon."

"We can't know everything," Morgan said.

Morgan, Tad Winfrey and Cy Black split up and went off to alert the men to the expected onslaught. Morgan, after a visit to the sharp shooters on the court house roof, rounded up the big Chinese, Cho Ping. He, Morgan and three other men, manhandled the Gatling gun into a new position to cover the southwest. Morgan anticipated a two pronged attack, one from the southeast and one from the southwest. He didn't believe either force marshalled against the town would take the time to move north. He underestimated Carbona's former cavalry troops.

Once Morgan was satisfied that everything that could be done was done, he returned to the saloon. He found a tearful Felisa Marin and he soon learned why from Tammy Winfrey.

"Teresa slipped away to meet her father and try to find out his plans and the agreements he made with Carbona."

"Dammit! I know she meant well, but her showing up right now could stop Marin in his tracks. If he smells a skunk we're through." Morgan poured himself a shot of whiskey and downed it. He eyed Felisa and added, "To say nothing about the danger to herself." He was thinking again of the day he'd been in bed with the two sisters and shook himself for having such thoughts at a time like this.

A few miles south, Joaquin Marin halted his troops.

"Teresa?" Joaquin Marin dismounted and ran along the road. Teresa Marin rode to meet him. She slipped from her horse into his arms and she wept. He comforted her. Slowly, she regained her composure.

"Daddy . . . I," she paused, "Felisa, she's, I . . . I killed her. She shamed us and helped the *Yanqui* dog." Teresa had always been her father's favorite and could elicit from him almost anything she wanted. Now he nodded his head in a gesture of understanding and he held her close to him.

"She is free of his spell now," he whispered "and you did what God dictated. He used your hand to strike this evil from our family."

Teresa looked up. "We must avenge her death. Morgan must die." Teresa had once loved her father very much but the death of her mother had changed him, and the fever for gold and power had made his mind sick.

"We ride now to cleanse the town of his evil and he will die and Felisa's spirit, too, will be free of him."

"They have many guns," she said, "straight ahead." Marin smiled and nodded. "Yes, my daughter, I know. Soon, we will hear them all and then Don Miguel will sweep down upon them from the north." Teresa looked up, smiled and kissed her father.

"I wish to go home now and rest. May I go home, Father?"

"Yes, of course, my daughter. I will send two men to escort you."

She shook her head. "No, please father, no. You will need all your men and I wish only to be alone." Marin hesitated but then realized there could be no harm to her behind his force. After all, Don Miguel was a long way off by now. He nodded.

Teresa rode off to the south and the troops began their northward movement again. A mile south, Teresa left the trail, wheeled her mount north and spurred it to an all out gallop. She reached a ridge a quarter of an hour later and looked down. She was fifteen or perhaps twenty minutes ahead of her father's force. It was, she knew, enough.

She made her report to Morgan and merely

smiled at his anger for the risk she had taken. It had paid off in a big way and both of them knew it. Morgan rounded up Cho Ping for the second time and with three other men, moved the Gatling gun for the last time, to the northwest quadrant.

Cy Black and Tad Winfrey both expressed concerns about the attack's coordination. Even with their knowledge and the loss of the element of surprise to the enemy, they were still faced with two fronts to cover. Morgan had already thought about it.

"We'll entice Carbona's force into attacking too soon. We're about to make a little noise of our own."

Cy grinned. "How much fireworks do you want?"

"Tell 'em to cut loose with everything they've got," Morgan said, "give me a couple of minutes worth." Cy nodded. Tad Winfrey said, "I'm going up to the roof of the courthouse and keep an eye on the results." Morgan nodded.

The barrage cut loose just eight minutes later and Tad caught Morgan on his way to the north end of town. "Thirty men I'd guess," Tad said, "headed right into the Gatling."

"Ride with me, Tad, I've got another little surprise for them. I sent a few men out last night with some dynamite." Morgan grinned. "North, a whole damned line of it about a hundred yards from the city limits."

Carbona's men rode down on the town in a

single line. They were certain that the firing they'd heard was that of Marin's attack. They were shooting as they rode in, not hitting anyone or anything and not really caring. Morgan and Tad reached the Gatling gun which was covered with a tarp and set up behind a well in the middle of the street. Morgan had put four of the best rifle shots on rooftops, two on each side of the street. A moment after Morgan and Tad arrived, the riflemen cut loose.

The dynamite went up with the inconsistency with which it was buried. Five or six sticks at a time and then one or two.

Carbona's line of men was by no means a straight line. The result was that a dozen or so of them were already inside the line of dynamite when the first of it went up. Four or five men and at least three horses died in the initial explosions. The rooftop riflemen then went to work on the harassed riders. The dozen or so who got into town, turned onto the street and Morgan yanked the tarp from the Gatling.

The deadly, rapid fire gun took a terrible toll in the opening volleys. Men on either side of the street, Morgan among them, then singled out riders with rifles. The butchery was all on one side and without Carbona's personal leadership, the attack floundered, slowed and finally halted. Seventeen men, all afoot, marched themselves into town and surrendered to five. Three or four simply fled. The balance lay dead.

South of town, Joaquin Marin cursed when he heard the first shots. He thought his point patrol had gotten careless and been spotted. As Marin pondered the possibilities, his patrol returned in force, riding in from the east!

"*Señor* Marin, Carbona has lied. We saw him and some of his men riding east. We followed them." The man pointed. "They ride to the Cargo Muchacho!"

Marin's face flushed with anger. Just then, they heard the explosions and firing off to the north. Marin was stymied.

Joanquin Marin was a meticulous man with an eye and a head for detail. As an army officer, he had been criticized only for being, perhaps, too cautious. The argument was weak since he'd never been defeated in battle. Memories flooded back to him now, however, and he came as close as he ever had to panic.

"Charge! Attack," he screamed as he drew his field saber. "Attack the town!" The line of men was not in the attack position however and the result was a lack of coordination. The men in town waited out the first scattering of Marin's force and allowed them to cross the first dynamite barrier. The second line, in nearly twice the number, was decimated by the dynamite. The first attackers reached the second line of dynamite and they too were badly bloodied.

Back in town, Lee Morgan pulled Carbona's top man into the saloon. The others were about to be stripped of their arms and ammunition when the leader spoke to Morgan.

"It is Marin" he said, "he has tricked us. We will fight for you. Put us in the line of defense and Marin will die."

"Yeah? Why don't we ask your boss about that?"

The Mexican frowned. "Don Miguel is not here. I lead. I am uh . . . the boss. Don Miguel rides to the Cargo Muchacho."

Cho Ping, almost alone, moved the Gatling gun back to the south end of town. A little at a time, Marin's men, more than eighty of them still remaining, prepared to charge and fight their way into town. More dynamite awaited them and a Gatling gun about which they knew nothing and seventeen more men than before.

No longer among the town's defenders was Lee Morgan. He had left Tad Winfrey and Cy Black in charge and he was riding hell bent for leather toward the Cargo Muchacho and the Peralta treasure. Less than two miles out of town, Morgan ran headlong into Marin's reconnaisance patrol. Five men who were charged with finding a weak spot in the town's defenses.

Morgan reined up about a hundred yards from them and assessed his situation. They were spread into a single line facing him and perhaps fifty to seventy-five feet apart. Two of them reacted quickly, drew rifles and took some shots at him. Morgan grabbed what he thought he would need, leaped from his horse and assumed a kneeling position on the sand. Shots dug up the ground around him and he watched the leader raise his arm and then bring it down in a signal to charge. Morgan shocked his attackers with back to back rifle shots which cut their numbers from five to three. The remaining three fanned out and dropped low to their saddles.

Morgan laid the Winchester aside. He was more than a little familiar with the skill of well trained Mexican cavalry. He would have to shoot their horses to stop them. The flank riders were to approach him simultaneously and thereby give the center man a chance at a shot. Too, in their scissor-like charge, the flank riders would both be in a position to get off a shot and their hapless victim would do well to get only one of them.

The center man fired, Morgan raised up, stiffened and fell. A few seconds later, the flank riders came within a few feet of Morgan, both sitting high in the saddle and looking down. Morgan came up and unleashed the blacksnake whip. The first rider took the tip of the lash across the face and howled with pain, jerking so violently, he lost his tenuous balance and tumbled from his horse. The second lash struck exactly where Morgan placed it, on the second rider's mount. The animal's flank just behind the saddle. The flesh wasn't broken and the animal wasn't hurt except for the shock of the moment. It snorted, whinnied and dug both front feet into the sand. The rider went ass over appetite over the animal's head.

The third rider, the center man, went by the action full speed, wheeled his horse and turned back. Morgan whirled around, dropped the whip, drew his Bisley and killed the man.

The Mexican with the whip-slashed face

never returned. The man who'd been dumped from his horse sustained a broken neck. Morgan recovered his gear and his horse and mounted up. Behind him, he could hear occasional explosions, the steady rhythm of the Gatling gun and a din of rifle and pistol fire. He knew the town's men were heavily outnumbered and he began to wonder if even their preparations, the turn of events and Marin's disorganization would be enough of an edge.

At the same time, he looked off toward the purple-gray ridge that was the Cargo Muchacho range and thought of Jake Ledbetter and four men who would sure as hell not be expecting fifteen Mexicans to ride down on them. "Hold the town," he said, aloud, "hold the damn town." Morgan knew he would make little difference back in Holtville. He could make all the difference to Jake. He wheeled his horse and spurred her to a hard run.

16

It was nearing dusk by the time Morgan arrived at the spot he recognized from the map formed by the four pistol grips. It led onto the single, narrow, rocky trail which wound its way downward into El Cavidad. During the last quarter hour of his ride, he'd had to cut his speed and he'd heard plenty of gunfire. In the rocks and gorges, determining the origin of the shots was impossible and by the time he arrived at the final trail, the gunfire had stopped.

A horse whinnied. Morgan whirled around.

"*Buenos noches,* Mr. Morgan."

"Shit!" He was looking at Joaquin Marin. Two men flanked Marin and both held guns on Morgan. "Okay Marin, you won yourself a town," Morgan gestured behind him with his thumb, "but I'm guessing you lost a treasure."

Marin smiled. "You are a formidable foe, Mr. Morgan, yes indeed, most formidable. No, I did not win a town. Many of my men were cut to pieces by your lines of dynamite and your Gatling gun but the *Federales Americanos* were the biggest surprise."

Morgan thought, 'What the hell is he talking about?'

"You look puzzled. Is it possible that you didn't know they were coming?"

"Okay, Marin, you've got me. What *Federales Americanos?*" Marin smiled. "The courts have ruled the Spanish land deeds are all legal. Those who hold them own both the land and that which is found upon or under it. Until the courts so ruled, the *Federales* could not act."

Morgan needed no pictures drawn for him as to the ramifications of that ruling. It meant Tad and Tammy's land, including the very spot where they now stood, and all the land owned and shared by Lita Peralta was theirs, free and clear.

"The troops were legally sanctioned by your American government and the state of California. Those of my men and those of Don Miguel who remain alive will be tried and perhaps hanged." He smiled. "The troops were led by your famous American Marshal, Wyatt Earp."

"Well I'll be damned. I'll be goddamed!"

"Unfortunately, Morgan, none of it benefits you. Perhaps I will lose also but behind you, down in El Cavidad, Don Miguel digs up the Peralta treasure. I will die before I let him get it and I cannot allow you to live either." Morgan eyed the two men with the drop on him. He knew what his chances were and he made his decision. He could take out Joaquin Marin before he died. He knew he was fast enough to do that.

"Father." Behind and to Morgan's right, hiding in the shadows was Teresa Marin. How she came to be there, for how long and why, Morgan didn't know. Neither did her father.

"Teresa? What . . ." Joaquin Marin looked at his daughter, then at Lee Morgan, thought back to their earlier meeting and suddenly everything came together. It was too late.

Teresa brought both arms up in front of her, cocked the pistol, steadied it and pulled the trigger. The two men flanking Marin were awestruck with the idea of a daughter gunning down her own father. Marin died instantly with a bullet through his brain. The two men's momentary distraction and Morgan's lightning speed signed their death warrants.

Teresa, it developed, had seen her father a second time that day and pleaded with him to give up the fight, save the town and go home. He promised that he would do so but she followed him. The trail ended here at the entrance to El Cavidad and a golden treasure which was forever stained with the blood of the Marin family.

"You stay here," Morgan cautioned her, "but if I'm not back by daylight, you ride back to Holtville. No questions, no last minute changes." Teresa nodded but Morgan wasn't even sure she'd heard him. After all, she had actually done what he could not bring himself to do once. She had killed her father.

The sun had to climb fairly high to bring daylight to El Cavidad. Morgan spent the night on a ledge, some fifty feet from the bottom of the gorge. When he finally woke up he got to his feet and looked into the hole below him.

"Goddam," he said, "goddam, what a sight! What a hulluva sight." Indeed it was a sight. What Morgan saw was five wagons loaded with bright, shiny metal. Gold and more gold! Hundreds of pounds of it, he reckoned. The Peralta treasure. Morgan let his eyes scan the canyon floor. He saw the body of a man, then another, then another. "Dammit!" Jake Ledbetter was sitting up, his back to a rocky wall. Next to him was a pile of gold trinkets and his Winchester and two wooden crates. Even at the distance, Morgan could see the blood on his face and where it had trickled down his nose from the hole in his forehead.

"Buenos dias, Morgan." Out of a small opening, not far from Jake's body, emerged Don Miguel Carbona followed by several men. "Before you act hastily and foolishly, look across the canyon." Morgan did. Opposite him, perhaps twenty-five feet below, was another ledge. It was wider than the one he was on and longer. Lined up on it were no less than ten men. All of them had rifles and they were all pointed at Lee Morgan. "You are a dead man, no *señorita* to save you now."

Morgan considered the small opening just behind him where he'd spent the night. He eyed the riflemen again. Hell, he thought, if one of them didn't get me directly, the ricochets would cut me to pieces.

"I didn't want you to be hasty, *Señor*," Carbona shouted, "because then you would die before I could show you just how rich you've made me." Carbona gestured toward the wagons with a sweep of his hand, "These carry only the small items, the baubles and trinkets of a lost race." He motioned to one of his men and several of them re-entered the cave. In a few minutes, they began coming out, carrying stack after stack of pure gold bricks. "You see, *señor*, you see how wealthy you have made Don Miguel Carbona."

Morgan watched as the Mexican bandit disappeared again into the cave. When he reappeared he was holding up a bottle of tequila. "Come, come down and let me toast you with a final drink." Carbona waved the bottle. "Or do you wish me to signal your death now?"

Morgan's eyes were roaming the length and breadth of the narrow canyon. His eyes returned once more to the body of his friend, Jake Ledbetter. Then, they moved slightly and he said beneath his breath, "Thanks, Jake." He waved to Carbona and shouted, "I'll drink with you, Don Miguel."

Morgan heard the levers of ten rifles lock into place. If he made any move which displeased Don Miguel, he'd be cut down at once. On the other hand, if he made no move at all, he was most definitely dead. He got up from his squatting position and eyed the little hole again. "If this don't fuckin' work, Morgan," he said aloud, "you're going to hate yourself in the morning."

Morgan waved to Carbona and then to the men across the canyon. He looked down again at Jake Ledbetter and the two wooden crates next to his body. Dynamite! Morgan had to be faster and more accurate than in any gunfight. He drew, dropped, fired twice and rolled into the hole. He released his pistol and covered his head.

Don Miguel Carbona saw Morgan's moves and he even had time to follow Morgan's line of sight just before the gunman drew and fired.

"Madre de Dios," were the last words ever uttered by Don Miguel Carbona. The explosions were ear shattering, first one case and then the second. Morgan could see very little opposite him except the rock wall falling away as though it was being pushed by some giant hand. The rock ledge supporting the gunmen went first but the noise of Morgan's shots and the explosions themselves drowned out the screams of buried men.

Morgan could only pray that there was no dynamite on his side of the canyon. Even then, the close quarters and unstable condition of the ancient rock walls didn't give him much room for error. He could only count on the explosions ripping away the base of the far side of the canyon. Indeed, that is what occurred but when Morgan finally got to his feet and the choking dust had settled, there was no more El Cavidad.

"Sonuvabitch!"

Between the fund raising dance held by the good people of Holtville, a Federal and a State bounty and a token gesture from Wyatt Earp, Lee Morgan earned himself a fee of $759.82. He grinned to himself, there had been a few fringe benefits.

He said his goodbyes to the Winfreys and to

Felisa Marin. Wyatt hung around Holtville long enough for them to tie on one good drunk, or Morgan anyway. Wyatt didn't drink. Part of his great fortune went at the poker tables. He stayed around Holtville for another two weeks and then he spent another two hundred of his money, on supplies.

On a sunny morning nearly two months after the affair had come to an end, Morgan was packing the last of his possibiles. A knock came at his door. He walked over, pulled it open and found himself staring into the face of Estralita Peralta.

"Well I'll be damned." He stepped back. She smiled and entered his room. "I never figured to see you again." She turned to face him.

"Why, because of the treasure?"

"Seems to me that would be reason enough."

"You did the only thing you could do. I left Holtville the very night Marshal Earp arrived. I went to Sacramento and filed my claims and those of the Winfreys. We have land and I want you to have some of it."

Morgan shook his head. "I've been paid."

"I heard what you were paid."

"Gold I'll take, land, no thanks. I've had my fill of land."

"What are your plans, Morgan?"

Morgan ran his tongue into his cheek and glanced at the floor. He looked up again and grinned, rather sheepishly. "I've got a friend back in Missouri who's a mining engineer. I kinda thought I might go spend the winter with him and then ride back out this way along around next spring."

"And do what," Lita asked, smiling, "some treasure hunting?"

"Mebbe."

"Well I had another reason for stopping to see you too. Are you in a hurry?"

"Well, some. Why?"

"I just wanted to show you how grateful I was for your help." Morgan walked over and closed the door.

"My engineering friend doesn't know I'm coming. I can be a day or two late." Lita smiled. Two days turned into five. Morgan didn't know anyone could be that damned grateful.

On the fifteenth day of January, Morgan came down for breakfast at the home of his friend, Daniel Jennings, in St. Louis. Dan said nothing but handed Morgan that day's copy of the *St. Louis Globe-Democrat*. He jabbed a finger at an item near the bottom of page one. Morgan read the headline and sub-headlines. They were all he needed to read.

"Earthquake Rumbles Across Southern California Desert. No Loss of Life Reported and Only Minor Property Damage. Major Alterations Occur to Cargo Muchacho Mountain Range.

Morgan tossed the paper aside, looked up at Dan Jennings and said, "Sonuvabitch!"

PEACEMAKER PASS

1

Denver had changed and Lee Morgan wasn't at all certain he liked what he found. There were too damned many people, too many tall buildings and not nearly enough breathing space.

"Another drink, sir?"

Morgan was staring out of the window. It was a huge window, framing a panoramic view of the Rocky Mountains some forty miles distant. The view was breathtaking.

"Mister Morgan, sir. Another drink?" The barkeep spoke a little louder and Morgan's head jerked. Still, it took a moment for the question to soak in.

"Yeah, sure, why the hell not?" Morgan replied, smiling. "Somebody else is picking up the check."

In spite of the pleasant state of his current situation, Morgan was growing both restless and angry. He had been ensconced at the Golden Inn Hotel for nearly ten days. The man he was supposed to have met nearly a week ago had still not shown up. Morgan couldn't get any answers to his questions either, since the telegram he'd received had been unsigned.

The young gunman had wintered alone in a mountain cabin in the Grand Tetons, then moved down to spend the spring in Cheyenne. After a winter of solitude he was ready for some civilization, so he played a lot of poker and, for a change, Lady Luck had bedded with him. He came away with more than three thousand dollars. He also had some fond memories of a few very special nights spent at the Cheyenne Social Club. It was reportedly the most lavish bordello west of the big river. Morgan wouldn't have argued the point.

It was getting on into summer, the 22nd day of July, when the telegram came. It was short and simple.

Mr. Morgan,

Use the accompanying funds to get yourself to the Golden Inn west of Denver. All will be furnished, ready and waiting for you. I'll join you within two days of your arrival. If I am late, be patient. Enjoy!

Morgan had followed the instructions to the letter. He reasoned that he had nothing to lose. He found exactly what the telegram implied and he had, in fact, enjoyed. Now even that was wearing thin.

He was beginning to think about trying to do some backtracking of the telegraph's origins. It was something with which he was not altogether unfamiliar. He'd learned more than a little about such procedures in several episodes with the Pinkerton Agency. He finally opted to wait one more day before trying to unravel his good fortune.

"Hello. Would you be Mr. Lee Morgan?"

Just the voice could have produced an erection. It was soft, no question of gender, and the words dripped from a pair of very sensuous looking lips.

Morgan finished his drink, eyeing the girl from top to bottom as he did so, and then he said, "If I wasn't, I'd sure as hell lie to you about it."

The girl smiled and licked her sensuous lips. She pushed a vacant barstool aside and slithered between it and Morgan.

"I'm Mariellen Chapel."

Morgan had to fight back the urge to chuckle. He was asking himself how long it had been since he'd been in a chapel.

"You are Lee Morgan, late of Cheyenne?"

"I am, if you're the one who sent me a telegraph cable."

"I didn't, but I'm here on behalf of the man who did. Can you prove you're Lee Morgan?"

"Can you prove you're here for the reason you say?"

"I like you, Mister Morgan," Mariellen Chapel said, stepping back from him now, "so don't do anything that would make me change my mind. Chotauk wouldn't like that even a little bit."

Morgan assumed a quizzical expression and then turned in the direction of Mariellen's pointed finger. By the doorway into the hotel's lobby there stood what Morgan could have very easily mistaken for an adult male polar bear. The Eskimo was six-and-a-half-feet tall and Morgan reckoned about 240 pounds. He looked a little foolish in an ill-fitted, store bought, blue pin stripe. Still, Morgan didn't think it would be healthy to comment on the man's appearance.

"Chotauk?" Morgan asked, pointing and smiling.

"Chotauk," Mariellen confirmed.

"In my room," Morgan said, "I've got the proof." He stood up and made a somewhat dramatic and gentlemanly gesture. "Shall we?"

"I think not," Mariellen said. "You get the proof and bring it here." She glanced around, spotted an empty table in the far corner of the room and added, "Over there will be fine."

Morgan shrugged and said, "Whatever you say, Miss . . . uh, Chapel, wasn't it?"

"It was, Mister Morgan, and it still is." She smiled that sensuous smile and added, "That will make Chotauk very, very happy."

By the time Morgan returned, Mariellen Chapel was very much engaged in devouring a two-inch thick cut of beef and all of the frills. She was dainty and feminine enough about her eating habits but her appetite looked more like it should belong to the big Eskimo.

"Coffee, Mister Morgan?"

Morgan wasn't sure if it was a question or a demand. He nodded, Mariellen poured, refilling her own cup at the same time. She sipped a little of it and then sat back. "Your proof, please."

He handed her a sheaf of papers and she studied each with the intensity of a spider examining the latest victim trapped in its web. Morgan suddenly felt like the fly.

After nearly a quarter of an hour, with Morgan getting a little more disgusted with the passing of each minute, Mariellen removed two of the sheets and handed Morgan the balance.

A wave of her arm brought Chotauk to the

table in about five strides. She handed him the papers and he eyed Morgan, then nodded.

"He may have a little trouble checking those out," Morgan said, "they go back aways."

"You'd best hope he doesn't, Mister Morgan. If he finds any discrepancies, he'll kill you."

"You'd order him to do that?"

Mariellen smiled. "I wouldn't have to," she said and then leaned forward and added, "and once he started, I couldn't stop him."

Morgan considered the girl. Really she was more a girl-woman. There was much about her that appeared young and innocent, but there was an equal part of a mature, shrewd and very hard lady.

"When do I meet the bossman," Morgan finally asked, offhandedly. "Or are you the boss lady?"

"If you are who you claim to be, you'll be on my payroll, Mister Morgan. If you're as good as my friend tells me you are, you may even live to spend your wages."

"And what if I don't want the job?"

"One step at a time, Mister Morgan, one step at a time."

Mariellen ordered some after dinner wine and this time she didn't ask if he wanted any, she just poured. A moment later, she broke out a shiny, hand engraved silver case. Somewhere out of sight there was a catch release and when she pushed it, the lid popped open. "A cigareet," she asked.

The cigareet, as Mariellen called it, wasn't half bad. Morgan made a mental note that he'd have to buy some of these store bought smokes. This one was his first. He was just finishing his second glass of wine, and feeling an inside warmth which was a dangerous mingling of the wine and the proximity of Mariellen Chapel, when her face broke into a very wide smile.

"I'm glad you are Morgan," she said, a little quiver of lightness in her tone, "very glad."

Morgan frowned and Mariellen pointed. Morgan saw Chotauk was back and he was also smiling, a toothless smile.

"I checked out."

She nodded.

"Then it's my turn to ask the questions."

"Not yet, Mister Morgan, not quite yet." She got to her feet and Morgan started to rise but she held out her hand. "Stay put, finish the wine, enjoy yourself. This is your last evening in Denver and it's going to have to serve you for quite a spell. Goodnight, Mister Morgan."

Morgan said nothing. He could only wonder about Miss Mariellen Chapel. What he wondered was not all printable, but then it was the only safe way to do anything where Mariellen Chapel was concerned. Morgan watched Mariellen go up the stairs. Chotauk was only a few feet behind.

Morgan found a Keno game and dropped two hundred dollars on it. He walked around two or three of Denver's blocks and then returned to the hotel. He asked a few of the bellhops and two or three of the people behind the desk about Mariellen. They would say nothing, although he was certain that most of them were lying. He was certain she was in the hotel, and he was damned certain he wanted to know her better. At that moment, his reasoning had little else to do but remember the rise and fall of Mariellen's blouse.

The girl he found was better than most, even in Denver. She was young, well proportioned and inexpensive. Morgan rarely needed the services

of a professional but it had been a long dry spell
and the whisky, beer, wine and visions of
Mariellen caught up with him.

They were settled nicely in Morgan's bed and
the gunman was just beginning to apply his skills
to the girl's breasts. He knew he'd locked the
door but it came open anyway, without breaking.
The tell-tale sound was the little squeal in one of
the hinges when the door was about half open.

Morgan rolled to the side of the bed opposite
the door, landed hard, his pistol in his hand. The
girl's scream was cut off.

The light of the lamp flared up and Morgan
peeked cautiously over the edge of the bed.

"I'm sorry, Mister Morgan, for having to spoil
your fun, but business is business and you
represent a considerable investment."

"Sonuvabitch," Morgan said, softly but aloud.
He got to his knees. In the hallway behind Mariellen Chapel, he could see the struggling girl. She
appeared the size of a rabbit in the clutches of
Chotauk. "Lady, you're pushing me a helluva lot
harder than any man would get away with, but
I've got a limit even on that."

Mariellen ignored Morgan and continued
tearing at the bedding. She finally found one of
the girl's red garters. She eyed it and then
Morgan, noticing for the first time his rather
unmanly position. She smiled and tossed his
longjohns and pants.

"Did your lady friend mention anything about
a drink?"

Morgan got his pants on and walked around
the end of the bed. "Yeah, something special
after we finished." He was surprised that Mariellen knew, surprised and mad all at once.

"It would have been special indeed," she said.

He frowned.

The garter was decorated with a tiny locket. Inside there was a pinch of white powder.

"I'd guess powdered quinela. That's enough to kill a horse."

"Are you telling me that, uh, young lady, was a set up?"

"I'm not telling you anything, Mister Morgan, except what I told you earlier. My suggestion is that you get back in that bed and try to get some sleep. You're going to need it."

Morgan was awake for nearly two more hours but only because he was trying to make some kind of sense out of what he knew at that moment. It was damned little and it made no sense at all. He finally drifted off and slept fitfully until the first rays of the new day's sun poked through the window.

Morgan washed, shaved, dressed and made two vows to himself. He'd begin the day with what could be the last really good meal he'd be getting for awhile and before the sun was gone again, he'd have some answers. Either that, or he'd be gone.

2

"Good morning, Mister Morgan." Mariellen Chapel spoke as she glanced up at the big wall clock in the hotel's dining room. There was a dirty plate in front of her and a half empty coffee cup. "Will you have breakfast?" she asked him, grinning, "or lunch?"

"You sure as hell look good for a lady who couldn't have gotten that much sleep."

"I don't require much," she said.

"Sleep?"

Mariellen smiled. "Yeah, sleep. Isn't that what we were talking about?"

By the time Morgan got his hat off and seated himself, the waiter had arrived with a pot of fresh coffee.

"Breakfast, sir?"

"He'll have the same as I had," Mariellen said. "A cut of your best beefsteak, two eggs on the sunny side and some black bread."

The waiter poured the coffee, nodded and was gone before Morgan could protest.

Mariellen seemed to sense that he was going to

15

do just that so she made her next revelation. "The young lady you so graciously took into your room last night hung herself this morning. Got up on the roof," Mariellen said, pointing straight up, "lashed a rope around an air vent, tightened the noose around her neck and jumped."

"Lady," Morgan said, his tone harsh now, "I'd better get an awful lot of the right answers in a very damned short time."

"Or what, Mister Morgan?"

"Or you can send off another telegraph cable and see what the bait brings this time."

Mariellen smiled and glanced toward the door. Morgan understood her meaning and took her by the wrist, hard. "And if the polar bear tries to stop me, ma'am, I'll kill him."

Chotauk moved almost at the same instant Morgan took a grip on Mariellen's wrist but he stopped when Mariellen raised her other hand. "I believe you'd try, Mister Morgan, I really do."

"You can count on it. Now, how about some answers?" Morgan detected the first doubtful look he'd seen in the girl's face.

Nonetheless, she smiled and recouped quickly. "One more little extension, Mister Morgan, just bear with me for a little longer." She glanced toward the kitchen. "Just until you've finished your breakfast."

"You stay put in the meantime, right there where I can keep an eye on you, Miss Chapel, and you've got yourself a deal."

"Agreed," she replied, tentatively.

Morgan ate his breakfast in silence. Mariellen smoked two of the cigareets, and drank two cups of coffee.

Morgan accepted another of Mariellen's smokes to go with his last cup of coffee. He noted that she had begun to fidget and glance, frequently, toward the door.

"You expecting company?" he finally asked.

She was about to answer when her face took on the sudden glow of a big smile of relief. Morgan jerked his head around and saw Chotauk pointing toward the table. Standing next to him was a tall, slender, distinguished looking gentleman, armed, as far as Morgan could see, with an official looking attache case.

Mariellen got to her feet and half ran to meet the man. She threw her arms around his neck and gave him a kiss on the cheek. Morgan wasn't surprised when Mariellen introduced him.

"Morgan, this is my uncle, Harrison Chapel. He hails all the way from Alexandria, Virginia."

Morgan got to his feet and took the man's hand. It was soft, almost feminine to the touch. This man was not a westerner, not a laborer, of those things only, Morgan was certain.

"Please," Harrison Chapel said, "sit down and finish your breakfast."

"I'm finished," Morgan said, "at least with breakfast."

"I owe you an apology, sir. I am usually more punctual."

"I hope so," Morgan replied, reclaiming his chair. The girl moved over one chair and Harrison Chapel took her old spot. He immediately unlocked and opened the attache case, removed a document and handed it to Morgan.

Agent Agreement

The following agreement is hereby entered into between the Colt Firearms Mfg. Co. and Lee Morgan. This agreement will not be bound by date or time and will

commence upon signing by Lee Morgan. It
will remain in force and in effect until a
termination of the duties requested, or the
permanent disability or death of Lee
Morgan, or a decision by two-thirds of the
then acting Board of Directors of the Colt
Firearms Mfg. Co.

The Company agrees to a recompense for
Lee Morgan as follows: All expenses
incurred in the line of his duties, plus
$25,000 severance bonus.

Morgan looked up, eyed both Harrison Chapel
and Chapel's niece and looked down again at the
paper. There was room on the bottom for three
signatures. His own, he reckoned, an agent for
the Colt Company, and likely a witness.

"I was told last night that if I accepted the job
I'd be working for you, Miss Chapel."

"You will, at a regular wage. That's the only
way you'll be able to move around and have half
a chance to do the job for my uncle."

"You work for Colt?"

"I'm a special representative in the territory."

"What territory?" Morgan asked.

The Chapels, for the first time, looked at one
another with expressions of doubt. Harrison
Chapel finally looked back at Morgan, sighed
heavily and said, "Alaska, Mister Morgan. My
company wants you to go to Alaska. We've got
big troubles up there and they will only get
worse unless we can find a man good enough to
stand up to the country and the evil in it."

"That's real damned pretty talk," Morgan said,
shoving his chair back from the table. His eyes
shifted from Harrison Chapel to Mariellen and
he gestured with his head, adding, "And you've

got some real pretty bait, too." He stood up. "The only thing you don't have is guts enough to come straight out and ask a man to do a job." Morgan tossed some money on the table and turned to walk away. He paused, turned back and added, "And the other thing you don't have is Lee Morgan."

Chotauk was already moving in Morgan's direction but Morgan didn't stop. Behind him, Mariellen Chapel held up her hand, Chotauk stopped and stepped aside.

Morgan hadn't broken his stride and as he drew parallel with the big Eskimo he spoke once again, loudly enough to make certain he was heard. "That was a damned smart thing to do, Miss Chapel." He looked squarely into Chotauk's eyes as he passed by.

Morgan wasted no time in packing his gear and making ready to ride out of Denver. He wasn't certain just where he'd go but he'd had enough of the easy life to last him awhile. It made a man soft and careless and if the man was Lee Morgan, that was dangerous. He'd made a lot of enemies of his own and those who didn't know him personally knew him by reputation, one not altogether of his own making. He was, after all, the son of no less a gunman than Buckskin Frank Leslie. One of the best or the worst of a breed, depending on which end of his gun you had to face.

Morgan couldn't help but think of Mariellen Chapel as he packed. He wouldn't be any kind of a man at all if he could ignore what he was certain was under the silk and satin. Between her and twenty-five thousand dollars, he could have quite a bulge in his buckskin britches. He could also end up in the clutches of that polar bear in the pin stripe suit or pushing up flowers in a six-by-six hole in Alaska.

The knock at the door was hard enough to tell Morgan that whoever was doing it wasn't trying to keep it a secret. Still, he was cautious. "Yeah, who is it?"

"Delivery, sir."

Morgan frowned and thought that the Chapels were making a last ditch effort. "Return it," he said.

Morgan heard the delivery boy or bellhop or whoever the hell was outside, walk away. He was also certain he'd heard them put the package by the door. He opened it and his suspicion was confirmed. The package was about three feet by two feet and some ten inches deep. Morgan looked both ways but saw no one. He moved the package carefully with the toe of his boot. It was heavy.

"Damn," Morgan muttered.

He picked it up and took it inside his room. He put it on the bed and then stared at it. His curiousity had led the young gunman into more adventures than he cared to recall and he figured it would, one day, be his downfall. "A parting gesture of good will from the Chapels," he said aloud, grinning. "Bullshit! Another temptation." He couldn't help but wonder if the package might contain twenty-five thousand dollars. He decided to stop wondering.

The holsters were matched as beautifully as were the weapons reposing in them. The case's lining was satin and velvet, a soft purple in color. The two weapons were nickel plated, ivory gripped Colt .45 Peacemakers. The grips displayed his initials on each and the outside barrels were also engraved.

Presented to Lee Morgan for Services Rendered to the Colt Firearms Mfg. Co. in Alaska, U.S. Territory

Morgan hefted the weapons and quickly realized their quality. The balance was perfect, the grips seemed almost as if they had been personally molded to his hand. He was not a two gun man but here were weapons that any man would be proud to own, to wear or simply to display.

He felt the warmth on his cheeks, the warmth of his anger. Most of it was anger that he was directing at himself. He was a loner, he always had been. He was set in his ways. He liked to be approached openly. Unsigned telegraph cables, sudden confrontations with beautiful women, threats from their bodyguards, young girls who tried to poison him and then tossed themselves off of rooftops, and business representatives who were a week late with appointments did not make up his idea of good business conduct. Still, he was flattered by the offer from so prestigious a firm as Colt. Too, he couldn't deny what had happened, someone had tried to kill him. He'd never been to Alaska, another reason to slow his judgment down. Then, of course, there was Mariellen Chapel.

"Damn," Morgan mumbled.

3

During the next several weeks, Morgan had plenty of time to digest the information he acquired from Harrison Chapel. He learned that Chapel had been in the employ of the Colt Company for more than a decade. During that time he had served the company in nearly every capacity, from demonstrating new guns and new designs, to negotiating with foreign governments in an effort to secure contracts. Never, during all of that time, had Chapel failed to deliver on his assignment. Never, that is, until two years ago.

Chapel was to carry the Colt name to the last frontier, Alaska. The gold and silver strikes in the raw, hard territory were only just beginning and every form of life, high and low, four legged and two, was scrambling to get in on the boom.

The Colt Company, of course, was by no means the only weapons maker anxious to cut a sizeable share of profit out of the frozen tundra but, at first, it was the only one willing to do it above board. The decision had taken four lives to date.

At the outset of the effort, Chapel was

confident he could quickly secure a base of business for the Colt Company. He had the expertise, and something else which his competition did not have . . . a resident representative.

Mariellen Chapel's parents had been killed on the 31st day of May, 1889. They were two of a reported two-thousand who died on that fateful day in the sleepy hamlet of Johnstown, Pennsylvania. Flood waters took their lives and their remains. As it happened, 19-year-old Mariellen was visiting her aunt and uncle at the time.

Mariellen had had a promising career in nursing and medicine. There had even been talk of her attempting to enter medical school to become a doctor. None of it mattered to her after the disaster, and one day she was simply gone. Three years later, Harrison Chapel got the first word of her whereabouts. She was in Alaska and was known far and wide as the Queen of the Klondike.

When the time came for Harrison Chapel to open the market for the Colt Company, he sent his best man to Mariellen. His best man ended up dead. So did the three men who followed. Mariellen's own troubles increased as well when the word began to circulate that she had a contact with the Colt Company.

Harrison Chapel made the trip north, personally did some investigating of his own into the problem, and then decided upon a course of action.

Chapel's plan was simple enough. First he had to restore the credibility enjoyed by his niece. Mariellen had built her reputation as Queen of the Klondike, in part, on greed. Chapel could only put his own man in place if he was able to convince the locals that Mariellen had also turned on him. He managed that with a highly visible and carefully orchestrated confrontation. Mariellen emerged the apparent victor and enjoyed an even more powerful position than before.

Now, almost nothing moved between Skagway and Dawson without first passing through Mariellen Chapel's fingers. The word was quickly spread that newcomers would be better advised to tackle the infamous Chilkoot Pass in winter than defy the Queen of the Klondike.

Harrison Chapel then delivered his *coup de grâce* by aligning himself with no less a figure than Mariellen's predecessor to the territory. She was known as Skagway Annie. In fact, she was Annabelle Thompson, and one of the most colorful characters ever to appear in the territory.

While her background was obscure, her appearance in Skagway had preceded even some of the hardiest men. She smoke cigars, chewed a tobacco named M.D. which the locals dubbed "Moose Dung" and turned the air blue with her expletives.

Morgan knew that much about the operation he was getting into by the time he arrived in San Francisco, the first week in September. Once there, he learned that the next available passage to Juneau was three weeks away. He spent that three weeks living in luxury in a prepaid suite at the Mark Hopkins Hotel. On his last day in San Francisco, he used the telephone instrument to order up room service. After a supper of steak and champagne, he poured himself a real drink, then walked over to the window to look out over the town. He held the glass up to the window and made a quiet toast to the city.

"A few weeks from now I'll be ass-deep in snow, so if I'm indulging myself a little now, I got it comin' to me."

On September 25, Lee Morgan, gunman and special representative for the Colt Company, boarded the steam packet *Arctic Mist*. He was told by the purser that it would be a trip of fifteen days.

The *Arctic Mist* was crowded with men who were going to Alaska to hunt gold.

"They say in Nome you can scoop it up right on the beaches."

"Nuggets big as robins' eggs, they say."

"Heard of a fella from Seattle went up there, spent just two months, come back with enough money to live in luxury the rest of his life."

"I got me a system, guaranteed to find gold. I'll be willin' to sell it to anyone wants it for a hunnert dollars. A hunnert dollars'll get you ten thousand, I guarantee it."

He was ten days out when he saw the envelope. It had been slipped under his door from the passageway. Morgan had been lying on his bunk with his hands folded behind his head, wondering what lay ahead, so he didn't see it right away. He just happened to look over and there was the envelope.

The confusion as to how the envelope got into his room was nothing compared to the confusion as to why it was pushed under his door. When he picked it up it was totally empty. It did have a rather unique mark . . . not a postmark, but a type of official seal. He opened the door and looked out into the passageway, but saw no one. There was no one on deck either. He walked over to the rail and looked out over the deep blue sea toward the distant horizon where the merger was

so indistinct that there was no line of demarc-
ation between sky and sea. He felt as if he were
suspended in a great, blue bowl, and he turned
away from the rail wishing he had a horse under
him and a mountain in front.

At Juneau he caught a mail packet up to Skagway. His arrival in Skagway was hardly spectac-
ular. It was already dark, though it was the
middle of the afternoon. He didn't know his way
around, and nobody had bothered to meet him.
He got less than a pleasant reception from the
few men he queried about the location of
Mariellen's place. He knew it only by name, "The
Queen's Throne."

He learned right off that anyone asking its
whereabouts was quickly recognized as a new-
comer, therefore an outsider, therefore competition, and therefore, unwelcome as hell.

Mariellen was in her office. The man who
escorted Morgan from the front door did so
without a word, walking slightly behind him.
Morgan was, briefly at least, sandwiched
between the sullen doorman and an old friend.
Or perhaps acquaintance would be a better
word. Chotauk looked down on Morgan from
lofty heights, nodded at the doorman and then
opened the door.

"Come in, Morgan," a woman's voice called
from within the room. Morgan eyed the Eskimo,
then stepped around him to get inside. He saw
Mariellen hunched over a ledger book.

"You knew it was me?"

"I knew you were in Skagway when the boat
docked."

"Yeah, well, thanks for the warm welcome,"
Morgan said, though he knew his sarcasm was

lost on her. She neither stopped working, nor looked up. Instead she said, "Fix yourself something to drink. I'll be a few minutes yet, then we'll talk."

Mariellen's few minutes turned into half-an-hour. Morgan went through three drinks and one of her cigareets. Finally she slammed the book shut, shoved it aside, sat back in her chair, smiled and said, "You read my uncle's report?"

Morgan nodded.

"Questions?"

"Just one for now. Who the hell are you fighting?"

"That's why you're here Morgan, to find out."

"Your uncle seems to think it's his competition. Remington or Winchester or that English outfit, uh, what's their names?"

"Huntington Armory."

"Yeah." Morgan shifted in his chair. "I think he's wrong."

In fact, Morgan hadn't formed any opinions at all yet but he wanted to test the waters. He got a surprise.

"So do I. I think he's dead wrong."

Morgan frowned.

"None of those people believe they can dominate the sales in Alaska any more than they could back in the States."

"Colt did a pretty good job of it for quite awhile."

"No they didn't, and you know it, Morgan. They got more publicity for a while and they sold more of one or two models than some of the others, but they never came close to all of it."

"Yeah, you're right," Morgan said, getting up and pouring himself another drink. "Who then, if not the competition?"

"Somebody who wants complete control of Alaska and if they control enough weapons and men they can get what they want."

"Somebody like the Queen of the Klondike?"

"Somebody who really is what I'm supposed to be."

"And how do I know you aren't what you seem to be?"

"You don't Morgan," Mariellen said, getting to her feet. She walked around the desk.

Morgan eyed her. She had on a full, heavy cotton skirt, plaid wool shirt and vest. It didn't flatter her but his memory was too vivid to be blotted out by cold weather wear.

"You don't know much of anything about anything right now and worse, you don't know this country or the people in it. We're a different breed, Morgan. You have to be, or the Klondike and the Yukon will swallow you whole."

"I heard the same tale about Texas, New Mexico, Arizona and the Oklahoma badlands."

"That's the difference," Mariellen said, smiling, "down there you hear tales. Up here, you see the real thing."

Morgan considered her. He took off his hat, scratched his head, looked down and then up again, up into Mariellen's eyes.

"Your uncle may be right, maybe he's wrong, but at least he's got an opinion. What have you got?"

"A long hard day tomorrow, Morgan, so I'll say goodnight."

"I hope you don't end up making me wish I was back in San Francisco."

"Chotauk will show you to your room."

Morgan smiled. "He going to tuck me in, too?"

Mariellen walked to the door, opened it, turned

around and said, "Only if you need tucking in, Morgan."

As the young gunman passed Mariellen, she gently touched his arm. He stopped. Maybe, he thought, she will soften up just a little.

"Beginning tomorrow, unless we're strictly in private, you address me as Miss Mariellen. Is that understood?"

Morgan smirked, looked at his boots and shook his head. "You bet it is," he said. Then he looked into her face again and added, "G'night, Miss Mariellen."

The room was at the front of the building, a corner room with a good view of the main street of Skagway. It was a town which rarely slept, and Morgan sat in the dark for some time just watching the men below coming and going. He had started to doze off when he heard the click of the doorknob. His pistol was at the ready when the door slowly opened.

He could see the trim figure of a woman. He waited until she had closed the door before he rose and turned up the lamp. She was more girl than woman. She smiled and handed him a note.

> I owe you this from Denver.
> Enjoy her and sleep well!
> The Boss Lady

"You come with me," Morgan said, his face warm with a building anger. The girl had to double time it to keep up with him as he headed down the long hallway. Mariellen Chapel's private quarters were at the far end of the building. When he turned the corner, it dawned on him that she would be well protected. Indeed, there was a youngster in front of her door. He realized that even Chotauk had to sleep sometime.

The youth looked up but when he saw the girl he just smiled. "Evenin', Clara," he said, grinning.

The grin faded when Morgan stopped directly in front of him.

"Wake up Miss Mariellen," Morgan said. He properly judged the boy and already had the barrel of his gun jammed into the boy's belly. "No arguments."

The kid reached behind himself and pounded on the door. Instantly, the next door down the corridor opened and Chotauk stepped through it. Almost at the same time, Mariellen opened her door. Morgan shoved the girl past her, stepped into the room behind the girl, and then slammed the door closed with the heel of his boot.

"We need a few things understood, boss lady," Morgan said. "I pick my own bed partners or they pick me, and then it's by mutual consent. Right now, you don't owe me a thing."

"I meant no offense."

The door opened and Morgan's Colt flew into his hand as he spun around. Chotauk stood in the doorway. Morgan eyed Mariellen.

"It's alright," she said.

The Eskimo eyed Morgan, eyed the pistol, grinned and backed out, closing the door as he did.

"No," Morgan said, holstering the gun, "it isn't alright. A helluva lot of things are not alright. I'll work for you and I'll do the job. If I don't, you don't owe me anything but you never *own* me, lady. Let's get that straight right now."

"Is that what you think I want to do, Morgan, own you?"

"Yeah, as a matter of fact, that's exactly what I think you want to do. Just like you own Chotauk." Morgan walked over to her. "I'm not Chotauk and I'm not one of your hired gunnies."

"Then why did you take the job?"

"That's my business. You don't like me being the way I am, I'll be on the next boat south, no obligations on either side."

Mariellen Chapel smiled at the girl and then nodded her head in the direction of the door. The girl smiled and quickly took her leave. "My uncle hired you, not me, but it has to look right."

"I'll make it look like whatever is necessary," Morgan said. "I just don't want you to forget that it's just acting, not the real thing."

"I don't know you well enough to judge the real thing, do I?"

Morgan slipped one arm around Mariellen's shoulders and the other around her waist. He pulled her to him and kissed her, hard and full and long. He felt the sensations and they quelled his anger. She did not struggle or protest.

He stepped back. "Start with that," Morgan said. He moved quickly to the door and then turned around, "I've got a busy day ahead," he said, grinning as he echoed her words, "so I'll say goodnight, Miss Mariellen."

4

It seemed to Morgan that all he had done lately was receive odd messages from anonymous authors. One had been slipped under his door during the night. This one had not been accompanied by a girl.

> I'd take it kindly if you'd
> breakfast with me. I'll find
> you. Thompson's Cove. 7:30.

Skagway didn't look much different to Morgan than any other boom town he'd seen. Indeed, the Klondike could have been almost anywhere in Colorado. He paused outside Thompson's Cove and looked north. There, he thought, is the difference. North of Skagway was the Yukon territory. Across a bit of British Columbia and over the Chilkoot Pass, north and east to Whitehorse and back northwest along the rugged trail to Dawson.

Thompson's Cove was different than anything Morgan had ever seen. It was, he thought, a

Herman Melville narrative carved from spruce, pine and cedar. It would have been right at home in Boston, Morgan imagined, or in the legendary seafaring town of New Bedford.

"You've a table waitin' for you, Mister Morgan."

Morgan eyed the speaker. He was bearded and he looked, for all the world, like he'd just stepped off the deck of a four-master.

Morgan was still looking around. This was not the saloon of a frontier. No batwing doors, no gunmen lining the bar, no card sharps dealing house games at the tables.

"At whose invitation?" Morgan finally asked.

"Miss Annie Thompson," the bearded man replied, and then grinned and said, "Miss Skagway Annie to you."

The man gestured toward the table and Morgan moved to it. The table was private, reposing beneath an archway along the east wall. There were several of them. The place settings were already there. The silver trappings and linen cloth were all mongrammed.

"Thanks," Morgan said, removing his hat and ducking a little in order to slide into the seat.

The man left, replaced by an attractive young girl attired in a peasant blouse and pinafore. Morgan's eyes followed the gentle undulations of her breasts as she poured his coffee and made ready the dishware for the serving of the food. She caught him looking once and smiled. He smiled back.

"Lee Morgan. You're younger than I thought. Younger than I heard, but then Chappy is probably not the best judge of men anyway. Guns maybe, but not men."

Morgan looked up.

Annie Thompson was, by Morgan's reckoning, on the sunset side of forty. Her face was a giveaway. There were none of the luxuries in Skagway which kept a woman looking younger than her years. Conversely, Skagway Annie had the body of a woman ten years her junior. Nothing back home to keep a woman fit and trim, Morgan thought. He also thought that her bust measurement would probably be a match for her age. He started to get up.

"Don't bother," she said. "You go and get gentlemanly on me and I'll come to expect if from the rest of the flotsam that drift in here. That'll just upset me, 'cause I won't get it." Annie sat down.

Breakfast arrived at once and while Annie ate, much like Mariellen Chapel, Morgan rather picked at his food. He caught more than one look of disdain. A man who couldn't devour half a polar bear and a quart of bad whiskey for breakfast, so Morgan had been told, would never survive in the Klondike.

"I hate to be pushy," Morgan finally said, "but just why am I here?"

"Because I invited you," came the reply, "and turnin' down an invite from Skagway Annie is mighty bad for a fella's well bein'. Matter o' fact, it's proved plumb fatal in a case or two."

"So you invited me just to see if I'd come and now that I have you can lay claim to having saved my life." Morgan leaned back. "That makes me obligated, doesn't it?"

Morgan's tongue-in-cheek assessment of Annie's motives took her aback for a moment and then she burst out laughing.

"By God Morgan, I like you, I really do like

you. I'll be honest, when Chappy told me about you, I didn't think I would. I mean, I was *sure* I wouldn't. Another driftin' gunhand come to God's country to right ever'body's wrongs."

Morgan finished his coffee. "What do you want, Miss Thompson?" Morgan set his cup down and leaned forward.

"I want you to come to work for me."

"Not interested, I've got a job."

"No you haven't. You're on a payroll over to that high classed whore's place. I'm offerin' you a job."

"I'm not interested."

Now it was Skagway Annie who leaned forward. They were nose to nose across the table. "Then get interested, Mister Morgan, or get out of the Klondike."

"No other alternatives?"

"Just one. You can get interested, or get dead."

"Why do you want me working for you?"

"I don't," Annie said, "Chappy does."

Morgan had assumed, correctly, that the "Chappy" to whom Annie was making reference was, in fact, Harrison Chapel. He assumed also that the meeting was a part of Chapel's plan to further promote the alleged feud between himself and his niece. Morgan sensed that the feud between Skagway Annie and The Queen of the Klondike, Mariellen Chapel, didn't need any help.

Morgan got to his feet. "Like I said before, I'm not interested."

Annie got to her feet, carefully considering the young, handsome gunman. "Tch, tch," she muttered, "too bad. The whore probably pays better, but I offer benefits she can't begin to match."

"No reason we can't be friends," Morgan said, putting on his hat.

"Yeah there is. I don't dally much with dead men."

Annie turned on her heel and walked away. Morgan watched her go back upstairs. He eyed the man who'd met him at the door and then realized two other men had drifted in while he and Annie were breakfasting. These men didn't look like they belonged in a place like Thompson's Cove. No, Morgan thought, they looked more the cut of men he was used to seeing. Both wore hip pistols, tied down rigs with weather worn holsters. They were some fifteen feet apart, standing at the bar. Morgan headed for the door.

"Hey you."

Morgan kept walking.

"Hey! I'm talkin' to you mister, you with the fancy hatband."

Morgan had spotted two bannister poles at the head of the stairway when he came in. Atop each was a small, hand carved parrot. By his estimate he would be about sixty to seventy feet away from them when he reached the door. They were also well above him and would require careful placement of shots if he was to do what he was thinking about.

"Unfriendly sonofabitch, ain't he?" The observation came from the second man.

Morgan reached the door, his back to both men and the stairway. He'd loaded the sixth chamber on the Bisley Colt before he kept his appointment. Now, he was ready. He stopped, bent his knees ever so slightly, drew in a blur, whirled and fired. Left side, right side, gun returned to holster, all in a single, quicker than the eye movement. The parrots were gone. Morgan straightened.

"Either of you gents want to see it again?"

The men's faces gave Morgan his answer.

Annie, with Harrison Chapel at her side, now stood at the head of the stairway.

Morgan glanced up. "You saved one life this morning," he said, looking straight at Annie, "I just saved two. Now you owe me."

He looked back at the two gunmen. One of them, the one who'd made the demeaming comment, was toying with his gun butt.

"Don't even think about it," Morgan said.

"You threatenin' me, mister?"

Morgan's face broke into a broad grin. He shook his head, glanced up again and then back to the man. "Not at all. Just a bit of friendly advice from an unfriendly sonofabitch!" He turned and walked out.

Upstairs, Skagway Annie Thompson had a frown on her face. Though neither of them had seen what had happened, both she and Harrison Chapel had seen the results. Chapel was smiling. "I was right, by God! He's our man, that's sure."

Annie looked up at him, still frowning. She looked at the evidence of Morgan's work and then at her two men. She was still frowning and she didn't comment on Chapel's observation.

Morgan spent most of the rest of the morning just sizing up Skagway and its male population. The only men he had seen so far who looked like possible trouble were the two at Thompson's Cove. He finally went back to Mariellen's place some three hours later.

"Where the hell have you been?"

"Keeping an appointment," Morgan replied, calmly. "I had breakfast with Skagway Annie."

Mariellen glanced around, there was no one close. She smiled. Her uncle had baited the trap.

"You have the regular breakfast?" Mariellen asked, grinning and looking into Morgan's face, "or the house special?"

"The regular I'd guess, but with a last meal option."

Mariellen looked puzzled for a moment and then said, "Cole and Pascal? Gun hands? One older gent an' a smirky lookin' kid?" When Morgan nodded she said, "They're both pretty good."

"I wouldn't know. All I did was kill a couple of wooden parrots."

Mariellen considered him for a moment, then laughed and shook her head. "Well, no matter. You're back and you're breathin'. Now, I've got a job for you. I've got a shipment of supplies comin' up from San Francisco. They'll be unloaded at Juneau on Friday. I want you and Chotauk to take the mail packet down, and be there waitin'."

"I don't need a nursemaid."

"You and Chotauk," Mariellen repeated, her tone firm. "Friday at Juneau. I want you to keep a close eye on the shipment coming back. Half of it is guns . . . rifles, mostly."

Morgan would rather have gone alone, but if he had to deal with the big Eskimo, better that he be on the boat with him.

"I'll watch it," he promised.

* * *

The trip down was about as exciting as a funeral. Chotauk never said a word. He just stood on the deck watching the wake roll out from the bow. He looked around at Morgan, disapprovingly, only once. That was the time Morgan started humming, "Sweet Betsy from Pike."

Juneau was the San Francisco, or, if you preferred, the New York of the territories. Almost nothing could reach the citizens deep in the Klondike or the Yukon which did not first pass through Juneau. It wasn't nearly as cold as Skagway, even though the distance between them was not that great. The difference in temperature came from the fact that Juneau, like Seattle, was warmed by the Japanese current. It was wild and wooly, tough and beautiful, dangerous and damned expensive.

When they got off the boat in Juneau, it was late Thursday night. Chotauk led the way to a big hotel with the rather unimaginative name of Midnight Sun. It was the only tri-story building in Juneau and one of only half a dozen which was built partially of brick. Morgan got his first surprise.

"You stay," Chotauk said. "I go back to boat."

"What the hell's the matter with you staying too?"

Chotauk frowned at Morgan's incompetence. "No allow Eskimo," he said simply. He turned and walked back toward the dock. Morgan looked around, catching a few expressions of disapproval for even being seen in company with an Eskimo.

"You don't really want to stay in this hotel, do you, mister?" a kid asked. He was about ten.

The kid was a hustler. Morgan eyed him and remembered back to his youth and his work as a stable boy. He, too, was a hustler, working on the streets of Grover, Idaho.

"I'd planned on it, yes."

"If you do, you'd better hire someone to keep a watch on your room. Else when you go out for dinner someone'll come along and take your tack."

"I see," Morgan said, smiling at the boy. "And do you happen to have any idea of who I might get to take care of that little job for me?"

"Me," the kid said. "I'll do it."

"I just thought you might. And how much is this going to cost me?"

"Ten bucks."

"Ten dollars? Isn't that a little high?"

"This here is Alaska, mister, an' ten dollars is a lot cheaper'n the other way."

"What other way?"

"You leave your stuff in your room and it gets stole. Then you'll wind up freezin' to death."

"I only have two choices, is that what you're tellin' me? Pay you ten dollars to watch my room and gear, or not pay you and have it stolen."

"There is another way."

Morgan frowned. "That right? And how's that?"

"You come stay at my house with me an' my sis an' you pay twenty dollars and your stuff is safe."

"What do they call you, son?"

"Name's Allen. Sis calls me that, most what know me call me Li'l Al 'cause o' muh daddy. Them what don't know me calls me Tukoolok. That's Eskimo meanin' talks a lot."

Morgan looked at the hotel again, then turned away from it. "I'll call you Took," he said.

Al frowned and then grinned. "That's okay," he said, nodding his approval. "Yessir, that's okay. Jist short for Tukoolok."

"Not quite," Morgan said. "It fits because I think I got took." Morgan ran his hand through the kid's hair. "You follow?"

Al laughed. "No, you follow," he said, and he started down the street with Morgan trailing behind. Morgan liked the boy and he'd rather stay in a private house than a hotel anytime.

5

Li'l Al, or Took, turned out to be Allen Gastineau, second born of Allain Louis Gastineau, one of the founders of the city of Juneau and one of the first white men to set foot in the territories.

Big sister was Micheline and she was all French and all woman. The clothes she wore did little for her femininity but neither could they hide it. She was dark, with almond shaped eyes and skin the texture of maple paste. They talked until near midnight with Morgan, finally turning the conversation to the subject of their father.

"He was one of the founders of Juneau," Micheline said, proudly. "He was the tenth white man to set foot in the territories. He wanted to bring government, law and order to us. He was," she paused and took a breath, "killed, ambushed."

"When?"

"Two years now. He was on his way to Prince Rupert." She looked up and smiled. "That's in British Columbia. His hope was to get some

British assistance from the Mounted Police until Alaska could form its own government and fund its own police."

"Sounds like somebody didn't much care for his idea."

"I wonder."

Morgan looked quizzical.

"It's just that he had so much support and no one knew exactly when he was leaving on that trip and yet they were waiting for him."

When Micheline finally showed Morgan to his room, he found it to be clean, quiet and comfortable. He also realized he was dead dog tired and he laid back and was almost asleep. He was jarred awake quickly.

"Mister Morgan." The voice was Micheline's.

Morgan hadn't realized she was still there.

"I didn't tell you," she said, "but I had a husband. He went off to Dawson in the Yukon eight or nine months back. He got caught in an avalanche." Her dress slipped from the maple hued skin and seemed to float to the floor. "I don't give myself to every boarder but my brother says, you, well, you're different."

Morgan couldn't help but think that Micheline was being pimped by a ten year old, but neither could he resist what stood before him. He'd worry about justifications later.

Micheline's breasts were small, firm and reminded the Idaho gunman of two persimmons. He kneaded them gently and Micheline responded with throaty whispers of "yes" and "good" and "don't stop." He didn't, but instead replaced exploring fingers with an exploring tongue.

The girl's nipples hardened under his ministrations and she seemed to melt onto the bed. Once there, she was at Morgan's mercy and he released weeks of pent up desire upon her.

Micheline's responses seemed to indicate that her previous experiences had been almost totally one sided. No man in her life had apparently ever given her anything, only taken. Morgan's almost frenzied application of his skills heightened his own desire for complete fulfillment.

He positioned her on the bed with her buttocks at its edge, her thighs splayed in a most unlady-like position and her arms pinned beneath her by her own weight. She didn't care, she didn't protest, she only closed her eyes and her head was rolling back and forth with each new spot Morgan found.

He let his tongue work its way along the inside of her legs from just above her knees, upwards. He alternated, getting higher each time. There was no change in the girl's response because this had never been done to her before and she could not imagine what was about to happen.

Gently, Morgan spread the folds of flesh reposing just below the silky fine covering of hair. He let his tongue find the moistness near the bottom of the slit and then he moved his head, slowly, upwards. His tongue went back and forth in rapid, short, firm motions. Micheline's breath came in little gasps. "What are you . . . oh, oh. OH . .. AHHHH!"

He struck home. He tightened his grip on her thighs and flicked his tongue faster.

Micheline climaxed, Morgan was certain, for the first time in her life. Her body shook and convulsed with each and every sensation. He stepped back and let her relax after the force of the pleasure. Her leg muscles quivered and jerked spasmodically. Once she had completely drained herself of the event, he leaned down, gently touching her breasts. Her breath immediately returned to short gasps. She opened her eyes, looked at him and smiled.

Morgan slipped his hands beneath her armpits and scooted her up on the bed. He mounted her and now she was anticipating an experience she had known before. He slipped inside her and her hips reared up to meet him, grinding bare flesh against bare flesh.

"Make me finish again, please," she begged, "make it happen again."

He did, careful to tease her clitoris with each thrust and adding the stimulation to her hardened nipples. His efforts had brought him to the very edge more than once and he struggled to stave off a premature release of his own.

They pushed against one another for a very long time, slowly at first, then faster, then slow again, draining from one another all of the pleasure each had to give. Slowly the sensation built until neither of them could restrain themselves any longer. In a single moment, two bodies became one.

The next morning, at the end of Main Street in Juneau, Morgan found the government dock, the packet boat *Golden Gate* and the Eskimo Chotauk. The big Eskimo was inside of a circle of men, eight or nine, and a barrel chested deck hand was circling around him warily. Morgan noted that the sailor had both hands free and held a big Bowie in the right one. Chotauk, by contrast, had only one hand free and no knife.

Morgan eyed the spectators carefully as he

moved nearer to the circle of men. He finally
edged between two of them and they glanced at
him only briefly. Chotauk spotted him.

"You call it this way?" Morgan asked.

Chotauk shook his head.

The man on Morgan's right suddenly realized
that Morgan was an ally of the Eskimo. He
reached for his gun. Morgan's was already in his
hand but he didn't plan to shoot anybody if he
didn't have to, and he didn't. Using the barrel of
the Bisley like a club, he smashed it into the
man's jaw and sent him reeling. At the same
instant, Morgan's left elbow shot back and found
the paunch of the man to his left. Morgan
followed up on that one and dropped the man
with the Colt's barrel laid over the top of his
head.

Then he stepped back and cocked the Bisley.

"Now untie the Eskimo's other arm and get rid
of the knife."

The man didn't move fast enough and Morgan
fired a shot between the man's feet. They were
bare.

"You'll lose a toe the next time."

The deck hand complied, tossing the knife
aside after he cut the rope binding Chotauk's
wrist to his belt. The deck hand eyed Morgan and
then his eyes shifted from one man to another
around the circle. Suddenly, he found no interest
in his plight. Morgan had reholstered the Bisley
but none of the sailors were gunmen and they
weren't about to test their skill against what
they'd already seen.

The deck hand had two brothers and the trio
had been charged with unloading the supplies
for Mariellen Chapel, under the watchful gaze

and direction of Chotauk. They had decided against taking orders from an Eskimo. Two of them quickly realized the error of their judgment, ending up in the water with cooled tempers. The third brother decided on a little more equal match.

Morgan motioned for the circle of men to spread apart somewhat and they did. That done, he nodded. The deck hand moved first and moved fast, spinning around. He charged, bull-like, head down, into Chotauk's middle. The Eskimo grinned, not even grunting. He simply back peddled to keep his balance until he could wrap his huge arms around the man's chest. Once he had locked his fingers together and lifted, the fight was all but over. He continued applying the pressure until the deck hand's face was about the same color as a ripe tomato. Chotauk turned him loose and the deck hand dropped, gasping for breath.

"Need men," Chotauk said to the others. "Five, all work there." He pointed to a cargo net full of crates. "Load onto packet boat, there." He pointed to the mail packet that would be going back up the Taiya Inlet. "Three hours all loaded."

Seven men, not five, answered the call.

Chotauk nodded his head with self satisfaction and then walked over to Morgan. "Chotauk would have won fight. Didn't need help."

Morgan considered him for a moment, smiled, and slapped Chotauk on the arm. "Yeah, I figure you could have, but I thought I'd offer anyhow. You didn't have to take the help if you didn't want it."

Morgan turned to walk away and Chotauk put

a big, meaty hand on Morgan's shoulder and pulled, half turning the gunman around. Morgan frowned.

Chotauk was grinning. "Chotauk like Morgan. You small man with big courage and big gun. Chotauk like Morgan." Chotauk took his hand away and Morgan completed the turn on his own.

This was the first time he'd felt halfway good about Chotauk, but the Eskimo had a postscript to add to his observation. "If you good man to go with courage and gun," he continued, jabbing first Morgan's chest and then his own, "you and Chotauk, we friends." The Eskimo's face suddenly turned hard and he leaned down, close to Morgan's face. "But if you bad man to Lady Boss, you sorry. You fight Chotauk. You shoot Chotauk with big gun and you drown in Chotauk's blood before he die." No further comment was needed.

"Can you handle the rest of the loading?" Morgan asked.

Chotauk nodded.

"I've got a few things to do while I'm here."

"You stay breathing. Lady Boss need Morgan. You die, Chotauk no like."

Morgan looked up, shook his head in despair and smiled. He said, "I wouldn't be too fond of the idea myself Chotauk, and you've just given me another incentive to stay alive. I wouldn't want you on me, even if I was already dead."

Chotauk responded with a broad grin.

Morgan made his way to what constituted downtown Juneau. It was also the territorial capital at the moment and Morgan had government business to attend to. He found his way to the office of the Canadian representative in the territory. The man's name was John R.L.D. Lycoming. He was a stringbean of a man with Lincolnesque features and thick, pure white hair. He gestured Morgan to a seat and then, himself, closed the door. Morgan noted that he stood by it for a few moments, just listening. The action puzzled Morgan but a minute later, Lycoming was smiling, pleasant and all business.

"Welcome to the territories, Mister Morgan."

"Thanks," Morgan replied.

"Your first trip to the land of the midnight sun?"

"I don't know why the hell everyone keep's sayin' that," Morgan said. "In the whole time I've been up here I haven't seen the sun more'n a couple of hours a day."

"Oh, that's because it's gettin' on toward winter. By mid-December you won't see it at all. In the summer the days get longer and longer until the sun never does go down, it just sort of dips. Tell me, what do you think of the place?"

"I haven't formed an opinion, Mister Lycoming. I've been just a bit too busy dealing with some of the less neighborly residents."

Lycoming's expression turned dour, his eyes shifted away from Morgan's face and finally he leaned back in his chair. "Well then, old fellow, what can I do for you?"

Morgan reached into the vest pocket of his buckskin shirt and produced the envelope that had been pushed under his door during the voyage up from San Francisco. He handed it to Lycoming.

"Someone pushed this under my door on the trip up," he said. "There is no postmark, but there is a small red design on the envelope. I was hoping you could tell me what it was."

Lycoming frowned. He eyed the envelope and asked, "The letter, sir, or whatever the contents, didn't tell you anything?"

"There was no letter or anything else. When it was slipped under my door, it was just as you see it now."

Lycoming nodded and then asked, "What brought you here for help?"

"Mail, at least where I come from, is government regulated. This is mail, you're government, and I was told this originated from somewhere in the territory. Territorial mail, I was told, is under Canadian jurisdiction. Was I told wrong?"

"No, no you were not, sir." Lycoming eyed the envelope again, leaned forward and handed it back to Morgan. "In this case, I'm afraid I can't be of much service to you. The red design doesn't indicate where the letter may have been posted."

"Does it tell you anything?"

"Oh yes. Whoever posted it is either in service of, or has access to, the official seal of the Mounted Police." Lycoming reached out and touched the red design with the tip of his finger. "That little stamp is the identification of the RCMP serving the territories."

"This came from the Mounties?"

Lycoming frowned. "Two things, Mister Morgan, in answer to your query. First, we don't call them Mounties. Not up here. Second, I didn't say it came from them, I said whoever placed it in that envelope had access to the stamp."

"Just how easy is that access?"

"Not easy at all old fellow, but there's no assurance that it is official simply because it's on there."

"You've lost me," Morgan said, somewhat irritably.

"The RCMP codes its written communications with a seal or design. Black, for instance, signifies that the point of origin is a regional headquarters such as you might find in Calgary or Edmonton. Green would tell you that the comminque emanated from a district office such as you will find in Prince George, British Columbia. No one would have access to these stamps."

"But the red is different?"

"Different is hardly enough, Mister Morgan. The red is possessed by only a handful of the most experienced field operatives. Men who work in the wilds and take great risks incognito. The only way that you, for instance, would have of coming into possession of the red stamp is by killing the operative to whom it was issued."

"This came from a Mountie, uh, a Royal Canadian police officer who may well have been working out of uniform?"

"That," Lycoming said, "or from the person who killed that officer." Lycoming reached into the top drawer of his desk and removed a file folder. He held it up. "The information is confidential, Mister Morgan, but suffice to say that this folder contains the names of five such operatives, all dead, all killed by person or persons unknown, and all within the past two years. That, sir, is why I can't be of much help to you in your quest."

"I appreciate what help you have given, Mister Lycoming, and I'm working up in Skagway, staying at The Queen's Throne Hotel. If you think of anything else that might be helpful, I'd appreciate knowing about it."

Morgan got to his feet and Lycoming followed suit, extending his hand as he did so. Morgan shook it and Lycoming walked him to the office door and then opened it.

Then, Lycoming spoke again. "There is one other thing you might do, Mister Morgan."

"Yeah? What's that?"

"You might ask yourself the same question I'm asking myself right now."

Morgan looked quizzical. "And what's that, Mister Lycoming?"

"Just what would a special operative for so prestigious an agency as the RCMP want with a second rate American gun fighter?"

There was a time Morgan would have taken the question as an insult but Lycoming was very British, very suspicious about anything American and, for the moment at least, not worth Morgan's time. Nonetheless, Morgan's nature precluded simply ignoring the statement. "I can think of one damned good reason, Lycoming."

The tall man's brows raised. "Really. And what, sir, is it?"

"Maybe he'd like to learn how to stay alive."

6

Mariellen Chapel found Morgan taking his breakfast. She sat across the table from him and he
knew at once that she was unhappy. He figured it
was probably because he and Chotauk had
arrived too late the night before to unload. They
had simply put the crates from the packet boat
onto wagons and drove the wagons into the
storage barn, opting to wait until daylight to
unload them.

"You got a beef with me?" Morgan finally asked.

"You do somethin' to give me cause to have a
beef with you?"

Morgan grinned. Mariellen seemed to make a
habit of answering a question with a question
and it was a sure sign she had a beef. He shook
his head. "Not as I know of."

"If you'd gone down to Juneau alone, I'd have
you shot by now, or sic Chotauk on you. As it is,
he already told me that you both kept an eye on
the crates all the way back."

Morgan frowned.

"There's not one damn thing in those crates
but rocks."

Morgan had a bite of food at mouth level. He paused and then the fork lowered. "You've got enemies aboard the boat up from San Francisco."

"Or at the dock in Juneau, or at the loading docks in San Francisco, or anywhere in between that you can think of."

"Yeah," Morgan said, "and that's a lot of places." He shifted his weight and pushed back from the table, keeping only his coffee cup. "What were you hauling?"

Mariellen considered Morgan carefully. He could tell that she was still uncertain about him. Chotauk had told her everything which had taken place and she knew her uncle put great stock in Morgan's reputation. She also knew, or at least believed, that every man had his price.

"You really don't know?"

"I really don't," Morgan answered. "Should I?"

"Guns."

Morgan leaned forward. "Guns? Nothing but guns?" he asked, incredulous.

"I've been bringing in extra supplies, small amounts of necessities, for months now, building up the stock. It was all so I could have one free load for guns." She rubbed her forehead and cursed under her breath. Mariellen looked up. "Colt pistols. The latest models of the Peacemakers and plenty of ammunition to go with them."

"How many?"

"Fifty."

"Jeezus! Who knew?"

"Me, my uncle and the factory," she paused, "I thought."

"What do you plan, uh, or should I say what *did* you plan to do with fifty Colt Peacemakers?"

"Arm the men I need to hold onto what I've got, Morgan. It's real simple."

Morgan's eyebrows raised and he looked around, gesturing with little bobs of his head. "This place? Fifty men?" He looked into Mariellen's eyes. "It's nice," he continued, "but who in hell wants it that bad? Surely not Skagway Annie?"

"Right church, Morgan," Mariellen replied, "wrong pew. Our problems, mine and hers, are not in Skagway. They're up in Dawson and they're not friendly, they're damned scary."

"What the hell is up in Dawson, more gold?"

"There's gold. Silver too, and copper, and God knows what else Morgan, but our money isn't dug up. It comes from men not mines. They need everything men need and they don't much give a damn who supplies it."

"Look," Morgan said, glancing around to make certain they were still alone, "I'm supposed to be working for you and I'm supposed to be on the outs with your uncle. We both know better. It's Colt I'm really working for," he said. He leaned forward, squinting steely eyes at Mariellen's face and then added, "Isn't it?"

"It is, Morgan, that's the truth of it. They wanted their weapons on the last frontier and they tried the usual methods without success. They finally left it to my uncle to make a deal. He did."

"You're not talking about the deal he has with me, Mariellen. As I see it, I'm an enforcer, nothing else."

"Right again, Morgan. The deal is this. Colt gets a solid foothold in the Klondike and the

Yukon through my uncle and I get all future supplies at special prices because I can purchase them by using the Colt name."

"Sounds like a flim-flam."

"On a smaller scale Morgan, like one little town back down in the states, it would be. In the territories it could mean millions of dollars. Canada, the Mounted Police, all of British Columbia and the rest of Alaska as it opens up." Mariellen leaned back, finished her coffee, put out her cigarette and looked hard. "And it will open up, Morgan, big and powerful and raw and mean but it will open up."

Morgan nodded. He knew she was right. "And Skagway Annie Thompson stands to gain the most if you can't keep your deal, that right?"

Mariellen shrugged. "Who else? We're the two biggest operators in Skagway. No reason for it to be different in Dawson."

Morgan got to his feet. "I've got a little trip to make," he said, smiling and adding, "Lady Boss."

"Morgan," Mariellen licked her lips and swallowed, hard, "be careful."

He nodded.

As he headed for Skagway Annie's place, he mulled over what he had just heard. In many ways, what Mariellen had revealed posed more questions then it answered. On top of that, it was obvious that the lady was scared. He hadn't seen it in her before but there was sure no mistaking it. Morgan began to wonder just how big a game he'd been asked to join. He didn't know yet but he knew one thing for damned sure. No matter how big, he didn't like the hand he was holding.

Morgan reckoned that if Skagway Annie Thompson was behind the theft of the guns, her next move would be to eliminate any possible problems she might encounter with somebody trying to get them back. After her offer to him and his refusal, he seemed the logical target for her efforts. Lee Morgan wasn't a man who liked to sit around and wait for somebody else's next move. If he was supposed to be on the outs with Harrison Chapel and Skagway Annie, he figured he might as well make it look good.

Morgan entered Thompson's Cove and looked at once toward the table where Annie Thompson usually had breakfast. He was either too late or just a shade early. He glanced toward the second floor. One of the two men he'd confronted on his earlier visit stood at the head of the stairs. He was armed with a shotgun. Morgan's eyes met those of the man and this time it was the man who felt safe. The shotgun was cocked and ready and even Morgan's speed wouldn't keep him from a load of shot.

Morgan reached up and tugged at the brim of his hat in a mock gesture of greeting to the man, then he turned on his heel and walked out. The man grinned. Morgan slipped into the walkway between Skagway Annie's place and the only store in Skagway which sold ladies' hats. He caught himself pausing to stare at such an unlikely item as was displayed in the store's window.

Morgan reached the back of Thompson's Cove and found both what he'd expected and what he was looking for. The second man with whom he'd had the earlier run in was now posted outside the second floor doorway. No getting in the backway, in silence anyhow. Morgan had expected it. He also found an outside ground

floor window which led into a storage room.
Morgan had hoped for it. He knocked out the
glass and yanked open the window.

"Who's there?"

Morgan had already stepped back into the
walkway. Now he eased forward.

"Who's down there?"

The man had come down about half the stairs.
Like his counterpart inside, Skagway Annie's
man was armed with a shotgun. Morgan eased
forward a little more and then pressed his back
against the building and edged around the
corner. He was now beneath the wooden stairs
and the guard had stopped. Morgan was ready
and he tossed an empty bean tin through the
broken window.

The man on the stairway acted predictably and
took two more steps. As he began the third,
Morgan's right hand closed around the man's
boot at ankle height.

"Goddam," the man yelled.

He was already pitching forward, face down.
He reflexively pulled the trigger on the shotgun
and Morgan took advantage of the noise to move
back out to the street.

A moment later, the Idahoan eased in the front
door and glanced toward the head of the stairs.
No man, no shotgun.

"Don't bother, barkeep," Morgan shouted.

The barkeep had not reacted quickly and by
the time Morgan reached the top of the stairs, it
didn't matter anymore. Morgan's gun was drawn
and aimed toward the back bar.

The barkeep, his eyes as big and round as beer
mugs, put both hands up and waggled them as he
backed slowly away. Morgan smiled and nodded

his approval.

"Very good Mister Morgan, but no cigar. Sorry."

Morgan had heard nothing behind him. He whirled. The gun flew from his hand as one of two hulking men in sailor's garb lit in on him. The voice belonged to Skagway Annie and she seemed to be enjoying Morgan's plight.

The smaller of the two men had struck first, knocking Morgan's gun away and then catching the gunman with a solid blow to the mid-section. The second man, much bigger, grabbed Morgan by the collar of his buckskins and whirled him in a half turn. Only Morgan's recuperative skills and his own speed kept the situation from being worse. As it was, he took a solid blow to the jaw and couldn't keep his feet.

Morgan faked a roll to his right hoping to gain a few moments. It didn't work. A third man slipped ham sized hands beneath Morgan's armpits and literally hefted the gunman to his feet, pinning his arms at the same time. The smaller of the two sailors went to work on Morgan's belly at that point. When he finally took most of Morgan's wind and maybe a rib or two, the bigger man moved in and put the lights out with a single, crashing blow to Morgan's jaw.

Morgan sucked in his breath, winced at the pain on his left side, and felt a moment of panic when his hands found solid wood only a few inches from his face. He was on his back.

"Buried alive," Morgan whispered to himself.

A moment later, his hand found open space to his left, then still more. He eased his feet to the left, more space. He was in the confines of a ship's bunk! Shanghaied! He swung himself down to the deck, again wincing with the stabbing pain in his left side. He also instinctively reached for his gun. It wasn't there.

Above him he could hear men's feet on the deck and after gathering his senses and getting his bearings, he also realized they were already at sea! Where? In what direction? How long had he been unconscious? He had to get some answers and he sure as hell wouldn't get them down in the darkened hold of a ship.

His eyes had somewhat adjusted to the darkness but there was damned little light. He did catch enough rays of sunlight for him to determine that it was still daylight. The same day? Now that he couldn't be sure about.

He found a ladder and went up it as far as he could, then put his neck and shoulder to the task of trying to open the deck hatch. It was to no avail. He began pounding on the hatch. He did so, hollering as well, for the next quarter of an hour. No one responded. Morgan found a corner, sat down and wished that he had one of Mariellen's cigareets.

When the hatch finally did open someone was standing at the top looking down at him. It was light outside, but it was the dim light of early morning or late afternoon and all he could see was a silhouette. He tensed, ready to defend himself.

"Morgan, I'm sorry, old boy, but if you'll come up on deck, I'll explain everything."

Chapel? What the hell was going on? Morgan got up, rubbed the back of his head, and moved cautiously to the ladder. Harrison Chapel moved away from the hatch as Morgan ascended slowly and finally emerged. He quickly glanced around, sizing up the deck hands. He was also looking for the trio who'd put him under in the first place. There was no sign of them and the deck hands present all seemed plenty busy.

"Chapel, your niece and I had a talk, uh, damn! How long was I out?"

"You were brought aboard yesterday," Chapel said.

"Yesterday? Yeah, well, as I was saying, Mariellen and I had a talk. I went to do something about it and this is where I ended up. Anyway, she told me a lot I didn't know. I figure the rest of the answers are ones you can supply."

"We have to be careful, Morgan, but consider this. If I didn't plan to give some answers, why would you be here, alive?"

"With all due respect, Chapel," Morgan said, "I've done nothing but answer all sorts of damned questions. Now, I don't plan on going anywhere until I find out just who's sitting in on this little game, and who's staking who."

"I have your weapons and personal things below, Morgan. I did what I did to put the finishing touch to our little charade."

"I don't much care for your approach."

Chapel smiled but at the same time raised his eyebrows at Morgan. "What did you have in mind just before Annie's men jumped you?"

"I'm not sure, exactly," Morgan said, "but I take your meaning. I don't quite understand why you'd go to the trouble you went to and then end up on the same damned boat with me. Isn't that a little risky?"

"It is unless you get dumped over the side in a canvas bag."

"That what you've got in mind?"

"With your cooperation, in the right place at the right time, yes Morgan, I do. I think it would completely free you to do what has to be done."

"Which is?"

"Find out who's against Colt. Who and why."

"Did Mariellen tell me right about the deal with the Colt Company and the battle for Dawson?"

"She did."

"I gather you think that the answer, or answers, to your problems are up in Dawson."

Harrison Chapel shrugged. "In the Yukon territory somewhere, yes." He pooched out his lower lip in an expression of mixed surprise and ignorance. "As to Dawson, I don't know, Morgan. Mariellen tends to be a bit melodramatic at times."

"As far as you're concerned, the trouble could be coming from one of your gun competitors, is that what you think?"

"Why not? Any deal Colt can make, anyone else can make. Can't they?"

"I guess," Morgan said, "if they had the money and the manpower and the contacts."

"There are plenty of all three up here, Morgan."

"How about Skagway Annie? What's her stake in the game?"

"Pretty healthy," Chapel replied, "and there really is no love lost between Annie and my niece but I don't think either of them would have the stomach for murder, outright, if push came to shove."

"Uh huh. Just whose life are you betting on it, Chapel?"

Harrison Chapel considered Morgan for a

moment and then moved again to the hatchway. "Come, I'll show you to your gear and you can get something to eat. I'll join you for some coffee and outline what I have in mind."

"If I'm supposed to be working for Mariellen and I end up supposedly dead, what will she have to do to keep up appearances?"

"It's covered, Morgan," Chapel said, smiling. "She'll be mad, she'll do something to Annie's place, or try. Before it gets too serious, I'll let her in on it."

"You're playing a damned dangerous game, Chapel. You could turn what sounds like a little friendly competition into an all out war."

"Yes, Morgan," Chapel said. "I could, and then supply the guns to fight it to the highest bidder." He gestured below. "Shall we?"

"One more question first, Chapel. What happened to the load of Peacemakers we were supposed to have picked up for Mariellen? We ended up with two crates of rocks." Morgan paused. "Or did you know all of that already?"

"I knew. I arranged it with Colt's. I had to make the first situation look good to, well, uh, you know, whoever is behind this." Chapel looked down. "I wish I could have told you."

Morgan edged past Chapel and went below. When the tall gentleman finally ducked low enough to work into the little room, Morgan had another question ready for him. "You really did make a pretty good show, but where are they?"

Chapel, obviously preoccupied, frowned.

"The pistols you arranged to have stolen."

"Oh yes," Chapel chuckled, "seems like a fair query, Mister Morgan. Well, they are safe, I assure you. They never left San Francisco."

Harrison Chapel moved across the small cabin and fished into a foot locker hidden beneath some woodwork and a blanket or two. From it, he eventually pulled Morgan's gun and holster, possibles he'd been carrying, and the monetary content of his wallet. "Your belongings, Morgan."

Morgan took them in silence, eyeing each with the scrutiny of a man distrustful of everything. This particular plan had smelled sour almost from the beginning. Everything he wanted to check out had proven to be just a little tainted. He was half afraid to check anything, and far too smart not to check everything. Satisfied that his belongings were intact, Morgan turned again to Harrison Chapel.

"Just how realistic a plan do you have in mind for me?"

Chapel grinned. "It will look good, Mister Morgan. I promise you."

Morgan nodded. "I was sure it would. Now, how about reality?"

"You'll find everything you need when we put you ashore, Morgan."

"Since most everybody hereabouts will think I'm dead, or at least hear that I am, just what is everything I need, Chapel?"

Harrison Chapel smiled broadly, walked across the room, slapped Morgan on the upper arm and said, "Transportation my friend, to Dawson, Yukon Territory."

7

The canvas bag was full of body, just as it was supposed to be. Morgan's buckskin outfit and crumpled hat supplied proof of identification. Chapel made certain that the bag was towed in close enough to shore to get caught in the tide. It was found two days later by some fishermen just off the fishing community of Yukulat. The local constable was duly informed.

Morgan had been put ashore some miles away in an isolated bay which led directly into a heavily wooded area near the base of Mt. Fair-weather, the highest point in British Columbia. There, Harrison Chapel had promised, transportation would be made available.

Transportation was desperately needed because Morgan was going to have to travel north and east towards Skagway, though he must avoid the town since everyone there, including Harrison's neice, thought he was dead. From there he would bear due north through the treacherous and infamous Chilkoot Pass and into the Yukon territory. He would pass through the tiny settlement of Klukshu and then go east to Whitehorse. After Whitehorse, bearing north-west, Morgan faced two-hundred miles of the most desolate scrub woods in the world. His destination would be Fort Selkirk. Resupplying and resting there, he would then undertake the final leg of his journey, another hundred and fifty miles of desolation, until he reached Dawson.

In Dawson, he was to find a room and await contact from someone known only as B.J.C. Morgan assumed the last initial might stand for Chapel, a third member of the clan, but the con-sideration was minimal. In his business, and particularly under his present circumstances, assumption of anything could buy him a six-by-six plot of Yukon ice.

But all that was in some distant, undefined future. The first thing he had to do was get there, and for that he would have to use the transporta-tion that was here for him. Too, he would also need equipment and clothing for staying alive under these conditions.

An old Tlingit, with a face that looked like the side of a mountain and legs that seemed to be only half the normal length, took Morgan in tow and showed him to the sled and team he would be using.

The Tlingit took great pride in showing him the sled, a sixteen-foot, basket-type vehicle lashed together with sinews. The runners were of wood, the harness for the dogs of rope and rawhide.

Morgan learned that the rigging had to be just right so the sled would pull even and travel a straight course. He was also shown how to navigate by the stars. He had learned since coming to Alaska that he couldn't count on the

sun rising in the east and setting in the west.
Here it rose in the west and it set in the west
after making a tiny arc of only a few hours across
the lower part of the sky. But the moon and stars
were exceptionally bright in the crystal night air,
and the white glare of the snow made long
distance vision possible, even in the middle of the
night.

As important as the sled and team would be the
equipment he would have with him. An inventory
of equipment disclosed the following:

    1 lantern
    1 gallon of kerosene
    1 tarpaulin
    1 axe
    1 small stove
    1 box of matches
    1 skillet
    1 fur lined sleeping roll
    2 woolen blankets
    1 large caribou skin
    1 Winchester .44-.40
    2 boxes .44-.40 cartridges
    2 weeks supply of dried deer meat for himself
    100 pounds of dried salmon for the dogs

The old Tlingit told Morgan that a caribou
skin, placed skin down, was the best thing to use
as insulation against the snow. The caribou hairs
were hollow and formed an insulation between
the snow and the body.

The clothing Morgan would wear was of equal
importance to the sled and the equipment he
would carry. He was outfitted in a fur parka and
pants. He would wear mukluks, which were fur
boots made of caribou and wolf.

Morgan started to put on a pair of red

"longhandled" underwear, but the Tlingit stopped him.

"No . . . you wear, you freeze and die."

"What do you mean?" Morgan growled. "I've worn these in Montana winters and they aren't easy winters. These things kept me warm."

"You work with sled, you get hot, you sweat," the Tlingit said. "Then you get cold, sweat freeze . . . you die."

Morgan rubbed his chin and considered what the Tlingit told him. He had learned long ago to listen to the natives . . . be they Apache telling him how to survive on the desert, or Tlingit telling him how to survive in the frozen wastelands.

"All right," Morgan said. "You're the one who knows. The longhandles stay off."

The Tlingit grunted and some of the lines on his face rearranged themselves. It might have been a smile.

There was almost disaster at the very beginning of the trip. With the sled packed and ready, Morgan was about to step onto the runners, when, from out of nowhere, a female wolf appeared. The lead dog, perhaps sexually aroused by the unexpected appearance of pulchitrude in the wild, started after her, pulling the team with him. The old Tlingit made a grab for the sled as it whizzed past him, and managed to jump on. He worked the brake handle and yelled at the dogs at the top of his voice. It took him just a moment to regain control, and a few minutes later he had the sled still, waiting for Morgan to catch up.

"Holy shit," Morgan grunted. "What if they do that while I'm out in the wild?"

"Shoot lead dog," the Tlingit said.

"If I had my way I'd shoot the sonofabitch now," Morgan said. He stepped onto the runners, released the brake as the Tlingit had showed him, and the sled was off like a runaway train.

The temperature was about fifteen below zero.

The old Tlingit trotted along with Morgan for the first couple of hours, sometimes shouting at the dogs, sometimes pointing out things to Morgan to make the sledding easier. Then, when he reached a long, smooth plain where nothing but level snow stretched ahead of him for as far as he could see, the Tlingit grunted something and turned away. Morgan waved at him, then realized that he was all alone.

Morgan had been alone most of his life. He had crossed the most treacherous stretches of desert in the U.S. and Mexico, and he had ridden and packed through the most rugged mountains. But in both cases he had been in his element, working with horses and in the case of the mountains, mules. Dogs were creatures who lay around on the front porch, or by the back door of saloons. They were white, furry little creatures in pink ribbons in the parlors of bawdy houses, or they were slab-sided hounds who ran out to snap at your stirrups when you rode into fly-blown towns. They were even things to eat in some of the Indian villages he had been in . . . but never before had he depended upon them for his very life. But these ten animals running before his sled were his lifeline, and he was damned uneasy about it.

Above and all about him stretched the very universe, overhung with the black curtain of the long, long night, lighted by the moon and the reflected glow from the mantle of snow. Its stark austerity was more awesome than anything he had ever experienced. By comparison, last winter in the mountain cabin seemed like it had been an encampment in the lobby of a downtown hotel. Some might go crazy under such solitude, but Morgan actually found the experience pleasant.

The second day out, Morgan learned that one of the dogs was a shirker. It had simply quit pulling in the harness and leaned back to trot, effortlessly, along. Morgan tried to get the dog to work, but it refused. The Tlingit told him what to do in such a case. An unalterable law up here was that a dog worked, or it was shot. There was no room for a shirker. Reluctantly, Morgan took the dog out of the harness, then shot him.

On the third day, Morgan encountered a stinging wind which whipped up the snow into an artificial blizzard. The wind and snow stung and burned his face so that he could no longer look ahead to where he was going. The Tlingit had told him, however, that the lead dog could find the trail alone. Morgan decided to test the theory and for one entire day he kept his head down, out of the blowing snow, while the lead dog continued the run.

On the fifth day, one of the dogs went vicious. Somehow he managed to chew his way through the harness and once he was free, instead of bounding away into the wild, he suddenly turned and leaped on Morgan, his teeth bared, his eyes red and angry.

The attack was totally unexpected and Morgan was knocked off the sled by the animal. Morgan put up his arm and the thickness of the parka kept the dog's teeth from tearing through to his flesh, though the dog's bite was so strong that it was like having his arm caught in a vise. Morgan rolled in the snow with the dog, all the while reaching for his gun. The draw that was so fast that many a gunman had gone down in the wink of an eye, was now slowed by the fact that he was down, in the snow, and fighting for his life with a would-be killer dog. Finally he got his pistol out, put the barrel under the dog's chin, and pulled the trigger. Blood and brains burst from the top of the animal's head and the vise-grip suddenly relaxed. The animal flopped over in the snow, a fan of red spattered out on the pristine white.

The other dogs reacted to the one gone wild and started snapping and growling at him. Morgan got a length of rope and started after them, beating them until they submitted. After a few well placed lashes, the dogs lay on their bellies with their paws by their noses, looking up through frightened eyes. Once more he was in control.

"All right, let's go," he growled, after he had readjusted the harness. He was down to just eight dogs now. "And no more of this shit. If I have to I'll leave every damned one of you on the trail and walk into Whitehorse pulling the damned sled myself. Now, mush, goddamnit, mush."

8

Morgan had an unaccustomed growth of whiskers when his sled pulled into Whitehorse. Several people turned out to look at him as he arrived. They weren't drawn to him by his appearance . . . dog sleds were common and he had learned enough on this trip to handle the team and sled without calling undue attention to himself. But he had arrived from nowhere, and he had arrived alone. That, in itself, caused some interest.

He was a stranger, and that aroused more interest. Who was he, and what had driven him to the nearly unheard of feat of coming through Chilkoot Pass this late in the year?

Whitehorse may not have been much of a town, but it was a town, with the promise of cooked food, whiskey, and a bed. Morgan decided he would spend a couple of days here. The town didn't seem that much different from Skagway, though Morgan did notice that fewer men seemed to be wearing pistols. That didn't mean they were unarmed, though. Almost everyone he saw was armed, but they were carrying rifles. They had the look of mountain men and prospectors, he thought, not gunmen.

Morgan found a board for the team and a place to park his sled, then he had a look around at the town. He needed a place to stay and he finally settled on a place called the Nugget.

The Nugget was the best place in Whitehorse, a dubious honor considering the other candidates. It was rough hewn of Alaskan timber and the furnishings came from the leftovers. There were no fancy trappings but Morgan concluded that the surroundings were at least on a par with the occupants.

"Howdy mister, and welcome."

Morgan looked up and found himself staring into a cherubic faced girl of about twenty-five. Her hair was coiffed in ringlets and hung down far enough on both sides to frame her face. He guessed her height at about five feet, two inches but nothing else was in proportion.

"Ma'am," he said.

"May I?" She gestured toward a chair as she spoke and Morgan nodded. She held out a lily white, petal soft hand. "I'm Lizzy McCutcheon and this is my place."

Morgan took her hand.

"You must be the fella who come in with the team this morning."

"Word spreads fast."

She smiled. "There are no secrets in Whitehorse, Mister, at least not where strangers are concerned. You bound for Dawson?"

"I can see why there are no secrets," Morgan said, "if you get answers to all your questions."

"I do, one way or another."

"Yeah," Morgan said, "I'm Dawson bound." He

noticed she was eyeing his hands and she glanced toward his hip.

"You're sure as hell no prospector and you wear a piece like you know how to use it." She looked up.

"If I have to use it, I can. I'm no prospector and my business is just that, mine."

"Your handle part o' that business?"

Morgan eyed her. He had agreed with Harrison Chapel to use his father's name, Leslie. As to a first name, Chapel came up with Hank. To Morgan, it made no difference.

"Name's Hank Leslie."

Lizzy McCutcheon motioned for the barkeep and when he reached the table, she said, "I'll have a scotch. Anything else for you, Mister Leslie?"

"Another bourbon."

"These are on me." The barkeep withdrew. "Who you workin' for, Mister Leslie?"

"I told you, I keep my business mine."

"Not up here you won't. Oh, you can keep it quiet for a spell, but as soon as you try to do whatever it is you do, the word will go out. Once it does, the price of your hide goes up."

Morgan looked puzzled.

"It's easy," Lizzy continued, "this land is tough enough for the best of men without having to compete with each other. I figure it would be downright miraculous if you were tryin' to do something somebody else hasn't tried."

"I'm not," Morgan said, "I'm trying to make some money. I can't imagine anybody who hasn't tried that, or isn't trying it right now. No miracles where I'm concerned."

"How would a thousand dollars appeal to you?

Half now and half when you complete the job?"

Morgan's first instinct was to say no but he caught himself. He was supposed to be a man looking to make money. Turning down a chance to do that without at least hearing how would smell a little rotten.

"I don't much care for half payments," Morgan said. "If you don't trust me to do it, you shouldn't ask."

Lizzy McCutcheon grinned. "I agree. I just can't pay you more than I've got and all I can spare from here is half. The other half is up in Dawson at my other place."

"Why'd you pick on me?"

"You're the only man in Whitehorse who's headed to Dawson with an empty sled."

Morgan considered her. "What makes you think it's empty?"

"I knew it was empty fifteen minutes after you got into town and at least that much before you walked in here. Most men peddlin' somethin' got goods. You got nothin' except what you need to get to Dawson and up here that's a damned sin."

"A sin?"

Lizzie nodded. "Need a lot up north. Man ought not go empty handed."

Morgan eyed the girl and then leaned back and said, "That seems like a fair amount of money for one sled full of supplies."

"It's ten percent of the value of what you'll be hauling for me."

"Which is?"

"Now that's my business, Mister Leslie. Isn't it?"

"Not if I'm hauling it," Morgan said. "I figure you approached me because you spotted me for a gun hand, not a prospector. You're hiring my gun, not me." Morgan looked around. "There's a dozen men in here right now who know the country better and know everything there is to know about a sled and team. Unless you figure on trouble, one o' them would already be on the trail."

The girl got to her feet, scooted her chair back under the table and then said, "I'll buy you a venison steak this evenin' Mister Leslie, and we'll talk some more. We can both decide after that. Seven o'clock suit you?"

"I don't recollect any better offers since I hit town. Seven's fine."

Morgan watched the girl walk away and his mind shifted from her offer to the sway of her hips. It was a hell of a long ways to Dawson and fresh memories were about the only company he could imagine having on the trail.

"That was good," Morgan said, wiping his mouth. He tossed the napkin aside and took a swallow of coffee. "I never much cared for deer meat but that was good."

"You learn lots o' things about cookin' in this country," Lizzie said, "when you don't have much to work with. One day, I plan to try to bring in some honest to God beef."

Morgan frowned. Lizzie's comment stirred a faint memory. "Seems to me that somebody tried that once."

"So I've heard," Lizzie said, "gent from Wyoming a few years back." She laughed. "He got paid well enough, that's sure, but he never lived to spend it."

"Runnin' cows in this country would be next to impossble."

"Nothin' is impossible Mister Leslie, unless them what tries it don't believe it. He got the cows here, he just didn't have any plans after that."

"Speaking of plans, I'd like to know what yours are for me."

"Upstairs, Mister Leslie," Lizzie replied, getting to her feet, "and I'll do better than tell you, I'll show you."

Morgan considered her, looked around the room, and realized that no one was paying them any mind. He nodded and stood up.

Lizzy McCutcheon's room was pleasant, warm and feminine with the low notes of her perfume hanging in the air like an invitation. The bed was a big four-poster, hand hewn like the rest of the furniture, but by a craftsman who took pride in his work. In addition to the bed there was an overstuffed chair, a rocker, a fine china cabinet, and a spinet. Morgan took the overstuffed, tossing his hat onto a straight back chair nearby.

"Do you like wine, Mister Leslie?"

"Good wine, yes."

Lizzie poured two glasses and handed one to him. The color was a deep, rich burgandy, glowing as if it had captured inner fire. Morgan sniffed it, then tasted it, and found it was as good as any he had drunk in San Francisco.

When she saw the expression of surprise on his face she smiled. "I do what I can to make life bearable up here," she said. She sat on the edge of the bed. "I've got three big wooden crates in a storeroom downstairs, Mr. Leslie. They're full of dynamite."

"Dynamite?"

"As you might imagine with all the prospecting and mining going on up here, that's one of the most precious commodities in the territories."

"I can see that," Morgan said. "I can also see that it might be difficult to hang on to something like that."

"Hard enough," Lizzie said. "I haven't tried to ship it yet because of that very thing. There are people who will try and get it, and they don't give a damn how they do it. That's where you come in."

"The job seems to be worth a little more than a thousand dollars," Morgan said. Their eyes met. "Wouldn't you agree?"

"Yes," she said, pausing, "but there is a bonus."

"A bonus? Like what?" Morgan asked.

"Like me," Lizzie replied.

Morgan wasn't disappointed. His imagination had, if anything, underestimated what was hidden beneath the unflattering clothes. Indeed, little else was in proportion to Lizzie's height. Her breasts were full and firm, and the hue and texture of her skin was that of a woman much younger. Morgan had bedded many women half the age of Lizzie who had less to offer.

Lizzie took the role of aggressor and did so with zeal and class. She didn't flaunt herself like a whore, but neither was she the timid housewife who only made love once a week, on her back, after a bath.

Lizzie explored Morgan's muscular body, first with her fingers, and then with her lips. She advanced quickly to her tongue after determining his most sensitive areas. The Idaho gunman relaxed and let nature and Lizzie take their respective courses.

She found his considerable manhood and

began a sensual stroking of it, first with tongue, then with her hand and then a combination of both. He was quickly aroused but she positioned herself so that she could control any involuntary movement.

Each time Morgan tried to respond with a touch or reaction of his own, Lizzie bore down her weight and stopped him. She wanted to give, not receive. Morgan finally accepted the situation and succumbed. Lizzie McCutcheon had both a sense of what a man liked, and a feel for just how far to go with it. Several times, Morgan was certain that she was about to take him to a climax, but each time she stopped and left him hanging in space, breathing hard, completely vulnerable.

After several times like this, Lizzie suddenly got up. "Now," she said, "give me what I want." She moved to the end of the bed, reached out and grasped the posts with each hand, then bent forward from the waist. At the same time, she planted her feet wide apart. Morgan needed no further coaching or invitation. He was rock hard and ready.

He bent his knees slightly and carefully inserted himself into Lizzie's depths, now well lubricated with her own juices. She moaned as she felt him make the insertion. He steadied himself with a small adjustment in his own position and then he began to thrust, slowly. At the same time his hands went down to grasp her breasts. He fingered the nipples and Lizzie moaned again. He stroked and kneaded them.

"Oh, God, yes, that's it, yes! That's what I like. Do it! Don't stop, keep doing it. Do it for both of us."

Morgan did it for both of them, for a very long time.

"Finish it this way," she moaned.

Morgan did finish it that way in a sudden, gushing burst of sperm and sensation. Lizzie's whole body stiffened and even in his own passion, Morgan could sense Lizzie's climax and her juices released. She was, he thought, a different kind of woman. She climaxed almost like a man.

When it was over, Morgan slipped from her, but he continued kneading her breasts and kissing her bare back, working down her smooth skin until he could gently kiss her buttocks. She sighed and swayed gently, but made no protest to his post climax display. He finally straightened and stepped back and Lizzie stood up and turned around. She stepped up to him, pressing her nakedness against his own. Kissing him, she stepped back and said, "I was wrong, Mister Leslie."

"Wrong about what?"

"I promised you a bonus. But it was I who got the bonus."

Morgan returned her smile. All this, he thought, eyeing her, and class as well.

If every other facet of his makeup was lost during the lovemaking process, Morgan's thinking processes remained ever sound, ever searching. Something was bothering him and it finally surfaced.

"Did I hear you right?" he asked, pulling on his boots. "Did you say my fee was ten percent of the value of what I was hauling?"

Lizzie, still dressing, turned to face him. "That's what I said. Damned expensive dynamite, isn't it?"

Morgan stood up. "Yeah, even up here I'd say ten thousand dollars is damned expensive dynamite."

"There are two commodities in very short supply in this country, Mister Leslie. Dynamite and handguns. If you have dynamite, you'll need handguns to protect it. If you have handguns, you've got to figure a way to get them where they're needed, without losing them."

"Wait a minute. Are you telling me you have pistols in this load? Pistols packed in dynamite?"

His face became stern, but before he could pursue the matter, Lizzie replied. "Who'll bushwhack a load like that and risk losing both?" Lizzie smiled confidently at her own query. It smacked of a certainty.

Morgan wasn't so sure. "What make of hand guns?" he asked.

Lizzie looked puzzled that he would ask such a question. "Remingtons. Why?"

"Well, if I was working for, say, Colt Firearms, this kind of shipment would be made to order for me. I wouldn't give a damn about blowing up a load of dynamite and my competitor's handguns with it." He strapped on his rig and tied down the holster. When he looked up, Lizzie was still considering his last observation.

"You're suggesting that representatives of these gun manufacturers, men who have to have government clearance to even come up here, would go to such lengths?"

"I've never known greed to be picky about who it infects, and with what's at stake in this country, I don't know many men whose resistance is that high."

"But the territorial government restricts American gun sales. And every representative has to undergo a full investigation of his background."

"So I understand," Morgan replied, smiling, "but who investigates the investigators? Are you trying to say that the investigators are so noble and fine that they can't be tempted if enough money is waved in their face?"

"My God! I never considered the possibility. The raids, the murders, the trouble we've been having, it could have been—" she let the sentence dangle as she paced across the room. She turned back and looked at Morgan with a troubled expression on her face. "I just figured it was locals trying to horn in on the market."

"Tell me, how do you manage to deal in guns?" Morgan thought about his question, then added, "Legally, I mean."

"I was the first business in Whitehorse to make the request. I went through weeks of filling out forms, answering questions from RCMP people, everything it took. I had no competition to speak of, but even that didn't assure me of a license."

"You got those Remingtons legal then?"

"Legal as hell, Mister Leslie. And very costly. I'll lose my ass if those guns are bushwhacked."

"Yeah? Carrying guns packed in dynamite, I may literally lose my ass before this is all over," Morgan said.

"I . . . I guess I didn't think of that," Lizzie said. She brushed her hair back with her hand. "It's just that the situation is critical right now."

"You must be pretty desperate to select a total stranger and then tell him everything. You don't know me," Morgan said, moving a little closer, then adding, "or do you?"

"I don't," came the quick reply. "And I can't afford the luxury of getting to know you. You're a gamble, Mister Leslie, a crap shoot. I'm out of time." Lizzie McCutcheon then made a statement which, under other circumstances, would have caused Morgan to burst into laughter. "Hell," she said, "for all I know you could be working for the Colt Firearms Company."

Morgan didn't respond to her observation. Instead he asked, "Who's your contact with Remington?"

"Fella by the name of Parmenter. Oliver Parmenter. I checked on him myself," she said. "I mean, besides what the RCMP and the territorial government did. He's legitimate."

"And your buyer in Dawson?"

Lizzie grinned. "Now him, I got no worry 'bout, Mister Leslie. He's been up there, so some say, since the first day of creation. He's half Eskimo and half polar bear. Fella by the name of Crowder. Big Ben Crowder."

Morgan's mind clicked. His contact in Dawson was someone with the initials B.J.C. Crowder . . . Ben Crowder. "What's his middle name?"

Lizzie wrinkled her brow and nose in a look of complete puzzlement, then she laughed. "Hell, Mister Leslie, I don't know. It was only three months ago that I found out Big Ben had a last name."

"Is he the only buyer in Dawson?"

"Only one I've got, and the only one I know anything about."

"Then he'd be a buyer from anyone coming in with a load of guns, no matter the make. That right?"

"I reckon it is, but Big Ben is honest. He wouldn't play both ends against the middle. If I show first, he buys from me. If Colt or somebody else shows first—" Lizzie shrugged.

"Why are you so certain about this fella, Big Ben?"

Lizzie McCutcheon played her ace. "My daddy was not much of a man. Too much whisky, too little backbone. Ever' shortcomin' he had was reason to hit my mama, and he had a lot of shortcomin's. He did it once too often, I guess. I only know what I heard. I reckon I was about two years old. Anyway, Mama grabbed me an ran, an' daddy was hot after her, and they both run headlong into Big Ben. When it was over, Daddy was dead and mama was grateful."

Lizzie walked right up to Morgan now, and looked him straight in the eye. "Big Ben Crowder is my step daddy, Mister Leslie."

9

Lee Morgan had been in tight spots before. Hell, he'd lived most of his adult life moving from one tight spot to another, but this particular one rubbed and chafed and raised welts everywhere. He was supposed to have gone to work for the Colt people, but he didn't. He ended up working for a hellion named Mariellen Chapel. He was supposed to have a feud going with her uncle, but he didn't. Now, he was supposed to be dead, but he wasn't. And topping off the whole thing was a new job for another hellion named Lizzie.

When Morgan left Whitehorse, he had a lot more confidence in his ability as a musher. He had been taught the most basic elements of the craft by the Tlinget Indian, but he had actually learned from the best teacher of all, experience. Having spent two weeks on the trail with nobody or nothing to depend on but his own skills, he was now as comfortable on the runners of the sled as he would be on the seat of a wagon. Hell, here was nothing about dog teaming that a reasonably intelligent, well coordinated, physically fit man couldn't handle. Morgan fit all those requirements, so dog sledding became routine for him.

On the third day out when he figured he was no more than a couple of hours from Dawson, Sheba, his lead dog, suddenly pulled up. Her snout went up in the air, she pawed, she growled, then she died. At almost the same instant the dog next to her rolled to his right as the bullet that had just killed Sheba ripped into his right, front shoulder. By the time the sound of the first shot carried to him, another dog was down.

The Idaho gunman didn't waste time trying to figure out what was going on. He might be in the frozen wastelands of the Yukon, but he had been under fire enough times to have already picked out the true sound of the rifle from the many echoes that were reverberating back from the low scrub trees. He grabbed his Winchester and, crouched low, ran, hell bent, for a low lying spiny ridge of ice and rock about fifty yards off to his left. Oddly enough, no one bothered to even shoot at him. They were after his dog team and he heard yelps of pain and surprise from the animals as one by one they were taken down by hidden riflemen.

When Morgan reached the scanty security of the ridge and dived over it, he had counted three separate rifles in action. That meant there were at least three men out there, maybe more. He turned around and looked back toward his team. By now all ten animals, including the two replacements he had picked up in Whitehorse, were down. He could see a widening pool of blood as the animals bled their life out on the snow, betrayed by the humans they were trained to serve.

"Sonofabitch!" he swore softly.

He couldn't see a damned thing, but he knew that whoever was out there had to be pretty good shots. They had taken out his entire team and he was certainly a bigger target than any of the dogs. He also knew he wouldn't be going anywhere for a spell, and when he did go, it would be on foot. The guns and the dynamite he could forget about. Whoever was behind this attack was playing for keeps, with no concern about life, either human or animal.

"Hey, mister!" one of the assailants called. "Mister, iffen you'll throw down that rifle we seen you pick up, an' walk up to the sled with your hands up, we'll let you get some food an' water. You can make it into Dawson on foot iffen you got some supplies."

Morgan didn't answer.

"All we want's what's on the sled," one of the others called.

Still no answer.

"This here's rough country," the first assailant yelled again. "You ain't gonna survive 'lessen we let ya'."

"All right, you bastards," Morgan whispered, "it's your territory and it's rough. But rough is rough, whether it's up here or back where I come from. I'll just wait you sonofabitches out."

"Mister? You gonna take us up on our offer?"

Morgan raised up as the last man was calling and he saw what he was looking for, the little wisp of vapor that came from the hardcase's mouth, drifting over the rock and purpling in the dim light of the sun, setting now after its brief sojourn across the sky.

"You know what I think?" Morgan shouted back. He levered a round into his Winchester and pointed the rifle toward where he had seen the vapor.

"What do you think?" the vapor asked.

"I think you can go to hell." Morgan drew a bead and waited. He knew the sonofabitch would raise his head to have a look and that was all he needed, just a split second.

A head raised up above the rock, just far enough for the eyes to look over the top, though since he was wearing a parka, the eyes couldn't be seen. Morgan put the front blade sight of his rifle even with the gate sight at the rear, and right in the middle of the shadow of the parka hood where he imagined the eyes were. He let out half his breath, then he squeezed the trigger.

The rifle barked and kicked back against his shoulder and he saw a little mist of blood spew out of the dark shadow. The man fell to his left, flopping out into the snow with arms akimbo. Morgan knew he had killed him with one shot.

"Holy shit! Did you see that?"

"Shut up, you stupid bastard. It was a lucky shot."

"Carter? Carter, where are you? Do you see 'im?"

Morgan heard the heavy bore boom of a big Sharps .50. The bullet crashed through the snowy spine in front of him, taking out a chunk of ice the size of a man's head. This was a new player in the game. He had spotted the other three men, but this one he knew nothing about. The thing that shocked Morgan the most, however, was that the bullet came from the rear! Carter, whoever he was, was behind him.

Morgan couldn't stay here. The man with the Sharps had his range. The next bullet would find its mark and with a .50 caliber it didn't much matter where he was hit. Even a leg wound could kill him out here. Morgan got up and started running. The two smaller rifles across the way opened up on him. Morgan clutched his gut, spun once, then fell.

"I got 'im! I got the sonofabitch!" one of the men yelled excitedly.

"You got 'im? What do you mean you got 'im? I had a bead right on 'im."

"Hell, maybe we both got 'im."

No one got me, you bastards, Morgan thought. At least, not yet. Morgan, who was unhit, eased his head out of the snow and peered toward the sled. The two men from the other side of the clearing were moving toward it. He could hear the third man, the one with the Sharps, coming up from behind him, his boots crunching through the crust of the snow.

"Carter? Roll 'im over, Carter. See'f he's got two bullet holes in 'im or just mine."

Morgan looked toward the sled. The two men were almost there, the third was on him. Morgan waited until he felt the boot on his side. He felt the pressure as Carter rolled him over to check for bullet holes. Morgan rolled over on his back and smiled up at Carter.

"Surprise," Morgan said.

"What the hell?" Carter shouted. He tried to raise his big Sharps into firing position but he was a trifle slow. Morgan's pistol cracked and Carter died, clutching at the sudden hole in his neck.

"Jesus!" one of the two men at the sled shouted.

Morgan grabbed his rifle and rolled once in the snow, levering a shell into the chamber as he did so. At almost the same time the two men at the

sled fired and their bullets came so close that
Morgan felt a sting of snow in his face from the
near miss.

Morgan rolled over onto his stomach, then,
from the prone position, fired at the black,
bulging blob that was his sled.

Craaaack! The rifle spit out its missile, and
almost at the same moment there was a bright
red-orange flash, followed by the shock wave and
stomach shaking boom of an explosion.

Morgan covered the top of his head with his
arms and buried his face in the snow as debris
began raining back down from the explosions.
He felt the stinging impact of dozens of tiny
pieces falling on him, though there was not one
piece of anything large enough to do more than
sting.

When the final echo was but a rumble, like far-
away thunder, Morgan raised his head and
looked over to where the sled had been. The snow
was scattered with black objects . . . pieces of sled,
pieces of guns and the crates the guns were
packed in, and most gruesome of all, pieces of
the two men who had been standing over the
sled.

Morgan looked down at the body of the one the
others called Carter. Carter's eyes were wide
open but they had already taken on the glazed
look of death. His hands were still clutched over
the hole in his neck and the blood was already
congealed, moments away from being frozen.

Morgan looked through Carter's pockets.He
found one-hundred dollars in ten dollar bills, but
nothing else. A check of the first man he killed
disclosed the same thing . . . one-hundred dollars
in ten dollar bills, but nothing else. Morgan
looked around on the snow for a few minutes,

then found what he was looking for. A ten dollar bill. Then another, and another after that until he managed to recover an additional 120 dollars, all in ten dollar bills. He also saw the charred remains of a couple of bills.

"Well, gentlemen," he said to the men who had ambushed him. "It would seem that you were paid one-hundred dollars apiece to steal my load. Now that you've had time to think about it, do you think it was worth it?"

With $320 more than he started the trip with, Morgan decided to go on into Dawson. He wasn't looking forward to the long walk, then he happened to think of the men who had ambushed him. They sure as hell didn't walk out here. How did they get here?"

Morgan followed their tracks for a short distance, then he found their horses. Smiling, he mounted one, then turned the others free.

"You want to come back in town with me you can," he said. "But I'll be damned if I'm going to lead you."

As if they understood, the horses followed obediently along. Morgan returned to the dog sled trail. The horse was sure footed and used to the snow. The last part of his trip to Dawson was a breeze.

10

After several days in the wilderness, the appearance of Dawson was quite a contrast. A booming little city of ten-thousand people, Dawson had fifteen saloons, five bakeries, two laundries, twelve general merchandise stores, fruit, cigar and confectionary stores, a meat market, a printing shop, four hotels, six restaurants, two bathouses, two barbershops, a hospital and a bank.

The appearance of the bank gave Morgan an idea. The ten dollar bills he found on the bush-whackers were American. Surely a bank in the Yukon, part of the Canadian Northwest Territories, would be able to tell him who had drawn four-hundred dollars in American currency. He stopped in front of the bank, swung down from the horse, and went inside.

The bank was well lighted and busy. In addition to the tellers' cages, there was an asseyor's desk for gold, and a land claims desk. Two wood burning stoves roared in the center of the room and Morgan, who had been cold for

three weeks, walked over to stand by one of them
for a moment. A few people looked at him as they
entered or left the bank, but no one gave him a
lookover that he would characterize as unusual.
There were so many prospectors being drawn to
the Klondike by the promise of gold that one
more new face in the crowd aroused no
abnormal curiosity.

When Morgan felt the warmth beginning to
come back to his fingers and hands, he stepped
away from the stove, then went up to the window
marked currency exchange.

The man behind the window had thin,blond
hair and rimless glasses. He looked up at
Morgan. "American for Canadian, or Canadian
for American?" he asked.

"Canadian for American."

"How much?"

"Four-hundred dollars."

"The exchange is $440 Canadian for $400
American." The clerk started to count out $400,
counting it out in ten dollar bills. Morgan took
$440 of the Canadian money he had been paid by
Lizzie, and counted out·for the exchange.

"Have you made this exchange before?"
Morgan asked.

The clerk pointed to the sign over his window.
"Currency exchange, that's what I do," he said.
"Of course I've done this before. Do you think I
don't know the exchange rate?"

"No, that's not what I mean," Morgan said.
"What I mean is, I'm looking for someone . . .
someone who might have made this exact
exchange in the last few days . . . $440 Canadian
for $400 American."

"That's not an unusual amount," the clerk
said. He finished counting out the bills, then took

the money from Morgan. "Will there be anything else?"

"No," Morgan said. He put the money in his pocket, then left the bank. So much for that piece of detective work. It got him absolutely nowhere.

When he stepped out front, he saw someone looking very closely at the horse he had ridden in on, the horse that had belonged to one of the ambushers.

"Something about that horse interest you, mister?"

"What? No, no, I was just admirin' him, that's all."

"Where's the livery?"

"Right down the street."

"Thanks."

Morgan rode the horse down to the livery, dismounted, then led the animal inside. He was met by a short, round man, bald on top, but with a bushy white beard.

"Board your horse, mister?"

"Yeah, I guess. You the only livery in town?"

"The only honest one," the man said. "They's a few folks claim they can board 'an keep your horse for you in a lean-to they got behind their shanty. I wouldn't count on 'em iffen I was you." The stableman looked at the horse pretty close, then looked at Morgan. Morgan saw in his eyes that he recognized the horse.

"You know this horse, do you?"

"I reckon I do."

"Whose horse is it?"

"Mister, you tell me it's yours an' board 'im here, far as I'm concerned, it's yours."

"It's not my horse," Morgan said. "I found him on the trail comin' up from Whitehorse. I'd like to know who he does belong to."

The hostler rubbed his whiskers and stared at the horse for a long moment. "Well, sir, he was rode into Dawson by a fella the name of Carter Lane. But from what I observed of Mister Carter Lane, that don't mean he owns the horse . . . it just means he rode 'im in."

"You're not givin' this fella, Carter Lane, a very high recommendation," Morgan said.

"I wouldn't want him guardin' my hen house," the stableman said. "Iffen I take the horse, who'll be payin' his fare?"

"What's the boarding fee?"

"Five dollars a day. That includes his feed."

"Five dollars a day? My God, I could stay in the finest hotel in San Francisco for five dollars a day."

"You ain't in San Francisco, mister, an' this animal don't eat frozen salmon. He eats hay an' oats an' ever' ounce has to come up the Yukon River, an' that means they ain't nothin' come up since the first week of October, an' there ain't nothin' else gonna come up 'till the middle of May."

"That's five bucks Canadian, I hope," Morgan said, remembering the unbalanced exchange rate.

"Yeah, Canadian," the liveryman said with a broad, yellow toothed smile.

Morgan counted out twenty dollars. "I'll come back before this runs out to let you know if I'm gonna keep him here any longer. Say, you don't know anybody who runs with this fella, Carter Lane, do you?"

"No, but try over at the North Star Saloon. I seen Lane over there a few times."

"Thanks," Morgan said.

He started to turn when he suddenly saw something in the liveryman's eyes, a widening of the pupils, a narrowing of the lids. There was a barely perceptible quickening of the liveryman's breath.

"Uh, yeah, be seein' you," the liveryman said. The tone of his voice was half a pitch higher, as if his throat had involuntarily contracted.

Over the years, Morgan's survival had been dependent upon his ability to interpret and use every sensory input. Many thought the Idaho gunfighter had a sixth sense, and in that he had an exceptional ability to use the five normal senses, one could almost say that he did have a sixth sense. That came into play now, for he knew that someone was behind him, and he knew that someone was about to try to kill him. Morgan took one step to the left, then hurled his body to the right. The would be killer's gun roared even as Morgan was in mid-air. The bullet hit the wood of the nearest stall, sending splinters flying. The horse neighed and reared up in fear, while the liveryman dived for cover. As all this was happening, Morgan twisted around so that he could see the assailant. By the time Morgan hit the ground, he had his Colt in his hand.

"You sonofabitch!" the bushwhacker yelled.

Morgan saw him move the gun toward him, saw him thumb the trigger back for a second shot. He never got the second shot off, for Morgan's own pistol was blazing then, and his bullet caught the hardcase right in the breast-bone. The impact of the bullet knocked the hardcase through the door of the livery, out into the hard packed snow of the street. He fell in a pile of horse turds; then, his feet still working, he pushed himself on his back for a few feet as if that way he could escape.

Morgan was back on his feet instantly and he hurried over toward the wounded man with his gun out in front of him. He kicked the wounded man's gun away, then, satisfied that there wasn't another weapon available to the man, he holstered his own pistol and looked down at his victim.

Blood was bubbling out of the hole in the man's chest, and Morgan could hear the wound sucking air. Morgan dropped to one knee beside the man.

"Why'd you try to bushwhack me?" he asked.

The man coughed. "You . . . you go to hell," he said.

"You're dyin', mister," Morgan said. "It can't matter to you now. Who are you? Why did you try to kill me just now?"

The man coughed again. "I needed a grubstake," he said. "I got a hunnert dollars to do this."

"Who gave it to you? Who, man?"

"The mountie," the man said.

"The mountie?"

"Yeah, you know. The Canadian law." The man broke into a coughing seizure. "I mean, he ain't wearin' that red suit or nothin', but he's a mountie, I seen the papers."

"But why?" Morgan asked. "Why would a mountie pay you to kill me?"

"He said you was wanted by the Canadians, said they was a price on your head. I'd get a hunnert now an' the reward when he told headquarters."

"Who is this mountie? What's his name?"

The man reached up and grabbed Morgan's arm, then squeezed it hard. "Mister," he said. "I got me a terrible hurt in my gut. It's . . ." He dropped his arm, his head rolled to one side and his eyes stared ahead blankly. The sucking sound in his chest stopped.

Morgan stood up. By now there were two or three dozen men gathered around, looking down at the dead man. More were coming down the street, materializing out of the dark. He could hear them talking quietly as they approached.

"Anybody know this fella?" Morgan asked.

"Figured you must," one of the men said. "You killed him."

"Never saw him in my life 'till he opened up on me," Morgan said.

"That there's the truth," the liveryman said. "I seen it all. This fella on the ground come sneakin' up behind this man. Next thing you know they was both blazin' away at each other. Onliest thang I don't know is how you know'd he was there," the liveryman said.

"You told me," Morgan said.

"Mister, you must be loco. I never told you a goddamned thang."

"Who is it?" Morgan asked again.

"The only thing I ever heard him called was Sourdough Mike," someone said. "He mostly stays out prospectin', he don't get into town much."

"He should'a stayed out there," someone else said.

"Out of my way. Out of my way, please," an authoritative voice was saying.

As the people parted to let the new man pass,

Morgan saw the red coat and black trousers of a Northwest Mounted Policeman. The policeman looked at Morgan, then pointed to the dead man. "Are you the cause of this?"

"You might say that."

"I'll take your gun." The mountie held his hand out.

"I'm not ready to do that just now," Morgan said.

"Mister, I am ordering you to surrender your gun to me."

Morgan looked at the policeman and smiled. The policeman not only didn't have a gun in his hand, the flap over his holster was snapped down so that anything close to a quick draw was absolutely impossible. And yet he had *ordered* Morgan to turn over his weapon.

"Now how the hell do you think you can make that order stick?" Morgan asked.

"I can make it stick because I have the authority of the law behind me," the policeman said. "Now please hand over your pistol to me, sir, or stand arrested for resisting the law."

"Constable, I can tell you, this here fella was just defendin' himself," the liveryman said. "The man layin' there come up behind him with no word o' warnin' or nothin'."

"If that is the case, you will be released to your own recognizance in a very short time. Provided you offer no resistance now."

Morgan thought about it for a moment. "Constable, I want you to know this is the second time today someone's tried to bushwhack me, and I don't know why. So you can see I'm not too keen on givin' up my gun."

"You will be in my custody," the constable

said. "And under my protection. No one would dare assault you while under custody of the law."

Morgan sighed, then handed his gun over with a wry smile. "Now, why doesn't that make me feel safe?" he asked.

"Come along," the constable said, sticking Morgan's gun down in his belt. He waved his arm at the crowd. "Give way, here, give way," he said. "Give way in the name of the law."

11

Constable Edmond Bannister returned Morgan's pistol.

"I've checked your story, Mr. Leslie," he said. "There was another witness in addition to the liveryman and he verified what happened. You are free to go."

"Thanks," Morgan said, buckling his pistol around his waist.

The constable tossed a few chunks of wood into the little stove, then held his hands over the top. He eyed Morgan carefully. "We don't see too many gun rigs like that up here," he said. "Are you an American gunfighter?"

Normally, when someone called Morgan a gunfighter, he made some deferential statement. But this wasn't a statement of accusation, nor was it the utterance of a thrill seeker. Constable Bannister was a no-nonsense lawman, asking a sensible question. Maybe, if Morgan was frank with him, he would be helpful to Morgan.

"Yes," Morgan said with a sigh. "I am what you might call a gunfighter."

"I see," the constable said. "And why are you

101

in Dawson?"

"Constable, I don't know what you know about gunfighters," Morgan said.

"Not too much, I'm afraid. But from what I do know, I don't think I'd care to know one."

"There are some who hire their guns out to the highest bidder," Morgan said. "They market their skill and they don't care who buys them."

"Are you telling me you aren't like that?"

"Yeah," Morgan said. "I'm telling you I'm not like that."

"But you do hire your guns." It wasn't a question, or even an accusation. It was a statement of fact.

"Yes, I hire my guns. But I've never killed a man who wasn't trying to kill me. I don't live with the ghosts, Constable."

"Would you care for some tea, Mr. Leslie?"

Morgan would rather have been offered coffee, but anything hot would taste good now.

"Yes, thanks. By the way, my name isn't Leslie."

"Oh?" The Constable looked up at him as he poured two cups of tea. "Isn't that the name you gave me?"

"That's the name I was going by," Morgan said. "My name is Morgan . . . Lee Morgan."

"Lee Morgan?" The constable walked over to his file cabinet and rummaged through a few papers, then picked one up and looked at it. "Mr. Morgan, according to the information I have, you are supposed to be dead. You were abducted from Skagway and your body washed ashore near Yukalat."

"That wasn't me," Morgan said.

The constable took a swallow of his tea and

studied Morgan over the rim of his cup for a moment. Finally he spoke. "Would you care to tell me the story?" he asked.

"I will, I'll tell you everything," Morgan said. "But first, I would like to ask a few questions, if you don't mind."

"All right. I'll answer what I can."

"First of all, the man I killed tonight. . ."

The constable smiled and held up his hand. "This afternoon," he said. "It was only half past three when you shot him. The darkness is confusing to new people."

"Yeah," Morgan said. "Yeah, I been up here a couple of months now and I'm still not used to it. Anyway, the man I killed told me he had been paid one-hundred dollars to kill me."

"I see. And did he say who paid him this money?"

"He said he was paid by the mountie."

Constable Bannister knitted his eyes together.

"The mountie?"

"That's what he said."

"Good heavens, did he tell you I was the one who paid him?"

"No. He said it wasn't a uniformed mountie. He said it was someone else. Supposedly, I am wanted by the Canadian law."

"No, Mr. Morgan, you are not wanted by the Canadian law, neither as Lee Morgan, nor as Hank Leslie. That part of his story is patently false, as is the part that he was contacted by a member of the Northwest Mounted."

Morgan reached in his pocket and pulled out the envelope that had been pushed under his door during the voyage up to Skagway. He handed the envelope to Constable Bannister.

"Does this mean anything to you?"

The constable looked at the envelope for a moment, then looked up at Morgan. "Is this it?" he asked. "An empty envelope, no address, no postmark?"

"This is it," Morgan said. "It was pushed under my door just as you see it."

"The red seal is an official seal," Bannister said. "And it is the seal of the plainclothes officers who—" Bannister stopped and looked at the seal more closely. Then he pulled open the middle drawer of his desk and took out a magnifying glass. He examined the seal closely through the glass. "Damn," he muttered.

"What is it?" Morgan asked.

The constable motioned Morgan over, then held the glass over the seal.

"Look in the upper right hand corner of the seal," he said. "Do you see the break in the line there?"

"Yes."

"Timothy McCutcheon."

"What?"

"This seal belonged to Constable Timothy McCutcheon."

McCutcheon, Morgan thought. Lizzie McCutcheon. At last . . . at long last, two pieces of the puzzle fit together.

"Where is McCutcheon?" Morgan asked. "I'd like to talk to him."

"Oh, I'm afraid that's quite impossible, Mr. Morgan."

"Look, I know these plainclothes agents have to keep low. I don't plan to expose him or anything. I just want to talk to him, to find out if he knows anything about this envelope."

"You don't understand," Bannister said. "It's not to protect his identity that you can't talk to him. You can't talk to him because he can't talk to anyone. You see, he's dead."

"Dead?" Suddenly Morgan remembered the news the constable in Juneau had told him . . . how four of their operatives had been killed in the last year.

"Yes, he was killed last spring while investigating the disappearance of . . ."

"Let me guess," Morgan interrupted. "He was investigating the disappearance of a shipment of guns, right?"

"Right you are, Mr. Morgan," Bannister said. "Now, I have answered all your questions. I believe you promised to tell me a story?" The constable refilled Morgan's cup and he held his hands around it, enjoying the warmth of the brew, even before he drank it.

"All right," Morgan said. He started then, beginning with the mysterious telegram that summoned him to Denver, and ending with the shootout on the trail in which he left four men dead and the remains of a shipment of guns scattered on the snow. He left out all the names, identifying them only as his "contacts."

"My," Bannister said. "That's the adventure stuff of a Beedle novel. And you say each of the brigands on the trail had one-hundred dollars in American money?"

"Yes," Morgan said. "At least, I think so. I found the money on the two who weren't blown apart by the dynamite, and I found another $120 lying scattered about on the snow. I'm sure the other two had a hundred apiece but it was destroyed by the blast."

"And one-hundred dollars American on Sourdough Mike," Bannister said. He stroked his chin. "Whoever is trying to kill you has certainly established the price."

"Yeah," Morgan said. He smiled. "But I'm gettin' expensive for the sonofabitch."

"Maybe that will be a break in our favor," Bannister suggested. "He may decide that he will have to pay a much larger sum to ensure that the job is done. If the sum is large enough, the news of the offer will have to get around."

"Yeah, could be," Morgan agreed, though he had no desire to wait around as bait while the offer increased. He remembered the man he was supposed to meet for Lizzie. "Do you know a fella named Big Ben Crowder?"

Bannister looked up sharply. "What about him?"

"Nothing," Morgan said. "I just wanted to know if you knew him, that's all."

"Yes, I know him. Funny you should ask. He was Timothy's stepfather. That's an interesting coincidence, don't you think?"

"Yeah, I guess it is."

"Of course, they never got along."

"Why not?"

"Mr. Crowder is what you might call an enterprising fellow. He is making a great deal of money out of the gold rush, yet he has never so much as picked up a nugget. We have a saying up here. Some folks get wealthy mining the hills, others make a fortune mining the men."

"And Crowder mines the men?"

"Yes."

"Is he dealing in guns?"

"Yes, as a matter of fact, he is. He has a license.

Of course, that was one of the things he and Timothy had difficulty over. Mr. Crowder thought that he should be given a license out of hand, just because he was Timothy's stepfather. Timothy, on the other hand, thought it smacked of corruption to have a relative—even an indirect relative such as a stepfather—get a license. I'm afraid Timothy fought against it . . . almost got it stopped."

"You don't think Crowder—"

"Had anything to do with young Timothy's death?" Bannister finished the question for him. He shook his head. "No, I don't think so. Of course, I did look into the matter. It was my duty, after all, and there had been that disagreement between them. Too, I have learned, Mr. Morgan, that despite the sudden eruption of gunfire between two armed and angry strangers, that the greatest number of homicides are committed by people who knew each other and, more often than not, are related. So, it wouldn't have been a great stretch of the imagination to believe that Ben Crowder could have killed Timothy. But my investigation convinced me that that wasn't the case."

"Where might I find Ben Crowder?"

"If I were looking for the gentleman, I should try the North Star Saloon," Bannister said.

"Thanks," Morgan said. He started toward the door then looked back. "By the way, does Ben Crowder have a middle name?"

"A middle name? No, not that I know of. Oh, wait, yes, I remember now, I did see a middle name when he applied for the license to handle the firearms. Just a moment, let me look it up." Bannister opened a file drawer and looked through several papers until he found what he was searching for. He pulled up a folder, opened it, then ran his finger down the page about halfway. He smiled. "Ah, yes, here it is."

"What is it?"

"Jacques," Bannister said. "Benjamine Jacques Crowder."

12

The North Star Saloon was a brightly lighted
edifice with all the comforts of home. During the
summer months riverboat traffic on the Yukon
was so thick that some made the comment a
person could walk from Dawson to Whitehorse
without once getting his feet wet. That same
river traffic brought all the necessities of life,
plus many of the niceties. As a result, the North
Star Saloon had a piano, a chandelier, and a
huge, bevel edged mirror behind the bar.

The liquor was flowing freely and a piano
player was grinding away a song as Morgan
stepped into the place. He saw a table near the
back wall and walked over to take it. A round
faced man with a half-smoked cigar came to see
what he wanted.

"Do you serve food in here?" Morgan asked,
realizing that he had eaten nothing but jerky
since the vennison steak he had with Lizzie
several days ago.

"We got some caribou stew," the man said.

"All right, bring me some. And a beer."

The man turned away from the table but
Morgan called to him and he turned back.

"You know a fella name Big Ben Crowder?"

"What do you want with him?'

"I got a message from his stepdaughter,"
Morgan said.

"Yeah, I know 'im."

"Would you point him out to me?"

The man looked around, then shook his head.
"He ain't in here."

Morgan grunted, then let the man go to take
care of his order. A moment later he had the beer,
and a few moments after that, a plate of
something hot and steaming called stew by the
man who put it on his table.

Morgan lifted a piece of the meat with his fork
and tried to identify what else was in the stew
but he had no luck. He raised some of it to his
nose and sniffed.

"Hell, mister, if you ever et dog, you can sure
as hell eat this."

Morgan looked up to see a man who had to be
Big Ben Crowder. He remembered Lizzie's description, half polar bear, half Eskimo . . . or in
this case, half Athabascan Indian. Morgan, like
many of the new visitors, called all Alaskan and
Northwest Territory natives Eskimos. In fact, he
learned there were four major groups . . .
Eskimos, who were around the northern and
northwestern rim of Alaska, Alieuts who were
out on the island chain, Tlingits, around the
southern rim and coastal areas of British
Columbia, and Athabascans in the interior.

"You'd be Big Ben Crowder," Morgan said.

"I heard you was lookin' for me," Crowder
said. He pulled a chair away from the table,
turned it around backwards, then sat on it,

leaning on the back to look at Morgan. "You're the fella shot Sourdough Mike, aren't you?"

"Friend of yours?"

Crowder guffawed loudly. "Mister, Sourdough never had no friends. No family neither, I don't reckon. Folks say he was birthed by a caribou and suckled by a she-wolf. He was mean as they come an' they won't nobody be sheddin' no tears at his wake."

"That's good to hear. I wouldn't want anyone tryin' to get even for him."

"That ain't gonna happen. Some folks is liable to get a mite put out with you for not bringin' in the dynamite an' pistols like 'you was supposed to. Me included."

"How'd you know about that?" Morgan asked, his eyes narrowing in curiosity.

"Charley said you was lookin' for me, had a message from my stepdaughter. She had a shipment of dynamite an' guns she was sendin' up here. I figure you're the one she sent them by."

"That's right."

"But you lost 'em, right?"

"No," Morgan said. "I still got 'em."

"What? Where?"

"I cached 'em out on the trail a ways," he said. "I got jumped once, I figured I might get jumped again, so I hid 'em out."

"Mister, the word I got is they's blood an' shit lying all over the snow out there. I figured you blowed ever'thin' up when you was jumped."

"One case of dynamite, about four handguns," Morgan said. "I got everythin' else."

Crowder rubbed his chin and studied Morgan for a few moments. "Uh, huh," he said. "And what kind of handguns would them be?"

"What difference does it make?"

"None, I don't reckon," Crowder agreed. " 'Course, iffen they was Remingtons, I'd figure you was tellin' the truth an' you brung 'em in for my stepdaughter. But if they was Colts, I'd be figurin' you for Harrison Chapel's man, the self same man I'm supposed to be meetin'."

"Your stepdaughter said you wouldn't be particular about whether you bought from her or the Colt representative," Morgan said.

"My stepdaughter's a smart girl. She knows I ain't gonna let family get in the way of business." Crowder suddenly smiled. "I'll be damned," he said.

"What is it?"

"You got both of 'em, don't you? You're representin' Remington and Colt."

"What makes you say that?"

"I'm s'posed to meet a man here," Crowder said. "A man who's workin' for Harrison Chapel. Would you be that man?"

"I might be."

Crowder laughed. "Yes, sir, it's just like I said. You're representin' both companies. Now, how do you like that?"

"Since you've had so many questions for me, now I'll ask you a couple."

"Go right ahead."

"Who set up the ambush out on the trail? Who tried to have me killed?"

"Hell, that could be one of half a dozen men," Crowder said. "Anyone who wants the guns bad enough could do that."

"How did he know they were comin' in?"

"Ever'body knew they were comin' in. Lizzie hasn't exactly been keepin' it a secret. She was ready to sell to the highest bidder, no matter what that might be."

"I see. All right then, that explains why the ambush on the trail. I had the guns, somebody else wanted them. But why the ambush down at the livery stable?"

"That, I can't help you with," Crowder said. He took off his fur cap and rubbed the top of his head. "I have to confess, I don't understand that at all. Folks don't normally go to all the trouble to kill a man, 'lessen there's somethin' in it for them. I guess the question you got to ask yourself is, who wants you dead? An' why?"

"I don't know," Morgan said. "But I intend to find out."

Morgan saw someone standing at the far end of the bar. It was the same man he saw showing so much interest in Carter's horse when he came out of the bank. "Excuse me," he said abruptly. He got up as if he was going out, then when he was next to the man at the bar, he suddenly stepped right up to him. His gun was out in a flash and he jabbed the barrel into the man's side. The whole thing was done so quickly and so smoothly, that no one else saw a thing. Not even the patrons standing closest to the man at the bar knew what was going on.

"Mister," Morgan hissed. "You and me's gonna take a little walk."

"What?" the man asked, gasping aloud. "What are you talking about?"

"You know what I'm talking about. And you know what this is in your side, don't you?" When the man didn't answer, Morgan shoved the barrel harder into his side, hard enough to make the man catch his breath. "Don't you?"

"I . . . I reckon I do," the man said.

"Move," Morgan said.

"Move where? Where are we going?"

"We're going to do a little horse trading," Morgan said.

At Morgan's insistence, and nudging, the man left a half-full glass of whiskey on the bar and walked out the door. The two of them tramped through the snow and dark down to the livery barn.

"Mister, I wish you'd tell me what the hell you're up to," he said.

"You'll find out soon enough. Push the door open and go inside."

The man opened the door and stepped into the livery barn. Morgan came in too, then closed the door behind him.

"You gonna tell me what this is all about?"

"No, mister, you're gonna tell me," Morgan said. "I want to know why you were so interested in the horse I rode in on."

"I told you, I was just admiring the animal. He's—"

That was as far as he got, because Morgan backhanded him. Surprised, the man took a couple of steps backward, then reached a hand up to his lips to feel the blood from the blow. "What'd you do that for?"

"I don't like bein' lied to," Morgan said. "And more important, I don't like bein' bushwhacked."

The man stared at Morgan sullenly.

"Empty your pockets," Morgan growled.

"Oh, I see. You're robbin' me, is that it? Well, I don't have much money but you're welcome to what I do have." He stuck his hand in one pocket and pulled out a roll of bills. "I've got a little over forty dollars."

"Turn 'em all out," Morgan said.

The man began emptying his pockets, making a little pile of his belongings on the flat top of a post. He had a pocket knife, a couple of keys, some change, and two little pieces of paper. Morgan recognized the papers, they were exactly like the paper he had been given by the bank when he converted Canadian money to American money. Morgan picked up one of them.

"Exchanged by the Dawson Canadian Security Bank," the receipt read. "Received from customer, $440 in Canadian currency . . . given to customer, $400 in American currency." The paper was dated two days earlier. Morgan put that one down and picked up another one. This one was dated today, and it exchanged $110 Canadian for $100 American.

"Well, now," Morgan said. "I find this very interesting. This is exactly the amount of money that's been paid to have me killed."

"That . . . that doesn't prove a thing," the man said.

Morgan's eyes grew flat and cold. "You're a dumb sonofabitch, aren't you?"

"What do you mean?"

Morgan raised his pistol and pointed it at the man's head.

"Mister, this isn't a court of law," Morgan said. "I don't need to prove you tried to kill me. All I have to do is believe it. I'm the judge and the jury. I believe you did it, and I'm going to kill you."

"No! No, wait!" the man said, raising his hands and crossing them before his face, as if by that action he could stop the bullet. "Don't shoot me, please, for God's sake, don't shoot me. I'll talk . . . I'll tell you everything."

"What do you mean you'll tell me everything? I already know you're the one who paid the money to have me ambushed. What the hell else do I need to know?" He cocked it.

"No!" the man screamed. "I was workin' for someone else! If you kill me, you still won't know who's after you!"

It was what Morgan wanted to hear, and the reason he had taken such a drastic step in the first place. He had no real intention of killing the man, but the man didn't know that. Morgan hesitated for a moment, pretending that he was thinking about it.

"Hell, mister, don't you understand? They's someone tryin' to get total control of all the guns that come into Alaska and the Territories." He laughed, a terrified, insane cackle. "You think those few guns and dynamite you was carryin' was the only loot in this whole deal? Mister, they's millions in this. Millions! Whoever winds up controllin' all the weapons controls everything."

"Are you telling me one of the legitimate gun manufacturers, Remington, or Colt, or somebody like that is behind this?" Morgan asked.

"Shit . . . they don't know nothin'," the man said. "What do they know? All they know is how to make the guns. They don't have any idea what's goin' on up here. The only one that did suspect somethin' was Tim McCutcheon, and he got hisself kilt soon as he started pokin' aroun'. Same as you . . . only you didn't get kilt."

"Right," Morgan said. "I didn't get killed. But someone is trying awfully hard, and mister, if you don't tell me in one second who it is—"

That was as far as Morgan got before the lights went out. He felt a crushing blow to the top of his head, and he went down like a sack of flour.

13

Like a cork surfacing from far beneath the surface of the water, Lee Morgan slowly floated back to consciousness. When he opened his eyes he saw that he was lying in a bed, well covered and warm. A kerosene lantern burned on the bedside table, the wick turned down so that the flame was a subdued glow rather than a bright glare.

Morgan tried to sit up but a sharp pain on the top of his head and a quick nausea made him lie back down. He turned his head from side to side to try and figure out where he was. There was nothing in the room to give him a clue, though he was fairly sure it wasn't a hotel room.

The door opened and someone came into the room carrying a tray. There was a steaming bowl of broth on the tray and even in his condition, Morgan appreciated the aroma, remembering that he had not finished his stew earlier. Today? Yesterday? When? This accursed constant darkness was enough to drive a man crazy when it came around to trying to figure time.

The woman carrying the tray was a large boned, round faced, Indian woman. She set the tray down on a table next to the bed.

"I have to admit that looks good," Morgan said.

The woman didn't respond, either by word or expression.

"Where am I?" Morgan asked.

The woman started to leave.

"Hey, wait a minute!" Morgan called to her. "Who are you? What is this place? Where the hell am I?"

The door was suddenly blocked out by a gaint of a man and for a moment Morgan thought it was Big Ben Crowder. Then, as the man stepped through the door, Morgan saw that it wasn't Crowder, it was Chotauk.

"Chotauk!" Morgan said. In his surpise he tried to sit up, but again the pain pushed him back down. "What the hell are you doing up here?" he asked.

"This my home," Chotauk said. "Woman who feed you is my wife."

"Well I'll be damned," Morgan said. Moving more slowly, he was finally able to sit up. There was a crust of hot bread near the broth and he broke a piece of it off and popped it in his mouth. He didn't think he had ever tasted anything more delicious.

"Miss Chapel think you were dead," Chotauk said.

"Yeah," Morgan said, rubbing the top of his head gingerly. "Well, for a while there I thought so too."

"No, not this bump on head," Chotauk said. "Before. Men come, say fishermen find your body."

"Yeah, well Chapel said he would explain all that to his niece," Morgan said. "That was his idea, not mine. Wait a minute . . . you mean he didn't tell her?"

"No," Mariellen said, coming into the room at that moment. "The only word I got was that you were dead."

"Damn," Morgan said. He started to reach for the broth, but Mariellen came over and sat on the bed beside him.

"Let me do that," she said, picking up the bowl and spooning some into Morgan's mouth.

"Been a long time since anyone did this," Morgan said.

"Your mother?"

"No. Some girl down in Abiline," Morgan teased.

"Uh huh, maybe you'd like me to spill this on your lap."

"No, no," Morgan said, laughing gently.

He noticed that Chotauk had withdrawn. Mariellen spooned another bite into his mouth and he took it and studied her for a long moment. There had been the girl down in Denver . . . the one who was going to poison him, then the girl in Juneau, and Lizzie McCutcheon. But Morgan realized now, probably for the first time, that every one of them had just been substitutes. Mariellen was the one he wanted, and had wanted since he first met her down in Denver more than two months ago.

"I'm glad," Mariellen finally said.

"Glad?"

"That you aren't dead."

"Why, thank you, Miz Mariellen," Morgan said.

"You don't need to do that here."

"That's good."

Mariellen gave him another spoonful.

"What are you doing up here?"

"Chotauk and I brought in a load of handguns this morning."

"Where did you get them? The shipment Chotauk and I picked up at Juneau was nothing but rocks."

"Oh, didn't I tell you? I had another shipment ordered besides that one," Mariellen said. "It came in three days later without a hitch."

"Your uncle didn't tell me anything about that shipment."

"My uncle didn't know," Mariellen said. "We had a disagreement about how to get the guns up here. I wanted to show him my way would work so I tried it."

"And it worked?"

"Yes."

Morgan chuckled. "I'll bet you're the talk of the town right now," he said. "Everyone's been trying to get a load in and you're the only one to succeed."

"Oh, no one knows they're here yet," Mariellen said. "Chotauk hid them."

"What about Skagway Annie?" Morgan said. "Didn't she get a little curious about where you were going?"

Mariellen laughed. "Poor Skagway Annie. I'm afraid I wasn't very nice to her when I thought she was responsible for your disappearance. There was a fire . . . terrible thing, actually, it destroyed her hotel, saloon, why, would you believe that the flames even leaped two blocks away, sparing everything else but landing on a laundry she happened to own?"

"Sounds like a pretty educated fire to me," Morgan said.

"Yes, wasn't it? Tell me, Mr. Lee Morgan. How is it we found you lying on the snow in the livery with your head cracked open? Who hit you?"

"I don't know," Morgan answered. "Was there anyone else there? A thin, hooknosed, beady eyed man with a scraggly beard?"

"Should there have been?"

"I was talkin' to him when I got hit," Morgan said. "He's the one that's been trying to have me killed ever since I got here. He was just about to tell me who was paying him when the lights went out. There are a whole lot of things that just don't add up, Mariellen, but I figure that man has the answers."

"Yeah, well, you're going to have to find them somewhere else."

"Somewhere else? Why? What do you mean?"

"They found someone fitting that description down by the river," Mariellen said.

"Dead?"

"Shot right between the eyes."

"Damn."

"His name was Billy Joe Collins," Mariellen said. "That mean anything to you?"

"No, not really, I never . . . wait a minute. What did you say his name was?"

"Billy Joe Collins."

"B.J.C."

"Is that supposed to mean something?"

"Well, I don't know. I thought I had that part worked out. Now I'm not so sure."

Mariellen laughed. "Mr. Morgan, would it be possible that your brains are all scrambled up, like a mess of pork brains and eggs?"

"I don't know, maybe it doesn't make any sense," he said. He waved away another bite. "I've had enough."

Mariellen put the bowl down, then looked at him with eyes that were smoldering. "It's about time," she said. "I've got another treatment in mind now, and it has nothing to do with food."

"Oh? What sort of treatment would that be?" Morgan asked.

Mariellen began unbuttoning the fastenings on her heavy wool shirt. "It's a little hard to explain," she said. "I'm going to have to show you."

Morgan lay back on the pillow and watched as Mariellen removed her shirt, then the undershirt beneath it, then her undergarments.

Morgan wasn't a poetic man, he was not one to put into words things he felt, but he did have a sense of appreciation for things in a way that some men would say were poetic. He liked the sight of a lone candle in a window on a dark night . . . the sound of a swiftly moving stream of water . . . clouds when they were underlit by the setting sun . . . flowers in the wild. These were things that were special to him, though he could never say so. But if he ever did get around to making a compilation of what made life sweet, he would have to add to the list what he was seeing right now. Mariellen Chapel, her skin pink and glowing, her nipples drawn tight by the cold, the hair at the junction of her legs shadowed in mystery, was standing before him in all her nude glory.

Morgan had seen his share of naked women, some beautiful, some functional, and some whose nudity gave meaning to the word obscene. He may have even seen women more beautiful than Mariellen, but in the sum total of things, in this place and in this time, no one in the world could have made a more pleasurable impact on his senses than this girl did.

"Aren't you going to take off your shirt?" Mariellen asked.

"I intend to take off more than my shirt," Morgan said.

Mariellen laughed, a low, throaty laugh. "I don't think so," she said.

"Oh? Why not?"

"You don't have anything but a shirt on," Mariellen said.

Even as she spoke, Morgan felt his erection rubbing against the sheet. He realized now that it had been growing, unrestrained, from the moment she started stripping for him. It was just that he had been so appreciative of what he was seeing that he didn't realize it.

"Let me take it off for you," Mariellen said, and she leaned over to grasp the shoulders of the shirt in her hands.

As she did so her breasts swung forward and the nipple of one of them brushed against Morgan's lips. He opened his mouth and took her nipple inside, sucking on it, running his tongue over the congested little nub. She moaned in pleasure, and leaned into him for just a moment, the she pulled the shirt over his head and tossed it aside.

Morgan's penis was as hard and as rigid as stone. Already so engorged with blood as to be petrified, it was ready to perform whatever task he asked of it, to give no quarter until the sensations that had turned it to stone waned, allowing it to return to flesh again. Mariellen went to him, flushed and panting. She was trembling in every limb and her eyes were awash with tears of excitement. She pulled the covers back exposing Morgan, looking down at the organ which stood like a raised arm.

Without a word, Mariellen lowered to her knees, opened her mouth, closed it over his penis, and slid it a good way down her throat. Morgan brought his hands up to rest lightly on her soft hair. She moaned, then moved on down until her lips surrounded the very root of his member. Morgan looked down at her. Her eyes were half closed and fluttering, her cheeks deeply dimpled from the suction she was beginning to apply. Then she lifted one hand and gingerly cupped his balls, lolling her tongue around with the instinctive skill of a hungry calf. Morgan reached down and, with thumb and forefinger, teasingly pinched and pulled at her nipples. Through her left breast he could feel the wild pounding of her heart.

With a talent born of her desire, she sucked and lolled his penis, at the same time massaging his scrotum, moving along his member with varying pressures from base to tip, then swiftly reabsorbing him to its hairy hilt. Morgan could feel a familiar sensation deep in his loins, a sensation which grew stronger with her every movement and touch.

Then, exerting a little pressure on her head with his hands, he stopped her, and with a tortured sigh, she rose to her feet. "Don't you like?" she asked.

"Yeah," Morgan grunted. "But I wouldn't want to spoil our fun by finishing too fast."

Mariellen smiled at him and then threw a leg over his chest, mounting him as if she were mounting a horse. "Well, then," she said. "Maybe you can do it to me for a little while now."

Morgan waited expectantly as she moved the swollen, foam flecked lips of her sex to his mouth. With his first good taste of her he felt a frenzy of excitement, reaming her with his tongue as she quivered against it and squeezed it until the very roots hurt. Finally she pulled away from him.

"I want you in me now," she said. "I want to feel it deep inside."

Morgan rolled her over, noticing almost as an aside that his head no longer hurt . . . that he felt no more nausea from his movement. He thrust himself in her, shoving it up and in, hammering against the furthermost membrane of her being. She gnashed her teeth and rolled her eyes until only the whites showed and contorted against him as she was ravaged by her climax. Then, when she was in the middle of her orgasmic throes, he ejaculated, sending vast quantities of semen gushing into her to comingle with her own juices, then to drip out onto the bedsheet beneath them.

When he awakened later, she was sleeping curled up next to him, her head nestled against his shoulder, her leg thrown over his, her hand curled possessively around his flaccid member. It was dark, but that didn't mean a thing in this damned country. It could have been three o'clock in the morning, or three o'clock in the afternoon. It didn't matter. For the moment, the rest of the world could go to hell.

This was nice. This was really nice.

14

"Lee? Lee, are you awake?"

Morgan opened his eyes and realized that he was still in bed. Mariellen was standing just inside the door of the bedroom, as fully dressed as if she were going to church. For a moment he had to force himself to realize that the woman he was looking at now was the same woman who had been so much a part of his primordal urges a little earlier.

"Uh, yes," he said. "Yes, I'm awake."

"There is someone in the parlor to see you," Mariellen said. "Do you feel up to it?"

Morgan sat up. The pain was gone and only a small amount of the dizziness remained. He swung his legs over, realizing as he did so that he was still nude.

"I'll, uh, wait in the hall," Mariellen said quickly, and Morgan noticed that she actually blushed. He smiled at that. How could she still blush after everything they had done together, and for each other?

A few moments later, Morgan stepped out into

the hall, fully dressed. Mariellen was waiting for him.

"Who is it?" Morgan asked.

"An old acquaintance of yours, I believe," Mariellen said.

Morgan followed Mariellen to the parlor of Chotauk's house. There, he saw Big Ben Crowder waiting for him.

"So," Ben said, smiling and extending his hand. "I learn that the man who called himself Hank Leslie is actually Lee Morgan?"

"Yes," Morgan admitted.

"And you are a representative for Colt Firearms?"

"Yes," Morgan said again.

Crowder laughed. "So much for my step-daughter's innocent faith in you," he said.

"Crowder, I never told your stepdaughter I wasn't working for Colt Firearms. And I planned to make good on that delivery for her too. I was bushwhacked, if you remember."

"Ah, yes, I do remember."

"Anyway, you knew I was working for Colt Firearms. You did have instructions to meet me, didn't you? Aren't you B.J.C.?"

"Yes," Crowder said. "I'm sorry about the initials, but when I realized that Billy Joe Collins and I had the same initials, I thought I might be able to use that. Unfortunately he's dead now, so he'll be of no further use to me."

"Who killed him?"

"Yes, yes, that's very good," Crowder said. "Keep sayin' it just that way."

"Keep sayin' what?"

"Why, that you had nothin' to do with killin' Billy Joe Collins, of course."

"I didn't kill him."

"Morgan, this is Big Ben Crowder you're talkin' to, remember. We were sittin' together when you suddenly left the table and went up to Billy Joe at the bar. A moment later you walked out with him. I was just naturally curious, so I followed you to the livery."

"All right, you followed me. So what?"

"I heard a shot 'bout halfway there, so I commenced to run the rest of the distance. When I come up on the two of you, you was lyin' there with your gun in your hand an' Billy Joe was just across from you with a bullet hole 'twixt his eyes an' a zap in his hand."

"A what?"

"A zap. That's a little sack made out of hide, filled with lead balls. A good rap on the head can do a man in. Lucky for you, Billy Joe didn't kill you."

"Goddamnit, Crowder, Billy Joe didn't hit me. He didn't hit me, an' I didn't shoot him."

"I'm only tellin' what I seen an' done," Crowder said. "Anyhow, I seen the two of you lyin' there, him dead, you purt' near that way, so I done what I figured should be done. I got a'holt of Billy Joe's body an' I carried 'im outta the livery an' dumped him down by the river. That way, when you was found, folks thought someone just come up on you an' give you a good rap on the head."

"That is what happened, and I'm tired of you makin' more of it."

Crowder held out his hands. "Look, you don't have to convince me o'nothin'. I ain't the law. 'Sides which, I'm in this here thing as deep as you are now. I'm the one carted the body away, remember? An' I also put a bullet back in your gun so's no one could tell you'd just fired it."

"Goddamnit, I didn't fire it."

"Maybe not, maybe somebody else did an' put it in your hand," Crowder said. "Anyhow, I told Constable Bannister that I seen someone runnin' away from the livery. 'Course, that was when he was tryin' to find out who hit you . . . he didn't know nothin' 'bout Billy Joe then. That didn't come 'till later when someone found his body right where I put it."

Morgan shook his head, then he thought of something. "Tell me, Crowder, what about the liveryman? Where was he all this time?"

"Did you see him?"

"No."

"I didn't either. Fac' is, I hear tell the constable is lookin' for him, but he ain't found him neither."

"He's the key to all this," Morgan said. "If we could find him, he could tell us what happened . . . who it was that hit me from the rear."

"Yes, well, I don't reckon it matters none now," Crowder said. "I took what money Billy Joe had, so the constable thinks he was murdered an' robbed. He ain't put the two of you together at all. We can jus' let that drop an' get on to other business."

"What sort of business?"

Crowder smiled broadly. "Why, gun business, of course," he said. He looked over at Mariellen who had been present for the entire conversation, but had said nothing. "You have told him about the guns, ain't you?"

"He knows that Chotauk and I brought up a load, yes," she answered.

Crowder chuckled. "Ain't that somethin'? A

woman bringin' in guns like that, after so many others have failed? We been waitin' six months for a shipment of guns, and here this little ole' gal brings up a load." Crowder rubbed his hands together as if anticipating a feast. "Tell me, Miss Mariellen, how many guns did you bring?"

"One hundred and fifty."

"A hunnert an' fifty? What kind? Was they all handguns?"

"Peacemakers, every one of them," Mariellen said.

"Good, good. Them's the best kind," Crowder said. He leaned back in his chair and crossed his arms across his chest. "You hear that?" he asked Morgan. "Peacemakers."

"I heard."

"This here is your lucky day, Miss Mariellen," Crowder went on. "I'm gonna give you one-hundred dollars apiece for each an' ever' one of them guns."

Mariellen didn't say a word.

"Didn't you hear me?" Crowder asked, smiling broadly. "A hunnert dollars apiece. That's fifteen thousand dollars."

"Yes, I can do my math," Mariellen said.

"Well, I was beginnin' to wonder if you heard me there. I guess you was just took back over how much money you just made yourself. Yes, sir, let these here fools break rocks for their gold. This is a much better way, don't you think?" Crowder stood up. "When will you be bringin' the guns to me?"

"I haven't said I'll do it, yet," Mariellen said.

The smile froze on Crowder's face. "What do you mean?"

"I thought the meaning was quite clear, Mr.

Crowder. I haven't accepted your offer.''

"Why the hell not?" Crowder exploded. "You ain't plannin' on gettin' no better offer from anyone, are you?"

"I don't know. I suppose that's a possibility. I would like to wait and see."

Crowder got up from the chair and walked over to the halltree where he recovered his parka. He started putting it on. His eyes narrowed as he looked over at Mariellen.

"It was my thinkin', Miss Chapel, that we, meanin' me an' you, an' your uncle, had us a understandin' about all this. We was gonna stake out a marketplace for the Colt Firearm Company."

He looked over at Morgan. "Hell, you're supposed to be a representative for Colt Firearms. What do you say to all this?"

"You're telling us this is all out of loyalty to Colt?" Morgan asked.

"You're damn right it is. When Big Ben Crowder makes a business deal, he sticks to it. I said I would sell Colts in the Klondike, and I will."

"If that's the case, Crowder, why were you so willin' to take the shipment of Remingtons from me?" Morgan asked.

"You know why I was takin' 'em. My step-daughter was tryin' to make a few dollars an' I was willin' to help out, that's all. 'Sides which, I figured to buy 'em and take 'em off the market."

"Yeah," Morgan said. "Well, you weren't the only one wantin' to take 'em off the market. That's why Billy Joe Collins sent the welcomin' party out to meet me."

Crowder had his parka and fur hat on now, and

he looked at Morgan in puzzlement when Morgan said that about the welcoming party.

"Look here, are you tellin' me that Billy Joe was the one tried to have you ambushed?"

"That's right."

"I'll be damned. I never figured him for much more'n a cheap crook. Didn't figure he had enough sense to get involved in anythin' this big."

"He wasn't in it alone," Morgan said. "That's what I was talkin' to him about. He was about ready to tell me who was backing him, when I got hit over the head."

Crowder stroked his chin for a moment. "All right, maybe you didn't kill him," he conceded. "All I know is what I found an' to me it looked bad . . . so bad that I figured I ought to change it before someone else seen it. If I done wrong, I'm sorry . . . but I was just tryin' to do you a favor."

"Yeah, well, I hope that favor don't come back to haunt me," Morgan said.

Crowder started toward the door, then looked over at Mariellen again.

"Miss Chapel, I think you're gonna find that there's plenty of money to be made up here, iffen we don't none of us get too greedy. What we've got to do is all of us got to work together . . . just like me an' your uncle has done . . . and just like I done for you, Morgan, when I carried off Billy Joe's body. I hope the two of you think some about what I'm telling you. I'll see you around."

"I'll be damned," Morgan said, after Crowder left.

"What?"

"He didn't make me an offer for the guns he

thinks I've got hid out."

"Do you have some guns hidden on the trail?" Mariellen asked.

"No, but he doesn't know that. Just before I had my run-in with whoever knocked me out, I told Crowder that I had off-loaded some of the guns before the ambush. He was so anxious to get the guns from you, why didn't he make me an offer?"

"I don't know," Mariellen said. "You just told him you had guns hidden, but you didn't really, is that right?"

"Right."

Mariellen laughed. "That's funny," she said. "That's really funny."

"Why is it so funny?"

"I don't have any guns either."

"Would you mind tellin' me why the hell you're letting it be known that you have guns if you don't?"

"Simple," Mariellen said. "If you want to catch whose been raiding your hen house, you set out a chicken. I'm just dangling a little bait, that's all."

"You were part of the bait," Morgan said.

"I suppose I was."

"If you've spent any time around traps, Mariellen, you notice that even when you catch what you're after, the bait nearly always gets eaten. You were taking an awful risk."

"I had Chotauk with me."

"One of the men who came after me on the trail had a .50 Sharps," Morgan growled. "A .50 Sharps will drop a buffalo, a polar bear, a grizzly, and, Miss Mariellen, it will drop Chotauk."

"What about you?" Mariellen asked. "You did

the same thing, didn't you?"

"That's different."

"Why? Because you're a man and I'm a woman?"

"That might have something to do with it," Morgan agreed.

"Lee Morgan, they call me the Queen of the Klondike for a very good reason," Mariellen said. "I run this country up here, and I run it because I know how, and when to take chances. I'm not some little schoolmarm from Denver, I'm an arctic she-wolf. And I remind you that a bullet will go through you just as easily as it will through me. So don't tell me how to run my business."

Morgan laughed and held up his hands in mock surrender. "All right, all right," he said. "But, if we're both going after the same critters, with the same bait, then the least we can do is work together."

Mariellen smiled sweetly. "Now, Lee Morgan, you are making sense. You'll find I'm a lot easier to get along with when you're working with me, instead of against me."

15

"I must say, you and your lady friend have created quite a furor in town," Constable Bannister said as he poured a cup of steaming tea, first for Morgan, then for himself.

"Yeah," Morgan replied. "I never knew that many people were gun fanciers."

Bannister laughed. "Gun fanciers, oh that's good," he said. "Yes, that is good indeed." He blew on the surface of his tea then slurped it over the rim of his cup. "You are both in quite a bit of danger, you know," he added.

"I suppose so," Morgan agreed.

"Tell me, Mr. Morgan, why do I get the distinct impression that this is exactly what you wanted?"

"Constable, there have already been several good men killed while trying to open up the market for handguns. I don't think they were just isolated cases. I think there is a grand design behind it all."

"To what end, Mr. Morgan?"

"Do you know how much money a single

handgun can bring in this town?"

"Yes, I do. I was quite astounded to hear that people are willing to pay up to $150 for a pistol."

"That's a lot of money," Morgan said. "You could sell two thousand pistols here in Dawson, at least that many in Whitehorse, and in all of the Territorites and Alaska, probably as many as twenty-thousand handguns. Are you adding all that up?"

Bannister let out a low whistle. "That's three million dollars," he noted.

"Yes, and it's a hell of a lot easier than blasting holes in the sides of mountains or panning an icy stream."

"And you believe there is someone behind all this, trying to corner the market?"

"Yes."

"You may very well be right, Mr. Morgan." Bannister got up from his chair and walked over to a file drawer. He opened it, then looked through the papers until he pulled out a large, brown envelope. He brought the envelope over to Morgan.

"What's that?"

"This, Mr. Morgan, is something that I could get into trouble over, if it were known that I shared it with you. It's the last report submitted by Timothy McCutcheon."

Morgan opened the envelope and took out the single page report. It had been composed on a typewriting machine and was very easy to read.

REPORT ON UNSOLVED MURDERS
IN TERRITORIES AND ALASKA
SUBMITTED BY
FIELD AGENT TIMOTHY McCUTCHEON

1. In the last year there have been five (5) unsolved murders in portions of the Northwest Territories and U.S. Alaska.

2. The method in which each of these men were killed, and the events leading up to the discovery of their bodies, have differed in every case. Two of the victims were long time residents of the north country, three were newcomers.

3. There has been one thing common to all five murders. Each of the victims were engaged in gun dealing, either in the introduction of weapons into the territories, or the distribution of guns already available.

4. It is the conclusion of this agent that the murders are not random, but rather the design of a person or persons who, for their own nefarious scheme, wishes to eliminate all who deal in firearms.

5. My personal investigation has led me to believe that Mr. Frank Church, a local businessman, should be questioned about his possible involvement in this.

Morgan put the report back into the envelope, then looked up at Bannister. "What did headquarters say about this report?"

"Nothing," Bannister said.

"Nothing? Why not?"

"They never received the report."

"Why not?"

Bannister pointed to the envelope. "You'll

notice that the report was done on a typewriting machine?"

"Yes."

"And it wasn't sighed," Bannister went on. "Without McCutcheon's handwritten report, or, at the very least, his signature affixed thereto, this isn't a valid report. As it was done on one of those machines, it could have been prepared by anyone . . . for any reason. Therefore, officially, the report doesn't even exist."

"What about unofficially?"

"Unofficially, I tried to submit it," Bannister said. "I sent it under the cover of my own letter, handwritten and signed, by me, attesting to the authenticity of the document. But regulations are regulations, Mr. Morgan, and I'm afraid it was to no avail. The document came back to me with a note saying that it would not be received."

"But you said it would get you in trouble if you showed it to anyone."

"Yes, even though it is not a valid document, it is still the official property of the Northwest Mounted Police, and therefore not authorized to be viewed by any civilian."

"What about this man, Frank Church? Have you spoken with him?"

"I've tried . . . believe me, I've tried. He has an office in a small room above the mercantile store, but he hasn't been seen there for several months now."

"Any idea where he is?"

"He left word that he was going to spend the winter in the States. He asked the mercantile store to hold his mail for him."

"Did you take a look at his mail?"

Bannister smiled. "I did," he said. "I had no

authority to do so, but I feel that sometimes investigations, if they are to bear fruit, need not necessarily be restrained by lines of authorization. Therefore, I managed to take a look at the mail once, when the proprietor of the mercantile store wasn't looking."

"What did you find?"

"Nothing of any help, I'm afraid. A few responses from mail order houses, a calendar from a Denver bank, and a bill for some engraved stationery. No personal letters, nothing to give a clue as to where he might be, or when he might be coming back."

"I wish I knew what made McCutcheon suspect him," Morgan said. He looked down at the report again, and noticed crease lines across the paper where it had once been folded. Curious, he refolded it, then reached in his pocket and removed the envelope he had been carrying ever since it was slipped under the door on board the ship coming up. The envelope too, had been folded over once, and the crease line in McCutcheon's report fit exactly with the crease line in the envelope.

"My word," Bannister said when he saw what Morgan had done. "It would appear that the report was once in that same envelope."

"Yes," Morgan said. He rubbed his chin as he looked at the envelope, now with the report inside. He tapped it with his finger. "Are you a betting man, Constable?"

"No, not really."

"Too bad, because I would be willing to bet a ton that this is the way the envelope was meant to reach me. But somehow, someone got to it before I did and they removed the report."

"But . . . how could that be?" Bannister asked. "The report is right here and has been all along."

"Go over to your file drawer and pull out three other reports," Morgan said. "No, pull out five."

Bannister looked puzzled. "Reports about what?"

"About anything, Constable," Morgan said. "It doesn't make any difference."

Shaking his head in confusion, the constable did as Morgan requested. He pulled out five reports and dropped the big, brown envelopes on the desk in front of Morgan.

"Open the envelopes and pull them out." Morgan suggested.

Bannister did so, then looked up at Morgan, still as confused as before.

"What do you see?" Morgan asked.

"Well, this report is asking for an increase in the allotment for food for the dog teams . . . this one deals with illegal gambling on the riverboats during the summer months . . . this one—"

"No," Morgan interrupted. "Don't look at what's on them, just look at them. What do you see?"

The confusion stayed on Bannister's face for a moment longer, then he suddenly smiled as he realized what Morgan was getting at. He pointed at them.

"They are all flat," he said. "Not one of them has been folded."

"Right. I realized as soon as I saw the large envelopes that it was so the reports wouldn't be folded. And yet this one was. Someone got in here, took the report out, folded it, and put it in this smaller envelope."

"Then that same person, or another person, took the report out of the small envelope and returned it to the large one," Bannister concluded.

"It looks that way," Morgan said. "Who else, besides you, can get into the files?"

"No one besides me, Mr. Morgan," Bannister said.

"Someone sure as hell did."

"Perhaps it was the person who gave you a whack," Bannister suggested.

Involuntarily, Morgan rubbed the top of his head. "I sure wish I knew who that was."

"Yes, well, the only witness we have is Mr. Crowder who found you lying on the ground and saw someone running out the back. Of course, the liveryman could substantiate that if I could just talk to him, but so far I haven't been able to do that," Bannister said. "I was hoping he might be able to tell us something, even if it was just to give me a list of people he saw at the stable that day."

"You still haven't found him?"

"No," Bannister said. "To tell you the truth, I'm beginning to suspect foul play. He hasn't been seen by anyone in four days."

"Has he ever left his stable that long before?"

"Oh, yes, frequently, when he goes to White-horse or someplace like that. But always before he has made some arrangement for his business. This time, he didn't appear to do that."

"Maybe he did see who whacked me over the head," Morgan said. "Although I don't remember seeing the liveryman around."

"Yes, and then there is the case of Billy Joe Collins," Bannister said. "I have to tell you, Mr. Morgan, had you not been found unconscious in the stable, you would have been my prime suspect in that case. You were seen leaving the

North Star with him."

"He had some information I wanted," Morgan said. "I was talking to him when someone hit me."

Bannister's eyes widened. "You were? See here, I wasn't aware of that."

"Were you aware that Billy Joe Collins is the man who paid to have me bushwhacked on the trail?"

"No."

"And were you also aware that he was the one who posed as a mounted policeman to pay the fella to try and shoot me at the livery stable the day I arrived?"

"No, I didn't know that either. Mr. Morgan, I hope you realize that the more you tell me now, the more you are piling suspicion upon yourself for his death."

"Yeah, but we come back to the same thing, don't we? I was lying unconscious on the ground in the livery, he was found dead down by the river. I sure didn't kill him there, then come back and hit myself over the head."

"Unless you killed him by the river, then came to the livery bent on taking your horse out to make good your escape, at which time you were attacked."

"Do you believe that's what happened?" Morgan asked. "Do you think I killed Collins?"

Bannister studied Morgan for a long moment, then shook his head slowly. "No, Mr. Morgan. I don't think you did. But I'll tell you what I'm afraid of."

"What?"

"We're going to find the liveryman just the way we did Mr. Collins. Belly up in the snow."

16

Clayton Summers urged the dogs on. There was a storm coming and he wanted to make as much time as he could before he was forced to stop. He'd heard there were Indian villages spread out all along the trail . . . no more than fifty miles apart, people said. He wouldn't know about that. He had never come this way before, nor had he ever traveled by dogsled. He had always come and gone by boat, leaving Dawson only in the summer months when travel was relatively easy.

He'd ventured up from Kansas a few years ago, intending to stay four years. His plan was to return home with enough money to buy a farm. He didn't quite have four years in Dawson yet, he had six months to go, but recent events made it seem like a good idea for him to leave while the leaving was good.

He thought back to what had happened four days ago. He had been lying in one of the stalls, wrapped in blankets and skins, keeping warm with a bottle of whiskey, when he heard Morgan and Collins come into the livery. He raised up when he heard Morgan threaten to shoot Collins. What happened next, happened so fast that Summers was taken totally by surprise. A man suddenly came out of nowhere to bash Morgan over the head. The man had his back to Summers, and he was dressed in furs so that it was impossible to tell who it was.

"Am I glad to see you," Collins had said.

"Don't be," the man replied.

That was when Summers saw the flash from the pistol, saw the black hole appear between Collins' eyes, then saw him go down. He got up then, and ran toward the back of the barn.

"Hey, you! Come back here!" the killer had shouted, as if Summers was crazy enough to actually do it.

Summers hadn't kept his money in the bank. It was a foreign bank and he didn't trust foreigners, so it was easy enough for him to go to his cache and take out the money he had saved. It was a little more difficult for him to get a dog team and sled together to leave. He had to pay twice what they were worth, and as dogs were the only means of transportation in and out of Dawson for several months at a time, they were worth a great deal.

Summers hated the damned dogs. Give him a horse anytime. The problem with a horse, of course, was that there was no way he could carry enough food for the animal. He had heard stories of horses dropping dead on the trail from starvation. Dogs would eat frozen salmon, that made them manageable, but as far as Summers was concerned, it sure as hell didn't make them any more desirable.

Summers urged the dogs on to greater and greater speed. He wanted to get away, to get all the way down to Juneau of possible. There, he would take the next boat south. He wondered how far he had to go, and he looked around to try and get his bearings.

Where the hell was he?

He had purposedly avoided the main trail because he was afraid that the killer would come after him, and since Summers was inexperienced with dog teams, the killer would have no difficulty in overtaking him. But since he left the trail, he was having more and more difficulty with navigation. He tried using the stars, but the sky had been so overcast for the last several hours that he had been unable to take a sighting. And now it was beginning to snow. The situation was getting much worse.

Manquit was on the route from a remote Athabascan village to Dawson early the next day, as soon as the storm had passed. He was a young, powerfully muscled Athabascan Indian, but even Manquit, who was used to such conditions, found it hard going on this steep, and little used trail. Then, as he topped one particularly steep rise, he came upon a pitiful sight.

A man, frozen stiff, his face blanketed with snow, huddled on the ground alongside a pitiful heap of frozen sled dogs. Manquit didn't know the name of the frozen white man, but he did recognize him as the one who ran the livery stable in Dawson. Using his knife and hatchet, Manquit managed to break the frozen body loose from the ice and load him into the sled for the journey back to Dawson.

The mysterious death of Clayton Summers was the talk of the North Star Saloon. At every table his name was mentioned, stories were told about him, and speculations were advanced as to why he would have taken his entire poke and just skedaddled in the middle of the winter like that. The fact that he was off the main route added fuel to the speculation, though many said that was just a result of his inexperience with dog teams. A few pointed out that the murder of Billy Joe Collins was still unsolved, and wondered if there was any connection between the two. Even Morgan's name was mentioned as he had been found unconscious in Summer's livery, and no one could recall having seen Summer since that time.

Morgan heard his name on a few lips as he went into the saloon, but he made no effort to hear what was being said or who was talking about him. He knew that he was the center of attention right now and, for his purposes, it didn't bother him. If he was right in the middle of things, he would better be able to see what was going on around him. He stepped up to the bar and ordered a whiskey.

The bartender poured him a drink, then moved down the bar to attend to another customer. Morgan turned his back to the bar and looked out over the room. There were two stoves roaring in the middle of the room and though they turned back the sub-zero weather, it could hardly be said that the saloon was comfortably warm. In fact, everyone here continued to wear their parkas and caps, though the heavy mittens were removed to facilitate drinking and handling of cards. Or guns, Morgan thought, though as he looked around he noticed that not too many men were actually carrying pistols, evidence of the need for the product he was representing.

Ensconced at his regular table across the room

near the wall was Big Ben Crowder. When Morgan looked toward him, Crowder invited him over. Morgan took his drink with him and crossed the room to join the big man.

"Well," Crowder said. "I'm sure that by now you and Miss Chapel have talked to each other and she knows that you've also got some handguns up here."

"We've talked," Morgan said.

"I figured you would," Crowder said. "I didn't bring it up in front of her 'cause she seemed to be tendin' to you pretty well an' if she knew you was in competition with her she might not be so friendly to you."

"It's good to know you were just lookin' out for my interests," Morgan said dryly.

"Yeah, I know, you don't believe me," Crowder said, "but it is true. Now I think it's time you an' me come to some sort of agreement. I want to buy those guns from you."

"What about your stepdaughter?"

"What about her?"

"Technically these guns are hers. They are a part of her shipment."

"No, they're not," Crowder said. "Her shipment got blown up in the bushwhacker's attack. These guns are yours and she don't even come into the picture. I'm willing to buy them from you."

"How much?"

"One hundred-and-twenty-five dollars," Crowder said.

"Why are you being so generous to me?" Morgan asked. "That's more than you offered Miss Chapel. Why not raise the offer to her?"

"Oh, for a very good reason," Crowder said,

smiling confidently. He leaned back in his chair and folded his arms across his chest. "I want you to tell her that you sold the guns to me for seventy-five dollars each. When she realizes that you have undersold her, she'll be forced to come down in price in order to do business."

"What makes you think I would do such a thing?"

"Because, Mr. Morgan, in the short run, it's good business. In the long run, it will even be good for Miss Chapel. She'll sell her guns at a fair profit . . . not a gougers' profit mind you, but at a fair profit. And, she'll have a foothold in Dawson for her guns."

"It's good to see that you are looking out for everyone," Morgan said.

Crowder chuckled. "Well, like I told Miss Chapel, there's plenty enough money up here for all of us to get rich, if we just don't get too greedy over it. Now, what do you say? Do we have a deal?"

Morgan stroked his chin for a moment, then nodded. "Yeah, Crowder," he said. "We've got a deal."

"Good, good," Crowder said, rubbing his hands together eagerly. "Now, how many guns do you have? And what kind are they?"

"Remington Frontier .44s," Morgan said.

"Ah, yes, just like the Peacemaker."

"They don't have as good a balance," Morgan said.

"Well, you should know. But believe me, Morgan, I could sell flintlock pistols up here."

"I'm sure you would."

Crowder laughed. "Oh, yes, I would if I had them. Now, how many of these guns do you have?"

"Twenty five."

"Let's see, that would be $3,125," Crowder said. "All right, Mr. Morgan, you deliver the pistols to me and I'll pay you, cash on delivery."

"You'll have them by nine o'clock," Morgan said. He started to get up from his seat when a big, meaty hand suddenly, and roughly, pushed him back down into the chair.

"No! You no cheat Lady Boss!" Chotauk said.

"You stay the hell out of this, you goddamned Eskimo!" Crowder shouted, standing up across the table.

Chotauk brushed Morgan aside as if he were no more than a fly and went after Crowder. Crowder didn't give ground and the two men met in the middle of the table which had suddenly turned into kindling wood.

Chotauk drove a right into Crowder's jaw, knocking him back against the wall. Though a large man himself, Crowder wasn't quite as large as Chotauk, but he did have a leathery toughness about him, and he was a man who had been tried many times so that he was a skilled barroom fighter. He also had a killer instinct, and such an instinct served him exceptionally well in a fight where there were no rules.

Crowder drove a low, whistling right into Chotauk's groin, catching him by surprise and numbing him with the ferocity of the blow to his balls. Chotauk let out a bellow of pain and dropped both hands to protect himself. Crowder smiled, confidently. He was confident, but he was no fool. He knew he would have to get in a telling blow quickly, so while Chotauk was still doubled over in pain, Crowder slammed a fist into Chotauk's Adam's apple. Chotauk staggered back toward the bar and Crowder followed him, hitting him two more times with blows that would stun a buffalo. Finally, Chotauk went down to his knees, so far having thrown only one blow . . . the first one of the fight.

"Come on, you big Eskimo, get up and fight!" some of the crowd shouted.

"Finish 'im off, Big Ben," others encouraged.

In fact, very few cared who won the fight. They were watching it as a diversion and bets were rapidly placed as if this were a match put on by the gaming commission.

News of the fight spread fast and more than a dozen new men rushed in through the door to see the collision of the two giants.

Crowder, intending to make quick work of Chotauk, drew back for one final, telling blow to put him away. Though Crowder had gotten the upper hand, temporarily, Chotauk wasn't out of it, and he saw Crowder get set for a roundhouse right. At the last possible instant, Chotauk jerked his head to one side. Crowder's hand slid past and slammed hard into the bar, crashing through the front and temporarily holding him, like a bear with its paw caught in a trap. That gave Chotauk the opportunity to send a short, brutal right into Crowder's belly, drawing a loud grunt and knocking Crowder loose from the bar, sending him backwards with quick little steps to keep him from falling down. Chotauk used that opportunity to jump to his feet.

By now Crowder realized that he had lost his advantage. His only hope over the big Eskimo had been to take him out by surprise, but Chotauk had taken everything Crowder could dish out and was now coming at him on even terms. Desperately, Crowder sent a left jab toward Chotauk, but Chotauk slipped it easily and countered with a short right hook to Crowder's jaw. It was only the third time Chotauk had swung at Crowder, but all three punches had landed with telling effectiveness.

Crowder tried another left jab, hoping to set Chotauk up for a roundhouse right. Chotauk took the jab in order to get in close. He hooked Crowder with a left, then caught him flush with a hard right, and Crowder went down.

"Get up, Big Ben. Get up!" some of his supporters were yelling. "Get up, get up!"

Crowder struggled to his feet, then reached for a chair. Raising it over his head he started for Chotauk. Chotauk stood his ground. He had a clear, unobstructed shot at Crowder's jaw, and he put everything into a roundhouse right which lifted Crowder from the floor, then sent him crashing through another table. Crowder lay on the floor with his mouth open, his jaws slack, and his eyes closed, totally unconscious.

"Holy shit, did you see that?" someone asked.

"You reckon he broke his neck?"

"Naw, look at the bastard. He's sleepin' like a dog in the sun."

Chotauk looked over at Morgan and pointed at him. "You no cheat Boss Lady," he said. "We go get guns, bring them to town, sell them ourselves."

17

Skagway Annie stood at the window of her room, Room 212 of the Klondike Hotel, and looked down on Main Street. A few minutes earlier she had seen several people running across the street to the North Star Hotel and she sent Cole and Pascal to find out what was going on.

The three of them had arrived this morning. They came to Dawson when Annie found out that was where Mariellen Chapel had gone. She had a score to settle with the bitch who called herself the Queen of the Klondike, and if she had to follow her to hell to take care of it, she was willing to do so. So far, Mariellen didn't know she was here, and that was the way she intended to keep it. She heard a pounding on the door and walked over to open it. Cole and Pascal were standing on the other side.

"Well, did you find out what was going on?" she asked.

"Yeah. There was one hell of a fight," Cole said.

"I thought it might be something like that,"

152

Annie said. "Well, that's none of our concern. What we need to do is find out where—"

"You might be interested in it," Cole interrupted. "It was between that big Eskimo that follows Miss Chapel around all the time, and a fella they call Big Ben Crowder."

"Yeah," Pascal said. "And it was over guns. Lots of guns."

Annie smiled. "Really? It could be that our luck is changing," she said. "What did you find out?"

The two gunmen told of the conversation they had overheard between Morgan and Crowder . . . about the guns that were hidden somewhere. And they told of the big Eskimo's challenge to Morgan.

"That's what he said? That he and Mariellen would get the guns and bring them in to sell themselves?" Annie asked.

"That's what he said."

Annie's eyes flashed with excitement, and she walked back over to the window to look down on the town again.

"Well, now, ain't that a lucky break for us? Looks to me like we're gonna kill two birds with one stone. We can follow Queenie and her polar bear out to where they have the guns, take care of them, and get the guns."

"How do you want to take care of them?"

Annie looked around from the window. "Take care of them," she said coldly, but without elaboration.

The two gunmen looked at each other and smiled. Further elaboration wasn't needed. Annie turned back to the window and her eyes grew cold and distant. "I'll teach that bitch to burn me out," she said.

* * *

When Chotauk and Mariellen drove their dog team through the middle of Dawson, there wasn't a person in the entire town who didn't know where they were going. And there were quite a few who gave a passing thought to following them, to discovering for themselves where the treasure trove of guns was hidden. Rumors had been flying about town ever since she arrived, and some were saying there were as many as one-thousand guns buried in the snow out there, though how one-thousand guns could have been brought up on one dog sled, no one stopped to consider.

They did stop to consider whether or not they wanted to follow her out though. The ones who hadn't actually witnessed the fight between Chotauk and Crowder had heard of it, and no one wanted to go up against Miss Mariellen Chapel's bodyguard.

No one, that is, except the two gunman who were being paid by Skagway Annie Thompson to follow, and take care of, Mariellen Chapel and her bodyguard. And, in the process, bring back the guns.

Cole and Pascal waited a full half hour before they left with their own team. They left casually, heading east, as if they were going up into one of the Indian villages to trade for pelts. Mariellen and Chotauk had been heading south when they left town, so Cole and Pascal were positive that the different directions would throw off anyone of a suspicious nature.

No more than a mile out of town, Cole and Pascal turned south. They were both experienced dog sledders and they felt that by pushing their team, they would quickly cut the trail of the people they were following. They would stay back, far enough that they were completely out of sight, so Mariellen and Chotauk wouldn't suspect they were being followed. That way there would be no hesitancy about getting the guns. It wouldn't be very productive to catch up with them before they got to the guns, because then they would lose out.

Morgan had built a snow shelter and he was waiting in it, wrapped in caribou robes to keep warm. He heard the dogs approaching and he stood up to meet them.

"Anyone following?" he asked.

"I don't know," Chotauk answered. "I see no one."

"Maybe no one came," Mariellen suggested.

"Don't say that," Morgan said. "That would mean we put on that little show for nothing."

"Wait," Chotauk said, holding up his hand. "I hear dogs."

The three of them were silent for a long moment, then Morgan heard it, the long, thin yap of dogs on the trail.

"All right," Morgan said. "Someone did take the bait. You know what to do?"

"Yes," Mariellen said. "We'll be digging in the snow over there, while you're hidden out here."

"Right."

"Lee, I don't suppose I have to remind you that we're depending on you to not let anything happen, do I?"

Morgan chuckled. "Doesn't it make you wish you had been nicer to me when we first met?"

The barks grew louder and Mariellen and

Chotauk hurried over to put on their act. There were, of course, no guns at all. The *argument* between Chotauk and Morgan had merely been to call attention to the suggestion that there were guns, and Chotauk's assertion that he and Mariellen would bring the guns in to sell themselves was to see who they could get to fall into their trap. Now, it appeared that someone was about to do so.

Morgan hurried into a place of concealment, being careful to take a wide route around so that footprints would not give away his position. He waited until the uncoming dog sled approached.

There were two men on the sled, but they were so bundled up that Morgan couldn't see them well enough to identify them, even if he knew them. As the sled approached, one of them pushed down on the brake, a little spade device that dug into the snow, and the sled stopped. Chotauk and Mariellen looked around at them.

"Well, now, lookie here what we have," one of the two men said. "If it ain't the Queen of the Klondike and her pet polar bear."

"Cole, Pascal," Mariellen said. She said the names loud enough for Morgan to hear them, warning him in that way that these weren't just a couple of sourdoughs out to make an easy dollar. These were professional gunfighters. "What are you doing up here? I thought you were down in Skagway."

"Yeah? What would we be doing down there?" Cole asked angrily. "You burned half the god-damned town before you left."

"Yes, I do seem to recall a fire," Mariellen said.

"Have you dug 'em up yet?" Pascal asked, pointing to the snow.

"Dug what up?" Mariellen asked innocently.

"Look, sister, don't play dumb with us. We know you come out here lookin' for the guns you got hid. So be a nice girl an' dig 'em up for us."

Chotauk took a step toward the two men and they both had their guns out, amazingly fast considering the fact that they were so bundled up against the cold.

"Tell the polar bear to stop or we'll see how many bullets it takes to stop him," Pascal growled.

"Chotauk," Mariellen said quietly.

The big Eskimo stopped.

Pascal grinned. "Yeah, I like to see that. I like it the way you have him trained."

"Don't judge Chotauk by yourselves," Mariellen said. "He's a loyal friend. He's not a lap dog the way you two are to Annie Thompson."

"Yeah, well he's gonna be a dead friend if he takes another step. Now, dig up them guns."

"There are no guns."

"Don't give me that. Ever'one in town is talkin' about 'em. Now dig 'em up and load 'em on the sled. And be quick about it, we ain't got all day."

"I told you, there aren't any guns."

"And I told you to quit lyin' to me. Load 'em up."

"She isn't lying," Morgan suddenly said, appearing behind the two men.

"What the?" Cole asked, spinning around with his revolver in his hand.

"No, don't," Morgan shouted, and he pointed his pistol right at Cole's head. "Unless you want to be dead."

"Cole, remember them two wood parrots he shot?" Pascal warned.

"Yeah," Cole growled. "I remember."

"I'm glad you remember," Morgan said. "I'm even better at shooting lap dogs."

Mariellen and Chotauk both laughed.

"The lady was right, you know," Morgan went on. "There are no guns."

"But I don't understand. Why have you been tellin' ever'one you had guns out here?"

"We were just baiting the trap to see who we would catch," Mariellen said. She smiled, prettily. "And look who came waltzing in."

"Yeah," Morgan said. "The only thing is, we set bait for a fox and we caught a couple of weasels."

"You mean you don't think they are the ones?"

"No. They aren't smart enough to be the ones we're after."

"But they work for Skagway Annie. If's she's not smart enough, nobody is," Mariellen protested.

"Oh, I agree, Annie is smart enough, all right. But she's not the one we're after. My guess is these boys were after something entirely different from our mastermind."

"Just what were you going to do out here?" Mariellen asked.

"We was supposed to take care of you then bring the guns back to Miss Thompson," Cole said.

"Cole, shut the hell up," Pascal ordered. "You don't have to blabber everything you know."

"I don't intend to take the rap all by myself," Cole defended.

"When did you three arrive from Skagway?" Morgan asked.

"Yesterday," Cole said.

"Can you prove that?" Mariellen asked.

"Prove it? No," Cole said. He looked confused. "I don't understand, why the hell should I have to prove when I got here? There ain't no law against comin' up here if I want to."

"Do you believe him?" Mariellen asked.

"Yes," Morgan said. "He's too goddamned dumb to lie about it."

"What do we do with them?"

"Chotauk, get their guns," Morgan said. "About the only thing we can do is send them back."

"You can't take our guns away from us," Pascal complained. "You can't turn us lose up here with no way to defend ourselves."

"Why you two no account bastards," Morgan said. "There are more people up here without guns than there are with. And by taking your guns away from you we've made those people a lot safer."

Chotauk took the guns, then looked at the two disarmed men and laughed. "Too bad we not learn," he said.

"Learn? Learn what?"

"How many bullets you can put in polar bear, before polar bear kill you," Chotauk said easily.

18

"And nobody showed up?"

"Only the two hardcases that work for Skagway Annie," Morgan said. "And I don't think they are the ones we're after."

"Don't you think they are capable of killing?" Constable Bannister asked.

"Oh, yes, not only capable, but I'm certain they've done their share," Morgan said. "It's just that they aren't behind all of this, and neither is Skagway Annie."

"That leaves us right back where we started," Bannister said.

"Not quite, I have a few bumps and bruises I didn't have when all this started," Crowder said with a chuckle.

"Well, you said it yourself, Ben, you wanted to make the fight as real as possible," Morgan said.

"Yes, well, I guess I said that because I thought I could whip him. It's all right to make the fight real if I'm going to win. But if I'm going to lose, that's something else again."

Both Morgan and Bannister laughed at

Crowder's observation.

"I'm sorry I couldn't tell you earlier that Crowder was the one who tried to get the report to you," Bannister said. "Of course, since it was all unofficial, that was the only way it could be done."

"It was all arranged," Crowder went on. "Bannister let me know by a certain signal that he would be gone from the office for five minutes. That was all the time I needed to sneak in and get the report."

"And the envelope it came in?"

"That was easy," Crowder said. "I got it from my stepson's files. Then I put the report in the envelope, dropped that in another envelope, and mailed it to you."

"Why did you use another envelope?"

"Simple. I didn't want anyone seeing the RCMP seal on the outside envelope, because if the wrong person saw it, it would be a simple matter for them to intercept it. I included the RCMP envelope so you would realize that the report was authentic."

"Of course, what we didn't anticipate was that someone intercepted your mail anyway," Bannister explained. "They opened it, took out the RCMP envelope, then took out the report that was inside, and slipped the RCMP envelope under your door."

"That's what I don't understand," Crowder said. "Why didn't they take all of it? Why did they give him the envelope?"

"It was probably just their way of having some fun with me," Morgan said. "But it backfired on them because it has led me this far, and now I've read the report they didn't want me to see."

"Yes," Bannister said. "You can imagine my

surprise when the report turned up in my mail a short while later. I didn't know what to do about it, so I merely put it back in the original envelope . . . although, of course, it now had creases, as you so cleverly observed."

"Frank Church," Morgan said. "It all boils down to who he is . . . and where he is."

"Yes, well, I've been thinking about that," Bannister said. "Have you ever considered synonyms, Mr. Morgan?"

"Synonyms?"

"Yes, synonyms. Sometimes a clever criminal when constructing a new identity for himself, will—"

"Constable! Constable, come quick!"

Bannister stood up and moved quickly to the door of his little office. "What is it?" he asked.

"There's a couple of galoots in the North Star gettin' awful nasty. They done shot one man, an' they're layin' the claim that blood's gonna run in the streets before they're through."

"What has them so riled up?" Bannister asked.

"Somethin' about how many bullets it takes to kill a polar bear."

Morgan stood up quickly when he heard that. "Constable, you'd better let me handle this," he said. "That's Cole and Pascal, and the polar bear they're riled up over is Chotauk."

"No, thank you, Mr. Morgan," Bannister said. He strapped his black leather belt and pistol holster on. As usual, the flap was buttoned down on the holster.

"But I know these men," Morgan said. "They are gunfighters."

"They are violators of the law, Mr. Morgan, and as such, are subject to my jurisdiction."

Morgan watched Bannister leave the office and walk swiftly, purposefully, toward the splash of yellow light that was the North Star Saloon.

"Surely he'll take out that pistol before he gets in there," Morgan observed.

"I don't think so," Crowder said.

Morgan looked at Crowder in disbelief. "You mean he'll walk right in there with his gun still in his holster to make the arrest?"

"He's a man that believes in the power of the law," Crowder said.

"Yeah? Well he's going up against two men who believe only in the power of the gun," Morgan replied. He pushed out into the street and started toward the saloon.

"Hey, wait, where are you goin'?" Crowder called. "Bannister won't let you interfere with his arrest."

Cole and Pascal were armed again, thanks to Skagway Annie. She berated them for their failure, and for losing their weapons, but she couldn't very well have bodyguards who were unarmed, so she paid $150 apiece for two Colt .44 Peacemakers. They were the same kind of pistols Cole and Pascal lost, so they were glad to get them back. They were so glad they began celebrating, and a few minutes ago the celebration had erupted into a shooting. Now one man lay bleeding on the floor and everyone else in the saloon was backed up against the walls, giving Cole and Pascal all the room they needed.

"Well, now, lookie here, will you, Pascal?" Cole said, deriding all the customers of the saloon. "There's not one man in town . . . not one man who'll step up to the bar with us and have a drink."

"They're yellow bellies," Pascal said, laughing. He took a drink of whiskey straight from the bottle and looked at everyone who was cowering against the wall. He made an imaginary pistol with his thumb and forefinger, then made a shooting sound with his mouth. The man he pointed his hand at shrank back in fear.

"Ha, ha! Look at that!" Pascal laughed, pointing at the frightened customer.

"Bartender, I thought you had men up here," Cole said. "You got nothing up here but yellow bellies and old women."

"Yeah, only old women got more guts than these yellow bellies," Pascal said. He "shot" another customer with his imaginary gun.

The front door opened then and a well groomed man of medium height stepped into the room. He wasn't wearing a fur hat like everyone else, he was wearing a blocked hat with a golden crest on the crown. Though he was wearing a parka, his red coat could be seen underneath, and he wore black pants with a red stripe down the legs. A pistol belt was fastened around his waist and a pistol, secured by a holster flap, was at his side.

"Well, now, gentlemen, that's quite enough, don't you think? I'm Constable Bannister."

Bannister heard a quiet groan and he looked at a man lying on the floor. When he looked around the room he recognized one of the town doctors.

"Doc, how about taking a look at this injured man?"

"I started to a moment ago," the doctor replied. "But they pulled a gun on me and made me get back."

"Really, gentlemen, you would deny an injured man medical attention? See to him, Doc."

"But they—"

"See to him, Doc," Bannister said again. "The law will attend to these two. You gentlemen surrender your firearms to me, now. You are under arrest."

Cole and Pascal looked at each other in momentary confusion, then they both burst out laughing.

"Arrest? You are putting us under arrest?" Cole said.

"Yes," Bannister said. "Oh, I assure you, gentlemen, you won't find it so amusing when you spend thirty years in one of our jails for attempted homicide."

"Attempted what?" Cole asked.

"It means attempted killin'," Pascal explained.

Cole laughed again. "Oh, we wasn't attemptin' to kill the sonofabitch," he said. "If we had really been tryin' to do it, we would'a done it."

"Yes. Well, nevertheless, you are both under arrest. Please surrender your firearms at once."

Cole pointed to the constable. "Mister, you're talkin' like somebody that ain't go no sense. Here you are with your gun in that shiny holster an' a flap down over it, tellin' us to give you our guns? Why, don't you know we could blow you to hell before you could even get your hand to the holster?"

"I am the law," Bannister said. "And I am ordering you to surrender your firearms."

"And I'm tellin' you we ain't gonna do it," Cole said.

"Very well, I can see that it will be necessary for me to enforce the demand," Bannister said.

He reached for the flap and unbuttoned it.

"Don't go reachin' for that gun, mister, 'cause if you do, law or no law, we're gonna have to shoot you," Pascal warned.

"I'm sorry," Bannister said. "But the law is quite specific about this. Now you are going to have to surrender your weapons at once." Bannister started to withdraw his pistol.

"I told you not to do that!" Cole yelled.

Undaunted, Bannister continued his slow, methodical withdrawal.

Guns appeared in the hands of both Cole and Pascal at nearly the same instant. Almost as quickly as the guns were in their hands, they were firing, and a billow of smoke pushed out from the barrels of the two Peacemakers.

Bannister was hit by both bullets and they slammed him back against the bar. He put his elbows back, trying to hold onto the bar, trying to stay up, but he couldn't do it. With a look of surprise on his face he slowly slid to the floor.

Morgan stepped through the door of the saloon just as Bannister slid down. The constable was in the sitting position and he looked up at Morgan with an expression of disbelief on his face. Morgan knelt on the floor beside the young constable.

"They defied the law," he said. "Don't they understand? Without the law we are nothing but barbarians." Bannister leaned his head back and closed his eyes. He took a few deep breaths, then opened his eyes again. "Barbarians," he said, then, with a sigh, he died.

Morgan looked back at Cole and Pascal, both of whom still held smoking guns in their hands.

"Did you see him?" Pascal said, pointing at the

dead lawman. "He was crazy. He started pulling his pistol against us, even when we warned him."

"It wasn't him pulling the pistol," Morgan said. "It was the law."

Cole laughed, derisively. "The law?" he said. He shook his head. "What the hell is this law? There's only one law up here and I'm holdin' it right in my hand." Cole raised the pistol for Morgan to see it.

Morgan was still on one knee beside the constable. "You heard the man," Morgan said. "Without the law, we are barbarians. Now, I'm going to ask you to do what he said. I'm going to ask you to turn over your guns."

"Goddamnit, man, at least when he asked, our guns were in our holster. Now they're in our hands. You're crazier than he was."

"Oh, no, there's one major difference between the constable and me," Morgan said.

"Yeah. What's that?"

"The constable believed in the power and authority of law. He believed that was all he needed to keep the peace. I don't believe that."

"What do you believe?"

"I think the only way I'm going to keep the peace with the two of you is to kill both of you," Morgan said.

Several of the onlookers gasped in amazement at the man who, on his knee, and with his pistol in its holster, had just threatened to kill two men who had their pistols in their hands.

"You're . . . you're crazy," Cole said. He made a cackling sound that might have been a laugh.

"This is the last time I'm going to tell you," Morgan said. "Put your guns on the table there, or I'm going to kill both of you, right here and right now.''

''Try it,'' Pascal hissed.

Morgan had his pistol out so fast that most people were aware only of a jerk in the shoulder. He fired two shots, so fast, and so close together, that people in the building next door thought they heard one shot . . . or at least, two guns going off simultaneously. There wasn't two guns going off at the same time, or even two guns going off at all. Morgan shot twice, neither Cole nor Pascal fired a shot. Both men were dead before they even realized what had happened.

''My God!'' Crowder gasped. ''I've never seen anything like that in my life!'' Crowder had followed Morgan into the saloon, arriving just as the constable died. ''What man can draw and shoot that fast?''

''I can,'' Morgan said, standing up and holstering his pistol. He looked down at the two men he had just killed, at the surprise on their faces. Then he turned away from them and left the saloon, pushing past the stare of the awed onlookers, walking out into the street to let the cold air clear his senses. He walked down the middle of the snow packed street, listening to the babble of voices in the saloon behind him, knowing they were talking about him, but purposely blotting out any specific words. He didn't want to hear praise right now, he didn't want to hear anything except the peaceful sigh of the night wind.

Morgan knew what nobody in the saloon knew. He hadn't killed the two men in a fair fight, though to everyone there it not only looked fair, it looked like the odds were tipped against him. It wasn't a fair fight at all.

Morgan didn't understand the technical terms for it, had never even heard the word reflex, but he knew that if someone was holding a gun on him and didn't start to pull the trigger until they saw Morgan begin to draw, they would never get the trigger pulled. For the longest part of a draw was the part where the brain thought about it, then told the arm, hand, and finger to move. Morgan's arm, hand, and finger were already moving. Before the message got from Cole and Pascal's brain to their fingers, telling the finger to pull the trigger, it was too late. Morgan had already shot them. They would be telling stories to their grandchildren about this gun battle, Morgan knew. He wondered how long it would be before anyone figured out that it wasn't a gun battle . . . it was an execution.

19

Harder and harder, again and again, Morgan lunged into her. Mariellen's hair, soaked with the sweat of their passion, lay pasted to the trembling mounds of her chest, half crushed beneath him. Her passion was building faster and faster, her turgid nipples digging into Morgan's flesh as she writhed in ecstasy.

Mariellen suddenly choked back a little scream of pleasure, then bit him on the shoulder. His hands searched her body, raking up and down her back to hold and squeeze her pounding buttocks. Her hands went to his head, her teeth chewing on his lower lip, her body writhing like a snake.

Morgan continued to drink the nectar of her lips as she thrashed and heaved beneath him. His own groans of ecstasy were absorbed by her hot mouth as she opened it wide and sucked his lips, crushing them with her teeth and inflaming them with her rapier tongue.

They clung to each other, kissing wildly, their hands searching, grasping, clutching, finding, tearing at each other, hers as eager as his. Her moans came steadily, her back arched, carrying him with her. He lunged harder against her, redoubling every ounce of effort he had left. His surge tore a wild cry from her as she bit him again. His body slammed to hers over and over until she cried out, "Now! Now!" and her throbbing hips arched upward as she tightened her legs around him. She flung her head back, her wild hair flowing past her shoulder, while her lower torso undulated, bucked, and jerked its harsh rhythm.

Morgan approached the ultimate moment, cupping her upthrust breasts, squeezing them unmercifully. He sighed, stiffening, as salvo after salvo of hot sperm spurted out. She gurgled and cried out his name and her features, which had been frozen by the agony of lust, softened and her lips parted. "That was wonderful," she said. "Just wonderful."

Mariellen stood by the window of the bedroom, looking out at the snow. Though a roaring fire in the little stove kept the room pleasantly warm, she was holding a blanket around her nude body. The blanket stopped at her waist and her naked thighs gleamed in the soft light. A breast peaked through the blanket's fold, its nipple still congested. She had been silent for a long moment, then she turned toward him. Her eyes were glistening with tears, one had started down her cheek, leaving a streak behind it.

"You won't come back to Skagway with Chotauk and me?"

"Not yet," Morgan said.

"But there's no need to stay up here now," she said. "Everyone knows who we are. They know we don't have any guns. Even if there is someone to catch, we have no bait for the trap."

"They aren't going to send a new constable in here until after the ice breaks up," Morgan said.

"But I don't understand. What's that to you?"

"I know you don't understand," Morgan said. "I'm not sure I understand myself. But I want to watch over things for Bannister. There was something about that funny little man . . . his insistance that we must be governed by laws . . . that got to me."

"You'll come down to Skagway in the spring?"

"Yes," Morgan said. "In the spring, I promise."

"All right," she said. She sighed. "It will probably be that long before we can get another shipment of weapons up here anyway."

"Tell Chotauk I thank him for letting me live here."

Mariellen suddenly smiled. "It's not Chotauk you need to thank. It's me. I could be very jealous, you know, leaving you here with another woman."

Morgan thought of the woman Mariellen was talking about, Chotauk's wife, as pie faced, bland, and round as any woman he had ever seen. He chuckled. "I'll say this about her. I've never known anyone who was a better cook. I may be as big as Chotauk by the time I come back."

The trip downriver was a lot easier than the trip Morgan had made upriver five months earlier. He stood on the desk of the *Maid of the Klondike*, a riverboat that served Dawson and Whitehorse, watching the water froth into foam behind the paddle. The ice was gone from the river, thousands of wild flowers bloomed in colorful profusion on both sides of the Yukon, patches of green fed the caribou and other foragers, while overhead the sun warmed the air to a balmy sixty-five degrees.

It was good to be out of the parkas and furs, to dress normally for a change. And it was good to get out of Dawson, though Morgan had to confess that the winter he had just spent was the most unique winter of his entire lifetime.

"Mr. Morgan, the dining room will be closing for the night soon," one of the crewmen told him. "If you haven't taken your supper, this is your last chance."

"Thanks," Morgan said. He looked out at the crystal clear sky, as bright as midday though it was already nine o'clock in the evening. He had just gotten used to living in constant darkness . . . now he would have to make the same accommodations for constant light. He left the deck and went to take his supper.

He bought a horse in Whitehorse and rode the animal through the Chilkoot Pass to Skagway. It was a much easier trip this time than it had been before, and days before he thought it was possible, he found himself descending the mountain trail into the coastal town of Skagway.

This was the first time he had ever seen Skagway without its mantle of snow. Without the element's softening effect, Skagway was a raw, rough, frontier town, a place of mucky streets and plank sidewalks. It's population was near ten thousand people now, and swelling every day as new prospectors came to the established gold fields, or flocked together to be fleeced like sheep by a coalition of corrupt government officials and hoodlums. Most of them poured off the ships and headed for the Klondike laden with supplies brought from the States . . . and many of these were murdered between the mud flats called Skagway Beach and the summit of White Pass.

The guns which were at such a premium in the interior of Alaska, or the Northwest Territories, were in more common supply here as the men brought their own. As a result of the accessibility to the guns, shootings were routine and armed robberies on the streets were common. This was, Morgan realized, frontier country, as real and as rugged as anything his father had faced in an earlier generation. Here, for the first time since coming to Alaska, Morgan felt in charge of his own environment. In a world where the gun was law, Morgan could argue his case in any court in the land, up to and including the Supreme Court.

Morgan rode by what had been Thompson's Cove. He knew it had burned down last winter, but he didn't know it had been replaced by another saloon. He dismounted, tied his horse off at the hitching rail in front, then walked across the boards to avoid the mud and went inside.

"We got some beer fresh in from the States," the bartender said.

"Sounds good," Morgan agreed. He looked around the saloon. Though functional, it certainly had none of the class of the old Thompson's Cove. "Miss Thompson around?"

"Who?" the bartender asked, setting a mug in front of Morgan.

"Thompson. Annie Thompson."

"No," the bartender said, his face drawn in confusion. Then it changed into recognition. "Say, are you talkin' about he woman they used to call Skagway Annie?"

"Yes."

"No, she ain't in Skagway anymore. I heard tell she went up to Nome, but I wouldn't know nothin' about it. She was gone long before I come here. She's just one of them stories you hear the old timers tellin' all the time," he said.

Morgan took a drink of his beer. My god, was he now considered an "old timer" up here?

"What they like to do," the bartender went on, "is take somebody just arrived . . . like you, say, an' fill his head with all sorts of tales. Don't believe none of it. Take this here Skagway Annie, for example. They're tellin' a story now 'bout the two gunfighters she always had with her, how they was kilt by one of them mounties. And get this . . . the story goes that they was two of 'em with the drop on the mountie, but he drawned his gun and kilt 'em both before they could even pull the trigger. Now if that ain't the beatenist story you ever heard?"

"I knew that mounted policeman," Morgan said. "His name was Bannister . . . and the story is true."

"Go on," the bartender said. "They ain't nobody that fast." Noticing Morgan had finished the beer he went on. "Care for another one?"

"Thanks, no," Morgan said. "I've got some business to tend to."

When Morgan tied his horse at the hitching rail in front of the Queen's Throne, Chotauk came out onto the porch to greet him. He smiled broadly and stuck out his hand.

"Well, Chotauk," Morgan said. "Your woman sends greetings."

"And my friend, Crowder?"

"Yes," Morgan said. "Your friend Crowder sends greetings as well."

"Boss Lady wait for you inside," Chotauk said,

holding the door open for him.

The Queen's Throne was crowded with customers, and as Morgan looked over them he was surprised to see how easily he could pick out the newcomers from the old sourdoughs. No wonder everyone who spoke to him last year knew immediately that he was a tenderfoot. From the clothes they wore, the language they used, even their very demeanor, it was as easy to determine who just got off the boat as if they were wearing large signs advertising the fact.

When Morgan started up the stairs to Mariellen's office, two armed men moved quickly to intercept him.

"Out of my way, clowns," Morgan growled, "or I'll break the two of you into little pieces."

"I'd like to see you try that, mister," one of them said.

"No, I don't think you would," a woman's voice called down from the top of the stairs. "This is Lee Morgan and if he says he can break you into little pieces, I'm sure he can."

Both of the guards backed away quickly.

"I'm sorry, Miss Mariellen," one of them said. "I didn't recognize him."

"No reason you should," Mariellen replied. "You've never seen him before. Well," she called down to him, "are you going to come up, or do I have to come down for you?"

Morgan smiled up at her, recalling her aloofness when he first arrived last fall. "No, I'll come up to you," he said. "I certainly wouldn't want to cause people to talk."

"I don't care if anyone talks or not," Mariellen said, laughing happily. She came halfway down the stairs and plastered herself against him with a long kiss. Her two armed guards looked away in embarrassment and, Morgan noticed, not a little envy. "Come on up to my office," she said. "We've got a lot to talk about."

In the office Mariellen poured Morgan a glass of wine, then curled up on a sofa beside him and listened as he told her of the winter spent in Dawson, and of the newly arrived constable.

"He's older than Bannister, and maybe a little more practical. I think he'll do just fine."

"And you and Big Ben kept the peace all winter," she said. "I thought you were dead set against wearing a badge."

"Oh, I didn't wear a badge," Morgan said. "And I had no official position . . . neither did Crowder, for that matter. I guess that's why I was able to do it without it going against my grain. In fact, the only thing that has stuck in my craw all winter is I still don't know who tried to have me ambushed when I went up there, and I still don't know who the mysterious Mr. Church is. When you come right down to it, I guess I didn't do that good of a job for Colt Firearms."

"Oh, that reminds me," Mariellen said. "I have a letter for you from Colt Firearms Company. I was told to hold it for your arrival." Mariellen got up from the sofa, looked through a little case, then brought him an envelope. "It came two weeks ago," she said.

"What's in it?"

"I don't know. As you can see it's marked personal and confidential. I didn't look."

Morgan opened the envelope and pulled out the letter. It was dated six weeks ago.

Dear Mr. Morgan,

Two-thirds of our board concurring, we are

hereby dismissing Harrison Chapel from all duties and responsibilities with our company. He is no longer our representative in Alaska, or the Northwest Territories, and is not authorized to speak for us in any capacity.

The reasons for his dismissal are of a confidential nature. The original terms of your own employment are still in effect, should you wish to continue working for us. We would also like to offer you the position once held by Mr. Chapel, and now void. Should you accept that position, you will then be told why we found it necessary to terminate Chapel's employment. In any case, whether you continue in your present capacity, or accept our offer of new responsibilities, you are no longer answerable to Mr. Harrison Chapel for any business regarding Colt Firearms.

"Has your uncle said anything to you about his work with the Colt Company?" Morgan asked.

"Do you mean do I know he has quit? Yes, I know."

"Why?"

"I asked him the same question," Mariellen said. "After all, he had been with Colt for a number of years and I was quite surprised when he told me about it."

"What was his answer?"

"He said why have a sandwich when he can enjoy the entire banquet."

"I see."

"Well, if you do see, I wish you would tell me. I swear, that doesn't make one bit of sense to me."

"It would if you understood synonyms," Morgan said simply.

20

"Well," Chapel said, greeting Morgan when he went to his office to see him. "So, you've come down from the frozen north to visit us."

"Yes."

"Mariellen told me a little of what happened to you . . . how you were ambushed on the trail up, hit on the head, and shot it out with Cole and Pascal. I must say, you've had quite some experiences since signing on with Colt Firearms."

"I hope that doesn't mean I'm going to have even more experiences now," Morgan said.

Chapel looked at him in puzzlement for a moment, then nodded in understanding. "You're talking about the situation between Colt and me, aren't you?" He opened the humidor and extracted a cigar, offering one to Morgan.

Morgan accepted. "Yeah. I received a letter from them."

"Well," Chapel said, biting the tip off his cigar, then holding a match to it. After his was lit, he held the match out to the end of Morgan's smoke.

"I suppose it's time you and I had a little talk, isn't it?"

"I suppose it is," Morgan said.

"No doubt Colt has told you why they fired me." Chapel took a deep puff, then blew out a cloud of blue smoke. "Fired me, after all these years of loyal service to them. Can you believe that?"

"I'd like to hear your side," Morgan said. Of course he hadn't even heard Colt's side yet, but Chapel evidently didn't realize that.

"Well, I told my niece I quit. I mean, I didn't want to tell her that a respectable company like Colt Firearms would do that to one of its most faithful employees."

It did not escape Morgan's notice that Chapel chose the word faithful over trusted.

"But it's all right that they fired me, I was going to quit sooner or later . . . I just thought it would make things go easier for me if I would continue to work for Colt as long as I could."

"But they wouldn't go along with that," Morgan said. It was a safe enough statement under the circumstances, and it helped to continue the illusion that he already knew why Colt had fired him.

"No," Chapel said. "They wouldn't go along with firearms exclusively . . . and any other dealings I might have with other companies was in violation of my contract. The fools."

Chapel's eyes narrowed in the smoke, but they gleamed brightly as he explained to Morgan his plans. "They are concerned with a few sales and protecting their name," he said. "They don't realize the money that could be made by controlling every firearm that comes up here. I don't mean just Colt arms, I'm talking about Remington, Winchester, Butterfield, Sharps, Deane and Adams, anybody you can think of. My God, there are few opportunities in a man's life when he can make a fortune . . . I mean a real fortune, like the monied giants back East, the Goulds, the Vanderbilts, the Mellons. I can be like one of them, Morgan, do you realize that? And all Colt is worried about is their precious name. They don't want to be involved in any scheme that would, in their words, 'defraud the public.' "

"Well, a respected name is a good thing to have," Morgan said.

"What the hell, you can buy a good name," Chapel said. "If I can pull this off, if I can make the money that I know is to be made up there, I can become a great friend of the people. One-hundred years from now there could be schools named for me like Vanderbilt, Stanford, and Cornell are named for their benefactors. Oh, yes, Morgan, I can buy my good name."

"I have to hand it to you, Chapel," Morgan said. "You do have ambition."

"What about you? Would you like to work with me? There's plenty of money up here for both of us."

"A full partner?" Morgan asked.

"Yeah, sure, a full partner. Why not?"

"Suppose I took you up on that offer?" Morgan asked. "What exactly would you expect of me?"

"The same thing I expected of you when we were working for Colt," Chapel said. "Morgan, the people who were killing off the Colt representatives, the people who tried to kill you, are still here, and the guns still make a tempting target for them, whether they are brought in by a large company like Colt, or by private enterprise such as ourselves. Quite simply I am buying your protection, just as Colt was."

"I see."

"Also," Chapel went on. "There is a shipment of guns at the docks in Juneau. I can't pick them up . . . I'm no longer a valid representative of the Colt Firearms Company. But you can."

"I suppose I can."

Chapel smiled broadly. "I knew we could do business together," he said. "I just knew it. Now, here's the plan. You pick up the Colt shipment and bring them to White Pass. I'll meet you there, and we'll take the guns on up into the gold fields. Morgan, they're paying over $200 each for them now."

"Two hundred dollars?"

"Yes. I knew that if we kept the guns out long enough the price would go up. That is exactly what I planned on. The only thing, I had thought to get the shipment from Colt before I quit. Well, no matter, you can get it for me, if you will."

"For money like that?" Morgan said. "Hell yes, I'll get them for you."

Chapel opened a cabinet and took out a bottle of brandy, then poured each of them a snifter. He held the drink out to Morgan.

"Let's have a drink to our partnership, partner, then you hurry on down there and get the guns. I'll meet you at White Pass in two weeks."

Morgan knew now that Alaska wasn't all glaciers and Yukon basin permafrost. The panhandle, warmed by the Japan Current, was no tropics, but in the summertime it would actually get balmy. Juneau was on the panhandle, the first boomtown of the Alaskan gold rush. It had sprouted beside a deep water channel beneath mountains where miners were routinely sluicing twenty-five dollars worth of gold a day.

Already tents and false fronted buildings had given way to the more substantial, more permanent structures, painted clapboard houses with shake roofs that would do credit to any town in New England.

In Juneau, Morgan took delivery of twenty cases of Colt .44 Peacemakers. Packed at twenty pistols a case, that was four hundred guns, which, at two-hundred dollars per gun, would make quite a sizeable start on Chapel's fortune. He transferred the guns to a boat going back up to Skagway, and three days later rode out of Skagway leading four pack mules.

Though the temperature in Skagway was warm enough to go about in shirtsleeves, White Pass, because of its elevation, was still covered with snow. Earlier travelers through the pass had broken a path of sorts, but there were still places where the snow came up to the chest of his animals, and sometimes Morgan had to dismount to lead them through. In a way it reminded him of the grueling dogsled journey he had made last year, only now he knew that when he came through on the other side it would be warm again.

And now he knew who his enemy was.

The first bullet could have killed him, but he had to take that chance . . . he had to expose himself until the other man made his move. Now the fat was in the fire. The bullet whistled by his head so close he could hear it passing by. He grabbed his rifle from the saddle boot and leaped off his horse into a snow bank alongside the trail. The snow bank wouldn't really turn aside a bullet, but it did provide him cover as he burrowed through it toward a nearby rock. He pulled himself up behind the rock, an apparition covered in snow, then peered out over the trail to see if he could spot his adversary.

It was bright out . . . a sparkling blue sky, a brilliant sun, and the bright glare of white snow. Morgan shielded his eyes and looked around.

"If you'll turn around and go on back . . . just leave the mules here, I might let you live," a voice called.

"Hello, Chapel," Morgan called back. "Or, should I say, Church?"

Morgan could hear Chapel laugh. "How long have you known?"

"Long enough that I knew better than to actually bring the guns with me," Morgan said. "There's nothing in the boxes."

"You don't really expect me to believe that, do you?" Chapel called back.

"See for yourself," Morgan said. "I'll send one of the mules through to you."

Morgan looked over at his pack mules, standing quietly by the trail. He aimed at the lead rope that connected the lead mule with the others, fired, and cut the rope with his shot. The mule bolted forward, running through the pass. Morgan watched until the animal reached the other side, then he saw a couple of men run out, grab the mule, and pull it off the trail.

"How many do you have with you?" Morgan asked.

"Enough to get the job done," Chapel

answered. There was a moment's pause, then
Chapel yelled again. "Goddamnit, you're right!
There's nothing in these boxes."

"I told you that, but you wouldn't listen,"
Morgan said.

"You should have followed the rules, Mr.
Morgan. I don't like it when people don't follow
the rules."

"What are you going to do about it?"

"Why, kill you, of course. I told you how big
the stakes are in this game. I don't intend to let
you do anything to mess it up."

Morgan looked up toward the head of the pass
and saw five men moving toward him, darting
swiftly from rock to rock, snowbank to
snowbank, never giving him a clear shot. Five to
one, he thought. Not very good odds.

A bullet suddenly hit the rock beside him, then
whined off into the pass. Morgan turned on his
side and saw three more coming down from a
different direction. Now the odds were eight to
one, and they were positioned so that if he took
cover from one group, he was exposed to the
other. He snapped off a shot at the three who
were coming down from his side, then rolled
away, just as the five men below opened up on
him.

Bullets were popping into the snow all around
him, kicking up little puffs to mark where they
hit. Some of them were close . . . damned close.

Morgan heard something, a deep throated
rumble, like thunder far in the distance. For a
moment the sound surprised him . . . there wasn't
a cloud in the sky. Where could the thunder have
come from?

A bullet hit the rock right in front of him, and a

piece of chipped stone nicked his face, drawing blood. He heard the rumble again, and decided it was just distant echoes from the rifle fire. He raised up his head to see how close they were, then saw something that suddenly made all the rumblings clear. At the very top of the mountain he saw plumes of snow drifting off, evidence that there had just been a small snow slide. It wouldn't take too much to get the slide started in ernest.

High up on the slope behind Chapel and the others there was a tree loaded with heavy, wet, snow. Morgan raised his rifle to his shoulder and fired into the tree. His first bullet popped through harmlessly, but his second dislodged a pretty good sized snowball.

"What the hell?" he heard Chapel shout, when Chapel realized what Morgan was doing. "Morgan, you fool!"

Morgan fired a third time, and this time the shockwave of the bullet dumped half the tree's load into the snow. That, plus the sound of rifle fire that had already destabilized the snow, caused a large slide to begin. The slide grew larger, and larger still, until the entire side of the mountain started down, rolling up into a huge wave, roaring with the sound of a thousand cannons. Morgan had started a full fledged avalanche!

The eight men who had been steadily advancing toward him suddenly stopped in their tracks and looked back up the mountain toward the huge wall of snow rushing down at them with the speed of a runaway freight train. Morgan was struck with how tiny the men looked under these circumstances . . . they looked like toothpicks, like insignificent flies to be brushed away.

One of them may have screamed . . . Morgan believed he heard Chapel's voice, high and thin against the deep throated roar, but the voice, like the men themselves, was brushed away, snuffed out in an instant of terrible rolling, snapping, roaring white.

Morgan turned and dived back down the path. Falling and sliding, he was moving fast enough to get away, and the farther back down the path he got, the further away the roar sounded. When Morgan finally got to his feet, five-hundred feet down the trail, he looked back to where he had been. The entire pass was blocked by a wall of snow, but there the avalanche had played itself out. The snow slide had quit, leaving a one hundred-foot-deep drift over what had been a cleared path just seconds ago. Somewhere under that one-hundred feet of snow, Morgan knew, lay the bodies of Chapel and the men who were with him.

He chuckled. Synonyms, Bannister had said. Two words meaning the same thing. Like church and chapel, or, put capitol letters to the words and they become Church and Chapel.

Morgan's horse and three of the mules had gotten away from the slide, and Morgan saw them standing quietly, shaking in fear, though not understanding what had just happened. He walked over to his horse and stood there for a moment, calming him.

A couple of travelers, just now approaching the pass, came up then. They looked at the closed pass in bitter disappointment.

"My God, look at that, Charlie," one of them said. "You was right, that was an avalanche. The whole pass is closed."

"Damn!" Charlie said. "All that gold on the other side an' we can't get to it!"

"Maybe there's another way."

"How 'bout you, Mister? You know another way?" one of them asked, hopefully.

"No," Morgan said. He started back down the path.

"Yeah. Well if you don't know any other way, then where are you goin'?" Charlie yelled.

"I'm goin' home," Morgan said.

SADDLER

The hardest-riding, hardest-loving cowboy whoever blazed a trail or set a heart on fire

#3: HOT AS A PISTOL by Gene Curry. Hated by the townspeople, Saddler had to work all day to keep the town safe from a renegade Irish family, a corrupt politician, and a deadly Confederate guerilla—and all night to keep himself safe from two criminally beautiful women.

__3037-3 $2.95 US/$3.95 CAN

#4: WILD, WILD WOMEN by Gene Curry. After killing a sadistic wagon master, Jim Saddler took over the wagon train carrying 50 buxom beauties to San Francisco. But after several deaths, torrential rains, and broken axles, it looked bad for the women and the wagons. But Saddler swore he'd get his women to California come hell or high water.

__3099-3 $2.95 US/$3.95 CAN

SPEND YOUR LEISURE MOMENTS WITH US.

Hundreds of exciting titles to choose from—something for everyone's taste in fine books: breathtaking historical romance, chilling horror, spine-tingling suspense, taut medical thrillers, involving mysteries, action-packed men's adventure and wild Westerns.

SEND FOR A FREE CATALOGUE TODAY!

Leisure Books
Attn: Customer Service Department
276 5th Avenue, New York, NY 10001